NO TIME TO LOSE . . .

"They wouldn't touch her," Peter said in a soft, savage voice.

"They would," Gabriel said. "They're looking for a virgin sacrifice . . ."

"I'll kill them."

"After we make sure Jane is safe," Gabriel said. "She's probably back at the tower with Lizzie right now, cursing all men. Come along."

Gabriel came to a halt a few yards from the base of the tower. "Someone's been here," he said. "A carriage and horses. And it looks as if someone was dragged . . ."

Gabriel disappeared into the shadowy tower, taking the steps three at a time. He stopped just inside the door as a feeling of cold, bitter fury washed over him. The place was a shambles of overturned furniture. Lizzie hadn't given up without a fight.

Gabriel didn't turn when Peter came up behind him. "They've taken her, Peter. I think they've taken them both."

"I'll kill them," Peter said with devastating calm. "If they've harmed a hair on Janey's head . . ."

"We've got to find . . . an icy calm voice. "The

BOOK YOUR PLACE ON OUR WEBSITE AND MAKE THE READING CONNECTION!

We've created a customized website just for our very special readers, where you can get the inside scoop on everything that's going on with Zebra, Pinnacle and Kensington books.

When you come online, you'll have the exciting opportunity to:

- View covers of upcoming books
- Read sample chapters
- Learn about our future publishing schedule (listed by publication month *and author*)
- Find out when your favorite authors will be visiting a city near you
- Search for and order backlist books from our online catalog
- Check out author bios and background information
- Send e-mail to your favorite authors
- Meet the Kensington staff online
- Join us in weekly chats with authors, readers and other guests
- Get writing guidelines
- AND MUCH MORE!

Visit our website at
http://www.zebrabooks.com

PRINCE OF MAGIC

ANNE STUART

Zebra Books
Kensington Publishing Corp.

ZEBRA BOOKS are published by

Kensington Publishing Corp.
850 Third Avenue
New York, NY 10022

Zebra and the Z logo Reg. U.S. Pat. & TM Off.

First Printing: December, 1998
10 9 8 7 6 5 4 3 2 1

Printed in the United States of America

Books have an unfortunate habit of taking their own sweet time to be born, and all the pushing and shoving and forcing simply won't hurry the process. Lots of thanks and love to the Merrie Midwives of Genie-Romex, in particular Saint Jo Beverley and Saint Teresa Hill, without whom I would have been in a major mess.

PROLOGUE

It was the first night of spring. April had come to Dorset, and there was no way that Elizabeth Penshurst could spend one more moment cooped up inside the parsonage.

Everyone was sound asleep. Her five half brothers, ranging in age from a sturdy seventeen to a precociously charming three and a half, were worn-out from their various exertions. Her father, the Very Reverend William Penshurst, slept the sleep of the righteous, his helpmate, Adelia, snoring softly by his side. No one would hear as Lizzie crept down the back stairs and out through the kitchen garden. The town of Wickham was a sober village of steady habits. No one would be up late, peering out the window to see the rector's outspoken daughter go flitting down the midnight streets to the forest. Even her nemesis, Elliott Maynard, had gone to London more than a week ago, and he wouldn't be anywhere near to spy on her.

Odd, that she would think of her most determined suitor as her nemesis. It wasn't as if she had anything against marriage in particular. Her father and stepmother seemed very happy with each other, and most of the people of her acquaintance seemed content with their lot.

But then, most of the people of her acquaintance didn't have a wicked habit of running off to the woods whenever they had a moment to spare. They didn't dance in the moonlight, converse with the animals, sing to the trees, or lie stretched out on the soft earth, breathing in the spring air.

The only one who did so was Old Peg, and half the village considered her some sort of witch. Old Peg had little use for the villagers, but she must have recognized a kindred spirit in the minister's dreamy daughter. For the last few years she'd welcomed Lizzie into her forest, taught her the lore of herbs and trees, taught her to find her home in the woods.

And now Old Peg was gone, decently if reluctantly buried in the churchyard, with all the proper Christian words said over her free spirit by the disapproving Mr. Penshurst. Old Peg would have hated it. Lizzie was the one who had found her body, of course. If she'd had enough strength, she would have buried Old Peg herself, but the old woman weighed a good thirteen stone, and Lizzie couldn't manage. Instead she'd had to stand by Old Peg's grave and weep, the only mourner.

It had been two weeks since Old Peg had been buried, two weeks since she'd sat and listened to Elliott's doleful pronouncements on mad old women and the dangers of the woods. Two weeks since she'd flatly refused his offer of marriage.

Her father had been deeply distressed. William Penshurst tended to see the best in people, and what better mate could be found for his daughter than his own curate? And surely his daughter was too fine a creature to be critical of Maynard's thinning hair, expanding paunch, or slightly fishlike profile.

It wasn't Elliott's unprepossessing appearance that appalled Lizzie; it was his small, critical nature and the way his moist eyes ogled her when her father wasn't around. The way he always found some excuse to touch her with his soft, damp hands. Never indecently, just possessively. Leaving Lizzie with the desperate need to scrub whatever portion of her anatomy he'd happened to grasp, be it her hand, her wrist, her elbow, or the small of her back.

But Elliott was gone, having taken his latest dismissal with a high dudgeon. Lizzie had little doubt he'd return to renew his courtship, and the thought of those upcoming battles was deeply unsettling. She loved her father and stepmother as well as her five little brothers, and she would have done almost anything to please them. Short of marrying Elliott Maynard.

As for the Penshursts, they viewed Lizzie as some sort of exotic creature, much beloved but never completely understood. She took after her own mother, a fey, impractical creature who'd had the bad taste to die in childbirth, leaving her husband with an infant daughter and no idea what to do with her.

Fortunately Adelia had appeared on the scene. She had loved Lizzie dearly, as much as she loved the five little pledges of affection she'd presented to her husband, but she was a woman entirely without imagination. And Lizzie had far too much of it.

On a warm spring night Lizzie's family's expectations were a distant worry, and Elliott's determined courtship was miles away. For tonight she could go back to the woods, where she hadn't been since Old Peg had been buried. She could go and say good-bye in her own way.

No one stirred as she crept down the narrow back stairs. The kitchen was huge and deserted, the two servant girls employed by the Penshursts lived in the village, and no one would be likely to notice that Lizzie wasn't in bed as a proper minister's daughter should be in the middle of the night.

It was the first truly warm night of the year, she thought as she slipped out into the kitchen garden. She hadn't even bothered with a shawl—there was no need for it. She wore her soft leather dancing slippers, but the ground was damp, and someone would be sure to notice if she tracked mud into the house. She took them off, setting them carefully by the garden gate, and took off toward the woods, reveling in the feel of the new grass beneath her bare feet.

The woods around Wickham weren't that large— really not much more than a thick copse bordering on a nearby estate. Old Peg had paid little attention to whose land was whose—she simply lived in the forest as was her right.

The moon was almost half-full, a rich, creamy crescent in the blue-black sky. Even on a moonlit night Lizzie could have found her way to the tiny grove where stones stood sentinel. It was a holy place, though she knew perfectly well her father would pale at such a thought. A magic place, where Old Peg's soul would linger, even as her body turned to dust.

She reached the center of the circle, tilting her head back to drink in the moonlight, feeling her unbound hair ripple down her back. Without hesitation she stripped off her plain wool dress and tossed it beyond the circle. She was clad only in a light shift, no proper boned corset, no restricting drawers, nothing but a filmy layer of cotton over her body. She raised her arms to the moonlight and began to dance.

She danced for her trammeled soul and the respectable future she wasn't going to be able to avoid for much longer. She danced for the moon and the stars and the soft breeze that tumbled her wicked red hair about her face. She danced for everything she could never have, and she danced for Old Peg.

This would be her last trip to the woods. Tomorrow she would become what her family wanted, a dutiful young lady of the parish, practical, pragmatic, a credit to her parents. Her mother's fickle blood would vanish, and Lizzie would become Miss Elizabeth Penshurst, a good, solid creature like her stepmother.

She would marry the first man who asked her, as long as he didn't sneak and lurk and disapprove like Elliott Maynard. As long as he didn't look like Elliott Maynard. She would marry and have children and leave the forest to the woodland creatures who belonged there.

But for one last night she would dance. She sang beneath her breath, old songs that Peg had taught her, songs of love lost and love found, and she whirled and swayed, turned and dipped, lost in the feel of the night air and the strength of her young body.

Until she turned and came to a dead stop, coming face-to-face with Elliott Maynard's smug expression. And her father's look of absolute horror.

It was April, warmer than usual for the demanding climate of North Yorkshire, and Gabriel Durham could stay inside no longer. He closed the ancient tome he'd been poring over and rose, stretching his long, lanky body. He'd weathered his first winter in more than a dozen years in the place where he'd spent his childhood.

It wasn't the place where he'd been born—he had no earthly idea where that was, though he presumed it was somewhere near London. It didn't matter. This was where he belonged, and it had taken far too long for him to realize it.

But realize it he had, coming back to his dubious heritage just as the first snows had begun to fly. Coming back to Hernewood Forest.

Now winter was over, and even though a chill still lingered in the air, the daffodils were blooming riotously, the sheep had begun to lamb, and the first of May was fast approaching.

He should have been looking forward to it. If it weren't for the presence of a group of bored, self-indulgent parasites whom he could only presume followed him in his retreat from London, he could enjoy the feast of Beltane with all his heart and soul. He had every intention of doing so anyway.

Beltane was one of the oldest festivals in the pre-Christian world that had once been Britain. Even though it was now dressed up as May Day, everything went back to a time when the Druids ruled Britain with a scholarly hand.

Of course, people like the Chiltons and their friends preferred tales of bloodshed and human sacrifice. According to the Roman historians, the ancient priests of Britain used to regularly herd large groups of people into wicker cages and set them aflame for no discernible reason. Gabriel had always taken leave to doubt such horrific tales. After all, the Romans had just conquered Britain—it was in their best interest to paint the powerful locals in an unflattering light.

But in the last few years all things Druidic had become immensely popular, and most people preferred the bloody tales as well. And Gabriel had no particular interest in being the voice of reason. He was fascinated by his studies for their own right, not because he had anything particular to prove.

He'd been a studious boy—it was no wonder his so-called father, Sir Richard Durham, avid sportsman who avoided the written word as if it were plague-ridden, had nothing but contempt for him. That contempt had only spurred Gabriel deeper into his studies, until he'd broken free in an act of desperate rebellion.

He'd tasted all the fruits of the flesh. And found, after a while, that they were empty. London was a noisy, clamorous bore, and he'd had his fill of society to last him the rest of his life. The simple people of Hernewood were far more to his liking. The simple life, alone in his ramshackle tower with his books and his solitude, kept him perfectly content. If he needed companionship, there was always his old friend Peter or Gabriel's sister Jane.

If he needed sex, he could find that as well, from any number of discreet, willing women in the area. But what he needed right now was peace.

The night air still held a taste of winter, but he didn't bother to return to the tower for a coat. He'd learned to endure hardship, both self-imposed and those put upon him by others, and he'd survive. He was seldom sick, and the deserted woods that surrounded Hernewood Abbey wouldn't harm him.

He moved through the moonlight, silent as a ghost, circling past the skeletal remains of the refectory. Hernewood Abbey had once been one of the richest abbeys in the country, before King Henry decided to be greedy. It was still unsurpassingly lovely, even in its ruined state. And it was, blessedly, his.

There were no ghosts roaming in the moonlight, he thought with a wry smile. The ghostly monks of Hernewood Abbey would profoundly disapprove of the rites of Beltane: the Maypole and the fires and the merrymaking. They were probably conferring with sepulchral gloom over the wickedness of modern civilization.

Still, he had the sudden longing for even a ghostly encounter. He cherished his solitude, he needed it as most people needed air and water, but for a brief moment in the heart of the midnight woods he felt achingly alone.

He closed his eyes and saw her. A faery creature from another place and another time, a long-legged sprite, with flame red hair and only a wisp of garment, dancing in the moonlight. When he opened them she was gone, a figment of his imagination, and he shook his head, managing a wry grin.

He had no need of scantily clad dryads, no matter how enticing. That blend of erotic innocence haunted him, but he needed no more ghosts. He had no need of anyone at all.

Just the same, perhaps a visit to the talented widow in York might be called for. Before the fertility rites of Beltane made him imagine far worse.

And made him actually long for something to disturb his quiet days.

CHAPTER ONE

Hernewood, Yorkshire, April 1765

Elizabeth Penshurst, twenty-year-old spinster of the parish of Upper Wickham, Dorset, climbed down from the traveling coach and looked around her. The day was crisp and cool, with a strong breeze coming down from the north, whipping her skirts around her legs, rustling the leaves overhead in some sort of whispered warning. Her box was set down beside her, and then the coachman climbed back onto his perch with a haste that seemed oddly suspect.

"You certain they know you're coming, Miss?" he asked in a gruff voice. "I could take you further, leave you at the Boar's Knees up ahead a ways. It's not a fit place for a lady, but neither are these woods, I'm thinking."

Elizabeth, sometimes known as Lizzie, looked at the towering trees surrounding the market cross. At one point there must have been a thriving village here in the center of nowhere, but now nothing remained but the old stone cross.

The forests were darker in Yorkshire, the trees taller, and in the distance she could see the towering ruins of an old building. She liked it, more than she would have expected.

"I'll be perfectly fine," she assured him, wishing she were quite so certain. "The Durhams know I'm coming today, and I'm sure they'll be here before long."

"That's all right then," the coachman said. "You watch yourself, then, lass. There've been strange goings-on around here, or so they tell me. The Dark Man's been on the prowl, and young girls have turned up missing."

"Missing?" Elizabeth echoed in a slight squeak. "Dark man?"

"Nothing for you to fret your pretty head about. It's two hours till dark, and you'll be safe and sound by then. And they say the ghosts are harmless old souls."

Elizabeth's panic began to fade. Dark men and missing girls could get her far too lively imagination in an uproar—ghosts were carrying things a bit too far.

"I'll watch out for the ghosts," she said solemnly, suppressing a smile.

"You don't believe me," the driver said mournfully. "Just as well. I've never seen them, few do. With any luck you won't even know they're around."

"And who's the Dark Man?"

The driver shook his head. "Old fairy tales, Miss. Nothing for you to worry your head about. You've never been to Yorkshire before, have you? They're a superstitious lot, and who can blame them? But don't let it trouble you. Like as not you won't see a thing out of the ordinary."

"Like as not," Lizzie echoed with dubious cheer.

"Well, all right then," the driver said, as if life had just been settled to his satisfaction. "Just stay here, don't wander off into the woods, and you should be fine." And before she could think of one more way to delay him he snapped the reins with a decisive gesture, and a moment later the coach had disappeared over the hill, leaving Lizzie Penshurst alone at the edge of the forest.

She shivered, suddenly nervous. Old Peg would be sorely disappointed in her. All her life Lizzie had wanted nothing more than to escape into the forest, away from proper behavior and stifling clothing and disapproving eyes. Now she was at the very edge of the wildest forest she'd ever seen, and she was silly enough to be nervous. This was an adventure, the kind she'd longed for, and she wasn't going to waste her time with regrets. Fate and her own scandalous behavior had brought her here; it was up to her to make the best of it.

She squared her shoulders, smoothed her skirts, and sat down on her abandoned trunk, humming softly beneath her breath. Not a hymn, which would scandalize her father, but an old tune that Peg had taught her, about faithless lovers and found love. She could hear the wind riffling through the new growth of leaves overhead. Her father's living was a good one, but she'd spent most of her twenty years in the county of Dorset, a much gentler, milder climate. It had been warm with the blush of spring when her father and stepmother had packed her onto the mail coach with stern warnings and strained affection. Their dutiful daughter had disgraced them, and the Penshursts were both hurt and mystified.

This afternoon the wind across the dales carried the memory of winter on it, and the towering trees were like nothing she had ever seen. It would get dark in

another hour or so, she suspected. Her father had
warned her of outlaws and highwaymen and heartless
seducers, all of whom might prey on a young gentle-
woman traveling alone. Not that she was the sort of
female to attract heartless seducers. She was only passably pretty, obviously devoid of any generous fortune,
with a deceptively calm, nonsensical manner guaranteed to frighten away most importunate gentlemen. And
the unimportunate ones as well. She'd grown accustomed to it. She had no interest in gentlemen. She had
no interest in anything at all but what she found in the
woods surrounding her native village.

She'd spent her entire life in the market town of
Wickham, and it was rare that she'd managed to escape
her stepmother's watchful eye and find her way into
the forest. It was on one of those occasions that she'd
first met Old Peg, and changed her life forever.

But the gentle woods of Dorset were nothing compared to the wilds of Yorkshire. And as Elizabeth sat
and waited for the carriage to come and carry her to
Hernewood Manor, she couldn't rid herself of the
notion that the driver's warning, while obviously well-
meant, was just slightly unnerving.

She'd never met a Dark Man, though she could
assume the driver hadn't been speaking of a dark-
skinned foreigner. She knew far more than any minister's daughter should know of legends, stories of woodland creatures and sprites and piskies and even the
Green Man himself, thanks to Old Peg. She'd never run
across any magick creatures in the boring confines of
Wickham, unless you counted Old Peg, who was reputed
to be a witch.

But if one were to meet magic anywhere, this green
and brooding place would be the spot to find it.

The light was fading now, and the wind had picked up,

stirring the folds of her sensible merino cloak, tugging at her tightly coiled hair. She was very careful to keep it pinned tightly to her scalp, subduing its wild waves even if she couldn't subdue its flame red color. She had brought only her plainest, dullest clothes, she was pinned and starched and tucked and covered, and no one would ever believe that one week earlier she had been caught dancing in a forest grove in the moonlight, barefoot, her hair rippling down to her hips, clad only in her shift.

She sighed. The scandal had shaken the entire town, and she knew whom she could blame for it. She'd always been very careful not to be seen when she ran off into the woods, but Elliott Maynard had watched her with a solicitude that made her ill. He had followed her, watched her as she shed the stifling layers of clothes and danced in the moonlight. And he had brought her father and a crowd of disapproving parishioners to bear further witness.

The scandal had been appalling. Mr. Penshurst had thundered, her stepmother had wept, her five half brothers had alternated between outrage and amusement. And wicked Lizzie Penshurst had been sent away, banished to distant relatives of her poor dead mother, as far away from Upper Wickham as could be managed.

Lizzie sighed. She had every intention of improving her wicked ways. She didn't know what it was that called her to the woods, but she fully intended to ignore that call. She would be a quiet, helpful guest at the Durhams, she would be meek and subdued, and when it came time for her to return to Dorset, people would marvel at how docile she was.

However, she had no intention of being docile enough to marry Elliott Maynard, despite her father's fondest hopes.

The wind was picking up a bit. Perhaps she was foolish to sit here in the middle of nowhere and wait. She couldn't very well drag her luggage around the country-side, but she was young enough and quite strong and used to walking, even in the tight boots and layers of wool. She could follow the narrow road into the darken-ing afternoon—sooner or later she'd have to come to a village, or at least a farmhouse where they might send word to the Durhams.

But what had the coachman said, in the midst of his dire warnings about Dark Men? The nearest pub was no place for a young lady, and as the night grew darker she might very well lose her way. At least the market cross was a well-known landmark. Someone would have to pass by, sooner or later, and it was getting to the point where Elizabeth would have gladly welcomed an outlaw or a heartless seducer. And her father's worst fears would be confirmed.

They had never thought that she would take after her mother, the wild and impractical Guinevere de Laurier. Elizabeth had always suspected it had been a relief when her beautiful mother had died of a wasting fever right after Elizabeth was born. William Penshurst had wor-shiped his well-bred, mysterious wife. He'd also been totally bewildered by her.

Adelia was a good, sturdy woman, and loving step-mother, dutiful wife, wise counselor, and solid tren-cherwoman. She was perfect for Elizabeth's sober father. For nineteen years Elizabeth had done her best to belong. It was neither of their faults that deep inside she had always felt like a faery changeling in their neat and practical house.

It would have been better for everyone if she'd never run into Old Peg during one of her solitary rambles. If she hadn't stopped to talk, only to have Old Peg fix her sharp eyes on her and announce in mysterious tones, "You're one of the old ones."

Considering that Old Peg was ancient and Lizzie was only just past her fifteenth birthday at the time, it seemed like a strange thing to greet her with, but Old Peg would never explain. Instead she told Elizabeth the tales of the woods, the old legends of Herne the Hunter, stories going back to the time before Christ, and Lizzie had listened, her determinedly dutiful, fettered soul enraptured by a world long gone that somehow felt like a lost memory she had lived in ages past.

Elizabeth had learned by then not to mention such things to her father if she wanted to keep the peace. She had helped take care of her five little brothers, assisted Adelia in the household duties, attended church with pious regularity, and kept her long, unsuitably red hair tightly coiled and her troublesome eyes chastely downcast. Except when she escaped the house, the watching eyes, and her confining life, and ran free.

All would have been well, and she would have slipped into the satisfyingly peaceful life of a spinster, had it not been for the Reverend Penshurst's weasely curate. Elliott Maynard was a pale, soft-handed, wet-lipped man eager to rise in the world. While the Penshursts had little money, the daughter came from good stock, with a respectable portion. Certain physical drawbacks could be overlooked. Elliott's courtship commenced immediately.

Unfortunately Mr. Penshurst approved the match. His dreamy daughter had always been a worry to him, and placing her in the care of another Man of God seemed the best way to assure her moral well-being. Mr. Penshurst considered it his duty to see the best in all of his fellow creatures, and he was serenely unaware that Elliott Maynard was a lecher, a bully, and a narrow-minded creature concerned less with his flock and almost entirely with his own betterment in society. He was also inordinately stupid.

When Elizabeth's polite demurrals had given way to stern refusals, Elliott had simply presented his suit to Elizabeth's father. And been warmly welcomed into the family.

Old Peg had been her only support. "Don't marry him, lass!" she'd said in a hushed voice. "He's not the man for you. He's waiting for you."

"Who is?" Lizzie had demanded, but Old Peg had refused to answer, closing her eyes and looking deep into the strange places where she always seemed to find the answers.

"The Dark Man," Old Peg had muttered. "You have to face the Dark Man. It's Him you'll be wanting."

That had been six months before, and her parents had kept on at her, determined that Elliott Maynard was the answer to her future. She might have been worn down, eventually, if she hadn't gone to the woods one morning to find Old Peg still and silent, lying amidst the leaves, her long life finished with her secrets taken with her. And the next time, when Lizzie went to dance in the woods, Elliott had followed her.

Elliott Maynard hadn't given up, despite Elizabeth's shocking fall from grace. He considered her visit to her second cousin Jane in North Yorkshire to be a minor setback, and he was prepared to wait. After all, there were few men willing to marry an ordinary young woman with such strange and pagan habits. It didn't matter that she had too clever a tongue and nothing more than a respectable portion. He could be patient.

He could be patient till hell froze over, Elizabeth thought with uncharacteristic violence, shivering in her thin cloak. She'd prefer the mysterious Dark Man to Elliott's soft-handed bullying.

And here she was, at a crossroads, and nearby a Dark Man lurked in these ancient woods. A spawn of Satan, or something else. Old Peg, for all her adherence to the Old Ways and the Old Religion, wouldn't have sent her to the devil, would she?

She hadn't heard a sound, only the ripple of the wind through the thick bower of leaves, the faint scurry of a small woodland creature. But she looked up, torn from her brooding thoughts, and saw him standing there, watching her.

He was no Dark Man, of that one thing she was absolutely certain. It had to be a mere trick of nature, that sent one solitary shaft of late-afternoon sunlight down to gild his tall, silent form.

For a moment she thought he might be the coachman from Hernewood Manor, but there was no comfortable conveyance, no horse nearby. He was dressed in rough clothes—a coarse knit shirt, open at the neck, and dark breeches that might have been leather or wool. His hair was far too long, as if he hadn't bothered to have it cut in years, but his face was clean-shaven. He tilted it to get a better look at her, and her breath caught in her throat.

His hair was a sun-streaked brown, his face tanned from the outdoors even this early in the year. His eyes were curiously light in his face, though she was too far away to see what color they were. His face was narrow, a watchful, clever face, and she wondered who he was. And if he knew about the Dark Man.

Her father had told her to beware strange men, and this still, silent creature who stood watching her was very strange indeed. But the darkness was closing in

around them, and she couldn't very well pretend not
to see him.

"Hullo," she said, and to her annoyance her voice
wavered a bit.

He didn't say a word, he simply moved closer. She
stared at him in astonishment. He didn't move like a
peasant. He was the most graceful creature she'd ever
seen, and the most silent. He crossed the rough ground
until he came very close to her, and she saw his eyes
were a clear, golden brown in his cool, still face.

His voice was the biggest surprise of all. She'd been
expecting the flat, broad Yorkshire tones she'd already
learned to interpret. His voice was low, warm, beguiling.
And she knew, instinctively, the voice of a gentleman.

"Who are you?" There was nothing rude in the question—he simply seemed curious to find a young woman
perched on her luggage in the middle of nowhere.

"I'm waiting for someone from Hernewood Manor to
fetch me. I don't suppose you've seen anyone nearby?"

"Hernewood Manor," he murmured. "That explains
it. And would you be visiting Jane?"

He didn't say Miss Jane, and Elizabeth wasn't fool
enough to correct him. Whoever this strange creature
was, he didn't fit in any of the normal, rigid social levels
she was used to.

"Miss Durham is a cousin."

"Indeed?" He sounded doubtful.

"Yes, indeed."

"And why have we never seen you in these parts
before?"

The conversation was beginning to make her as
uncomfortable as the mysterious man. "And who's to
say I haven't been here before?" she countered in a
practical voice. "You might have just missed my presence."

He shook his head. "I would have known," he said simply. He glanced around. "It looks as if they've forgotten all about you. That's not like them—the Durhams pride themselves on details and minding their manners."

"I'm sure they'll show up any moment now."

"I could see what's keeping them."

She was frozen to the bone, and all her father's warnings vanished with a shiver. "Would you?"

"There's only one problem," he said. "I don't know your name. Shall I just tell them a mysterious young woman is waiting at the market cross?"

"Miss Penshurst," she said. "Miss Elizabeth Penshurst."

He tilted his head to one side, a strange expression in his golden eyes. "Miss Elizabeth Penshurst," he repeated it, as if he were tasting the words. "Welcome to Hernewood, Miss Penshurst. Do you believe in magic?"

Stranger and stranger. "Not for an instant," she said flatly. She wasn't going to believe in magic any longer, she'd promised her father, promised herself.

His faint smile was ever so faintly unnerving. "You will, Miss Penshurst. Hernewood will make you believe."

There was nothing she could reply to such an extraordinary statement. He moved away from her. "I'll find someone and send them for you."

He walked away, she knew he did, like any other normal human being. But it still seemed to her overtired, overactive brain that he melted back into the dappled sunshine, vanishing from view as the darkness grew deeper and thicker around her. She wondered if she was a complete fool to trust him. She wondered if she'd imagined the entire encounter.

Less than ten minutes later the jingling of a horse bridle set her mind at ease. The small pony cart came racing down the roadway, pulling to a stop in front of her with a great flurry of dust and stamping horse.

The young driver was almost as surprising as her previous encounter. Tall and lanky, dressed in an enveloping coachman's coat, he jumped down and pulled off his cap, exposing a head of cropped black curls that was most definitely feminine.

"Dreadfully sorry!" she said in a breathless voice. "We thought you were coming next week!" She stuck out a large, well-made hand. "I'm your cousin Jane, you know."

Elizabeth had risen, and she looked up into her cousin Jane's plain, pleasant face. Her eyes were a warm brown, her black hair hacked off midway to her shoulders with a singular lack of style. But those eyes were the kindest eyes Elizabeth had ever seen in her life, and her smile was equally welcoming.

"I'm Elizabeth Penshurst," she said. "And you can't imagine how very glad I am to meet you."

"Yes, I can," Jane said cheerfully. "This place is a little strange for those who aren't used to it, and here we were, forgetting all about you. My father will have my head for this."

"Was it your fault?"

"No," Jane said. "But that won't matter to my father—he's a stickler for polite behavior, not to mention punctuality, and he can't very well blame the brats."

"The brats?"

"My younger brother and sister. Two absolute hellions who nonetheless fail to make my father appreciate my subdued manner." She laughed, a rich, hearty chuckle that was wonderfully infectious. She reached for Elizabeth's box, the box that had strong coachmen staggering under its weight, and heaved it into the back of the cart with deceptive ease.

"I gather you're in some sort of disgrace," Jane continued, climbing up into the pony trap and holding out her hand for Lizzie. "Was it with a man?"

"No!" said Lizzie, affronted. "I was simply walking in the forest, entirely by myself."

"What's so shocking about that?"

"I wasn't wearing much," she admitted.

Jane laughed, a full-throated chuckle. "Well, I'm always in disgrace as well. It sounds as if your crimes aren't much worse than mine, which usually include spending too much time in the stable and ripping my clothes. I expect we'll get along famously."

"Two unrepentant hoydens," Lizzie said. "I'm supposed to be mending my wicked ways."

"So am I. I think it's a lost cause in my case. My parents gave up on me years ago. I'm doomed to be an old maid, and just as happy." There was a trace of defiance in her rich voice.

Lizzie looked at her in surprise. "You don't want to get married?"

"Not if I can't have true love. Of course Gabriel says that true love doesn't exist, but he's being tiresomely cynical. I believe in it, I just don't believe I'm going to end up with that particular blessing." She shrugged. "I'm not going to worry about it though." She'd turned the pony cart onto a narrow track. "This isn't the main way to the house—Father would never stand for anything so shoddy—but it's the fastest way to get you there and warm you up. Just don't tell him I brought you in the pony trap, will you?"

"Why not?"

"He expected me to have the carriage set up, but that would have been another half hour, we'd have had to take the main road, and I wouldn't have gotten here until it was pitch-black. Thank God Gabriel found me."

"Gabriel? Was that the strange man?"

Jane laughed. "Strange, you think? I suppose I can't argue—there's no one on earth quite like Gabriel. Don't mention anything to my parents about him. They'll have the vapors."

"They don't approve of him?"

"That's putting it mildly."

"But who is he? I thought he was a servant at first, but once he spoke I realized he couldn't be."

For the first time the outspoken Jane looked uncomfortable. "Gabriel is simply . . . Gabriel. You won't be likely to run into him again—he keeps his distance from most people. Forget you ever saw him."

For some reason the memory of his haunting golden eyes danced back into her brain. "Certainly," she said briskly, in no means certain that she'd be capable of doing any such thing. "If you'll tell me one thing."

"Of course," Jane said blithely.

"Who is the Dark Man?"

CHAPTER TWO

William Frederick Randolph Lindley Gabriel Durham moved through the woods in silence, weaving his way through the towering ruins of the old abbey. He blended in with the dark and the shadows, blended with the silence and the ghosts, and no one would have seen him. He preferred it that way.

It surprised him that he'd left the benevolent haven of the woods to find Miss Penshurst sitting on her luggage, trying not to show her fear. He wondered if she were about to cry. He didn't think so. She didn't have the look of someone who cried easily. She looked both too practical and too fey, an odd combination.

He'd seen her from a distance, from the edge of the woods where she never would have noticed him if he hadn't wished it, and if he'd had any sense at all, he would have simply turned and gone back, somehow getting word to Jane that a forlorn young lady had been abandoned by the market cross. But he had never been

concerned with sense, he believed in tempting his devils
and satisfying his curiosity. That was all he intended
to satisfy with Miss Penshurst. He accounted himself
intellectually amoral, but he had certain standards, and
despoiling virgins, both the well-bred and the working-
class, was something he avoided.

For one thing, virgins were tedious, prone to tears,
usually frigid, and afterward always decided it simply
must be true love to have made them forget themselves
in his bed.

For another, he felt sorry for the poor creatures. They
belonged in bed with some stalwart, unimaginative husband, who'd give them babies and perhaps some inkling
of the pleasure that could be had. They didn't need
the temptation he offered. Most people were better off
not even knowing what kind of arcane delights existed
in the world.

What he didn't understand was why he was suddenly
thinking so determinedly of sex, and he could only
come to the entirely unwanted conclusion that Miss
Penshurst had set him off. She wasn't the most beautiful
woman he'd ever seen. She was passably pretty, but her
hair was bound too tightly to her well-shaped head,
covered by a plain bonnet, her eyes were too wary and
too wise, her mouth set as if she was afraid a smile might
escape. He wondered where she came from. He didn't
remember Sir Richard or Lady Durham ever men-
tioning a Penshurst connection, and while she was obviously well-bred, she wasn't of the highest echelons that
the Durhams usually pursued in their determination to
make their way in society.

A wry smile crossed his face as he rounded the corner
of the old kitchen area of the abbey. The stones were
almost gone now, carted away to build the huge house
that Richard Durham had managed to acquire, along

with his title, some thirty-three years before. Everyone believed the old abbey was haunted by the ghosts of monks who once lived and worshiped here. Anti-Catholic sentiment was so strong that many of the villagers believed babies had been sacrificed at regular intervals before King Henry had dissolved all the monasteries. They believed the souls of the guilty monks still wandered the ruins, searching for new victims, and Gabriel did nothing to dispel the notion. He liked his privacy. And he knew the truth of the matter.

The tower was at one end of the ruins of the old refectory, still intact. Smoke was pouring from the chimney, though he expected Peter had already left. If Sir Richard ever knew he attended the unwelcome heir of Hernewood Manor, Peter would be out on his ear. And while Gabriel had more than enough money to afford a raft of full-time servants, Peter had his own reasons for not wanting to leave the manor.

Elizabeth Penshurst, he thought as he climbed the winding stairs to the place he thought of as his lair. She looked like a Lizzie to him. He needed to stop thinking about her. He'd made his peace with Sir Richard, in his own mind if not face-to-face, and he had no need to drive one more thorn into his side. Even if seducing his innocent kinswoman would make Sir Richard squirm indeed.

He wondered how long she would be there. Yorkshire was far too rugged for most southern English girls—if she was like any of Edwina's friends, she'd run screaming for the doubtful comforts of civilization before a month was up.

But he suspected she wasn't like Edwina's pretty little friends. She'd sat alone at the market cross in the biting wind, looking deceptively calm, when Edwina would have had a temper tantrum. He could be wrong, but he suspected there was an inner steel to Miss Penshurst, the kind his sister Jane possessed.

He would indulge himself, long enough to find out exactly who and what she was. And what she was doing at the back end of nowhere with an influence-seeking baronet of dubious lineage. One who would sell his soul for a better title.

The circular stone steps were worn down beneath his soft leather boots, and here and there one had crumbled dangerously. He left it that way on purpose—one small trap for the unwary trespasser.

He wasn't sure why he spent so much time in the luxurious ruin of the still habitable tower when he had a house and estate of his own, far grander than Herne-wood Manor, just waiting for his attention. For some perverse reason he preferred to live at the very edge of Sir Richard's property, a tiny, stinging thorn in the old man's side.

He paused at the top of the winding stairs. The heavy oak door was tightly closed, but his senses immediately became alert. He had a visitor, and he had little doubt it was an unwanted one.

Only for a minute did he consider turning and heading back down those stairs and into the night. He was seldom in the mood for visitors, and tonight he was even less so. Besides, he had an uneasy suspicion who it might be.

Delilah, Countess of Chilton, was aptly named. She lounged against a pile of pillows, her beautiful eyes half-closed, her full, petulant mouth curved in a welcoming smile. "There you are, Gabriel," she purred in her deep, sensual voice. "I was wondering if you were ever going to show up."

Either Peter had still been there when she arrived, or she'd helped herself to his wine. There was another glass, and he took it, stalling for time. "I wasn't expecting you, Delilah."

"But aren't I a happy surprise?"

"Not particularly. Where's your husband?" There was no disapproval in his voice, just boredom.

"Oh, chasing after some lovely young creature. He doesn't care what I do, you know it as well as I do. I'm lonely, Gabriel." She looked up at him from the pile of cushions where she lay, artfully arranged to expose her best assets, and he viewed her dispassionately.

Her assets were indeed remarkable. She was a beautiful woman, small, delicate, with full, lush breasts semiexposed by her wispy, low-cut gown. Her hair was a midnight black, rich and tumbled around her feline face, and her expression was mocking, provocative, beneath the thick fringe of eyelash.

He turned his back on her, crossing the room to stand by the fire. The earl and countess of Chilton had arrived in Yorkshire some six months ago, and according to Peter they'd been hounded out of London for some unspeakable indiscretion. He could only imagine. Decadent and willful, they were the sort of people he had once sought out, the same sort of people he had come back home to escape. He'd had his fill of London and licentiousness. For now all he wanted to do was keep to himself, reading the ancient texts he'd found in his travels, studying the Old Ways, the Old Religion.

Unfortunately the Chiltons had followed popular sentiment and become enamored of the ancient British religions as well. Gabriel had no idea what they believed or why, and he preferred to keep it that way. He expected their constant invitations had little to do with scholarly interest and more to do with widening the scope of their perennial house parties and the variety of bed partners.

Either way, he was not interested in their bizarre entertainments.

He was admittedly human, despite the rumors they spread about him in the village. He could be tempted by a beautiful wanton as well as the next man, though the thought of the countess's effeminate husband left him decidedly unmoved.

But temptation and acting upon that urge were two different things, and Delilah Montgomery had always been a shade too eager for his tastes.

"I'm celibate, Delilah," he said wearily, staring into the fire.

"You don't need to be." He could tell by the rustle of clothing that she'd risen from her provocative pose and was coming toward him, and he stiffened his backbone, ignoring that other, annoyingly stiff part of him. Odd, but Delilah was more tempting than usual. Most times he was able to banter with her and then dismiss her, but tonight he could feel that long-smothered need. "Druids weren't celibate—far from it. They could be quite bawdy. Where do you think all the little Druids came from?"

She came up behind him, leaning against his back, and she smelled like a woman, like firelight and wine, and he knew if he turned he would kiss her, and then he'd be lost.

He turned anyway, impatient, reaching for her, and then stopped. She stared up at him in frustrated confusion, but it wasn't the face he was expecting. For some reason he'd pictured another woman standing behind him. Waiting for him. And he knew he could blame the young woman who'd stared up at him in dismay earlier that day. "Druids have been dead for more than a thousand years, Delilah," he said gently, taking her hand from his arm. "Go home. There's nothing for you here."

She had a delectable pout, and she knew it. She accepted her dismissal gracefully enough—she'd certainly had enough practice in her determined pursuit of him. "I came for a reason, you know."

He smiled faintly. "I can imagine."

"Not that reason, Gabriel," she said with a moue. "We're hosting a small party to celebrate May Day in a typically country fashion, and Francis and I were both counting on you to come."

"I seldom socialize, you know that."

"We're seekers as well as you are. We want to learn of the Old Ways, the Old Religion, and what better time than Beltane? I promise, I'd be a very apt pupil."

It was women like her who'd driven him out of London, back to the woods and the secrets. "You aren't interested in religion, Delilah."

"You'd be surprised what can interest me. The Druids were so delightfully . . . savage." Her smile was rich and full. "You know you aren't a holy brother anymore, Gabriel, and you aren't an archangel like your namesake. You might as well accept the world and all the lovely things it has to offer." She put her delicate hand on his arm, stroking him very gently through the rough cloth of his sleeve.

He controlled the faint shiver of desire that washed over him. He didn't deny it—he was a man who accepted all his strengths and weaknesses, and lust was a normal emotion when confronted with a temptation like Delilah Chilton. If it weren't for her husband, he'd probably give in. If it weren't for the cold calculation in the back of her fine blue eyes.

"You don't need to deliver your invitations in person,

my dear. You have servants," he said, stepping away. "Use them."

"I do. At every possible chance," she added with a ripe laugh. He'd seen the men and women employed at Arundel, all quite remarkably good-looking, and he had little doubt she did exactly as she said.

She'd been lying on her rich, fur-trimmed cloak, and she reached down and caught it, pulling it around her voluptuous figure. "Please come, Gabriel. Don't disappoint us. I promise I won't invite your father."

She was more than capable of doing just that, just to watch the ensuing debacle. "I'll send word."

"Or come yourself," she cooed, reaching up and pressing a kiss against his mouth. She left the oak door open as she descended the dangerous, curving stairs.

He stood there unmoving. A gentleman would have seen her safely down those stairs with a lantern to guide her. She would doubtless have a servant and a carriage waiting nearby, but if he had any decency at all he would see her safe.

He wasn't feeling particularly decent, and he knew full well if he went after her he might not be able to resist. He wasn't sure why it was so important to resist, when he'd spent his life indulging his appetites, his curiosity, and his intellect, but he trusted his instincts.

He heard a slight banging noise from beneath him, and he started for the door in sudden guilt.

"Don't go, lad. She's a deceitful wench, out to destroy you if she has half a chance. She won't fall and break her neck—it's only the good who die young. Haven't I warned you?"

Slowly Gabriel turned at the sound of the familiar voice. Brother Septimus, tall, thin, scholarly, and disapproving, stood by the fire that could never warm his bones, his monk's robe hanging loose on his gaunt body, his tonsured head bowed, his craggy old face creased in disapproval.

"You've warned me, Brother Septimus," he said wearily. "And I've listened."

"Good lad," murmured the Cistercian monk. "I'll be watching out for you." And he vanished, as silently and as swiftly as he had appeared.

"Damned ghosts," Gabriel muttered under his breath, and reached for his glass of wine.

Francis Chilton greeted his wife's return to the carriage with a faint smile, handing her a glass of wine without spilling a drop as they pulled away from the forest. Their driver was well trained.

"And how did it go, my precious? Will he join us on Beltane?"

Delilah took a sip, shivering beneath the rich animal throws that Francis draped around her. "He's being very stubborn, Francis. You'd think he'd realize what an important occasion this is—Beltane comes but once a year, and it's the most significant time for any number of reasons which he knows even better than we do. He's resisting."

"Of course he is, darling. That's what makes him so much fun. I have my utmost faith in you, precious. You'll triumph in the end, I know you will. You'll bring Gabriel Durham to me in good time."

"I'll do what I can," she murmured. "But I want him, too, Francis. You do realize that?"

"You'll have your chance, dearest. In the meantime, perhaps we ought to consider the sister."

Delilah leaned back against the squabs, a small, savage smile on her face. "Ah, yes, the sister. Such fun, Francis."

He leaned forward and kissed her mouth in a gentle salute. "Such fun indeed, darling."

Hernewood Manor was an imposing edifice, nestled in the heart of a steep valley at the edge of a forest. Made of white stone, it was nevertheless a dark, unwelcoming sort of place, Lizzie thought. And its inhabitants, with the sole exception of Jane, weren't much more hospitable.

Sir Richard Durham was an imposing figure of a man, a bluff, hearty country squire with all the subtlety of a bull. His wife, Elinor, was a pale, nervous woman, prone to saying "Yes, dear" as her sole means of communication, but they both seemed relatively free from malice, despite the waves of disapproval that seemed to reach across the room like a noxious cloud and envelop Jane.

"Good to have you here, Elizabeth," Sir Richard said gruffly, looking at her with faint disapproval, as if her red hair was somehow a personal affront. "I hope my elder daughter didn't keep you waiting for too long. God knows her mother and I have tried to drill punctuality and proper behavior into her, with blessed little cooperation, I might add."

Elizabeth allowed herself a furtive glance at Jane's calm expression. To her surprise Jane managed a quick wink before ducking her head in dutiful contrition. "But you haven't met the rest of my little family," Sir Richard continued, allowing no one else the chance to speak. "My wife, Elinor, who'll be a second mother to you, no doubt. Your own mother was her cousin, though they're nothing alike, thank heavens. The world couldn't have handled too many Guineveres in this lifetime. Or in any, for that matter," he said with a bark of laughter.

Elizabeth's gaze sharpened. Never in her life had she met anyone who knew her mother and was willing to talk about her in other than hushed, dismissive tones. Sir Richard didn't seem particularly inclined to let anyone else in the room speak, but later, away from his overbearing presence, Lady Durham might be persuaded to talk about her past.

"And these are my two little darlings," he added fondly. "Edward and Edwina, the twins. All that a parent could hope for."

Elizabeth received Edwina's limp hand in salutation. She was indeed the perfect daughter, at least by the Durhams' standards. With perfect blond ringlets surrounding a face of astonishing beauty only slightly marred by an expression of discontent, she looked to be about seventeen years old. She was flanked by her handsome twin brother, a young man just as perfect, just as spoiled-looking as his sister, and fully four inches shorter than his older sister. His greeting was even more lackluster, and both of them studiously ignored their older sister Jane.

"It does an old man's heart good to see his line carried on," Sir Richard continued. "Makes up for earlier disappointments."

"Richard!" Lady Durham's voice was horrified, and Sir Richard looked properly abashed. For a moment Elizabeth warmed toward the woman for defending her daughter.

"I meant Jane, of course," he said defensively. "Jane's a disappointment to us all, who can deny it? Nothing else, m'love."

Beware the Dark Man. The voice echoed in Elizabeth's head, irrationally, but loud and clear. It wasn't the voice of the coachman with his Yorkshire dialect. It was Old

Peg, telling her future, warning her. *Beware the Dark Man.*

Elizabeth managed a polite smile, casting a furtive glance beyond the leaded-glass windows to the dark woods beyond. If the Dark Man was somewhere out there, she'd keep well away from him. Peg had been her mysterious self, unwilling to tell her whether he was her doom or her salvation. And Elizabeth had sworn to behave herself.

Lady Durham had sidled over to her, her soft, powdered skin like crumpled tissue. "I'm sure we're delighted to have you," she said in her soft voice, clearly sure of no such thing. "We were so concerned when your father wrote and explained your delicate situation, and so pleased we could have you up to Hernewood Abbey for a visit."

"My delicate situation?" Elizabeth echoed, perplexed.

"But I'm sure with our good clean Yorkshire air you'll regain your strength in no time, and we'll soon be dancing at your wedding. Your curate sounds absolutely delightful. I could only wish the same for poor Jane. Alas, I'm afraid she's doomed to be an old maid."

For all that Lady Durham's voice was soft, it was also remarkably distinct, and from a few feet away Poor Jane made a wry face that her mother, fortunately, missed.

"I'm not engaged to anyone," Elizabeth said, astonished that her father hadn't revealed the true reason for her banishment. Doubtless his shame went too deep.

Lady Durham laughed in a particularly annoying way. "Your father said you were very shy about it. Don't worry—it will be our little secret. Such a modest girl you are—I wish Jane weren't such a hoyden."

Indeed, one of Jane's extraneous flounces was ripped, and there was a smear of dirt across the side of her fussy skirts, and Elizabeth knew a moment's instant envy. A longing for fresh air and moonlight and unfettered clothing.

"Good country air is the thing for you, young lady," Sir Richard boomed out from across the room. "Just keep away from the woods."

Lady Durham's smile was chilly. "Why doesn't Jane take you up to your room and get you settled? We keep country hours here, and our cook is very temperamental. He has a tantrum if the food is kept waiting, and we're lucky we were able to persuade him to come all the way up here." There was more pride in her voice concerning her cook than her elder daughter, but Jane seemed oblivious.

"You're very kind to have me, Lady Durham," she murmured politely.

Lady Durham waved a weak hand. "It's nothing, child. Just see if you can be a proper model for Jane."

"She can teach our Jane some ladylike behavior," Sir Richard boomed from across the room. "Elizabeth seems a quiet, pretty-behaved young lady—you'd do well to emulate her ways, miss."

Elizabeth managed to turn her surprised laugh into a cough. Her straitlaced father had been white with horror at the sight of his misbehaving daughter. If Sir Richard discovered how wild she truly was, he'd probably die of apoplexy.

She met Jane's laughing eyes. "I'll do my best, sir," she murmured.

And she wondered if Jane had ever danced barefoot in the moonlight.

CHAPTER THREE

"I never liked red hair," Cousin Edward announced with a remarkable lack of tact.

He was lounging inside her open doorway, trying to look sophisticated and failing utterly. Elizabeth resisted the impulse to poke at her tightly coiled hair, simply turning to him with a bland expression on her face. "Since God gave it to me, I'll have to suppose He does," she said mildly enough.

He straightened to his full height, which still made him shorter than his towering older sister. "Your hair doesn't go with the rest of you. You dress like a governess," he said spitefully. "Look like one, too."

She glanced down at her plain gray gown, the epitome of dull, conservative apparel, and told herself she was pleased. "I expect that's what I'll end up doing with my life. I'm very good at rapping the knuckles of rude young gentlemen." Her voice was dulcet. "How old are you, Edward?"

"Seventeen."

"Really? I would have thought you were younger." She smiled with utter sweetness.

His twin appeared behind him, her perfect mouth in a sullen pout. "I do hope you're not going to take too long in getting settled," she observed, looking at Elizabeth with a disapproving air. "After all, you can't be planning a long stay at Hernewood Manor, so there shouldn't be that much to unpack, and Papa detests it when dinner is late. Besides, we have servants for that sort of thing."

"Why shouldn't I want to stay here?" Elizabeth ignored the fact that this was, in fact, a punishment. "I've never been to Yorkshire before."

"If you had any sense, you wouldn't have come in the first place. It's a cold, wild, uncivilized place. Any sensible person would much prefer London."

"Have you been to London?"

"Many times," Edwina said. "It's a glorious place."

"It's a pigsty," Elizabeth said firmly. "Full of noisy, jostling people and no peace. You can't breathe the air."

"Maybe you spend your time with riffraff, dear cousin," Edwina said, her smile exposing pointy little teeth, "but we're accustomed to a better class of people."

"Not that there's any decent society up here, if you don't count the Chiltons," Edward added in a sullen voice. "And I wouldn't go traipsing off around here in search of fresh air. You're likely to run into things you're better off not seeing. Besides, the grounds are haunted."

Finally he'd managed to get to Elizabeth. "So I gather," she said serenely.

"Ghostly monks have been seen wandering the ruins," Edward said in a sepulchral voice.

Edwina looked uncertain. "Don't be ridiculous, Edward, you know that's probably just . . ." Her voice trailed off.

"Probably just the souls of murdering Catholics," Edward continued smugly. "Unable to rest because of their hideous crimes."

Elizabeth had never held with the notion of murderous Catholics, and this was more than she was willing to swallow. "More likely it's the Dark Man," she said calmly. "Gabriel, is it?"

She'd managed to shock the two of them into silence. "How . . . how did you know about him?" Edward stammered.

"How do you think she knows? That prattle, Jane, must have told her," Edwina said crossly, clearly the domineering member of the partnership. "If I were you, my little country cousin, I wouldn't say the name Gabriel in my parents' presence. They're likely to become quite apoplectic."

"And exactly who is Gabriel?" Elizabeth asked with admirable calm.

Edward snickered. "Let's just call him one of the ghostly monks. Brother Gabriel, another lost soul of Hernewood Abbey."

"He didn't look particularly lost."

Edwina let out a little shriek. "I don't believe you actually saw him! He's a hermit, and he hates women. Except for the ones he . . . well, you know."

"I can't imagine."

"She probably saw one of the laborers," Edward scoffed.

"Do they all have such astonishing eyes?"

"For heaven's sakes, don't mention his eyes!" Edwina

hissed. "Mother would probably fall down in a screaming fit of vapors. That was Gabriel all right. The least said, the better for all of us."

"Is he a monk?" For some reason Elizabeth found that notion to be completely unsettling. He didn't look like a monk. He hadn't looked at her like a man sworn to celibacy.

"Former monk," Edward corrected. "Now he follows a different master. He's a Druid. He dabbles in witchcraft and magick and the black arts. They say he performs blood sacrifice when the moon is full and reads the future from the way the blood falls to the ground. There have been mysterious disappearances in the area, you know. Animals found slaughtered, that sort of thing. People think Gabriel's behind it. And him named for an angel!"

"He's a demon," Edwina hissed.

"You'd best forget you ever saw him, little cousin," Edward continued, blithely ignoring the fact that he was three years younger and not an inch taller than Elizabeth. "He might go in for a little virgin sacrifice on the side. Slitting the throat of chickens and sheep probably gets boring after a while."

Edwina giggled and slapped him on the arm. "I don't think it's virgins that interest him, brother."

"Go away, you two, and leave Elizabeth alone." Jane's sudden appearance was like a *dea ex machina,* and Elizabeth just barely resisted the impulse to fling her arms around Jane's neck. A few minutes in the company of the twins was a few minutes too long. "She doesn't want to be bothered with your silly fairy stories. No one thinks Gabriel's behind anything. He's loved in this area, which is more than I can say for the rest of us."

"And who was the one who told her about the Dark

Man?" Edwina shot back. "And Gabriel the ghostly monk?"

"I certainly didn't fill her head with tales of magic and ritual sacrifice," Jane said sternly. "Go away, the two of you, or we'll be hours late for dinner, and Father will become dyspeptic."

"He's always dyspeptic anyway," Edward muttered, giving ground. "Don't listen to Jane, Cousin Elizabeth. She'll try to convince you there's nothing to worry about, but it will be a lie. Keep out of the woods. Keep away from Gabriel. If you have any sense at all, you'll go back to where you belong as soon as possible."

"If she has any sense she won't listen to a word you say," Jane said. "Shoo!"

The twins beat a hasty retreat, unwilling to stand up to their powerful elder sibling. "Beasts," Jane muttered under her breath. "I hope you didn't pay them any mind."

"They told me I shouldn't mention Gabriel or the Dark Man at the dinner table."

Jane barely blinked. "Well, since I already warned you about the same thing, I would think you'd pay heed. Gabriel's a sore point around here."

Elizabeth peered into a mirror trying to smooth her hair back into obedience. Her skin was even paler than usual, and she must have found just enough sun to bring forth pale golden freckles across her nose. "I'm sorry. It's none of my concern," she said apologetically.

"No, it's not," Jane said. "But that doesn't mean you're not curious."

"I shouldn't give in to curiosity," Elizabeth said stalwartly. "But you're going to tell me who Gabriel is, and why your parents quiver at the mention of his name, aren't you? You wouldn't let me perish of wicked curiosity."

Jane let out a weary sigh as she headed toward the door. She paused, looking back. "Who do you think he is?" she said wearily. "He's our brother. Dinner's ready." And she disappeared down the hallway, leaving Elizabeth to race after her, a moment after her initial shock passed.

Elizabeth wasn't sure what dragged her from a sound sleep that night. She'd been dreaming, of wolves roaming the dark woods with strange, translucent eyes, and she was running, barefoot through the thick grass, with the heat of the wolf's breath on her back and his paw between her shoulders blades, flinging her down onto the hard ground . . .

She sat up in bed, stifling a small scream, and for a moment she couldn't remember where she was. She was in the wolf's cave, and he was staring at her out of the darkness, his strange eyes glowing . . .

She blinked, and the fitful moonlight illuminated the recesses of her strange room, and she remembered where she was. In the small bedroom on the second floor of Hernewood Manor, dreaming of ghostly wolves.

The room was cold—the fire had died out long ago and it hadn't been a generous one in the first place. It was all done very subtly—a sly glance here, a faint expression there, but Elizabeth had no illusions that she was an honored guest, but rather a poor relation, taken in with a combination of resignation and duty. The Durhams seemed to have almost as little use for her as they had for their eldest daughter.

Not to mention their eldest son. Elizabeth was still reeling from the revelation that the mysterious man from the woods was in actuality Gabriel Durham, Jane's brother. He looked as different from his parents and the twins as night from day, and his resemblance to Jane was minimal except for their height.

But what was the heir of Hernewood Manor doing dressed in rough clothes, living in the woods?

She climbed out of bed, dragging a shawl with her and wrapping it around her shoulders as she peered out the window. Her room overlooked the forest, not the wide expanse of formal gardens, and at first she could see nothing but the thick trees. She leaned her forehead against the chill glass, and as she squinted she could make out the pale, moonlit stone of the ruined abbey. And a faint shadow of movement that might be a deer, might be a rabbit, might be a ghostly monk.

"There are no such things as ghosts," she said out loud in her best, most practical voice. Old Peg would be sorely disappointed in her—she'd always maintained that there were more things in heaven and earth than many even dared to dream of. And Elizabeth had believed, until she'd seen the shock and hurt in her father's eyes and determined to mend her ways.

"You won't be able to be who they want you to be," Old Peg had warned her that last day Elizabeth had seen her. "You can put shoes on your feet and drab clothes on your body, you can cast your eyes down and pin your hair close to your head and pretend you haven't seen with your soul things few people even dream of. But the truth will own you, Elizabeth Penshurst. No matter how you try to hide from it, the truth will own you."

But it wouldn't. She could be the proper child her father deserved. She would do her duty—she was a loving daughter with a loving heart, and while she wouldn't marry a slug like Elliott Maynard, she was perfectly willing to obey her father's wishes and find suitable employment. She would teach ungrateful children, she would keep a disagreeable old lady company, she would willingly do any number of things to lessen the burden on her father's slender purse. And she would turn a deaf ear to the call of the woods and the lure of magic.

But here she was, leaning against a cold window, staring out into the forest, her breath leaving a mist on the glass, her heart longing for the forest.

On impulse she opened the window, hoping the chill air would put a stop to her yearnings. It was cold—bright and crisp and clear—and she shivered within the cocoon of the shawl, and wondered if her feet would freeze in the cold wet grass.

She wasn't going. She was going to close the window and get back in bed and back to sleep, with no dreams to disturb her. She was strong-minded—indeed, her father often said she was too strong-minded. He would have been shocked if he'd ever learned of the hours she spent in the woods with Old Peg, listening to stories of ancient magic.

In the end she didn't even bother with her slippers. She moved through the house silently, finding her way through the dark, empty halls with such unerring precision that she would have suspected otherworldly help. If she allowed herself to believe in such things.

She was right, the grass was wet and chilly beneath her feet, and yet she moved forward, closing the terrace door behind her. The moon was only a quarter full, and she paused, listening. She had no idea why she was here instead of tucked safe in her bed. Indeed, she was doing just what she'd promised never to do again. Perhaps she was dreaming.

But her feet wouldn't be cold if it was a dream. She wouldn't feel the soft, cool breeze against her face. She wouldn't be wondering what had called her out into the darkness on her first night at Hernewood Manor.

Her reluctant hosts would be horrified if they discovered demure Miss Penshurst had a habit of going for midnight walks clad only in her night rail. She would likely be back on the next mail coach to Dorset if she were discovered, and her disgrace would be irreparable.

She didn't even hesitate. She moved through the trees toward the ruined abbey, ignoring common sense and firm resolutions. She moved through the trees like a ghost.

"What are you doing out here?"

The voice came out of the darkness, cool and unwelcoming, and she let out a tiny screech, shocked out of the strange daze that had entrapped her.

She turned, half expecting a ghostly specter, but the reality was worse. Even in the shadowy moonlight she could see him quite clearly, the glow of his eerie wolf's eyes as they moved across her body.

She clutched her shawl closer to her, grateful she'd thought to bring that much covering, and hoped he wouldn't see her bare feet in the dim light. He looked different in the moonlight than he had earlier that day. He was wearing some kind of dark robe, almost like a monk's habit, though she suspected the material was far richer, and he stood silhouetted against an arched stone doorway of the ruined abbey, watching her with an expression that was far from welcoming.

"Miss Penshurst," he said after a moment, his voice impatient, "I can't imagine why you're wandering out here all alone like a ghost, but I would suggest you get yourself back to the manor before anyone realizes you're gone. Sir Richard and Lady Elinor won't take kindly to a houseguest with a propensity for midnight walks."

"They don't take kindly to having me as a houseguest at all," Elizabeth said with unexpected candor. "I'm certain they'll think someone who sleepwalks is even less desirable.''

He blinked, and for some reason the phrase ''less desirable'' echoed in her head. ''Is that what you're doing?'' he asked. ''Sleepwalking?''

''I must be. No sensible woman would be wandering in the woods in . . .'' She almost mentioned her night rail, then decided such a comment could be provocative. ''. . . in the middle of the night.''

''You didn't look as if you were asleep. You looked as if you knew exactly where you were going.''

''You were watching me?''

''Since the moment you crept out of the house like a sneak thief.''

''But why?''

''I make it my habit to watch over the Durhams,'' he said.

''They're your family.''

He didn't look surprised. ''In a manner of speaking.''

''I know who you are,'' she said abruptly, annoyed.

His faint smile was less than reassuring. ''Do you? I wish I could say the same about you.''

''I've already told you, I'm Elizabeth Penshurst, Jane Durham's second cousin. And yours as well,'' she added belatedly.

''Don't assume any such thing,'' he said softly, looking at her. ''Now why would a sensible, well-bred young woman suddenly take to wandering the woods in her nightclothes and bare feet?''

She immediately bent her knees so that her plain white-cotton gown trailed in the grass, covering the shocking sight of her pale, bare feet. ''What makes you think I'm sensible?'' she inquired rashly.

''Do you believe in ghosts, Miss Elizabeth Penshurst?''

"No," she said firmly, resisting the impulse to look over her shoulder into the darkness.

"And do you believe in the Old Religion, in magic and mystery and things beyond mortal understanding?" His voice was low, silky, persuasive, and he'd somehow moved closer in the moonlit copse of wood.

"My father is an Anglican rector, sir," she said stiffly, avoiding the question. "Such blasphemy would horrify him."

His smile was wider now; he was genuinely amused by her. "That's what the Durhams call me, you know, when they can be persuaded to discuss me. Blasphemer, cynic, voluptuary. I am everything they abhor."

"You're their son!" she said, more shocked by this than any of the dramatic epithets.

"One thing you learn early on, sweet Lizzie, is that things are not always what they seem."

No one had ever called her sweet Lizzie before, and she was certain she didn't like it. Especially in his rich, soft voice that carried across the night air and wrapped around her like a shawl of velvet.

"I shouldn't be here," she said belatedly.

"Wise of you to realize that." He was closer now, so that she could almost see him clearly in the moonlight. "It's a dangerous place, Miss Penshurst. Ghostly monks wander the ruins. I thought you were one of them, with your ethereal white robes."

"I don't believe in ghosts," she said, not sure of any such thing.

"They're harmless. Brother Septimus and Brother Paul have lived here for centuries. I think they'd like you. They're quite fond of my sister Jane, though she's totally unable to see them."

"And you think I could?"

He was very close now, and she hadn't even realized

he'd been approaching. "Oh, quite probably. You aren't the starched, practical creature you pretend to be. Beneath that prim nightgown beats a wild and passionate heart, and gifts even I couldn't begin to fathom. They frighten you, though. Don't they?"

"Very little frightens me," she said stiffly.

His elegant mouth curved in a wry smile. "Now that is one of the first things you've said that I believe. A fearful soul wouldn't be wandering the haunted woods of Hernewood Abbey."

"I can take care of myself."

"Now that I take leave to doubt. There's danger here, and evil. From places you'd least expect, my girl."

"Ghosts again?" she scoffed.

He shook his head. His hair was too long, dark and silken against his face in the moon-shrouded night. "Ghosts are the least of your worries. It's the living who are evil."

There was a note in his rich voice that chilled her, far more effectively than the cool air or the cold wet grass beneath her bare feet. "Are you evil?" she found herself asking.

There was no humor in his smile. "Not entirely."

His answer failed to reassure her. She turned to go, suddenly uneasy as she should have been from the beginning of this strange encounter, when his rich voice stopped her.

"What brought you out here tonight?"

"I dreamt of wolves."

"That should have kept you safe in bed."

"I saw ghosts."

"An even stronger reason to stay put." He had moved, so close to her now that the hem of his robe brushed against her feet. Warm, soft velvet. "Don't come out here again," he said quietly. "Not alone."

"You said the ghosts were harmless, and there are no wolves. Who would hurt me?"

He touched her face, pushing her thick hair back behind her ear, and the feel of his skin against hers was shocking.

"I would," he said.

CHAPTER FOUR

Elizabeth was not in the mood for early rising the next morning. She heard her bedroom door open, and she bundled deeper into the narrow bed, devoutly hoping whoever it was would go away.

"I know you're awake," Jane said in too cheerful a voice for so early in the morning. "You can't convince me you're the sort who spends half the day in bed like the rest of my family."

Elizabeth didn't move. "Go away," she muttered.

"It's a beautiful day, cool and clear. Get up and eat something, and I'll show you the ruins of the old abbey."

Elizabeth sat bolt upright. "No!"

"You don't like historical ruins?" Jane said, perching on the end of the bed.

"Of course I do," she said, pushing a hand through her tangled hair. "I'm just . . . tired."

"Why?" Jane asked. "Didn't you sleep well?"

Elizabeth hesitated, looking at her. For some reason

she trusted Jane, and had done so immediately, but perhaps she ought to use a little discretion. "Do you ever dream, Jane?"

"Everyone dreams, don't they? I don't usually remember mine, which is probably just as well."

"I dreamt about wolves last night," Elizabeth said. "I heard them howling, and I saw them out the window, wandering through the woods."

"That was probably just the ghosts," Jane said calmly. "There are no wolves around here."

"It's not funny."

"I wasn't joking. The woods are haunted, as almost anyone can tell you. Even Edward and Edwina believe in them, though I don't think they've ever seen them. You're lucky, you know. Mostly they only show themselves to a special few."

"Lucky?" Elizabeth echoed. "I think I could have done without that particular piece of luck."

"At least you were wise enough to get back in bed and forget about them," Jane said. Her eyes narrowed. "Weren't you?"

There was a wet leaf on the floor by the bed, telltale proof that Elizabeth hadn't been nearly so wise. "Not exactly," she confessed.

"You didn't go out last night!" Jane said, clearly shocked at the knowledge that her new cousin had done exactly that.

"I'm afraid I did. I was curious," she added, trying to sound practical and failing completely. "You would have done the same."

"Certainly not," Jane said. "I'm afraid of ghosts."

"I didn't know they were ghosts," Elizabeth said in a pleading voice, trying to sound eminently reasonable and failing. "I thought they were wolves. And I thought you said the ghosts were harmless."

"Harmless compared to wolves. You don't want to be messing with the supernatural—Gabriel could tell you that much."

"He did."

"You saw Gabriel? In the middle of the night? Oh, my heavens!" Jane was clearly shocked. And then, as an afterthought, "You were properly dressed, weren't you?"

"I was decently covered," Elizabeth said, trying not to look guilty.

"I wouldn't have thought you'd be quite so trusting."

"I wouldn't have thought I'd need to worry about a cousin," she said, defensive.

"He's not . . ." Jane bit her lip, stopping abruptly.

"Not what? Not safe? Not my cousin?"

"With Gabriel, nothing is quite as it seems," Jane said tersely.

"I'm finding that true about Hernewood in general," Lizzie said, drawing her knees up beneath the covers.

"Believe me, Elizabeth, you're better off keeping out of the woods altogether. Away from Gabriel, and the ghosts, and the ancient stories."

"I'm trying very hard not to be a fanciful creature," she said, smoothing down her riotous red hair.

"I wish you luck," said Jane. "Hernewood Forest has the power to seduce even the most practical of creatures. I'm wise enough to keep my distance. You should do the same. Come with me for a ride this afternoon, and we'll shake off the cobwebs, go across the fields and keep far away from the forest, and if you're extremely lucky, you'll never run into my brother again during your visit."

Elizabeth didn't let any expression cross her face at that possibility. Doubtless it would be the best for everyone. "He never comes to the house?"

"Never. He seldom emerges from the forest. He's a hermit and prefers his life that way. You would be wise to keep away from him."

"I have no intention of seeking him out," Elizabeth said. "It was simply an accidental meeting . . ."

"Gabriel would say there are no such things as accidents, and I tend to believe he's right. He's a dangerous man, Elizabeth. Be wary."

"He already warned me," she said, throwing back the covers and scrambling from the bed. The room was chilly, and no maid had been instructed to tend to the fire. She shivered in her loose white nightdress.

"Be careful, Elizabeth. There are odd things happening in the woods." Jane rose, shaking her sadly wrinkled skirt. "We'll go for a ride, and you'll see that the fields and hills are far more cheerful than the forest."

Elizabeth paused in the act of taming her hair. "I like the woods, Jane."

"Well, you shouldn't. You're supposed to be practical, and the woods are dangerous. You never know what you might find there."

"Besides ghosts and the wicked Gabriel, what else would I have to worry about?"

Jane shook her head. "Just because you don't believe in something doesn't mean it doesn't exist. They used to practice black magick around here, and Druidry. Earth religions, and sacrifice, and really quite awful things."

For a moment Elizabeth didn't move, her thick mane of hair twisted in one hand. "Do you think your brother is involved in such things?"

"He's known to be an expert on the Druids," Jane said miserably. "People follow him up here from London to seek his wisdom. Wisdom, ha!" she said with sisterly scorn. "I'm a sensible woman, and I know well enough to keep out of the woods. Please, for your sake as well as mine, do the same. There's nothing but trouble awaiting you there.''

There was no way Lizzie could ignore Jane's concern. ''I've made it my new goal in life to keep away from trouble,'' she said calmly, plaiting her hair and pinning it neatly at the back of her neck. ''I think a ride would be just the thing.''

And she was rewarded with Jane's beatific smile.

It was likely that Jane wouldn't be smiling later, when she realized that not only was Lizzie one of the world's worst riders, but she was terrified of horses as well. On the ground she loved and understood them as she did all animals. Mounted on a horse's broad back, she lost all rapport.

But she could manage a sedate ride without disgracing herself, couldn't she? At least it would keep her out of the forests, away from the lure of the woods.

And the unexpected lure of the Dark Man, who lived within their shadows.

It was a cool, crisp day for a ride across the dales, and Elizabeth had managed the first part of their ride with admirable calm. Marigold seemed placid enough to the casual observer, though Lizzie knew otherwise. She understood animals, could look into their wise, liquid eyes and know what they were thinking. Unfortunately Marigold was thinking that she didn't want a stranger up on her back.

Not that Lizzie was about to explain such a far-fetched notion to her cousin. Jane was a different creature on a horse, graceful, majestic, at one with her animal. Gone was the awkward, overgrown young woman, and in her place was a girl of glowing health and beauty, confidence and strength.

Unfortunately Elizabeth could count on no such transformation for herself. Even learning to ride well wouldn't make her hair less red, and nothing short of a miracle could make her majestic. And Jane was in the mood for a gallop.

Elizabeth struggled to keep up with her cousin's neck-or-nothing pace, clinging nervously to her horse's reins as they raced across the countryside, and she almost wept with relief when Jane finally seemed to have rid herself of the demons that were riding her and slowed her reckless pace, turning to look back.

"I'm sorry," she said with a rueful smile. "I was in such a need of a gallop that I forgot you might not be entirely comfortable on a strange horse."

Elizabeth resisted the impulse to admit she wasn't entirely comfortable on any horse. The mare beneath her had slowed to a walk, and Elizabeth's heart was slowing as well. "She's a very nice horse," she said lamely.

"Marigold? She's a stodgy old thing, but even-tempered. We'll get you a more challenging mount, and then you won't have so much trouble keeping up with me."

"No!" Elizabeth's voice came out in a little shriek, and she coughed. "Marigold's just perfect for me. I really don't mind if she's a little slow."

"Gabriel says I ride like a man," Jane said. "Always looking for more speed and power. But there's nothing more glorious than racing across the dales with the wind in your hair, now is there?"

Elizabeth's disreputable hair was bound tightly around her head, and the last thing in the world she needed was to have it flying in the wind, but she managed a wan smile. "Glorious," she echoed.

"Now if we could just . . . oh, blast!" A high-perch phaeton had appeared around the corner, traveling at a reckless clip. It was bright yellow, and looked as if it belonged in a city like London rather than a country road in Yorkshire. The driver seemed to have no intention of slowing his dangerous pace. Elizabeth tried to sidle her horse out of the way, but Marigold proved suddenly stubborn, despite Elizabeth's kicks to her broad sides, and a moment later Jane swooped down on the reins and pulled them both to safety on the grassy sward.

The carriage pulled to a screeching halt a few feet beyond them, and Jane uttered a low, genteel curse beneath her breath as the door opened. "Come along, Elizabeth," she muttered. "Got to be neighborly, even to snakes."

"Jane, dear! What a treat to run into you!" The woman was tiny, dark-haired, and breathtakingly lovely, dressed in a bright peacock cloak. The man beside her was, if possible, even more beautiful, with wavy blond locks, a straight, perfect nose, pale, delicate skin, and an expression of utter boredom. He was dressed in puce.

"Actually, Lady Chilton, you missed us," Jane said in a caustic drawl. "May I present to you my cousin, Miss Elizabeth Penshurst?"

If Lady Chilton had thought to bring a lorgnette she would have certainly held it up to her bright blue eyes to shield her frankly assessing gaze. It took her only a moment to dismiss Elizabeth as someone of no earthly interest. Elizabeth wasn't sure whether she should feel affronted or relieved.

"Delighted, Miss Penshurst," she said, barely stifling a yawn. "And this is my husband, Lord Chilton." The elegant Lord Chilton waved a bored hand in her direction. "And what brings you to Hernewood, Miss Penshurst? You look like a healthy young girl—perhaps you were in search of bracing physical exercise? That's about all Yorkshire has to offer, unless, of course, you're interested in metaphysical matters."

"Metaphysical matters?" Elizabeth echoed, resisting the impulse to exert some bracing physical exercise on the tiny Lady Chilton. She had no idea why, but Her Ladyship's tone of voice had been lightly mocking, making Lizzie feel both overgrown and positively fat. She could only wonder at her effect on the lanky Jane.

"The Chiltons are followers of the Druid religion," Jane said in a noncommittal voice. "They came to Hernewood to consult my brother about his research."

"Gabriel is a font of wisdom and power," Lord Chilton said with a faint show of enthusiasm. "The world is blessed to have him."

Jane made a faint choking noise. "You'll have to forgive me—I'm his sister, and less impressed."

Lady Chilton wrinkled her tiny little nose. "A prophet without honor in his own land," she intoned. "I pray for the day that everyone will follow the true way."

"Did I happen to mention that Elizabeth's father is a rector?" Jane said cheerfully.

If anything Lady Chilton looked even less approving. She sniffed. "How interesting."

"Maybe Gabriel will decide to convert her," Jane continued mischievously.

Elizabeth opened her mouth in shocked protest, but her response was overridden by Lady Chilton's clear horror.

"Don't be silly, Jane," she said, her voice with its faint hiss sounding ominously snakelike. "Gabriel would have no possible use for a . . . for a . . ."

"A proper young cousin," Elizabeth supplied cheerfully. "Perhaps he wants me for a virgin sacrifice." She said it deliberately, to shock them, but the moment the words were out she regretted them. Her father would have been horrified to hear her pertness.

Lord Chilton turned to stare at her, a speculative expression in his pale eyes. "Perhaps," he said, eyeing her as if measuring her for a shroud. Or a sacrificial altar.

"Don't be ridiculous, Elizabeth!" Jane sounded absolutely horrified by her weak attempt at humor. "Gabriel doesn't believe in human sacrifice."

"I'm delighted to hear that," she said dryly.

"I mean, he doesn't believe the Druids practiced blood sacrifice at all. He thinks it was all a bunch of wicked lies perpetrated by the Romans."

"Or that's what he tells people," Lord Chilton murmured with a patronizing smile. "We followers of the Way know the truth, and do our humble best to relive the customs of our forefathers."

This didn't sound particularly encouraging to Elizabeth, but she wasn't sure she wanted to get into an argument about arcane and possibly bloody religious practices.

Jane wasn't similarly repressed. "I'm certain if Gabriel were interested in blood sacrifice it would be in honor of a juicy sirloin."

"The Druids didn't eat their sacrifices," Lady Chilton said softly, looking at Elizabeth with a singular lack of appetite.

It was a bright, crisp spring day, and yet suddenly Elizabeth felt suffocated, by the bright colors and eerie demeanor of the Chiltons, by the bloodthirsty discussion. Marigold moved restively beneath her, adding to her sudden queasiness, and she wondered how the ele-

gant Chiltons would respond if she spewed all over
them. She doubted they'd be pleased.

She cast a pleading glance at Jane, but her cousin
was oblivious. For the moment she was well and truly
trapped.

"You really should consider joining us in one of our
little meetings, Jane dear. It could open new worlds to
you," Lady Chilton said in her rich, dulcet voice. "And
your cousin would be welcome as well. Though of course
a follower of a limited religion like Christianity would
doubtless be bored by our quest for knowledge."

"I think not, though you're very kind to offer," Jane
said.

"Your brother has honored us with his presence on
several occasions, dear Jane. There's nothing to be
afraid of," Lady Chilton pressed her.

Elizabeth had had enough—of being ignored, of the
Chiltons, of Lady Chilton's soft, possessive tone when
she spoke of Gabriel. It was time for desperate measures,
and her nausea had passed. There was nothing else she
could do but give docile Marigold a surreptitious pinch.

Marigold's reaction was distressingly enthusiastic. She
let out a trumpeting shriek, rearing on her hind legs,
and it was all Elizabeth could do to throw herself down
on the horse's neck, clinging for dear life as the suppos-
edly sluggish mare took off like a bolt of lightning,
heading straight for Hernewood.

It seemed only a matter of moments before the dark
forest closed around them. It took all of Elizabeth's
concentration simply to hold on, uncertain whether
she'd be better off clinging to the wild creature or falling
to a certain death. It didn't help that she could blame
no one but herself for her predicament. The wind had
torn her bonnet from her head, her hair had pulled
free and was streaming behind her, and she couldn't

hear whether anyone was in pursuit or not. Doubtless Jane would come after her, but Marigold seemed possessed of supernatural speed, and together horse and rider seemed to hurtle through a tunnel of green darkness.

But Marigold was far from supernatural, and eventually she began to slow, almost imperceptibly at first, then gradually. The wind was no longer rushing past Elizabeth's head, and she slowly lifted herself from her crouched position, listening for the sounds of pursuit. She could hear nothing but the heavy breathing of the horse beneath her and the wind through the towering trees.

She reached down and stroked Marigold's neck, murmuring soft, apologetic words, and was gratified to find the mare slowing her pace even more, coming to a halt just as the path led into a small clearing.

"Good girl," Elizabeth murmured. "Good, strong girl, everything's all right, and we'll just find our way back . . ."

She'd spoken too soon. Something spooked the already-rattled horse, and this time when she reared up Elizabeth went flying, sliding off her back and into an ignominious heap on the forest floor. Marigold was kicking, and Elizabeth rolled quickly out of the way of the flying hooves, hearing her dress rip as she scrambled out of harm's reach.

A moment later Marigold was gone, tearing through the forest on another mad dash, this time riderless. And Elizabeth lay in the fallen leaves, bruised, winded, and dazed.

The silence of the forest closed around her like a shroud. Marigold was long gone, and she'd outpaced Jane's attempt at rescue. Lizzie was alone, lost in the middle of the forest, with no earthly clue how to find her way home.

She struggled to her feet, brushing the twigs and leaves from her sober brown dress. It was well and truly ripped, the gaping cloth exposing her pristine cotton chemise trimmed with lace. She should have known better than to wear a riding dress that was too small for her. At least it would prevent her from ever having to mount a horse again during her visit to Yorkshire. Unless some nimble-fingered soul could repair it.

She reached down and ripped it outward, tearing the fabric across the front as well in a triangle-shaped flap. *Fix that*, she thought defiantly.

Tossing her unruly hair behind her, she took stock of her surroundings. She was at the edge of a small copse, with what seemed to be at least three paths leading from it, including the one Marigold had brought her on. The clearing was surrounded by a ring of ancient trees. Lizzie took a deep, calming breath, but there was no peace in this place, and she wondered why.

She looked about her, unsure which path had brought her here. And which way led to Hernewood Manor. For all she knew she might have even left the Durhams' land.

She took a few steps toward the center of the clearing, then stopped, frozen. Something was wrong, something was very wrong with this place. She knew it with her senses, deep in her bones, knew it with a certainty that her father would have scoffed at and Old Peg would have approved. There was evil in this place, she could feel it. And Marigold, smart, annoying creature that she was, had felt it, too.

She saw it then, and tried to tell herself it was nothing. Simply a dead rabbit, lying in a welter of dried, brownish blood, stiff and still. It was set on a large flat stone that looked oddly like a table. Or an altar. She shook away the horrid thought.

But why would an animal be left to rot in the woods? There were plenty of scavengers, woodland creatures who would have made short work of a dead rabbit, and yet this one seemed to have been there for at least a day. And whatever had killed it would have normally eaten it as well.

Not whatever, she realized belatedly. Whoever. The rabbit had been slit from stem to stern with a sharp instrument, and the blood had fallen onto the rock in a bizarre pattern.

People needed to eat as much as the woodland animals did. Who would have had the luxury of simply killing one of God's creatures and then leaving it? Certainly not anyone who ever had to think about providing food for the table.

Which meant that whoever had slaughtered and abandoned the lowly rabbit was one of the landed families. Someone who could kill with impunity, knowing there'd be no punishment and no repercussions.

She forced herself to move closer, staring down at the poor creature. She wanted to touch it, to offer some comfort, but it was too late. The miasma of evil that surrounded it was powerful, and she wondered if that was what had spooked the exhausted horse. There was something about the pathetic little corpse that frightened away the other animals as well.

She stepped back, feeling the odd relief fill her as she increased the distance. She couldn't just leave it lying there to rot, she thought. If the animals wouldn't take care of it, then perhaps she ought to bury it.

"Don't be absurd, Lizzie." She spoke the words out loud, taking comfort in the sound of her prosaic voice. "You're in the middle of the forest with nothing but your bare hands. You need to concentrate on finding your way back home, not on burying rabbits.''

Resolutely she turned away, looking for an avenue of escape. And she told herself that it had to be an overwrought imagination that made her think the rabbit's dead brown eyes were watching her.

Catching her tangled hair in her hands, she fashioned it into an ineffectual knot at the back of her head and started toward the middle path with a dubious sense of assurance. For some reason it seemed utterly important that she appear certain. And that she didn't look back.

She had no sense of the hour. The forest was dark, timeless, looming over her. She could hear the rustle of the wind through the trees, the occasional call of birds, and those sounds of life provided her a measure of comfort as she made her way through the pathways, following the deep bite of the horse's hooves in the soft dirt.

And then she came to a fork in the path. She could either go to the right or the left. Common sense told her to go right, instinct tugged at her to take the left-hand path. And the telltale hoof marks had disappeared completely in the thick tumble of fallen leaves.

She was getting cold now, and she pulled her torn dress closer around her, shivering in the cool afternoon. "You have nothing to worry about, Lizzie," she scolded herself. "You're in the forest, where you belong. You're in Yorkshire, not in the wilds of Scotland, and three people watched the horse take off with you. People will be looking for you, beating the bushes.''

For some reason the thought of the so-elegant Lord Chilton beating the bushes in his puce wardrobe was ridiculous enough to make her laugh. But Jane would be hunting for her, and doubtless so would half the servants at Hernewood Manor. Her father would be mortified that his wicked, thoughtless daughter had caused such an upheaval, and she suspected neither Sir Richard nor Lady Durham would be greatly pleased with her fecklessness, but that was the least of her worries. Getting home safely was paramount.

She took the left-hand path, ignoring her practical self and following her instincts. The path to the right was wider, better traveled, the path to the left narrow and winding. She kept going anyway, her riding boots pinching her feet, her hair tumbling out of its makeshift knot.

She began to lose track of time. She might have been out there for half an hour, it might have been two or three. The darkness of the woods remained constant, both comforting and unnerving. There was peace and beauty in the woods. But in this woods there was evil as well.

Another fork in the path, and Elizabeth stopped cold, suddenly uncertain. She'd come no nearer to civilization by taking the left-hand course—by all common sense she ought to head toward the right.

She didn't want to. The path to the right, like the previous one, was wider and more recently traveled. She could see the broken branches, the unsettled leaves that carpeted the path. A number of people had been down there recently. Perhaps those who were in search of her?

She started down the right path, and that hideous sense of wrongness washed over her once more. She could hear Old Peg's voice in her head, warning her. *Stay away, Miss Lizzie. There's bad things down there. Keep away, love. Keep away.*

But Old Peg was long dead, and Elizabeth had lost all sense of proportion. She halted, peering down the wide path, and for a moment she thought she saw movement, a flash of white in the tall trees.

"Is anyone there?" she called out, her voice strong and clear. "Can someone help me?"

There as no answer. No movement. She'd made another wrong turn, she told herself. She should retrace her steps, go back.

Go back, Old Peg's voice whispered in her head.

I don't believe in ghosts, she'd told Jane earlier that day, in what now seemed like a different world.

Something was behind her now, something dark and unseen. She whirled around, but there was nothing there, just the forest closing in around her, the wide path suddenly narrow, darker, so that she had no choice but to keep going.

She stumbled backward, and something was soft, pliant beneath her foot. She went sprawling, landing on the soft, warm body, landing in the blood and torn flesh, the smell of death all around her, and when she opened her mouth to scream she saw Gabriel Durham standing utterly still, blood on his beautiful hands.

CHAPTER FIVE

"Please don't scream," he said in a world-weary voice. He'd moved with his customary effortlessness, reaching down to catch her arm and pull her from the bloody creature. She flinched at the sight of his bloodstained hand, but she was similarly covered in gore, and it was a waste of time to be missish. He pulled her to her feet, and if her knees felt a bit wobbly, she wasn't about to let him know it.

She forced herself to turn and look at the body she'd sprawled across, and let out a tiny sigh of relief as she recognized the good-sized doe lying limply in a pool of blood. It was newly killed, the blood was still draining from the body, the smell of fresh death was strong in the air.

"Thank God," she whispered under her breath. "I thought . . ."

"You thought it was a human?" Gabriel supplied,

leaning down and wiping his bloody hands on the fallen leaves. "You're a fanciful creature, aren't you?"

"Not particularly," she replied in her most calm voice. She always tried to sound very calm when she lied. "Getting thrown by a horse, lost in the woods, and falling over corpses would make anyone a bit nervous."

"I imagine so. How many corpses have you fallen over?" he asked casually.

"This is my second. There was a dead rabbit somewhere back in the woods."

"The poachers must be getting very sloppy."

She jerked her head up in surprise. "Poachers did this?"

"Who did you think? I don't have any weapons on me, and I find no pleasure in hunting. Sir Richard considers me unmanly," he added with a faint smile.

She could make no response that wouldn't put her into worse trouble. "Why would people poach and then leave their game behind? I thought the purpose of poaching was to provide food."

He shrugged, an elegant gesture belied by the rough cloth of his white shirt. "Someone might have interrupted them. I wander these woods quite often, and while the people around here should know I'm not about to go telling tales to Sir Richard, they're still unlikely to trust me. And then there are the ghosts."

"I don't believe in ghosts."

"So you've said. I'll have to introduce you to Brother Septimus and Brother Paul."

"No, thank you. I'm quite happy in my current state of ignorance," she replied. "What I would like is some assistance in finding my way out of these woods."

"You mean you didn't come in search of me, Elizabeth? I'm wounded. And don't bother telling me I can't call you Elizabeth—it would be a waste of time. I'll call you anything I please. I think I might prefer something a little more endearing. You're far too much of a starched-up creature as it is. I don't quite fancy you as a Beth. And Eliza sounds a bit too proper as well. I think I'll call you Lizzie.''

She allowed herself the luxury of glaring at him. "No one calls me Lizzie," she said sternly. Trying to ignore the fact that the last time she'd seen him she'd been scantily clad and barefoot.

"No one but yourself. I heard you off in the woods, muttering beneath your breath. Does Sir Richard know you talk to yourself? He might think twice about having such an odd influence on his darling daughter.''

"I'm unlikely to influence Jane . . .''

"Jane is not his darling daughter. He dislikes her almost as much as he hates me. I meant the perfect little Edwina.''

"Edwina has no use for me. Neither does Edward.''

"Ah," said Gabriel. "My esteem for you rises proportionately.''

"Does no one in your family care for another?" she demanded, horrified. Even though she had shamed her father, stepmother, and five brothers, she had no doubt of their unconditional love.

"Oh, to be sure," he said airily. "Sir Richard and Lady Elinor dote on the twins. The twins are devoted to themselves and passably fond of their parents. And Jane and I have a strong alliance against the pack of them, along with a dedication to watching out for each other.''

She shook her head, feeling the treacherous tangle of hair begin to come loose once again. "I don't understand you," she said.

"You weren't meant to, Lizzie. You'd be best keeping your distance from all of us, and keeping out of these woods. You spend far too much time lost in them. This is only your second day here.''

"I would do just that, if I could simply find my way home," she said with some asperity. "If you'll show me the way back to Hernewood Manor, I would be most grateful. And then you could see about having someone retrieve the deer. It's been a long winter, and there's a good deal of venison. It would be wicked to have it go to waste."

"No one will eat that deer, Lizzie. Any more than they would touch any of the creatures found dead in these woods."

"And why not?"

His smile was cool and annoying. "That comes under the topic of things you're better off not knowing." He glanced down at the dead deer. "I'll probably bury it once I see you safely back to Hernewood Manor."

"I don't need company, I just need directions."

"You'll get lost. These woods are not for the unwary." He held out his hand, and once again Elizabeth marveled at the elegant beauty of him. But she made no move to take it.

"I can . . ."

"You can be tiresome, Lizzie," he supplied. "There's a storm coming, and while a good soaking might wash some of the blood from that monumentally ugly dress, it won't serve your health any good. Come along and stop arguing."

"I'm not afraid of the woods."

"You should be. These have changed over the last few months; it will take time and care to exorcise the evil. Only the abbey ruins are still relatively safe."

She stared at him. "How do I know I can trust you?"

He sighed. "You don't. But don't you think someone would have warned you about me if I were any danger?"

"They did. They told me to beware the Dark Man. And I gather that's you."

He looked amused. "You didn't listen to the warnings though, did you? The first night you're here you go racing into the woods, looking for trouble. And you seem so prim and proper, so completely dutiful. Does your father the reverend know just how willful you are beneath that stern bosom?"

"Why do you think he sent me up here?" she countered, oddly comfortable talking so freely with a stranger. Standing in the midst of the forest, her outrageous hair loose about her, her clothes ripped and bloodstained, it seemed ridiculous to be formal. Besides, he didn't seem like a stranger.

"Were you undutiful?"

"Only in refusing to . . ." She stopped, belatedly cursing her wagging tongue.

" 'Only in refusing to' what? Did he want you to marry some boring young man?"

She stared at him in amazement. "How did you know?"

"It's logical. You're young and quite pretty, and a little past the age of marrying. Obviously he'd be trying to get you properly settled."

Elizabeth wasn't certain whether she should be gratified by the "quite pretty" or incensed about the reference to her advanced age. "Obviously," she said in a stiff voice. "Though he wasn't a boring young man—he was a lecher."

He laughed, and the sound was disturbing in a not altogether unpleasant way. "Lizzie, my pet, there's a lot to be said for lechery. I wish I were in a position to show you."

"I'd prefer to use my imagination," she said.

"And you've got an active one, haven't you?" The soft

breeze had stiffened, sending gusts of leaves whirling at her feet. "Why don't we imagine you homeward. Hernewood Forest is no place for a young lady. And I'm not fit company, as anyone would tell you."

He started down one of the paths with a surety she couldn't resist, and she followed him, skipping slightly to catch up with him. "I thought you were in holy orders," she said. "Surely that would make you fit company."

"I'm defrocked, my pet. For my sins of the flesh. I was never made for celibacy, I'm afraid, and my abbot knew it. I didn't even get to take my final vows—I was booted from the monastery for casting lascivious eyes at a merchant's daughter. It served its purpose, however. The Durhams were able to reject me with impunity, and while I'm still Sir Richard's putative heir, I am thankfully free of any claim they might have upon me."

"Then why are you here?"

He glanced at her over his shoulder. "Because this is my home. I belong to this place, to these people. Sir Richard doesn't own Hernewood Forest and the abbey ruins. He owns nothing but the manor house and the surrounding gardens. I own everything else, including a ramshackle estate on the northern boundary of Hernewood. Needless to say Sir Richard isn't best pleased with the situation."

"But how could that be?" She was struggling to keep up with him. He was tall, with very long legs, and he seemed to know his way through the torturous paths with absolute certainty. "I've always assumed that people's inheritances come from their parents . . ."

"Use your deductive reasoning, love."

"He's not your real father."

"Exactly. Though he's sensible enough not to announce it to the world. Sir Richard has made his choices in this life, and he's had to live with them. There's a saying—when you sup with the devil you'd best use a long spoon. Sir Richard wasn't so wise when he was younger."

The path had widened, and she caught up with him, slightly breathless from the determined pace he was setting. "Why are you telling me this?"

He paused, glancing down at her. "Sheer perversity, I suppose. I wouldn't want you making the dire mistake of taking Sir Richard at face value. He's a bitter, frustrated old man, and as such, he can be quite unexpectedly dangerous."

"Why would you care? Whether or not I take him at face value, that is?"

His mouth quirked up at one side. "Perhaps I have a weakness for redheaded sprites who wander my woods at odd times of the day and night."

She was spared the necessity of answering. Lightning sizzled through the sky, followed far too quickly by a crack of thunder that seemed to shake the trees around them.

"Afraid of lightning?" he asked her.

"Not particularly."

"You should be, particularly when you're in the woods. Lightning tends to seek out high points, and there are plenty of tall trees around us." He glanced ahead of him, a frustrated expression on his face. "I don't think we have time to make it back to the manor."

"I can't imagine there's a suitable alternative." It had begun to spit rain, a cold, wet mist that immediately soaked through her torn clothing.

"Suitable or not, it might save your life." He took her hand in his, and his grasp was strong, firm, warm. Unnerving. Before she could do more than choke out a token protest he was half-leading, half-dragging her through the woods, deeper along a narrow path instead of following the steadily widening one that instinct told her led to Hernewood Manor.

"I'm not going with you," she said, pulling back. Nature chose that moment to be particularly spiteful, sending another bolt of lightning sizzling through the thickening rain, and Gabriel turned on her, and for the first time she understood the phrase, the Dark Man.

"I may be a conscienceless bastard, but I'm not going to leave you out in the woods during a thunderstorm," he said. "Come along peaceably, or I'll carry you. And if you struggle too much, I won't have any qualms about knocking you out. Anyone will tell you I'm not much concerned with the niceties of polite behavior."

Her eyes widened. He looked as if he'd do just that—pick her up and carry her, or even knock her senseless if she put up too much of a fight. He didn't bother to wait for her assent, he simply turned and continued hauling her through the dark tunnel of the woodland path, ignoring the rain that chose that moment to drench them.

She could barely keep up with his wild pace, and she slid in the mud, going down hard. He didn't release her hand, he simply hauled her back upright and continued onward, dragging her behind him. The storm was thundering around them with a fury, and she could barely see in the unnatural darkness. All she had was his warm, strong hand, leading her to safety, and she gave up fighting, following him blindly.

He stopped without warning, and she tumbled against him. He put his arms around her and pulled her into darkness, into safe, warm, dry darkness, like a cave. He leaned back, pulling her wet, shivering body against his, holding her there in the musty gloom, and outside the storm raged around them with a fierce hunger.

She didn't know how long she stood there, safe in the shelter of his arms. He was warm and strong, his heart beat steadily against hers, and it took her long moments to realize the utter and complete impropriety of the situation. It still wasn't enough to make her break free of him. Even when he muttered "Lizzie" under his breath, and put his strong hand under her chin, tilting her face upward, so that he could kiss her properly.

She'd never been kissed by a man, and she'd been too dazed to realize that was what he'd had in mind. One moment she was peering up at him in the darkness, the next his mouth was pressed against hers and her eyes were closed as she savored the new experience.

It was dangerously pleasant, she decided. The firm pressure of his lips against hers, the feel of his strong arms wrapped around her. It was no wonder she had always been cautioned against such lascivious delights. One could become dangerously accustomed to the habit of kissing.

He lifted his head, and even in the darkness she could see the faint sheen of amusement in his beautiful eyes. "You kiss like a nun, Lizzie. Haven't you ever let anyone near that luscious mouth of yours? I've been thinking about it since I first saw you."

She didn't know what shocked her more. She grasped for the first thing. "A nun? When did you kiss a nun?" she gasped.

"On more than one occasion," he replied, and she realized he still cupped her face with one hand, and his fingers were slowly stroking the side of his chin. "Open your mouth, Lizzie."

"Why?"

"So you can learn to kiss properly."

She thought he'd been holding her closely. She'd

been mistaken. This time he slid his arm around her waist and pulled her tight against his body, so that she could feel the warmth of his skin through the damp cloth of his shirt, feel the hardness of his thighs through her wetly clinging skirts. She glared up at him mutely, but it was too dark for him to see her disapproval, and her hands pressed against his chest seemed to have little effect.

This time his mouth was open against hers, and she would have recoiled in shock if he weren't holding her so tightly. She tried to squirm, but it only brought her closer still to him, and he was inexorable.

"Don't panic, Lizzie," he whispered against her mouth. "It's only a kiss. I'm not stealing your soul."

She let out a faint sound of protest, and it gave him the advantage he needed. Cradling her head in his elegant hands, he tipped her face back to give him better access, and proceeded to kiss her with a thoroughness that left her heart racing and her knees week. He used his lips, his teeth, his tongue, in ways that had to be thoroughly indecent, and she could only stand there, trapped against his body, and let him do it. And tell herself the hot dizziness that swept over her body was simple disgust, not a warm, treacherous delight.

He released her, slowly, released her mouth, released her body, to let her lean up against what felt like a curved stone wall of some kind of tower. She leaned back, shivering, breathless, terribly afraid he might kiss her again. And that this time she might try kissing him back.

"That was a slight improvement," he murmured. "I don't suppose I can convince you to come upstairs and strip off your clothes for me?"

She should have slapped him for that, but she was still too shaken to do more than stand there in the cushioning darkness. Besides, it was dark enough that she couldn't be sure of her aim.

"I suppose it would be foolishly optimistic of me to take your silence for agreement," he added. "Why don't you come upstairs, and I'll have Peter make us a nice warming cup of tea while we wait for the storm to pass. Or better yet, I could ply you with French brandy and see whether I could change your mind."

"Why are you doing this?" she somehow found the courage to demand.

"I would think it would be obvious. You're young and female and quite luscious, and as I said, I have a weakness for redheads who roam my woods. And what else is there to do on a rainy afternoon?"

"But try to despoil your father's houseguests?" she supplied, gathering strength. "That's it, isn't it? Your dislike of Sir Richard runs so deep you'd do anything to shame him, including ruining a young woman under his protection."

"Oh, I'd hardly call it ruin," he replied. "I think you'd enjoy it immensely, if I could get you to relax. The brandy would do the trick quite nicely, I would think."

"No, thank you. I have no interest in illicit passion."

"You don't know what you're missing," he murmured. "And I suspect you aren't going to let me show you. At least, not now, more's the pity."

"I'm far more sensible than you think." She didn't know what to call him. She would die before she called him by his given name, but given his odd background she had no idea what his family name or title was.

"Unfortunately so," he said, and if there was a trace of amusement in his voice, she chose to ignore it. "Come upstairs with me, Lizzie, and you can wait out the storm in virgin safety. I promise you. On my honor."

"Do you have any honor?"

"My own brand, certainly. Besides, I can hear Peter up there. He'll provide an admirable chaperon. He's spent most of life trying to keep me out of trouble. You'll be as safe as you would be in your own bed."

It was too dark to see his face, but she could hear the irony in his voice. If she had any sense, she would stay put, not go anywhere further with him.

She did have sense, her fair share of it, but she also had instincts. If he promised he wouldn't touch her again, then she could believe him

"A cup of tea would be very welcome," she said in a small voice.

"Trusting soul, aren't you?" he mocked her.

"On occasion."

"Give me your hand, Lizzie, and I'll lead you to my lair."

She couldn't very well stumble after him in the dark. She'd made the choice to trust him—it would be foolish to hold back now.

She put her hand in his, once more feeling that odd tingle that sent a strange, clenching feeling to the pit of her stomach. "Good girl," he murmured.

And she hoped to heaven that he kept that in mind.

CHAPTER SIX

She followed him, in the dark, up the seemingly endless, winding stone steps of the tower. Outside the rain lashed against the walls, and thunder still rumbled at an encouraging distance. Inside her hand was caught in his, and all the universe seemed to center on that small expanse of flesh.

He pushed the door open, and light and warmth flooded toward her. She squinted in the sudden brightness, then swayed dangerously, as she realized just how high up they were.

"There you are, Gabriel," came a man's rough voice. "Your sister and her cousin have gone missing, and God knows what kind of trouble Jane's gotten herself into in this kind of storm. It's up to you to beat some sense into the girl—her father doesn't care a fig about her, and it's not my place to warn her."

"Jane doesn't listen to me, Peter. You know that,"

Gabriel said calmly. He was standing in the doorway, his tall body hiding Elizabeth.

"She'll listen to you more than she'll listen to anyone else. I don't want some flighty southern miss leading her into trouble . . ."

Elizabeth chose that moment to sneeze, three times, quite loudly. Gabriel moved out of the way, an enigmatic expression on his face, and Elizabeth looked across the room into the astonished face of the man called Peter. A man she recognized as one of the grooms from the manor house. "I'm not a flighty southern miss," she said with some dignity, then spoiled it by sneezing again. "I was riding a wild horse, and she ran away with me."

"Marigold?" Peter echoed. "She's the gentlest mount in the stable."

"Not with me, she wasn't."

"You're afraid of horses, aren't you, Miss? That will make all the difference. They sense when you're uncertain, and they'll take advantage," Peter said.

"Don't listen to him, Lizzie. He thinks his horses are perfect, and it's only us wretched human beings who muck things up," Gabriel said with a drawl. He moved over to the fire, holding out his hands to warm them.

"I'd take a horse over most humans any time," Peter said calmly. "Let me get you a blanket, Miss. You're soaked."

"Perhaps you can find something dry to wear. I wouldn't want her catching the ague while she's under Sir Richard's protection."

"I'm not about to change my clothes," Lizzie said in a dark tone.

Gabriel smiled. "No, to my regret, I imagine you're not. Find her a blanket then, Peter, and then if you insist, you can go running off looking for Jane. Though

I know it's almost impossible for you to believe, but Jane is more than capable of taking care of herself."

Peter approached her with something that looked suspiciously like purple velvet. "But she'll be searching for Miss Penshurst, all the while she's here with you, safe and sound."

"Convince Lizzie of that, would you, Peter," Gabriel murmured. "She thinks I'm some sort of lecherous demon, out to despoil her."

"You are," Peter said flatly.

Gabriel threw back his head and laughed. And then, to Elizabeth's mingled fascination and horror, proceeded to strip off his sodden shirt and toss it over a chair.

Elizabeth stood frozen in the doorway, too shocked to move. It wasn't as if she had never seen a man without a shirt before, after all, she had five brothers, and she lived in the country. But she'd never seen a man like this. One with smooth, golden skin that stretched like silk over bone and muscle. He turned to face the fire, seemingly unconscious of her embarrassment, and she could take no comfort in his back. It was as distractingly beautiful as his chest had been.

"Don't worry," he said without turning back to her. "I don't intend to take off the rest of my clothes with you watching me. You look as if you might faint as it is."

Any momentary dizziness vanished in the heat of annoyance. "I'm not quite that missish," she snapped.

"True. You didn't faint when I kissed you."

"You kissed her, Gabriel?" Peter demanded, profoundly shocked. "Are you out of your mind? You can't just go around kissing properly brought-up young women . . ."

"Why not?" he said casually. "You ought to try it. I

can heartily recommend it, even if Lizzie here isn't certain how much she liked it.''

"Don't be a fool," the man said shortly. He draped the warm throw around Lizzie's shoulders, and she caught it before it slipped to the floor. It was velvet, thick and lustrous and wickedly sensuous.

"Jane, for instance," Gabriel continued. "I think she might enjoy being kissed quite a bit. I'd go so far as to say she needs to be kissed."

"Sod off."

Elizabeth's dizziness had returned full force, and with great presence of mind she walked across the room and sank down in a chair, holding the velvet around her. The two men sounded more like arguing brothers than servant and master.

"Now you've done it, Peter," Gabriel said in a lazy voice. "Lizzie doesn't know what kind of bedlam she's wandered into. She's obviously trying to figure out why a servant would tell his employer to sod off, and whether she ought to warn Jane that she's in danger of being kissed by a sturdy young man."

"By a servant," Peter supplied.

"And, of course, she could always go running to my putative father and tell him that you're conspiring to seduce my sister. That might force you to take some action."

"I doubt he'd care. He'd probably be more concerned with losing a good servant than anything that might befall Jane." There was no missing the bitterness in Peter's voice.

"Maybe he'd let you have her, Peter," Gabriel suggested. "You're absolutely right—he values his horses more than he does his elder daughter."

"He values his pride and position more than anything."

"True enough," Gabriel agreed. "That has always been his downfall." He turned to glance at Elizabeth, who sat utterly still, listening to all this with astonishment. The moment she caught him looking at her she quickly lowered her gaze, but she could feel him watching her, and she knew the moment he started to move in her direction.

Don't let him touch me, she prayed to her father's stern, moral God. She held herself very still as he loomed over her, and then she had no choice but to look up at him.

He had a faintly quizzical expression on his face. "You're sitting on my shirt," he said.

She sprang up as if she'd sat on a tack, smashing into his chest with unexpected force. He caught her arms as she fell against him, and the warmth of all that bare, smooth skin was even more appealing than she could have imagined. She found herself wanting to touch him. To put her face against the smooth, silken flesh and taste him.

She tore herself out of his grip and stumbled back, overturning the chair as she went. He watched her for a moment, then reached down and picked up the shirt that had tumbled to the floor.

She turned her back on him, unwilling to look at him a moment longer. He disturbed her in ways she couldn't even begin to understand. He wasn't what she wanted in this life, he wasn't what she needed. He was strange and unsettling and all she wanted was to get away from him and regain some sense of equanimity. To remember her promises to her father and to herself.

"I think Lizzie needs to get back to the manor house, Peter," he said after a moment. "She's had far too busy a day. I'd take her there myself, but we both know I'm persona non grata. Besides, I know Jane will want to thank you properly for rescuing her."

"I might still be able to thrash you," Peter said in a warning voice.

"You're welcome to try."

"Please," Elizabeth said in a strained voice, "I need to get back. They'll be worried . . ."

"You heard her, Peter. Unfortunately she's not asking for anything I have to offer, much as it wounds me. You take her back to the house and tell them you found her wandering out in the woods. While you do that I'll go take care of the latest offerings before someone else stumbles over them."

"They've been at it again?"

"Why do you think the lady is covered in blood? I'm much neater than that, I promise you. She happened to trip over the freshly butchered corpse of a pregnant doe."

"She was pregnant?" Elizabeth demanded, oddly shocked.

Gabriel glanced at her. "They prefer it that way. It doubles the value of the gift."

She willed herself to meet his gaze. He was quite beautiful in the fitful glow of candle and firelight, and she'd never thought of a man as beautiful. She needed to get away from him, to put some distance between her odd, uncharacteristic emotions. The woods had always called to her. Not anything as ordinary as a man.

But then, she knew perfectly well that Gabriel Durham was no ordinary man.

She rose. "I don't know what you're talking about, and I expect I'm better off not knowing."

"I expect you're right," he agreed. He'd put the fresh shirt on, a rough, simple cambric shirt that looked oddly elegant on him, but he'd failed to button it. Probably because he knew it disturbed her, she thought sourly.

"You're very kind to spare me," she said.

"I would spare you a great deal, if I could," he replied, his voice oddly calm. "As it is, I don't think Peter will have to escort you back after all. Unless I miss my guess, my sister has arrived at the tower and will probably come tearing in here in a matter of moments. I'm guessing on the count of twelve. What do you say, Peter? You care to hazard?"

Peter was clearly not amused by Gabriel's facetious tone. He'd moved to the door, opening it into the chill darkness of the tower, waiting patiently as someone raced up the stone steps.

Elizabeth watched in utter amazement at the change that came over him. One moment he was arguing with Gabriel, in the next he'd become self-effacing, silent, a perfect servant. But there was no missing the look of deep, desperate longing in his eyes.

Jane stopped at the door, momentarily distracted from her goal. "Peter," she said in a hushed voice that told Elizabeth volumes.

Peter, obviously, was less observant. "Miss Jane," he said, in properly subdued tones, "we were hoping you'd come. Miss Penshurst has met with a bit of an accident."

It took Jane a moment to come to her senses and pull her gaze away from Peter's tall form. "Lizzie, are you all right?" Jane demanded as she spied Elizabeth standing near the fire. "Are you hurt?"

"No one calls you Lizzie?" he murmured in a soft voice that only reached Elizabeth's ears. "She's fine, Jane," Gabriel said in a louder tone. "She's merely had an adventure. I take it that wild steed Marigold made it safely back to the stables?"

"Marigold isn't wild," Jane said automatically, and Elizabeth resisted the urge to scream. "Dear Elizabeth, let me get you back to the manor and we'll get you taken care of. Is that blood on your clothes?"

"She scared off some poachers," Gabriel said easily.

"I'm still not convinced that's what they were," Elizabeth said. "I don't care what you say—poachers don't leave good food behind."

Gabriel cast her a warning look. "You've been remarkably silent for the last few minutes . . . pray continue to be."

But Jane had already turned pale. "They've done it again, Gabriel? I thought they were through with that sort of thing."

Elizabeth had had enough. "Who? What sort of thing?" she demanded.

"No one knows for certain," Jane said. "Though the Chiltons are the logical choice."

Elizabeth stared at her in disbelief. "You aren't going to tell me that those overdressed creatures have been tramping through the woods killing rabbits and pregnant deer? Why in the world would they do that?"

"Not for the sport of it," Jane said in a grim voice. "I told you, they believe they're Druids. They probably believe in blood sacrifice and all sorts of nastiness. They think Gabriel's some sort of high priest who'll lead them in their horrid ways."

"In point of fact they aren't actually Druids," Gabriel said in his lazy drawl, "but some sort of odd religion they've concocted on their own, taking bits and pieces of various arcane rituals and elaborating on it. Unfortunately Francis Chilton is quite bright and very well read beneath that useless exterior, and he's studied almost as widely as I have. He just happens to interpret things a little differently."

"Differently?" Elizabeth echoed, thinking of the pale, effeminate man who'd dismissed her with an elegant smirk.

"Francis and his coterie think by sacrificing animals

they'll bring favor to their various financial and romantic exploits. They also try to tell the future by the way the blood falls to the ground. But I wouldn't dignify them with the term *Druid*, Jane."

"All right, they're not Druids. They're evil," she said. "And don't bother coming up with any philosophical arguments about whether or not evil actually exists, Gabriel. It does, and the Chiltons are evil."

Elizabeth chose that moment to start another sneezing fit. She could feel Gabriel's strange eyes watching her, but she was too involved in trying to control her sneezes to read his expression.

"I'm not going to fight with you, Jane," he said after a moment. "I think the important thing is to get Lizzie back home."

"Lizzie?" Jane echoed, turning her wondering gaze back to Elizabeth.

"I'll make sure they get back safely, Mr. Gabriel," Peter said in that sudden, submissive tone he'd taken on the moment Jane had entered the room.

Gabriel's smile was mocking. "I expected I could count on you, lad," he said, his emphasis on the condescending term deliberate.

And Peter tugged his forelock with an exaggerated subservience.

"Are you able to walk, Elizabeth?" Jane asked. "We're actually not that far from the main house if we follow the most direct route, but I'm afraid there's no path wide enough for a carriage. I go could and bring back some horses if you'd prefer to ride . . ."

"No!" Elizabeth said in a heartfelt shriek. "And don't anyone dare tell me how gentle Marigold is. I'd prefer the safety of my own two feet."

"It won't take long to walk, Miss," Peter volunteered, holding the door.

Elizabeth struggled to her feet, pulling her sodden clothing around her and attempting to look energetic.

"You look like a drowned rat," Jane said, casting a critical look over her. "Your clothes are soaked."

"I tried to divest her of them, but she proved tiresomely resistant," Gabriel murmured. "And Peter was a disapproving hindrance as well. But I don't think she looks the slightest bit like a rodent. More like a wet, exhausted kitten."

There was the oddest note in his voice. A foolish woman might almost have called it tenderness, but Elizabeth was not going to allow herself to be foolish. No man had ever had such a strange, unsettling effect on her in her entire life. It confused her, but she refused to give in to it. She squared her shoulders, giving him a stern look.

"I'm neither feline nor rodent," she said flatly. "Merely in dire need of dry clothes and a fire." And she sneezed again.

"Take her away, Peter," Gabriel said with a wave of his hand, dismissing the three of them. "This is far too much company for a recluse."

Elizabeth was halfway out the door when she remembered her manners. For all Gabriel's outrageous behavior, he had rescued her in the forest and brought her to safety in his strange, ruined tower.

"Thank you," she said in a stiff little voice. "I'm in your debt."

His smile was brief and unnerving. "We'll find a way for you to repay me," he said sweetly. "I'm a very inventive man."

Jane had spoken nothing more than the truth—they were back at Hernewood Manor in a matter of minutes, the dark, rainswept woods fading into the mist behind them. Neither Peter nor Jane spoke one word as they made their way through the widening paths, and once they reached the courtyard of the massive building, Peter vanished, leaving the two women to make their way through a side entrance into one of the back hallways.

As luck would have it, Edwina was on her way down to dinner, a vision in pink-and-rose tulle. She took one look at the two soaked women and made a disgusted face. "Where in the world have you been?" she demanded. "You know Father detests having to wait for his dinner. He's not going to want to hear that you've only just returned."

Elizabeth sneezed again. She was miserably cold, despite the warmth of the house, and she couldn't seem to stop shivering. Jane put a protective arm around her shoulder. "Tell Father we won't be down for dinner. I'm certain we won't be missed."

Edwina shook her artful curls. "Will you never learn, Jane?" she said. "At your advanced age you should have learned proper behavior, but you're an absolute hoyden. You'll break poor Mama's heart."

"I doubt it," Jane said wryly.

Edwina made a moue. "You're doomed to be an old maid, Jane. You'll never get a husband, you won't be fit for anything but running a stables. No one will want you, and you'll spend the rest of your life alone."

Elizabeth felt the tremor that shot through Jane at Edwina's words, but Jane's face was emotionless. "I expect I'll manage, dear. It's kind of you to be so concerned."

Edwina flounced off without another word, and Jane pushed open Elizabeth's door, her face pale and set.

"What a nasty piece of goods your little sister is," Elizabeth said after a moment. The room was thankfully warm—someone had built up the fire, and she began fumbling with her cloak, her fingers numb from the wet and cold.

"She is, isn't she? She'll still manage to find herself some rich fool who'll be totally besotted with her. She's right, you know. I'm the one who'll end up alone. Who would want me?"

"Any man with taste and judgment," Elizabeth said. "Any man worth having, I would think."

Jane laughed. "And how few of them exist? I want a good man, honest and true. Even harder to find."

Elizabeth yanked off her bloodstained dress and left it in a wet heap on the floor. "We're probably better off without them," she said. Remembering the feel of Gabriel's hot mouth against hers.

"Perhaps," said Jane. But there was a faraway look in her warm brown eyes, one of longing.

One that matched the expression in Peter's eyes when he looked at Miss Jane Durham.

CHAPTER SEVEN

Peter Brownington took his mug of strong, hot, sweet tea and walked out into the early-morning sunshine. It was a cool April morning, and the rich smells of earth and manure filled the stable yard. Peter took a deep, appreciative breath and drank his tea. He loved the smell of the earth after a rainfall, the sound of the horses, whickering in their stalls, and the faint cry of the woodland creatures that lurked in the forest beyond the ruined abbey. He loved the cool air of the morning, the thick slabs of bread and cheese Cook gave him and the other menservants in the morning. He loved the spaniels that followed at his heels, he loved the wild Yorkshire land.

And he loved Miss Jane Durham.

He paused at the entrance to the stable, knowing he should turn and head back to the kitchen before she saw him. She was standing by Penelope's stall, her tall body leaning slightly against the wood as she talked in a low, sweet voice to her beloved mare.

He was a tall, strong man, but he liked a woman who could look him in the eyes. He liked her deep, rich voice, her strong hands, and her merry eyes. He loved her ways with the horses, her patience with her horrible family. He loved everything about her except the fact that she was born of the manor house and he was a servant.

She never treated him like a servant. But then, she never treated anyone badly—she was fair and friendly to everyone. She had no idea that he longed for her in every part of his body, no idea that he dreamt of her at night, long, slow, tempting dreams, where she lay in his bed and stared up at him with trust and desire. No idea that he ever had a thought above his station in life. And she never would.

He must have thrown a shadow across the doorway, for she looked up, squinting toward him, and shoved her hand through her unruly hair. "Good morning, Peter," she said. "I don't suppose you brought me a mug of Cook's tea as well, did you?"

Too late to retreat, he moved into the darkness, perfumed by horse and hay and Jane. " 'Morning, Miss Jane. And you know as well as I do that Cook would have my head if I gave you your tea in a mug like the servants. You need to drink from bone china with little flowers on it."

She smiled wryly. "Those cups don't hold enough. I need lots of strong, sweet tea in the morning, or I can't wake up."

So did he. He could see her in the farmhouse kitchen, sitting at the table with him, a mug of tea in her hand. He banished the memory sternly. "How's Penelope this morning?"

She turned back to her horse, a worried expression crossing her brow. "I don't know. I think I was a fool to have her bred. She's not doing well at all. Maybe she just wasn't made to foal."

"Of course she was. There's no reason to think she won't get through it just fine, Miss Jane. I admit she's been a bit restive during the last few months, but they say most women get that way during their time."

"I suppose so," Jane said, clearly unconvinced. "If it weren't for you, Peter, I wouldn't have had her bred. You're the best man with horses in the county, maybe in the whole of England. If you say she's going to be all right, then I trust you."

Trusted him, she did. He needed to remind himself of that when she accidentally got too close, accidentally brushed against him. "I do my best, Miss Jane," he muttered.

She ducked her head. "I love her, Peter," she said in a hushed, strained voice.

"I know you do, Miss."

"She's the only creature that's ever let me love her unconditionally. Who's loved me back without wanting anything from me."

"She wants something from you, all right," Peter said. "She wants food and a warm, clean stall and a good gallop every now and then. And you know your brother loves you."

Jane's smile was a bit wobbly. "Gabriel loves me on his own terms. He doesn't have much time for sisters."

There was nothing he could say to that. She turned away from Penelope, leaning against the stall to look at him out of her cool, shy eyes. "Lizzie's sick," she said abruptly. "I doubt it's anything serious, but you might want to tell him."

"Why would I want to do that, Miss Jane?"

An odd expression crossed his face. "Why do you call him Gabriel and me 'Miss Jane'?" she asked.

"Because you probably wouldn't answer me if I called you 'Gabriel.' "

She managed a faint smile at his weak attempt at humor, but she wasn't deterred. "That's not what I mean, and you know it. Why don't you just call me Jane? You've known me since I was a little girl—you used to keep an eye on me when I played with your younger sister."

"It wouldn't be seemly."

"To whom? You don't have to do it around other people, but when we're alone why can't you just call me Jane?"

Because it wouldn't stop there, he thought. *Because I need to call you Miss Jane so that I don't forget that you're not for the likes of me.* "I'll try, Miss Jane," he said in his most formal voice.

She shook her head, obviously knowing a stubborn Yorkshireman when she saw one. "And how is Sally? I haven't seen her since she married her young man."

"Expecting her third, Miss, come Whitsuntide," Peter said.

"Her third?" she echoed in a hollow voice. "And she's a year younger than I am."

He knew women well enough to understand what she was thinking, and ignoring his own pain, said, "You'll have a fine husband and babies of your own in no time, Miss Jane. We'll just be sorry to have you leave us."

"I won't leave you." The words were quiet, intense, but he knew there was no hidden meaning to them. She smiled then, a little too brightly. "So why haven't you married, Peter? Why don't you have a hopeful family and a pretty little wife waiting for you at home?"

"You're full of strange questions today, aren't you, Miss?" he said, turning away from her to set his empty mug on a nearby shelf. "All things in due time, I suppose."

"Is there anyone you're thinking of marrying?"

He wasn't a coward, but he wished to God he could find a way to escape her, escape her questions, escape her tempting presence. If he had any sense at all, he'd leave the Durhams' employ and spend his time with Gabriel. God knew how much work there was to be done at the tumbledown estate his friend had practically abandoned. Gabriel was supposed to be staying in the tower while they made the old estate habitable, but he'd done absolutely nothing to ensure progress. He lived in his tower at the ruined abbey, haunted the woods, and drove his poor parents mad.

Except there was nothing poor about the Durhams, and their love for anyone but themselves and the twins was nonexistent as far as Peter could see.

If he had any sense at all, he'd leave this place, travel down to the south, where everyone smiled and lied and a man could forget about things he could never have.

But he wasn't going anywhere. "I'm in no hurry, Miss Jane," he said. "Like as not I'll find someone to marry eventually."

"Will you love her, Peter?"

Jesus Christ, the woman is out to drive me mad! He looked at her, driven almost past endurance. "Servants don't think much about love, Miss. We find someone who'll suit, who'll make a good partner in life, a good partner in bed," he added deliberately, "and we marry. It's that simple."

"That simple," she echoed. "And how do you know someone will be a good partner in bed?"

He could think of only one way to stop her damnable

questions, and he moved up on her, suddenly, expecting her to back away from him in nervous confusion. She held her ground, and he stopped, so close that he could see the faint gold streaks in her warm brown eyes, so close that he could feel the body heat, see the pulse beating at the base of her throat. Beating fast.

"You try them out, Miss Jane," he said. "We don't have to marry for money or position or property, because men of my class don't have any to begin with. We marry to have a good life."

"Then you do marry for love."

He wondered what she'd do if he pushed her up against the stall and kissed her as thoroughly as she needed to be kissed. He'd often wondered that very thing, and he had no intention of finding out, despite Gabriel's gibes. "Call it what you like, Miss Jane," he said roughly. "Were you wanting to ride this morning, Miss?" He couldn't very well back away, but he needed some sort of distance between them.

She turned back to her mare, and he told himself he was imagining the troubled expression in her eyes. "Maybe later. I'm worried about my cousin. She didn't look at all well last night." She turned back to look at her mare. "You will call me when it comes time for Penelope to foal, won't you? You'll come get me?"

"I'll have someone inform you," he said.

"I want to be there, Peter. I need to be with her. I was there when she was born, I've raised her from a weanling. Promise me? No matter what time it is?"

She was looking up at him with pleading eyes, still shorter than his lanky six-foot-two. And there was no way he could deny her. "I'll come get you," he said. "I promise."

Her smile was warm, enchanting, and he wondered

how any sane man could resist it. "You're a good man, Peter Brownington."

"Get on with you now," he said with mock gruffness. "I've got work to get done."

With a small laugh she scampered off, pausing only to take his abandoned tea mug with her. "I'll give this to Cook," she said airily.

"There's no need ..." But she was already gone. Leaving him alone with the memory, the breath imprinted on his flesh.

She went in through the kitchen, knowing her mother would lecture her if she caught her. Not that she was likely to—Lady Elinor never went anywhere near the huge kitchens of the house. It was Jane's favorite place— the only spot in the entire house that felt alive.

"There you are, Miss Jane," Cook greeted her. "There's breakfast set up in the dining room, and no one's there to bother you."

"I'd like some tea," she said.

Cook looked surprised. "I thought you already had some. You've been clutching that mug as if it's a love token."

Jane could feel the color leave her face, and it was an odd sensation. "Love token?" she said with a hollow laugh. "An odd sort of love it would be, to have a kitchen mug as a symbol."

She practically ran from the kitchen. The hallway was deserted—the rest of her family were still asleep, and Lizzie was sick in bed. The servants were busy with their various duties—no one would come across her unexpectedly.

Jane leaned against the wall, taking a deep breath as

she stared down at the ordinary mug she'd brought with her from the stable.

And without thinking she put her lips to the rim, where Peter's had touched it, and closed her eyes with a long, blissful sigh.

CHAPTER EIGHT

It was close to midday and Gabriel Durham had the very devil of a headache. It was no wonder—he'd spent the night before drunk as a lord. Peter dumped a load of firewood by the hearth with a singular lack of regard for Gabriel's tender nerves.

"Curse you, Peter," Gabriel said weakly. "Do you have to be so damned noisy?"

"And just why were you drowning your sorrows, Your Lordship?" Peter responded. "It's no wonder you're suffering the aftereffects."

Gabriel glared at him. "Bugger His Lordship."

"No, thank you, Gabriel. You're not to my taste."

Gabriel emitted a bark of laughter. "You're too literal, Peter, and always have been. It's my sister who's to your taste, and we both know it. Did you take my advice last night and kiss her?"

"I did not. I wouldn't have had the chance with Miss Penshurst still reeling from having to deal with the likes of you." Peter took a seat by the fire. "I'm not about to put a hand on Jane, and you know it. She trusts me. Sees me as a loyal servant and nothing more, and I'm not about to be the one to disillusion her."

"You're too damned loyal a servant, if you ask me," Gabriel said, thoroughly disgruntled. "I don't know where you got such a conservative streak."

"From my mother."

Gabriel snorted with laughter. "Not that I'd say a word against Alice, but she's hardly the one to preach."

"Considering where I came from, you mean? Everyone's entitled to one mistake. I'm hers."

"I doubt she'd consider you one," Gabriel said, suddenly repentant. "I'm a right bastard, to tease you about it."

"True enough," Peter said without rancor. "That makes the two of us."

"Two right bastards. Actually three, if truth be known."

"Truth doesn't need to be known, Gabriel," Peter said, his voice carrying a trace of warning.

Gabriel leaned back and stretched his legs out in front of him. "A lovesick man is a pitiful sight, Peter," he said mildly.

"One I don't intend to inflict on your sister. Did you enjoy kissing Miss Penshurst?"

"What has that got to do with anything?" Gabriel demanded.

"I don't know. I just haven't seen you turn to the bottle for months now, and even Lady Chilton's special charms haven't tempted you. Yet Miss Penshurst is here for a handful of days and you take to roaming the woods, drinking too much, and doing all sorts of unexpected things."

"I wasn't roaming the woods looking for Miss Penshurst. I was afraid the Chiltons and their little coven might be out and about.''

"And you were right about that. I buried the animals, by the way. No sign of anything new, but there's no telling what they'll do next. Lady Chilton doesn't seem ready to take no for an answer.''

"No, she doesn't,'' Gabriel said, staring into the fire. "If I were noble and self-sacrificing, I'd let them have their way. I could lead their filthy little group, and I have little doubt I could distract them from their bloodthirsty practices. Or at least convince them to devote their rituals to farm animals awaiting slaughter. But for some reason I can't bring myself to join them. Must be getting squeamish in my old age. Something about the pair of them gives me the cold grue.''

"You never were particularly noble,'' Peter observed.

"And you, my boy, have far too much nobility, and my poor sister will suffer for it.''

"She won't suffer for any act of mine,'' he said gruffly.

"Even acts of omission?'' Gabriel said gently.

"Sod off, Gabriel.''

"That's the second time you've said that in the last twenty-four hours. Are we losing our close bond, dear Peter?''

Peter rose, heading for the door. "You do your best to drive everyone away from you, Gabriel,'' he said.

"It usually doesn't require much effort. You're particularly stubborn.''

"I'm a fool.''

"A loyal one. I don't deserve a friend like you,'' Gabriel murmured, keeping his gaze fixed on the stone floor.

"True enough. Contemplate that, when you're brooding on your sins.''

Gabriel didn't say a word as Peter left him, though

he was half-tempted to call out and stop him a moment before the door slammed shut. The problem was that Peter knew him too well. A liability, of course. He preferred to keep his secrets to himself. He rather fancied the person he presented to the world—brilliant, reclusive, cynical, and occasionally charming. A man who cared for absolutely nothing at all but his studies and his own well-being.

Peter had known him too long and too well to be fooled, however. During the bitter, lonely years of his childhood Peter had been more a brother than a friend, one of the few spots of human warmth in those long, bleak years.

At least Gabriel could be grateful for one thing. The Durhams had never shown him a moment of human warmth, kindness, or affection. They had treated him as a wealthy but unwanted guest in their house, and it wasn't until he was thirteen and Jane had arrived in the household that he understood why.

He'd endured it all in stoic silence, but Jane's appearance changed all that. She was four years old when she arrived, plain and shy and frightened, and the Durhams' straight-faced insistence that she was both their daughter and his sister brought the absurdity of his own situation home to him. Despite their contention, Jane was no child of theirs. And neither, thank God, was he.

Between the two of them, he and Peter looked after her. Peter taught her about horses, Gabriel taught her about the woods and the trees, he schooled her in Latin and Greek and French, much to her dismay. Lady Elinor gave up all effort at mothering her two changelings upon the arrival of the twins, and no one ever thought to school Jane in the various arts she would need to attract a reasonable husband. She knew nothing about ordering a household, about fashion or music or art beyond a passionate appreciation. Peter's mother Alice took Jane under her wing and taught her the rudiments of housekeeping, though her knowledge of cooking and mending were better suited to a farmer's wife than a lady. And Jane learned to love all by herself.

Gabriel leaned back and sighed. Peter was a block-headed fool not to realize how desperately Jane loved him. He was intent on being noble, but his nobility would do nothing but cause everyone pain. The best Jane's future would hold was a polite marriage to some boring widower. There was no passion in her future, only emptiness and duty unless Peter took a hand.

Or Gabriel gave them a little push.

All his faint hints had met with stony resistance. All his overt suggestions had been met with hostility. If it weren't for the problem of the Chiltons and their bloodthirsty band of false Druids, he would have dealt with his sister's happiness months ago. But now Elizabeth Penshurst had arrived to make matters even more complicated.

Lizzie, he thought to himself, closing his eyes and listening to the crackle of the fire. She'd tasted cool and sweet and damp from the heavy rain. She'd tasted like heaven. He'd forgotten that kisses could be quite so sweet, so disruptive to one's peace of mind. He'd long ago moved past the kissing stage, but there was something about Lizzie's soft, untutored mouth that made him think it was an occupation well worth pursuing.

He wanted to kiss her again, in the rain, in the darkness. He wanted to lick the raindrops from her eyelids, he wanted to taste the warm skin of her throat. He wanted to take her hands and pull her, laughing and dancing, into the rain-drenched forest, he wanted to strip off her clothes and lay her down in the wet mossy grass and take her in every way he could think of, sacred and profane. He wanted her with such a force that even the bottles of wine hadn't put a dent in his wild, irrational need.

And Peter saw him too well, damn him. Not content with mucking up his own life, he thought he'd mess with Gabriel's as well. There was a world of difference in their situations, one which Peter was unlikely to admit. Peter and Jane belonged together, and they could manage to forge a very happy life with each other if Peter would stop worrying about station and concentrate on what was right.

But there was no happy future for Gabriel. No sweet future in the arms of a loved one. He was infinitely unlovable, and he knew it. Not that Jane realized it—she was blind where he was concerned, firmly convinced that beneath his indifference he was a good man.

He wasn't quite sure what he was, but good certainly didn't suit him. He wasn't an evil man—if he were, he'd have deflowered Miss Elizabeth Penshurst without a second thought. He'd still be in London, on that tedious round of empty pleasures, instead of living in solitude in the wilds of Yorkshire, trying to make some sense of his life.

But then, his past had followed him, and the wicked deeds had come back to haunt him. The Chiltons were there, along with numerous other dilettantes and half-wits eager to trade their immortal souls for more power. And he knew, to his sorrow, that they weren't going to stop at the slaughter of a few helpless animals.

He could stop them. He hadn't made much of an effort yet, too lazy and too self-absorbed to waste his time on them. But the arrival of Lizzie in the neighborhood made it suddenly imperative for him to find distraction, and the Chiltons provided a powerful one. As long as he could count on his family to keep Elizabeth Penshurst at bay, he'd be just fine.

She was a young woman with a reasonable amount of common sense beneath that glorious mane of flaming hair. She'd keep out of his way if she could possibly help it, wouldn't she? And he was more than capable of avoiding her.

The question was, did he really want to? Or did he want to tempt fate just one more time? One more taste of that full, luscious mouth surely couldn't do any more harm. If he believed in hell, he was already damned for past sins. He could take one small taste of wickedness and survive.

As for Miss Elizabeth Penshurst, she'd be fine. He wasn't about to ruin a properly brought-up young lady, no matter how tempting she was. Besides, she didn't strike him as the type to let herself be ruined. She was much too strong-minded to be led astray by a ruthless seducer.

No, he could kiss her. Tempt her. Maybe even ruin her for any other man just by showing her the possibilities. He should regret such a notion, but he couldn't. He wanted her to remember him. In her dotage, with fat grandchildren at her knee, he wanted her to remember the man in the woods who'd kissed her to distraction, and know that nothing in her life had ever equaled it.

Yes, he was hardly a good man, no matter what his sister Jane thought. But he didn't care. He'd rid the area of the Chiltons and their nasty ilk, he'd come as close as he dared to seducing Miss Elizabeth Penshurst. And then maybe he'd take off on a grand tour and not return until he was old enough not to care.

Maybe he'd never come back.

It seemed as unlikely as any of his fancies. He was

tied to this place, to the land, to the people. He always came back here, whether he wanted to or not, and it wasn't the call of family that lured him. He belonged here, and there wasn't much he could do about it. He couldn't escape for long.

In the meantime, he could dream about what he could never have. Lizzie, lying in a pile of velvet and furs on the massive bed in his tumbledown house, her clothes scattered on the floor, her beautiful eyes looking up at him in complete surrender.

Somehow he couldn't see it. Even as he took her, even as he made her come, she'd be fighting him. She would put her arms around him and kiss him, and her eyes would be flashing fire.

He could love a woman like that. God help him.

"You're being maudlin, young man." Brother Septimus's disapproving tones echoed in his ear. He didn't bother turning to look—the monks seldom revealed themselves in the daylight, they simply whispered unpleasant reminders of his duty when he didn't want to hear them.

"He's not being maudlin, Brother Septimus," said gentle Brother Paul. "Can't you see the boy's in love?"

At that Gabriel swiveled around, driven past endurance. He could vaguely see their outlines within the dust motes, and he glared in their general direction. "I'm not a young man, I'm not a boy, and I'm most certainly not in love. I drank too much last night, and I'm suffering the consequences."

"So you say, my boy." Brother Paul's voice was annoyingly smug. "So you say."

And Gabriel picked up one of the logs that Peter had brought and heaved it at the shifting shadows.

* * *

Fever dreams. Elizabeth knew it, even as she fought against the constricting covers. She was burning up, her small room blazing hot, and some distant part of her consciousness found perverse annoyance in the fact that the ungracious Durhams had finally chosen to be generous with their fires when she no longer had need of additional heat.

They came and went, looking down at her from their long, elegant noses. They all had the same nose, she thought, blinking drowsily. Sir Richard and Lady Durham, Edwina and Edward had matching, slightly hooked noses, giving the four of them a faintly hawkish look. Jane and Gabriel didn't look the slightest bit like them.

"She'll die," Sir Richard pronounced, looking down at her without pity. "We'd best be off in case she's contagious."

"It's only an inflammation," Jane's stalwart reply came, though she was out of Elizabeth's limited view. "She'll be fine."

"I won't have my darling children exposed to it!" Lady Durham proclaimed.

"I'm not leaving her," said Jane.

"I hadn't supposed you would. Make her comfortable, and let us know when it's safe to return."

Safe to return, Elizabeth thought hazily, as the room grew still and quiet. *There is nothing safe about Hernewood.* Ghosts roamed the woods, bloodthirsty pagans performed horrid acts upon helpless animals, and worst of all, Gabriel was there, like a huge spider awaiting his prey.

Her faint laugh turned into another coughing spasm. Gabriel wasn't the slightest bit like a spider. He wasn't dark and hairy, he was smooth and golden. In fact, all she could think of was the silken expanse of skin he had no qualms about displaying. And nipples. She hadn't realized men had flat, dark nipples. There was no earthly reason for them. They seemed to exist merely to distract her.

Another coughing spasm ensued, and when she finally stopped, exhausted, she uttered a small, wicked curse beneath her breath. She hated getting sick. It happened so seldom, but then with such ferocity, that she made a miserable patient. She had always found she could court illness with a reckless abandon and emerge unscathed, but a midnight romp in bare feet, followed by a thorough soaking, had done its evil worst, and now she lay in her bed, wracked with chills and fever, coughing and miserable and unable to distract her mind from her illness by anything other than the insidious vision of Gabriel Durham.

At least she knew her illness wouldn't be of long duration. These things never were. The woods wouldn't kill her—they would make her stronger. She simply had to suffer through this miserable ague for another day, and she'd be well on the mend.

He came to her in the night. The house was still and silent, and Jane dozed in an uncomfortable chair by her bedside. Elizabeth could have told her such efforts were unnecessary. She certainly felt as if she might die, but she had no intention of truly doing so. She had what amounted to a monstrous cold, and nothing but time and rest would rout it.

But Gabriel was there, shimmering in the firelight, dressed as he'd been when she'd last seen him in that open white shirt, his hair loose around her shoulders, his eyes dark and glowing. He moved toward her bed, and she was burning up. She couldn't kick her covers free, but then, Jane was right there, and Gabriel certainly wasn't. He was a fever dream, and any impropriety was negligible.

She threw off the covers, but Jane slept on, unaware of her patient's restlessness. "Lizzie," he said, but his mouth didn't move, the sound of his voice echoing in her head.

It seemed as if she hadn't left the bed in days. She rose effortlessly, only vaguely conscious of the thin chemise that covered her body. She was never allowed to sleep in such light clothing—it must have been in deference to her fever. It didn't matter—he wasn't really there, and any sins would be sins of her imagination, not her body. Surely the punishment would be mild.

He stood in front of the fire, and she thought she could see the flames flickering through his white-gold body. She came up to him, closer than she would have ever dared, marveling at her boldness. She liked the freedom of this dream. He was watching her, his face still, silent, oddly solemn.

"Am I going to die?" she asked him. Her voice was soft, hoarse from coughing, a mere whisper of sound in the silent room.

He laughed. "You think I'm an angel, ready to take you to heaven?"

"No."

"I could take you to heaven, Lizzie. I could show you paradise on earth."

In such a lovely dream she should have swooned into his arms. But even in a fever dream she was still herself, doubting and pragmatic even as he called to her soul. "I can imagine," she said dryly.

"No," he said. "You can't. Touch me."

She didn't move, stunned by the heat, the need in his voice.

"Touch me," he said again, and she lifted her hand, slowly, tentatively.

His chest was smooth, sleek, warm in the firelight. She let her fingertips graze the surface, and she could feel the muscle beneath the silken skin. She flattened her palm against him, and his heart was beating, steady, fast, against it.

He reached up and put his own hand between her breasts, against the thin cloth of her chemise, and she knew her heart was pounding as well, in rapid counterpoint to his. She was sick, she told herself. She was dreaming. Perhaps she was even dying. None of it mattered.

All that mattered was his hand on her flesh, the warmth of it spreading outward to her breasts, spreading downward between her legs so that her knees felt weak and she wanted him to touch her, everywhere. She opened her mouth to speak, but no words came out.

His heart was beating more quickly now, pounding against her hand. She wanted, needed to get closer to him. She was suddenly cold again, wracked with shivers, and she knew the only way she could get warm was to press her chilled, almost naked body against him. He was so strong, so warm, that he would drive the chill from her body. She was encased in a block of ice, and he was the only one who could melt it.

He put his hand on her waist, and drew her toward him, and she came, slowly, letting the heat from his body flow over her like a thick warm blanket. He didn't kiss her. He didn't need to. His flesh against hers was a brand, a blanket of ownership and belonging that sank into her bones and claimed her.

He held her tight against him, and her body convulsed in a tiny spasm of reaction that shocked her. For a moment she tried to pull away from him, but his voice was low and hypnotic in her ear.

"You need more," he whispered. "You need me."

And the truth of it was so profound, so painful that her eyes flew open, and she was alone, lying in bed, covered with piles of blankets and a thin film of sweat, with Jane sound asleep beside her.

CHAPTER NINE

Delilah, Countess of Chilton, surveyed her reflection in the huge mirror that hung over her bed. She'd had it brought with her from London during their unwilling exile—she found she never enjoyed sex as much when she couldn't watch herself being pleasured by the partner of the moment. And on the rare occasions when she chose to sleep alone, there was nothing more comforting than waking up to the glorious reflection of exquisite beauty. Namely her own.

Of course, it had been her addiction to beauty that caused her unfortunate attachment to Francis. He was quite the loveliest human being she knew, apart from herself, and she had been blinded, smitten by the absolute perfection of face and form. She'd never had any illusions about his nature, of course. He was wicked, small, and venal, which made him a perfect consort for her.

He was also particularly interested in bedding other

men, but Delilah had assumed with regal certainty that
no man could ever resist her. No man could prefer a
pretty young boy to her own impressive charms.

But Francis had proven annoyingly difficult. He was
perverse enough to resist her simply because he knew
it annoyed her. When he could be persuaded to perform
he was quite gloriously inventive, and if some of his
particular talents involved pain, Delilah was more than
happy to cooperate. There was nothing more tedious
than unimaginative sexual congress, and two willing
partners tended to be one willing partner too many.

But in the end subjugating Francis was turning out
to be both too difficult and not worth the effort. He
was very pretty, to be sure. But Gabriel Durham was, in
his own way, even more devastating, and he had the
added piquancy of disliking her intensely.

He was also quite strong, almost disgustingly so. She'd
been watching him, covertly and at times quite openly,
and he had the body of a laborer. Skin colored by the
sun instead of the milky white of Francis's flesh. Sinew
and muscle that left the most entrancing pattern under
that tanned, golden skin. He was probably more than
capable of breaking a weakling like Francis in half. He
could probably crush her with no effort at all.

The idea excited her. She'd had sex with so many
men she'd long ago lost count, and for a while she'd
gone through a stage where she preferred the lower
classes. She started with the indoor servants, then went
to the stables, then had those servants prowl the streets
for her. She'd sampled chimney sweeps barely half her
size and age, she'd tried thieves and soldiers and even
the occasional female. She liked strength in a partner.
Almost as much as she liked weakness.

If only Francis had learned to control himself, they
wouldn't be in exile right now. If that wretched boy

hadn't died, they would still be in London, enjoying the fruits of civilization instead of stuck out here in the wilds of Yorkshire.

It wasn't as if children didn't die all the time, anyway. But there was a great difference between a homeless ragamuffin and the adolescent son of a shopkeeper. Shopkeepers were so tiresomely bourgeois. It wasn't as if the man didn't have other children, for heaven's sake. And Francis had offered him positively indecent sums of money to compensate him for the loss of one of his extraneous offspring.

There was, however, a silver lining to this dark cloud of boredom. Gabriel Durham had left London more than a year earlier, before either of the Chiltons could form a more than casual acquaintance with him. Getting as far away from London as possible had seemed an excellent choice for the Chiltons, and Hernewood, in North Yorkshire, was very far indeed. They could wait out their penance and renew their brief acquaintance with the world's foremost expert on arcane religions. If it weren't for Gabriel Durham's treatise on the ancient Druids of the British Isles, Francis and Delilah might never have found true meaning in their lives.

Gabriel had proven deliciously resistant to all their efforts at neighborliness, but Delilah thrived on challenge. The only question was, which Chilton would bed him first.

The rumors in London had been fascinating— Gabriel Durham was a man of powerful appetites and terrifying intellect, a man unburdened by conventional morality. It was little wonder, if the rumors about his parentage were true. He had the charming, arrogant disregard of the true nobility.

But overnight he had disappeared, leaving his companions, his mistresses, his gaming partners, and his creditors in the dark about his whereabouts. It was sheer luck that Francis discovered he'd returned home to Yorkshire, the one place he'd vowed never to go again.

And it was sheer luck that there was a suitable establishment just waiting for Francis and Delilah when circumstances forced them from their Hyde Park manor. A sign from the gods, Francis had said, though neither of them were particularly clear which gods they happened to worship.

Whatever god it was, he had a fierce appetite for blood and obedience. Not unlike the Chiltons themselves, Delilah thought with a lovely smirk. Perhaps, in their rituals, they were only worshiping themselves. She laughed out loud at the notion.

"That's an early sign of madness, darling," Francis drawled. He was lounging in her doorway, dressed in the palest of pink satins, his blond curls cascading over his shoulders.

She smiled winningly at him. "You know, dearest, that particular ensemble would be overdressed at Court. In the country it goes beyond absurd to comical."

He sketched a bow. "Always glad to amuse you, my darling, though I suspect that wasn't what you were giggling at when I arrived. Such a lovely, girlish giggle from such a wizened old soul."

She viewed her smooth, perfect complexion with a sigh. "As long as it is only my soul that is old and wizened, I am content," she purred. "To what do I owe the honor of such an early visit? I do hope you're not going to plague me with one of your nauseating attempts to beget an heir."

"I had no idea you found my attentions so tiresome, my pet."

"Your forays into traditional sex are tedious in the

extreme. It's your creative alternatives I find . . . entertaining."

Francis's pale, thin mouth quirked in a chilly smile. "Always glad to be of service, my precious, but I've not come for recreation. We have a problem."

"Indeed? None that we can't easily circumvent, I'm sure. You are soooo inventive, darling."

"That idiot Durham has taken his family off to London without the slightest bit of warning."

Delilah turned her back on the enchanting prospect of her mirror, facing her husband in dismay. "How dare he?"

"Indeed. Unfortunately he didn't see fit to consult with us," he said ironically. "I wish fate would stop attempting to plague us. Just when things were going so very well indeed."

"He took his impossibly silly children with him, I suppose?"

"Would I be complaining if he left them behind? Vapid, innocent Miss Edwina Durham is safely in London. We'll simply have to set our sights on an alternative prospect."

"No one who smells of the shop, Francis," she warned. "This gift must be absolutely perfect. A proper, innocent young female of respectable birth. Someone who is cherished. Someone who will be missed."

"But it makes things so much more dangerous, my dear," he complained lightly.

"But that makes it even more satisfying, my dear," she replied. "You don't like things to be too easy, do you?"

"You know me too well, Delilah."

"That's why we're so perfectly matched."

"Except for your inability to provide me with an heir."

"I rather thought it was your inability," she cooed.

"If you were quicker to conceive, we could have handled it properly." There was no missing the sulkiness in his voice. "You don't like it any more than I do."

"Nor do I like the notion of spoiling my looks with a great swollen belly. We'll have a child in good time, Francis. We will have everything we want."

"Not if we don't find a suitable sacrifice."

"Gift, Francis. She's a gift to Belarus. Sacrifice sounds so . . . so pagan." She turned back to twine her fingers through her silky black hair. "Tell me, did he take his elder daughter with him? Dear Jane?"

"I doubt it. I also doubt a long Meg such as she would be much of an offering."

"At least there's no doubt she's a virgin," Delilah said with a throaty laugh. "Who would want such an overgrown creature?"

"What about the red-haired bitch who was with her? Much prettier, though a bit too spirited. She could do with a taste of the whip."

"A taste I'm sure you'd be happy to provide. There, you see, problem solved. We have two well-bred virgins, left behind without any sort of protector."

"You're forgetting Gabriel. You think he'll sit by and let us sacrifice his own sister?"

"Perhaps not. But he doesn't have to know, does he? After all, he's kept his distance from us. Even if he decides to join us, we don't have to tell him everything. I doubt he has more than a passing sentimental fondness for her, if that. I doubt she's even his flesh and blood."

"You may be right."

"As for the other one, she's hardly his type, do you think? If he can resist me, what could he possibly want with a plain little creature such as her? With such distressing hair?"

Francis took her hand in his soft, limp grip and

brought it to his lips. "As always, my dear, you are a font of cold-blooded wisdom. I salute you."

Delilah smiled up at him, her full red lips curving in delicious anticipation. "I do my humble best." And she let out a small squeal of pleasure as his teeth sank into her hand, hard, drawing blood.

It was a very large house to be quite so empty, Jane thought wearily as she trudged up the back stairs, a canister of hot water in her hands. She'd greeted the departure of her family with well-concealed relief, but twenty-four hours later she would have welcomed a bit of company.

Sir Richard's tight-fisted ways ensured that only the barest of staff was left on at the manor. One elderly manservant who could only manage to bring wood to the first floor, and even that was taxing the poor old thing, and two scullery maids who bordered on the half-witted and whose thick Yorkshire accents were barely intelligible, even after Jane's lifetime in the north. She was on her own, as she had been before, but this time she had a sick young woman relying on her, and she had no notion of just how ill Elizabeth truly was.

A doctor had been sent for, but since Sir Richard felt it beneath his dignity to pay a physician for his services, it seemed unlikely Dr. Thompson would come. In the meantime Elizabeth slept and woke and dreamed and thrashed, and for all Jane knew she was close to death.

She didn't even dare leave her to find help. The half-witted Twickham sisters were utterly useless, and old George was too feeble and too superstitious to find his way through the woods to Gabriel's tower. And she hadn't seen any sign of Peter since she'd left him in the stable.

He had to be somewhere around, but he was making himself scarce. Sir Richard would have no qualms in dismissing the house servants for a fortnight or more while the important members of his family were in London, but he valued his horseflesh, and the stables would be properly attended.

Unless, of course, he took Peter with him to drive the coach. It hadn't happened yet—Peter had always declared his disdain for southern ways and cities, but one could hardly say no to an employer. Perhaps he'd abandoned her as well, Jane thought, moving up the narrow back stairs at a snail's pace.

She should have made one of the Twickhams carry the copper tub upstairs, but they were busy in the kitchen, concocting something that was likely to be barely edible, and she didn't want to confuse them with another order. Rose and Violet were of a very singular mind, and Jane suspected between the two of them they only shared one. She didn't want to task them too severely.

She paused at the top of the stairs, breathing deeply. At least she'd managed to move Elizabeth out of the tiny, cold room beneath the eaves into Gabriel's abandoned bedroom. It hadn't changed in the years since he'd left Hernewood Manor. It was still dark, opulent, and soulless. It was also possessed of the best fire and the warmest location, and Jane could sit by the window and search in vain for her brother or Peter to return.

She started forward, but her slipper caught on the worn carpet that Sir Richard thought suitable for the servants' quarters, and she went flying, the bucket of hot water streaming out ahead of her as she tumbled onto her face.

She'd hit her chin on the bucket and smashed her knee on the floor. She was soaking wet, exhausted, and utterly miserable. She was a woman who never cried, and yet she lay in the darkened hallway and let out a howl of pure grief and frustration that could have been heard through half the county, if anyone cared enough to listen. No one did.

She heard the footsteps from a distance, echoing on the thinly carpeted steps. Someone with a firm, measured tread, nothing like old George's wobbly gait or the Twickham sisters' clumsy scramble. She knew who it had to be, knew if she had any sense at all she'd leap to her feet and hide herself in the nearest bedroom.

She couldn't make herself move.

Any more than she could make herself stop crying. He thought she was strong, impervious, unimaginative, and boring. He probably didn't even realize she was female, Jane thought miserably, with all the weakness of the female sex. She could cry as well and as loudly as any woman, and she intended to do just that, and keep on doing that, and he could approach at his own peril, damn him.

She'd cradled her face in her arms as she sobbed, but she could feel him kneel beside her, feel the warmth of his strong, rough hands on her heaving shoulders.

"There, now, lass." Peter's voice was deep and rumbling. "What kind of fuss is this? You're not the sort to be weeping over a bit of spilled water, are you?"

She lifted her head and glared at him out of streaming eyes. The hallway was dark, so he probably missed the full glory of her rage and misery, but she wasn't about to spare him.

"I'm the sort to weep about anything I damned please," she wailed. "I'm tired, I'm wet, I hurt, and I'm alone, damn it." She liked the sound of that word, so she said it again between hiccuping sobs. "Damn damn damn."

His response was far from promising. She heard him

laugh, deep in his throat, and then he pulled her up from the floor, into his arms as he knelt beside her, just as if she were a frail slip of a girl, or a weeping child. "There, there, lass. Weep if you must. They say everyone needs a good cry every now and then."

Unfortunately being told she had every right to cry was the one thing likely to stop Jane's tears. That and the knowledge that her head was tucked against Peter's chest, and she could feel the warmth of his skin through the rough-spun cloth. Without thinking she buried her face in his shirt, blindly seeking some sort of comfort. Or something else entirely.

"You've had a hard time of it," he said in his rumbly voice. "I should have come sooner, but I thought the two of you would be fine once your family left, and your brother's been keeping me busy from morning till night. You should have sent for me, lass."

And what would that have done? she thought to herself, clinging to his shirt tightly. He'd have to pry her fingers loose—she wasn't letting go until she was good and ready.

He smelled wonderful. Like the stables, and warm skin, and cider, and leather. All the wonderful scents that made her think of Peter, and she started crying again, not making any effort to control herself.

His hand was stroking her short-cropped hair with the same gentleness he'd use on a foaling mare. "Lass," he said, and there was a trace of desperation in his voice. "You're breaking my heart. For the love of God, stop weeping and tell me how I can fix things."

You can kiss me.

He didn't hear her, of course. She didn't dare say the words out loud. She already had the best she could hope for. Peter was holding her in his arms, murmuring soft, meaningless words as he stroked her hair, and it was enough to treasure for the rest of her endless, lonely life.

"What's wrong with Miss?" She heard one of the Twickham girls' nasal voice inquire.

"She needs a cup of tea, and be sharp about it," Peter said crossly. "You haven't been taking proper care of your mistress. You ought to be ashamed of yourself."

"You know Miss Jane," the second Twickham girl said defensively. "She's as strong as a horse. Besides, there are only the two of us and old George in the house. We can barely manage to keep the fires lit. We can't be rushing around after Miss Jane."

"So instead she has to carry her own bathwater?" Peter said in a flinty voice.

"It was for Miss Penshurst." The Twickham who spoke obviously thought that was some sort of justification.

"Then why don't you and your sister take care of that little problem while I see Miss Jane to her room and make sure she's properly settled. And then you can bring her that cup of tea."

"Her room?" Twickham number one gasped. "You shouldn't even be up here, and you know it. You can't go to her room."

"Stop me," said Peter briefly, scooping his arms around Jane before she could protest.

He rose effortlessly despite the burden of her not inconsiderable weight, and when she tried to say something he simply crushed her against him to silence her. "Get along, you silly twits."

"Peter," Jane said in a weak, watery voice. "You can't . . ."

"I certainly can." He carried her down the dimly lit hall as effortlessly as if she were a newborn colt. She'd left her door only slightly ajar, and he kicked it open with his large, hobnailed boot, moving to the chair by the fire.

She would have thought he'd set her down in it, find her a shawl to warm her, but he did no such thing. He sat down in it himself, keeping her tightly folded in his arms, and she didn't bother to struggle.

She felt his hand reach down and catch her chin, drawing her tear-stained face up to meet his. It was brighter in her room—the light from the windows and the fire illuminating her misery far too clearly.

"Now tell me, Janey," he said softly, using the name he hadn't used since she'd reached adolescence and he'd grown suddenly formal. "Who's broken your heart, and what do I have to do to the bastard?"

CHAPTER TEN

Gabriel moved past the open door as silently as only he could. Not that Jane and Peter would notice him. Jane was too caught up in a totally uncharacteristic weeping fit, and Peter was trying manfully to deal with it. As far as Gabriel could tell he was doing a decent job of it for a change.

He shook his head as he continued down the deserted hallways of his childhood home. Life could be so simple for some people, if they stopped worrying about inconsequentials. Of course, Peter would probably say the same thing to him as well. Matters of rank and station were of absolutely no importance to someone like Gabriel, the unwanted bastard of a scandalous union. He was both outside society and above it, given his whispered connections, and he could do as he pleased.

It helped that he tried very hard not to give a damn about anyone or anything, with the possible exception of the two mismatched lovers in the other room. Peter cared too much, and therein lay his problem. He needed a good dose of Gabriel's remarkable selfishness.

He moved like a ghost through the deserted hallways. A ghost among ghosts. Not that his own personal ghosts ever journeyed to the manor. Brother Septimus and Brother Paul were bound to Hernewood Forest and the abbey ruins—they were unable to travel beyond a certain area. Though who could blame them for avoiding this cold, soulless house.

He hated this place with a fierce passion that resisted all his efforts simply not to care. He hadn't always been as distant and invulnerable as he was now. And the memory of his bitter, empty childhood lived on in this place, waiting to come out and snatch at the clothes of a lonely boy wandering the cold, sterile hallways.

He knew which bedroom they'd allotted Lizzie—they always put unimportant guests in the small, chilly room under the eaves. He considered himself noble indeed to avoid looking in on her. Better to resist temptation. She had an uncanny ability to distract him even when she was nowhere around.

His old bedroom was the finest in the house, larger than all the others, including the master bedroom belonging to the Durhams. As a child he'd wondered about that, as an adult he knew the answer. Large and fine meant absolutely nothing if the room was dark and gloomy, more a spacious prison than a place for a young boy.

He didn't need to go there, but he did, drawn by some random part of his nature that sought out remembered pain. He pushed the door open, then paused, shocked to see a bright fire burning merrily in the Italian marble fireplace.

The room was just as he'd left it. With the exception of the woman lying in his bed.

Even in the murky light he could see the bright flame of her hair spread out on the pillows. A sensible man would back away quickly, closing the door behind him before she even realized he'd been there.

He wasn't a sensible man. He stepped inside the hated confines of his old room and closed the door behind him, leaning against it, as he surveyed his surroundings.

She made a difference in the place. The dark walls and curtains, the heavy furniture were still the same. But the fire seemed brighter, more cheerful, lighting the oppressive darkness.

She lay very still beneath the pile of covers, and her face looked pale. He wondered whether he should be concerned, go and interrupt Jane and Peter, demand to know whether a doctor had been summoned. He resisted the impulse. He wasn't normally a man to worry over trifles, and she seemed to be resting peacefully, her breathing steady. His instincts told him she was on the mend, and over the years he'd found that his instincts were one of the few things he could trust.

There was a chair by her bed, but he avoided it, instead going to the large carved chair in the shadows cast by the blazing fire. He preferred shadows to bright light. He could watch and listen without being seen, at one with the darkness. He could sit in his old room with the ghosts of his childhood breathing down his neck and dream erotic dreams about Lizzie's lithe young body lying in his bed.

It was a pleasant enough occupation after an unpleasant day of searching the various wood groves for animal corpses. He'd tried to keep himself blessedly ignorant of the Chiltons' twisted permutations of the Old Religion, but there was no avoiding the fact that things were accelerating rapidly with the approach of May and the ancient festival of Beltane. The occasional dead animal had given way to sacrifices that occurred almost daily, and he had the wretched feeling that they were planning something particularly impressive for the coming week. And the Chiltons were entirely capable of moving beyond animals into the realm of human sacrifice. The troubling disappearance of three young women still bothered him when he allowed it to, though the villagers seemed to have accepted and dismissed it as nothing unusual. And it was true, young women took off for better opportunities all the time, and the missing girls were known to be flighty. Even if he couldn't understand why someone would willingly abandon Hernewood, he knew there were people who did.

There was nothing he could do about the Chiltons without cozying up to them, something he still fiercely resisted. He'd had enough of their kind of people, spiteful and shallow and utterly without redeeming merit. Neither of the Chiltons was particularly stupid, yet even a few minutes in their presence left him feeling both incredibly bored and ever so slightly unclean.

Unlike Lizzie. All he had to do was look at her, sleeping so peacefully in his bed, and he felt alive and refreshed and ready for anything. He'd had his first wet dream in that bed. He'd had the usual satisfying solitary fantasies any young boy could enjoy, probably more, since his appetites were powerful. But he'd never actually taken a woman in that huge, high bed.

And there lay a woman he wanted quite desperately. Granted, she was sick, but he didn't normally let such trifles interfere with his pleasures. He was a skilled man—he could make her forget all about her indisposition.

He didn't move from his seat in the shadows. There were times when temptation and anticipation were far more pleasurable than fulfillment, particularly in the case of well-bred virgins. He was better off fantasizing about Lizzie Penshurst than actually doing anything about it.

And so he'd keep insisting to himself, until he finally came to believe it.

When Elizabeth woke she was alone in a different room, with no idea how she had gotten there or how long she'd been lying in a strange bed. Her head pounded, her mouth felt as if she'd been chewing on rat droppings, and her entire body was a mass of aches, but she was undoubtedly better. She'd feel better still if she managed a bath and a hearty meal—she was utterly starving. At least the fire in the fireplace was uncharacteristically hearty. The Durhams must have been worried indeed, to sanction such a willful waste of wood, she thought as she managed to pull herself to a sitting position on the high bed.

It was full dark outside, and the house was still and silent, only the crackle of the fire breaking the quiet. She pushed her hair away from her face, and then she saw him, sitting in the shadows, watching her.

Obviously she wasn't feeling as well as she thought. More likely she was still asleep. Why else would she find herself in a strange room that she'd never seen before, warmed by a generous fire? She'd often had dreams about finding different rooms in familiar houses—this must be one of them.

However, she didn't usually see a beautiful man waiting for her in the shadows.

Part of her fever dreams, she reminded herself. She wanted more than the imagined touch of his body. She shouldn't have given in to the fantasy, she thought. It had just made her want more.

"Go away," she said in a rough, cranky voice. "I'm not going to give in to temptation this time."

"Am I tempting? You surprise me." His voice came from the shadows, a little more substantial than her previous dream, but still disembodied.

"You're not really here," she said. "Any more than you were last night, or whenever it was that you . . ." She wasn't quite sure how she could describe what he'd done to her, so she wisely let her words trail off.

"When I what?"

Even fever-induced apparitions could taunt, Elizabeth decided with a certain amount of irritation. "When you touched me," she said after a reluctant moment. "Do go away. This is my dream, and I don't want you here."

"If it's a dream, then why are you worrying about the consequences?"

"Because the last dream gave me nightmares." She shouldn't be having this conversation with a phantom, but then, what was the harm? Perhaps she had to deny the dream-Gabriel before she could resist the real one.

"Did it? Why? What have you got to be afraid of? The dreams had to come from inside you, Lizzie. I wasn't anywhere around."

"I'm not interested in arguing metaphysics with an apparition."

"I'm always interested in arguing metaphysics, whether I'm an apparition or not. Besides, I would think it would be particularly apt. What better person to argue with?"

"Go away," she said crossly. "If this is my dream, you might at least behave as I want you to."

"And how would you like me to behave, sweet Lizzie?" he murmured.

"I want you to go away and let me rest."

"Liar," he said softly. "You've had more than enough

rest. What do you want from me? Shall I lie beside you on the bed and soothe your fevered brow? You don't look particularly feverish right now, but I could be mistaken. Personally I think you're absolutely glowing with health."

"I can't be," she said. "I wouldn't be seeing you here if I were fully recovered."

"You still haven't told me why you're so angry with me? What did I do when I invaded your dreams last time?"

"You took indecent liberties with me," she said in a muffled voice.

"You're such an innocent I'm surprised your imagination was able to conjure up such things. What did I do?"

"You touched me," she said. "You made me feel very . . . odd. And you didn't even kiss me."

"You sound most disgruntled. Shall I kiss you now?"

"I'm sick."

"Apparitions aren't susceptible to contagion." He rose, and the firelight hit his tall body, illuminating it like an aura. "You can show me what kind of touching I did, though I expect I know just how it made you feel. Wouldn't you like to feel that way again? I could make it even better, I promise."

He was coming closer to the bed, and instead of shimmering away into nothingness he seemed disconcertingly solid. She looked up at him warily, waiting for him to disappear, and when he seemed to have no intention of doing so she scrambled off the bed, oblivious to the thin chemise that was her only clothing. Besides, the real Gabriel had seen her in not much more, when she'd made the mistake of wandering in the woods in her nightclothes.

"Keep away from me," she warned him.

He halted, the wide bed between them. He leaned forward, resting his hands on the rumpled sheet, and she stared down at them in fascination. He had beautiful hands, with long, narrow fingers. Strong, deft-looking hands. Very solid-looking hands. "Do you really want me to? After all, what harm can a dream do? Come back to bed, sweet Lizzie, and I'll show you how pleasant dreams can be."

She almost wavered. She looked across the wide expanse of the bed at him, at his lost, beautiful face, his elegant mouth, his haunted eyes, and she wanted to reach out to him, to feel the imagined warmth of his skin against hers once more. This was sin, hot and wicked, and she wanted to feel it.

At that moment the door to the room opened, and Jane stood there, flustered, a branch of candles in her hand. "You're better!" she said in relief. "I was so worried! But what in heaven's name is Gabriel doing in here? And why are you out of bed?"

Elizabeth could feel the hot flush of embarrassment sweep over her body like a flood. The bright candles illuminated the room far better than the flickering fire, and the man staring at her across the bed was no fever dream, induced by unspoken longings. He was real, he was there, and he knew exactly what temptations she'd been wrestling with.

He moved back from the bed, into the shadows once more, so she was spared his expression. "I found her sleeping in my old bed, Jane. I assumed she was a present for me."

"Go away, Gabriel," Jane said with sisterly annoyance. "Elizabeth's in no mood for your jokes. Go help Peter— he's in the kitchens trying to force some sense into the Twickham girls."

"Is that who's been left behind? The Twickham twits?

God help you." He skirted the bed, unfortunately coming very close to Elizabeth's rigid figure. Before she knew what he was doing he put his hand against her face, cool against her flushed skin. "She's hot, Jane, but I don't think she's feverish." There was a light of wicked humor in his eyes.

"Stop teasing the girl!" But Jane was across the room, and Gabriel was still touching Elizabeth, his eyes still caught with hers.

He leaned forward and brushed a kiss against the side of her face. "I wasn't teasing," he whispered. And before she had time to react he was gone, leaving the two women alone in the room.

"Back in bed with you," Jane said briskly. "I'm delighted to see you're feeling better, but despite what Gabriel says I still think you look feverish. I'm not certain you're ready to get up."

"I'm much better," Elizabeth insisted, letting Jane help her back up into the high bed. For some reason she kept seeing Gabriel's hands as they rested on the rumpled sheets, and she could feel her face flush even hotter. "I think I'd really prefer to get up. I feel like I've been lying in bed forever."

"It's only been two days," Jane said. She eyed her with a professional manner. "You know, Gabriel might be right. You do seem fine now. I don't understand it— just this morning you were utterly miserable. I was afraid it might go into an inflammation of the lungs."

"When I get sick I get quite sick, but I recover quickly," Elizabeth said, acutely aware of whose bed she was in. "I'm really feeling almost completely better, and I'm certain if I were able to come downstairs, I'd be completely cured."

Jane looked doubtful. "I suppose we can try it and see, though I can't promise you much of an improvement downstairs. George isn't strong enough to keep all the fires going, so we're making do with one in the kitchen and one in the library, and with the housekeeper gone there isn't much fresh food available.''

"Where is everyone?"

"Gone," Jane said succinctly. "My mother panics in the face of illness, and she was convinced both she and Edwina would contract a putrid disease and die immediately. Not that either of them is the slightest bit likely to become ill. For one thing, they came nowhere near you the moment they discovered you were feeling ill, and for another, the two of them are as strong as horses. Particularly Edwina.''

Elizabeth managed a rusty chuckle. "I don't imagine she'd appreciate being compared to a horse.''

"In truth I was giving her a compliment. If I had to choose between my younger sister and a horse, I wouldn't hesitate for long. Edwina may be absolutely lovely, but she's shallow, mean, and selfish, caring only for her own comforts. Horses are strong, brave, and noble creatures.''

"Even when they run away with you?" Elizabeth murmured.

"Marigold . . .''

". . . Is as gentle as a lamb. So everyone has informed me. I can only suppose she mistook me for some lamb-stealing wolf.''

"They know when you're frightened of them," Jane said firmly. "As soon as you're better I'll take you out again, and this time you'll have a chance to accustom yourself to Marigold. Learn to listen to her.''

"I think that as soon as I'm well enough to travel I should head back to Dorset." The notion was unaccountably depressing. "After all, my host and hostess have departed, and it would be rude for me to stay on.''

"It was rude of them to leave," Jane said flatly. "And they would want you to stay. My father expressly told me that I was not to allow you to return home. You must stay here, he said, and enjoy the peace and fresh air."

Dead animal corpses and pelting rainstorms and Gabriel Durham's eyes were not Elizabeth's idea of peace, but she didn't bother informing Jane of that fact. In truth, she didn't want to leave this place. Even if it meant riding that Devil Horse, Marigold, or tripping over more butchered animals.

She didn't want to leave Hernewood until Gabriel Durham kissed her, just one more time.

CHAPTER ELEVEN

She assumed, stupidly, that Gabriel would be gone. Elizabeth dressed in one of her plain, enveloping gowns and wound her long red mane of hair in a loose knot at the back of her neck, letting the length of it hang free. She couldn't find her hairpins in this new bedroom, and she didn't have the energy to go searching for them. Besides, she still had the remnants of a pounding head, and binding her hair tightly against her skull would surely make it worse. An excuse, she knew it, but the best she could come up with.

She couldn't find her shoes either, but going around in her stocking feet was more comfortable, and the shabby old shawl she draped around her shoulders was soft and warm.

She descended the back stairs, in search of food and warmth and companionship.

What she found was Gabriel, standing in the middle of the deserted kitchen.

She came to a frozen standstill a few steps from the bottom of the stairs, strongly tempted to turn and escape back to the confines of her room. His back was turned, and with luck he wouldn't even know she'd been there, and she should leave, fast, except that she couldn't tell what he was doing and she was, as always, regrettably curious.

"Are you just going to hover on the stairs, or are you coming in?" His voice was even, hardly curious, as he continued whatever he was doing. *So much for escape,* she thought, descending the last two steps into the warm room. It was hardly her fault if she kept running into someone she'd be much happier keeping her distance from.

"I'm hungry," she announced.

He glanced at her over his shoulder. "You may be the very first woman I've ever heard admit to such a thing. Sit down and I'll pour you some of this soup."

If Elizabeth had been surprised before, it was nothing compared to her current astonishment. Gabriel Durham was cooking.

"Sit!" he ordered impatiently, when she made no effort to move.

Elizabeth sat.

She hadn't yet ventured in the kitchen area of the manor house, and since she had no strong desire to stare at Gabriel's back she surveyed her surroundings with great interest.

"Never seen a kitchen before?" he murmured, looming over her. Bringing the tantalizing scent of chicken soup with him.

She allowed herself to look up, into his beautiful eyes, then focused on the earthenware bowl he was holding. "Not one of this magnitude."

He set the bowl down in front of her and took the

chair opposite her at the large, well-scrubbed worktable. "Eat," he said.

She dipped the spoon into the savory broth, then hesitated, stealing a glance at him. "Did you make this?"

"I did. It's not poison, I promise you."

"You aren't the type who would poison," she muttered, tasting it. The soup was sinfully good.

"And what am I the type for?" he asked idly.

The ritually slaughtered animals in the woods came to mind, but she quickly banished that thought, hoping it wouldn't show on her too expressive face. "I have no idea. I expect if you wanted to murder me, you'd probably use your bare hands. You've looked as if you've wanted to strangle me on more than one occasion."

He laughed, that soft, deep laugh that stirred her bones. "At least you don't think I'm about to try virgin sacrifice. Though there's a variation that might prove entertaining."

"Oh, really?" She was halfway through the soup, trying to keep from devouring it as she wanted to.

"One could always sacrifice the virginity but keep the former virgin. I can fancy all sorts of interesting rituals . . ."

She glared at him. "Why do you think you can get away with such insulting behavior? Is it because Sir Richard is gone, and there's no one to answer to?"

"Don't worry about it, my precious, my behavior is insulting toward everyone. In truth, I'm rather better with you than I am with most people I come across."

"I find that hard to believe. Why?"

"Why?" he echoed, considering it. "Probably because you entertain me. Very few people do."

"How gratifying."

"It's your temper, I think. It goes with your red hair, of course, but it's really quite delightful. You do your best to be demure, with your ugly little dresses and your downcast eyes, and perhaps an idiot like my foster father might be fooled by it, but I'm not. You're refreshingly hostile, my love, and it enchants me."

She stared at him, stupefied. "You're easily enchanted."

"Now that, I assure you, is not true. Tell me how you like my soup."

Safer subject ground, she thought with relief and regret. "It's adequate," she said.

"Adequate?" He let out a hoot of laughter. "Child, you are in the face of culinary genius, and you only consider it adequate? Obviously your palate is too unsophisticated to appreciate it. I need to take you in hand and introduce you to the wonders of the senses."

"You need to keep your distance. Where did you learn to cook?"

He leaned back in the chair, smiling benignly. "That would require that I tell you the story of my shamefully wasted life, and I'm not certain you're strong enough to hear it."

Elizabeth met his gaze calmly. "I'm stronger than you think," she said.

He shrugged. "Perhaps you are. I've lived a very colorful life, my pet. I'm afraid I'm cursed with an inquisitive mind. Durham was required to hire the best tutors, but I rapidly outstripped them in knowledge, and I was never one to accept the conventional answer when there were other possibilities. I believe Sir Richard had some vague notion of making me a churchman when I attained my majority. Anything to get rid of me. I'm afraid I went one step further and joined the Catholic Church. He and Lady Elinor were properly horrified." He smiled fondly at the memory.

"I didn't know one could convert," Elizabeth said.

"Ah, that's right, your father is a rector, is he not? I'm sure he's told you all about the horrors of the Catholic Church. I did my best to embrace them, but I'm afraid Catholicism is not much different from the Anglican Church. The rituals are rather more elaborate, but no babies are sacrificed, no Satanic rites performed."

"Is that what you were looking for?" she asked in horror.

"No, my pet. I was merely looking for some answers. I thought devoting my life to study and the stern, Catholic God would provide them for me, so I joined a monastery. The Durhams were, of course, delighted. Not only was I unable to own land or title, but now I was officially removed from their lives and with luck would never surface again. But I'm afraid the Durhams weren't so lucky."

"You can't really believe they didn't want you around. Even if you weren't their true son . . ."

"They wanted me dead," he said flatly. "Anyway, I'm getting distracted. You wanted to know where I learned to cook. It was during my years in the monastery in France. I can also bake bread, raise bees, tend a garden, and brew all sorts of herbal remedies. I could mix you up a powerful tisane for the headache I see still plagues you, but if you were that distrustful over chicken soup, you would probably refuse to drink it."

She didn't disabuse him of the notion. "How many years were you in the monastery?"

He smiled sweetly. "Five. Five years of sandals and praying and studying and hard labor. Five years of almost total silence, which failed to improve my command of the French language. It was astonishingly peaceful, until I came to the conclusion that I didn't believe in their God."

"What!" Now he'd truly horrified her.

"I've never been particularly attracted to the traditional notion of Christianity," he said mildly. "I told you, I have an inquisitive mind. I simply decided it was time to leave the monastery and see what answers I could come up with on my own."

"I didn't realize you could just do that. They let you leave monasteries?"

"And convents, in case you're ever tempted to join one, though I devoutly hope that sad day never comes. It would be a tragic waste." He took her bowl and went back to the fire, refilling it with more soup. "Of course I was excommunicated, which made me once again eligible to hold lands and title, but since that made Sir Richard furious, it had its uses."

"Why do you hate him so much?"

He sat back down, placing the soup in front of her. "Because he's a greedy, stupid, mean old man, who has no love for anyone but himself and his vapid children. He sold his birthright for money and title, and now he has no one to pass it on to."

"He has four children . . ."

"In fact, he has two. Jane and I are no kin of the Durhams. He and his wife accepted me as their infant in return for this place, a title, and a generous compensation, which seemed a worthy trade. Apparently I was a sickly child, and they expected I wouldn't live. Unfortunately for them, I did. I am legally his firstborn, and by law I inherit his lands, his title, and his wealth, with nothing left for Edward and Edwina."

"Or Jane, then?"

"I'll take care of Jane," Gabriel said coolly. "She knows she won't want for anything, though she's as far distant from the greedy Durhams as night from day. All she wants is her precious horses."

"I think there's something more she wants as well," Elizabeth ventured.

"Yes, she wants Peter." He glanced across the cavernous kitchen at the deserted stairs. "Unfortunately I can't give him to her. She'll have to figure out a way to manage that herself." He smiled briefly. "The course of true love never runs smooth."

"I'm surprised you believe in such things as true love," she said. The second bowl of soup was even better than the first, now that she was certain he wasn't going to poison her.

"Oh, it's admittedly rare, but I admit to it when I see it," he said lightly. "Speaking of true love, why are you here?"

She dropped the heavy metal spoon. "What are you talking about?" she said weakly.

"Jane says you're running away from an importunate suitor. What are you waiting for, a royal prince?" he drawled.

She picked up the spoon again, pleased to notice that her hand didn't shake. "There's a bit more to the story than that, but I don't intend to bore you with it."

"Why not? I've bored you with my life story. It would be only courteous to respond in kind."

"And you're so concerned about courtesy?" Lizzie replied, not fooled for a moment. "I was caught in a compromising situation."

Gabriel's eyes lit up. "Sweet Lizzie, you amaze me! I had no notion that a wanton heart beat beneath your prim exterior. Who was the lucky gentleman?"

"There was no gentleman," she snapped.

"Well, then, who was the lucky lady?"

She stared at him in astonishment. "You're joking," she said.

"Such things do happen. All right, if you weren't

caught *in flagrante delicto* with someone, how did you
manage your fall from grace?"

"I was dancing in the moonlight. In the woods.
Alone," she said, wondering why in heaven's name she
was telling him this.

"Wearing anything in particular?" he inquired
mildly.

"Not much." She couldn't read the expression on
his face, and she wasn't sure she wanted to. "So I was
sent away to meditate on my wanton ways, and when I
return home I shall be a perfect, dutiful daughter. I am
determined."

"That would be a tragedy," he said softly.

"Not for me. I'll stay out of the woods, behave myself,
and sooner or later true love will come along. I don't
intend to waste my time with anything less."

"An idealist? You surprise me, Lizzie. I wouldn't have
thought you'd even admit to such a thing as true love."

"I don't want to debate love with you, Brother
Gabriel." She used the name deliberately. "And I don't
want to discuss my tedious past—yours is a great deal
more interesting. Tell me what you did after you left
the convent."

"Monastery," he corrected. "If it were a convent, I
probably wouldn't have left. It did appear that I was not
a man made for celibacy. I did what any other healthy
young man would do. I went to London and made up
for those five long years."

"Indeed?" she said frostily.

He was enjoying himself, she knew, but there was not
much she could do to stop him. "Indeed," he said. "I
studied with scholars and academicians and theorists by
day, by night I studied the pleasures of the flesh. I must
admit I more than made up for five years of abstinence."

"How delightful."

"You shouldn't wrinkle your pretty little nose like that, Lizzie. I don't expect you to approve of my licentious behavior. I copulated with whores and duchesses, nuns and queens, priestesses and shopkeepers' wives. I learned tricks and techniques that could dazzle the most jaded courtesan. I'm very very good in bed."

She was getting hot sitting there. The fire was halfway across the room, and the air was pleasant enough, but she could feel a tingling in her breasts, a burning between her legs, and she shifted slightly, surveying him with a frosty look. "How pleasant for you and your partners."

"Alas, I've gone without partners for the last few months. I decided a bit of renewed celibacy would do my battered soul some good."

"I rejoice to hear it."

"Don't rejoice too soon, my love. Every time I'm around you I reconsider my decision."

She stared at him, the heat moving upward, over her breasts, covering her face. "Stop it," she said sharply. "You're just trying to make me uncomfortable. I don't know why you get such a perverse pleasure out of it, but I promise you, I'm immune."

"You don't look immune," he mused. "You look delicately flushed and just the tiniest bit . . . dare I say it . . . aroused. Do I arouse you, Lizzie?"

"Not likely."

He laughed. "I'm afraid, dear Lizzie, that you arouse me quite effectively. I'm afraid I want you to an almost desperate level, and when I want something I always manage to get it. Fair warning."

The heat was still there, but she felt a sudden chill as well. "A warning?"

His smile was brief, kindly, almost impartial. "It's time you went back to your safe little parish in Shropshire or wherever you come from. This is no place for a fey young virgin who roams the woods—there are bad people here."

"Including you," she offered.

"Including me," he agreed. "Everyone's warned you, but now I'll be more direct about it. If you don't go back to Shropshire . . ."

"Dorset," she corrected him.

"If you don't go back to Dorset, then I won't be responsible for what happens."

"You aren't responsible for me as it is," she said crossly. "I'm not afraid of you and your licentious boastings."

He reached across the table and took her hand. She tried to jerk it away, but his grip tightened, and she was trapped. His hold wasn't painful, but it was unbreakable, a reminder of just how helpless she really might be. "I would be the least of your worries, Lizzie. Go home while you still can."

"What are you doing, Gabriel?" Jane was standing in the hallway that led to the stables, a stern expression on her face.

He released Elizabeth's hand, taking a moment to stroke his thumb across the tender flesh. "Just giving Lizzie some well-intentioned advice. The same I gave you earlier. She should go back to her family, and you should leave here as well. I don't like what's going on around here."

"You're being ridiculous, Gabriel, and we all know it. There's nothing to be afraid of."

"Three girls have disappeared in the last six months," he reminded her.

"Girls run away from home all the time. One of the Twickhams tell me Maudie Possett was pregnant, and her father would have killed her if he found out. It was no wonder she took off. As for the others, they probably had just as good a reason."

"You're being willfully blind, Jane," he said in a stern voice. "I'm not so worried about you—between Peter and me we can make certain nothing happens to you. But little Miss Wander the Woods in My Nightdress is another matter."

"In your nightdress? You didn't, Elizabeth!" Jane said, scandalized. "It's no wonder you got sick."

"Tell her she's not welcome here, Jane," Gabriel demanded, all trace of humor gone from his rich voice. "She needs to go."

"I'll tell her no such thing!"

Peter appeared in the darkness behind Jane, stripping off his leather jacket. "What's going on, then?"

Jane turned to him. "Gabriel says that Elizabeth should leave here. He thinks she's in some sort of danger, though I can't imagine what. Promise me you'll look out for her as well as me."

Peter and Gabriel shared a long, silent look. And then Gabriel shrugged, lazy, charming once more, as if that moment of intensity had never existed. "So be it," he drawled. "Don't say I didn't warn you when you end up in a wicker cage."

"What are you talking about?" Elizabeth demanded.

"Some people think that's what the Druids used to do," Peter said slowly. "Take people and put them in wicker cages and burn them alive."

A sick feeling formed in the pit of Elizabeth's stomach. "And people say that you're the local high priest, Gabriel," she said. "Would you be the one to light the torch?"

He rose, towering over her, but she resisted the urge to rise as well. She stayed where she was, and he reached down and took her hand, the one he'd held captive.

She could see the marks of his fingers on her pale flesh, and to her shock he lifted it to his mouth, pressing his lips against her flesh. "I could think of better ways to set you afire, Lizzie," he murmured.

She made a shocked little noise, but he'd already dropped her hand and was heading for the door.

"Where are you going?" Peter demanded, sounding not at all like the servant he was purported to be.

"I feel the sudden urge to visit Delilah Chilton," he said lazily. "I want to see how they're coming with their wicker cage."

CHAPTER TWELVE

Violet Twickham was not in a very good mood that moonlit night. For one thing, she'd had a fight with her sister Rose, and she never felt good when they fought. It was Rose's fault, of course. She'd been making eyes at young Billy Tompkins over to the Boar's Knees, when she knew perfectly well that Violet had already decided he was absolutely perfect. Billy Tompkins was big as an ox and twice as stupid, but Violet had no interest in intellect. He would make a good husband, a good father, a strong provider. And Rose was nine months younger than she was. There was no way she was getting her hands on Violet's intended, whether Billy knew his fate or not.

She'd told Rose so, in plain and simple terms. Rose had replied in a manner that would have gotten her ears boxed if Ma had heard her, and then the two of them had had at it. Violet had a few bruises and a scrape across one arm, but fortunately Rose had a truly spectacular black eye and a nose swollen to almost twice its size. Billy Tompkins would think twice before gazing moonily at that.

The day had gone from bad to worse. Usually when the family left, Rose and Violet were free to do what they pleased. Miss Jane spent most of her time in the barn, and she never complained when no one saw to her room or her meals.

She was complaining this time, probably because of that ugly red-haired creature upstairs. Well, perhaps she wasn't truly ugly, though what man would want to come within miles of that horrible head of hair was beyond Violet's understanding. And she was too skinny. Violet weighed a good twelve stone, and she knew from experience that men much preferred a woman of substance, not some flyaway creature like Miss Penshurst.

But Miss Jane had had them dusting, and doing laundry of all things, and even cooking, when they were scullery maids, nothing more, nothing less. Of course, Sir Richard was so tight with a penny they were used to being sent all over the house to work, not like in a proper household where there'd be strict segregation between the upstairs maids and the parlormaids, the sculleries and the laundry girls. Cook had told them stories of the great houses where she'd worked, and both Violet and Rose considered the Durhams to be poor employers indeed, not to understand the niceties of social distinction below stairs.

So Violet Twickham was still peeved at her sister, angry with Miss Jane's silly demands, tired and hungry and entirely unwilling to spend the night up under the eaves with all those empty pallets and her angry sister. For all she knew Rose would smother her in the middle of the night, or even worse, Miss Jane would come searching for her, demanding she bring hot water or some such nonsense.

Well, if Miss Jane decided she needed a late-night bath, then she'd just have to count on Rose to haul the hot water. Violet Twickham had better things to do on a moonlit night in late spring.

It was time things were settled with Billy. He needed to know what his future was, and not go on making sheep's eyes at her sister. He worked for the Culvers over at the Boar's Knees, and slept above the stable. So far Violet had wisely allowed him a few hurried kisses and a bit of fumbling beneath her skirt. Enough to keep him wanting more.

She planned to allow him a lot more than that this night, and tomorrow she'd be engaged, and there wasn't a blessed thing her sister could do about it.

The night was dark and silent as Violet followed the narrow path that led away from the manor house. The quickest way to the tiny village was up a steep path, but Violet had already spent the day fetching and carrying, and she was in no mood for a brisk climb on a moonlit night. The path by the old abbey ruins would only take a few minutes longer, and it would be a lot less tiring. She needed to conserve her energy for more important things. Like Billy Tompkins.

She'd forgotten how eerie Hernewood Forest could be in the still of night. She could see the ruins rising stark and black in the moonlight, and she jerked her eyes back, suddenly uneasy. People said that ghosts walked the abbey ruins. Monks haunted the place, grieving for the loss of their home, maybe. Or grieving their damned souls. The vicar said that Catholics went to a special hell all their own, and if the vicar couldn't be counted on to speak the truth, who could?

She heard a sudden, rustling sound, and she stopped,

peering into the forest. It must be a wild animal, she told herself. A doe, perhaps, or even a rabbit.

Except that everyone knew that Hernewood Forest had grown very scarce of game in recent months, and the poachers had to look farther afield if they were to fill their family's pots come Sunday. Too many animals had been found slaughtered and abandoned, and the smell of rotting flesh had driven the other animals away.

The notion of rotting flesh was far from cheering, Violet thought with sudden nervousness, moving forward at a faster pace. Perhaps she should have stayed on at the manor house. She wouldn't have had to sleep with the disgruntled Rose—in a house that big with almost the entire staff dismissed there would doubtless have been a comfortable place for her to sleep. Cook had her own room, and probably a better bed than Violet had ever known.

She paused, staring back toward the house. It was hidden beyond the trees, and a thick mist had risen, obscuring things further. She hadn't realized she'd come so far already. Going back looked to be as much trouble as continuing on her journey, and it wasn't Billy Tompkins who was waiting at the manor house, it was sour-faced Rose.

She kept walking, her sturdy shoes making a crunching noise as she trod the ground. A chill had crept into her bones, and she was that glad she'd remembered to take Miss Jane's best cashmere shawl to wrap around her sturdy shoulders. Miss Jane didn't appreciate fine things—she was too caught up with her horses to notice when things came up missing. She probably didn't even remember she owned a cashmere shawl.

The fog was growing thicker, denser, wrapping around her like a heavy blanket, so deep that she could barely see in front of her. She'd walked this path many

many times in her eighteen years, she knew it as well as she knew the path out back of her father's cottage to the privy. There was nothing to be afraid of.

And if it were a year ago she wouldn't have been afraid, she thought unhappily. Sometime in the last year people from London had invaded their tiny little village. There was the Dark Man, whose own family had cast him off without a penny, who lived in the woods instead of in the fine house he'd inherited, who openly followed the Old Religion and ignored the vicar. She'd heard the rumors about the women. People said he bewitched women, touched them in ways that were unnatural and dangerous, made them weak and silly and unfit for any other man. Of course, she hadn't yet met any of those women, and a tiny part of her was admittedly envious. She was a healthy young woman, and the idea of someone touching her in such a way made her swoon. It would be worth a certain amount of risk to sample that kind of pleasure.

There was quality staying over at Arundel as well, though no one said much about them. London nobs, with their parties and their friends. They were free with the money, and that was all most people cared about.

The first animals were found about six months ago, Violet remembered, edging forward tentatively, blindly in the enveloping fog. People whispered they were found in the midst of an oak grove, and there were signs of the Old Religion all around.

It had to be the Dark Man, of course. He who admitted to studying the Old Religion, who turned his back on family and decency and faith. No one minded—the animals belonged to the landowner, and it was well-known that Gabriel Durham was the landholder of record.

But when the first girl disappeared people weren't

quite so happy. Josie Beverley was a wild thing, eager for the city, and everyone assumed she'd run away with the tinkers. Mary Hickey was dreamy, a little slow, and some thought she'd drowned one night, though they never found her body.

But Maudie Possett was another matter. She'd been a good friend of the Twickham girls, and while she'd not been best pleased at finding she had a bun in the oven, Violet had no doubt she'd be able to make Horace Rumsford marry her. Personally Violet couldn't imagine why a pretty young thing like Maudie would be willing to tie herself to a middle-aged widower with too much belly and not enough hair, and five children besides, but then, Maudie had been willing enough to crawl between the sheets with him. And the Rumsford farm was prosperous enough—Maudie could go a lot farther and do a lot worse.

But it seemed as if Maudie had just gone a lot farther. She'd disappeared two nights ago, and no one had seen or heard from her since. Rumsford was weeping into his stout at the Boar's Knees, and old Tom Possett was looking like murder. And the night of Beltane was drawing closer.

Not that that had anything to do with it, Violet reminded herself, trudging onward. They called it May Day now, and no one referred to it as Beltane except in whispers. Reverend Huston had put a stop to such pagan goings-on some sixty years ago, threatening everlasting damnation, and people still remembered and trembled. It was a hard decision—Hernewood was named for the old god Herne the Hunter, protector of the forests. People used to pray to him regularly, along with their Christian God, wisely deciding one couldn't have too many friends in the hereafter.

But now such blasphemy was forbidden. And most

people had forgotten all about such things, or if they happened to mention it were quickly silenced by wiser souls.

Still, May Day was fast approaching, no matter what you called it. And Maudie Possett had disappeared. And now Violet was walking alone in the blinding fog, the mist so deep the moon disappeared, and she knew with sudden horrifying certainty that she wasn't alone on the narrow path that traversed the border of Hernewood Forest itself. Something else was nearby. Something old and evil.

"Who's there?" she demanded in a quavering voice. The fog threw her voice back at her, startling her, and she froze, even more frightened. "You can't scare me," she said, the panic belying her words.

She could hear them, all around her, the whispers, the rustle of clothing, the sound of heavy breathing as they moved closer. They came at her from every side, and she could feel their hands reaching out for her through the mist, grasping, painful hands, and she was too frightened to run, certain she'd run straight into their arms.

And then she saw them ahead of her, more mist than substance, wavering in the light, and she knew there were indeed such things as ghosts. There were no monks left, and yet two of the creatures stood before her, neither solid nor air.

"This way." One of them spoke, without moving his mouth, and her terror increased.

"Be quick about it, girl," the other said. "Or you'll end up in the soup like others of your kind. Take this path, and run as fast as you can."

They were beckoning her toward hell, she knew that with blind certainty, and it would be madness to follow. But she could still feel the others surrounding her, creatures of darkness coming up behind her, breathing down her neck, and despite what the vicar said, these phantoms were men of God, weren't they? Surely they were safer than the creatures that crept up behind her.

"For the love of God, be quick about it," the taller one said in an irritable voice, though in truth there was no way she could know which one of them actually spoke when their mouths didn't move. He took a menacing step toward her. "Run!"

Violet ran. Something caught at her purloined shawl, ripping it from her shoulders, but she let it go without a moment's hesitation. Her heavy shoes thudded along the path, in time with her pounding heart, but she simply ran onward, blindly into the mist, trusting in instinct and the shades of creatures she had been taught to fear. She ran as if her life depended on it, knowing that whatever she'd left behind in the darkness, that unseen menace, was evil incarnate. A kind of evil that Violet Twickham had never even imagined. She ran, her heart pounding in her chest, her breath burning, her limbs shaking.

She ran, through the mist, until suddenly all was clear again, she was at the end of the pathway, the Boar's Knees Inn and Hostelry was in sight, and the evil had vanished into the darkness along with the two ghostly monks.

She staggered, weeping, into the common room. Her face was scraped, though she didn't remember how it had happened, and her sturdy gown was torn. But she was alive, and Billy Tompkins was waiting for her, and no ungodly creatures could grab her as long as he held her to his burly chest.

* * *

The wind had picked up, blowing Gabriel's hair in his face, and he pushed it back with an impatient gesture. He ought to cut it—according to Peter it made him too damned romantic-looking. Maybe he should shave his head and go back to wearing a wig like most proper gentlemen, but he wasn't ready to go that far. He couldn't be bothered with sartorial matters, and he certainly wasn't about to hire a valet if he could help it.

He heard them in the distance, that ghostly horde, moving away from the forest, back toward Arundel. From the muffled sound of their disgruntled voices they hadn't secured their sought-after prey. He wondered what they'd been in search of. Another doe, perhaps?

He hated to believe they would go so far as to interfere with any of the locals, despite the dark rumors that were circulating. He wasn't intimately acquainted with the Chiltons, and he much preferred to keep it that way, but he'd spent far too much time with their sort when he was in London. The bored, wealthy upper classes had nothing better to do with their time than play at blasphemy and witchcraft, and the latest interest in ancient British religions had caught on like wildfire. He'd attended more than one ritual, mainly out of curiosity. They usually involved copious amounts of wine, incantations, and a paint-daubed virgin who was obviously well paid and more than willing. The proceedings ended up as little more than an orgy, and after the first few he grew rapidly bored. He wasn't searching for sexual fulfillment in his studies. He could find that quite handily among the beautiful and the bored. He was looking for answers, and there were none to be found in London's various discreet and well-bred bacchanals.

The Chiltons were doubtless of the same ilk. While their London counterparts had been hard-pressed to

find suitable oak groves within the city limits, and any
ritual sacrifice had had to involve domestic livestock,
the Chiltons had found more fertile ground. The Old
Religions had never quite died out in the wild Yorkshire
countryside, and there were oak groves aplenty. If they
found some sort of entertainment in the ritual slaughter
of wild animals, he wasn't about to waste his time
interfering. He deplored the waste of good food when
so many were hungry, but not enough to exert himself.

Besides, he refused to believe the disappearance of
the three girls had anything to do with the Chiltons'
fun and games. Any more than he put credence in the
fact that Geoffrey Rumney's ancient father had been
found murdered a few months back, almost drained
of blood. Henry Rumney had been a mean-tempered,
villainous old sot, and any comeuppance he received
on his death bed was long overdue.

Nevertheless, Gabriel couldn't be sure the Chiltons
were quite as silly and harmless as he assumed. They
had guests arriving daily, among them several of Gabriel's more notorious former acquaintances and sybarites,
including the inaptly named Merriwether, as dedicated
a degenerate as Gabriel had ever met. And it might be
mere coincidence that the feast of Beltane was rapidly
approaching, but Gabriel never relied on coincidence
without considering even the most far-fetched of possibilities. It kept life interesting.

If the Chiltons were really intent on reenacting an
ancient Druid ritual, then there was no certainty as to
how far they'd go. And Gabriel's long-submerged sense
of duty was proving irritatingly intrusive. He supposed
he had no choice but to encourage the Chiltons enough
to assure himself they were basically harmless.

There had been a thick mist lying on the ground
when he first left the manor house, but he knew his

way through the abbey ruins by sheer instinct. The mist
had lifted now—blown away by the burgeoning wind,
and the trees rustled overhead in a warning whisper.

He bypassed his usual pathway to the standing tower,
more restless than usual. His house was less than a mile
away, and the night air was warm. It had been days since
he'd been home—it might behoove him to see how the
renovations were coming. To see if the old place was
growing any more habitable.

He could thank Sir Richard for its derelict state, a
petty act of revenge that doubtless brought the old bastard a fair amount of pleasure. Durham had chafed at
his devil's bargain all his miserable life—even the tiniest
of revenges must have seemed sweet.

Rosecliff Hall was larger than Hernewood Manor, a
fact that must have burned at Richard Durham's soul.
He and his childless wife had taken in the bastard infant
child and claimed it as their own, in return for a baronetcy and an impressive manor house in the heart of the
Yorkshire dales.

But the well-connected bastard had come with gifts—
money his father could never touch, a neighboring
estate that was far grander than Hernewood Manor, and
the unchangeable fact that Gabriel was heir to everything Richard Durham had attained. It was no wonder
the old man had despised him.

His revenge had been petty but thorough. Rosecliff
Hall had fallen into complete disrepair, untouched in
the last thirty years as the fierce Yorkshire winters had
taken their toll. And Gabriel had never known love in
his life.

It had taken inordinate amounts of money to begin
to bring the ruin back into something even slightly
habitable, but Gabriel had never lacked for financial
reserves. Peter had told him the west wing was relatively

comfortable, though the east wing might be beyond repairing. For some reason Gabriel seldom went there, content to live in the shabby luxury of the abandoned tower, happy among his books and the ghosts.

But tonight he wanted to see what kind of progress had been made on the Hall. Perhaps he should sell it, leave Yorkshire, and spend his life on the Continent, pursuing his studies and his pleasures without distraction.

There was distraction aplenty in Hernewood. The ghosts of his childhood, the Chiltons' bloody games. And a pale young woman with fire in her eyes, who needed to be kissed, quite often and most thoroughly.

Almost as much as he needed to kiss her. She was his bane and his delight, and the sooner he got away from her, the better.

He would check the progress on the Hall, and perhaps even spend the night in his own bed rather than the fur-strewn pallet in the tower. Tomorrow he would ascertain just how harmless the Chiltons truly were.

And then he would be free to run as fast and as far as he wanted.

If he could bring himself to leave the one place he had ever felt he truly belonged.

It made no sense, his attachment to this place and these people. He'd tried to fight it, tried to reason it away, but still the place called to him. The abbey ruins, the ancient forest, the no-nonsense people who didn't seem to care who he was or what he did as long as he treated them fairly.

But he'd dreamt of Hernewood during the long years of his travels. And he doubted he could bring himself to turn his back on the place for very long ever again.

Elizabeth was another matter. He could see her far too clearly, moving through the trees, her red hair brilliant in the misty light. Dancing in the moonlight, she'd said, and he was still haunted by the notion. He'd dream of her, curse him. And there was no way he could escape the strange spell she wove around him.

Short of running away.

CHAPTER THIRTEEN

"Oh, Lord," Jane said in the accents of utmost dread. "It only needed this!"

Elizabeth looked up from her ignominious position, squatting in front of the fireplace in the small salon. She was doing her best to coax a fire from the recalcitrant logs, but since the wood itself was green and damp, and there was no kindling or any coals from the previous fire, it was hard going. Even though the room was small, a damp chill had invaded it, and both women were dressed in bulky layers of clothing in a vain effort to keep warm. "It needed what?"

"The Chiltons," she said in tones of deepest loathing. "You don't suppose we could simply hide and pretend we're not at home?"

Elizabeth joined her at the front window. "Considering that they're looking up at us and waving, I don't think we can get away with it. You answer the door, and I'll see if I can do anything about the fire."

"I think it's a lost cause. Curse those wretched Twickham girls for abandoning us."

Jane was right, the fire was a lost cause. Elizabeth gave up, divesting herself of the wool blanket she had wrapped around her shoulders and trying to tuck her wayward hair into a subdued knot. She still couldn't find any hairpins, and Jane's short-cropped curls didn't require any that she could borrow, so she had no choice but to let the mass of it hang loose. It was an unnervingly delicious sensation.

"Miss Pennywurst!" Delilah Chilton trilled in her musical voice, moving into the room with a delicate grace and a swaying of her bell-like skirts. "I'm delighted to see you again. I heard you were ill, and nothing would have it but that I must bring you one of my own particular tisanes to help speed you on your recovery. But I must say you look quite recovered already, and I am relieved to know the reports on your ill health were quite exaggerated."

"Penshurst," Elizabeth said automatically.

Delilah blinked. "I beg your pardon?"

"My last name is Penshurst," she said, somewhat apologetically.

"Pish," said Delilah, dismissing it. "I'll simply call you Emily. And you must call me Delilah."

"My name . . ." At that moment her husband strode in the room, one arm tucked in Jane's, and the long-suffering expression on Jane's face was so comical that Elizabeth gave up. For the sake of peace she could be Emily Pennywurst.

"Miss Durham informs me their servants have decamped, dearest," Lord Chilton announced, drawing the reluctant Jane to the small settee. "Have you ever heard of anything so iniquitous?"

"Iniquitous," Lady Chilton echoed.

"Actually my father dismissed most of the staff when he took the family to London," Jane said. "He left a skeleton staff to look after us, but the two girls disappeared on Wednesday, and we haven't seen them since."

"Disappeared? Never say so! Have they been kidnapped like those other three girls? Poor creatures, I weep for them," said Lady Chilton, her pale, beautiful face entirely unmoved.

"No, they're home and not coming back. They're flighty, unreasonable girls who've become convinced evil things are lurking in our woods." Jane's voice was tinged with exasperation.

"My heavens," Francis Chilton murmured. "And are there evil things in your woods? I've heard stories myself, about ghostly riders and evil phantoms, but I'm not a gullible sort. I tend to dismiss such things as nonsense, though in this case I wonder if there might not be some truth in the matter. After all, there have been an extraordinary number of disappearances lately. I'm surprised your father allowed you to stay on with so little protection."

He was still holding Jane's arm, his soft white fingers absently stroking her. Elizabeth could almost see her quiver in distaste. "I've lived here all my life, and spent many long, happy hours in Hernewood," Jane said sternly. "This is all baseless rumor and superstition."

"I'm not certain it's baseless." Delilah seated herself opposite her husband. "After all, people have disappeared. If I were you, I would pack up my things and come join us in comfort at Arundel. We're fully staffed, and we can look after you both as you deserve."

For a brief moment a look of utmost dread flashed across Jane's face, but she quickly composed herself. "We wouldn't think of intruding . . ."

"It would be no intrusion. We're having a little house party at the moment, and there's always room for lovely young ladies such as yourself and Miss Pennywurst."

"Penshurst," Elizabeth muttered.

"Just a small group of my London friends, up to celebrate the coming of summer in a delightfully rustic setting. Though I must say it feels more like winter in this place." Lord Chilton allowed himself a theatrical shiver.

"We're very comfortable," Jane said, an arrant lie.

"Ah, the hardy Yorkshire stock," Lord Chilton said admiringly. "I only wish I were half so sturdy." He dropped Jane's arm and turned his pale, colorless eyes to Elizabeth. "You aren't Yorkshire born and bred, are you, my dear? Surely you can't be thriving in this cold, damp house. Especially after you've been so ill."

Elizabeth wasn't certain she preferred "my dear" to Emily Pennywurst, but she wasn't about to complain. "I come from Dorset, but I'm sturdy country stock myself. And I'm feeling quite well, thank you. The air is bracing."

"Bracing," Francis murmured with a theatrical shudder. "I'm sorry, but I must insist. In your father's absence I feel I should be in loco parentis, and it is my very Christian duty to take the two of you back to Arundel with us. I'll send some of our servants over to pack for you, but in the meantime you'll simply come with us."

"No, I couldn't possibly leave the horses," Jane said somewhat desperately.

Francis Chilton shrugged, rising from his elegant sprawl on the delicate settee. "Then we'll simply have to take Miss Pennywurst back with us. She's been quite ill, I gather, and this cold damp house will probably bring on an inflammation of the lungs. I know you wouldn't want to be responsible for that."

"No!" Elizabeth stammered in graceless panic. There was something about the Chiltons that unnerved her, particularly when Francis rose from his elegant sprawl on the delicate settee and advanced upon her. She held her ground, standing by the cold, empty fireplace, trying desperately to appear calm without being mannerless. "Truly, I'd much rather be here with Jane. We're quite comfortable, and I wouldn't think of abandoning her ..."

Lord Chilton put one of those pale, soft hands on Elizabeth's arm, and the relentless strength in them was shocking. "I'm afraid I won't take no for an answer," he said softly.

Elizabeth stared up into his colorless eyes, searching for some kind of clue, some kind of reason behind his insistence. He was stroking her arm, a soft, possessive caress, and yet she knew with absolutely sure instinct that he had no sexual interest in her. He wanted her, and he was determined to have her, but she couldn't possibly imagine for what.

"I insist, dear Elizabeth," he said softly, in a voice doubtless meant to be endearing. It gave Elizabeth a cold feeling in the pit of her stomach, one she couldn't reason away.

"You insist on what, Francis?" A new voice entered the fray, a low, elegant voice at odds with Lord Chilton's light, faintly lisping voice. Gabriel, like an errant angel, had come, Elizabeth thought with dizzy relief.

Francis made no move to release her. Instead he moved, to make certain his body didn't block Gabriel's view of his possessive touch. "I insist on taking this sweet young thing back to sample the delights of Arundel, Gabriel," he said, and there was a trace of mockery in his affected voice. "Dare I hope we can entice you to join us as well?"

"Oh, do say so, Gabriel," Delilah murmured, batting her eyes madly at him. "Several of your former companions are visiting, and I know you'd bring our little celebrations up to a whole new level."

Francis Chilton was still stroking her arm. The flesh on his hand was softer than hers, almost like an infant's. Pampered and white, yet she knew, with the instincts Old Peg had lauded, that this man was totally devoid of innocence. He flashed a triumphant smile at Gabriel. "What say you, Gabriel? Wouldn't you like to renew old friendships, enjoy old pastimes?"

"Let her go, Francis." The words were quietly spoken, and absolutely deadly.

Francis released her, seeming at ease, strolling back to the settee he'd shared with Jane. Jane sprang up when she saw him approach, practically hiding behind her brother's tall form, and Francis's pale mouth curved in a mocking smile. "You'd think we were monsters of depravity, dear Delilah," he addressed his wife in mournful tones. "We simply came over to offer our hospitality to these two orphans of the storm, and they act as if we're wicked degenerates with evil on our minds." The notion seemed to amuse him. "We're just being neighborly, dear Gabriel. Surely you can't fault us for that."

"I'm certain my sister and Miss Penshurst are touched by your concern, Francis, but I'm more than capable of seeing to their welfare. I'm here, aren't I?"

Elizabeth sank back into the shadows of the cool, damp room, watching the two of them in fascination. Their polite sparring hid something much deeper, much darker, and she found herself wishing she'd never made the dire mistake of coming into Yorkshire.

"You are, indeed, Gabriel. Entirely coincidental that you happened to time your visit with ours, isn't it? But what a happy coincidence."

"Actually, Francis, I watched your approach. Very little happens here at the manor that I'm not aware of. For instance, the loss of the Twickham girls was unfortunate, but not to be wondered at, considering someone or something chased the elder one through Hernewood a few nights past."

"Really? How edifying. I must admit I've never had a taste for servant girls, but *chacun à son gout*. Perhaps you're less fastidious than I am?"

"You haven't seen Violet Twickham," Gabriel replied in equally dulcet tones.

Elizabeth felt Francis's cold eyes slither over her. "No, you prefer to bed the bourgeoisie, do you not? Personally I always felt the middle classes to be extremely tiresome in the long run. Scarcely worth the bother."

"I feel quite confident that this is the safest place for my sister and her cousin," Gabriel said.

"I bow to your superior wisdom. Does that mean we can count on you to join our little party? I could console myself with the loss of the two young ladies if you would honor us with your presence."

"Oh, do say you'll come, Gabriel," Delilah murmured, cozying up to him, and Elizabeth surveyed her with strong dislike.

Gabriel looked down at her with an unreadable expression on his beautiful face. "Certainly," he murmured. "I've been finding country life a bit tedious recently. The lack of interesting company is appalling."

"Join us for dinner?" Delilah begged prettily.

"It would be my honor."

"But Gabriel, you were promised to us," Jane said swiftly.

"You are obviously in no condition to entertain, dear Jane," Delilah murmured. "I'm certain you'd want your brother to come when you have servants back in place. In the meantime we'll do our very best to keep him amused." She looked up at him, smiling prettily, and Elizabeth felt a strange, stinging pain somewhere near her heart.

"We were counting on his help," Jane said stubbornly.

Gabriel looked up from the enchanting prospect of Delilah Chilton's scantily clad bosom. "I'll leave Peter to assist you. I'm sure he'll provide much better company than I would." He didn't even look in Elizabeth's direction, as if unwilling to admit she even existed.

It was the perfect distraction for Jane. "We'll be fine without any help," she said grimly.

Gabriel smiled at her. "I insist."

"There, you see, everyone's working out beautifully," Lady Chilton cried. "We'll expect you at six, dear Gabriel. And of course, your sister and her little cousin would be welcome as well."

"They will remain here. But I wouldn't think of missing it. Let me see you out, since we're so woefully devoid of servants," he said smoothly, putting an arm around Lady Chilton's slender waist and guiding her from the room. Lord Chilton sauntered after them, a slightly querulous look on his pale, powdered face. He paused long enough to sketch a slight, mocking bow toward the two women. "Your servant, Miss Durham. Miss Pennywurst." And he was gone before Elizabeth's muttered "Penshurst" could reach his delicate ears.

Jane flopped down in a chair, looking shattered. "They are the most repulsive people," she said in a faint voice. "I cannot imagine what Gabriel sees in them."

"Perhaps he's just bored," Elizabeth suggested, trying to be fair.

"Gabriel is never bored. Not unless he's forced into company with people like the Chiltons. I do not know what possessed him to accept their invitation."

"I would think he was trying to distract their interest in you."

Jane looked surprised. "Why would they be interested in me? We have absolutely nothing in common, I despise them, and no one in society has ever sought out my company. Why would the Chiltons?"

"I don't know," Elizabeth said.

"I think perhaps it was you they wanted," Jane said thoughtfully. "You're very pretty, you know. For a moment I was afraid Lord Chilton was going to take you away by force."

"Don't be absurd. If Lord Chilton had the slightest interest in me as a female, I would be utterly astonished."

"Then perhaps they were just finding a way to make Gabriel bow to their wishes. They've been pursuing him since they got here, and barely paid the rest of us any heed. Though I do believe Father has spent a small amount of time with them. I can't imagine what they would have in common either."

"It scarcely matters," Elizabeth said. "I'm certain your brother will enjoy Lady Chilton's company, and we won't have to suffer them."

"Perhaps," said Jane, unconvinced. "Perhaps."

"I knew we would convince you," Delilah purred as Gabriel handed her up into the carriage.

"You're very astute," he replied dryly.

"Really, old man, we had no evil designs on your

sister. She's really better suited for the stable than the drawing room, don't you think?" Francis drawled.

Gabriel cast him an even glance. "Are you disparaging my sister, Chilton?"

"Heavens, no! Marvelous creature! I'm merely praising her equestrian talents," Francis replied with just a trace of nervous malice.

Gabriel felt a small amount of gratification. The Chiltons had won this round, but he wasn't going to let them have it scot-free. "I was certain you mean no disrespect," he said, letting a faintly threatening note slide beneath his polite tone.

"Of course not, of course not," Francis stammered, his smug smile fading.

"But what about that other creature, Gabriel? Your sister's little friend, with that ridiculous hair. She's quite pretty, actually, if you don't mind redheads."

"Can't abide 'em," Francis murmured with a shudder.

"Then you'll leave her alone." It was a mistake, the moment he said the words, and he could have cursed himself. It was never wise to underestimate one's enemy, and the Chiltons were undoubtedly his adversaries.

He'd been ready to break Francis Chilton's hand when he saw him stroking Elizabeth's arm. Her pale, frozen face had been scant comfort—at least he knew she wasn't enjoying it.

Such possessive rage was entirely new to him, and unsettling. If the Chiltons had known of it, he would have been at a definite disadvantage. They already knew he was vulnerable when it came to his sister. They would make endless profit of his foolish weakness for Elizabeth Penshurst.

"Leave her alone, Gabriel?" Delilah cooed, a flinty look in her huge eyes. "Why would you care?"

He made a swift attempt at recovery. "Simple manners, Lady Chilton. She's staying in my father's house, and in his absence I feel responsible."

Delilah smiled. "Is that all? I wonder." She leaned forward and pressed her full red lips against his, while her husband watched with no expression whatsoever. "If you want to keep them safe, you'd best prove it to me. *A bientôt*, Gabriel."

He stepped back, away from the carriage.

He stood on the steps of Hernewood Manor, watching as their phaeton moved swiftly down the curving drive. And then he reached into his breast pocket, pulled out a cambric handkerchief, and wiped her kiss from his mouth.

He glanced back at the house. He could see Jane in the front window, watching him, a worried expression on her face. She wasn't best pleased with him, he knew, but there was nothing he could do about it. The Chiltons had played their trump card, and there was no way he would allow his sister or Lizzie anywhere near them. He knew what sort of entertainments they had planned, and he preferred that his sister never even guess such things existed.

As for Lizzie, it didn't bear thinking about. He needed her safely back home, out of harm's way. Out of his way.

For the time being he'd simply keep the Chiltons and their ilk at bay. But the sooner Elizabeth Penshurst returned to her safe, happy home in Dorset or Devon or wherever, the happier he'd be.

Wouldn't he?

CHAPTER FOURTEEN

"Well," said Francis Chilton, absently picking at the nonexistent spot on his lemon-satin breeches, "I think that went rather well, don't you?"

Delilah was leaning back against the squabs, a discontented pout on her full, lovely lips. He had always enjoyed seeing her pout, and her current sullen expression was particularly gratifying, since she'd managed to get Gabriel to kiss her. "Well enough, I suppose, if it weren't absolutely clear that he's besotted with that ugly woman."

"He's besotted with his own sister?" Francis said, deliberately misunderstanding her. "But how deliciously perverse of him. There might be hope for him after all."

"Don't be absurd. I mean the girl. Pennywurst."

"Actually her name is Penshurst," Francis murmured. "And I hesitate to tell you, but she's far from ugly. As a matter of fact, the more I see of her the more I realize she's quite delicious in a rather out-of-the-ordinary sort of way. I might be tempted to try her myself if I grow too bored.''

"She's the wrong gender, dearest," Delilah cooed. "Though if you're waiting for Gabriel, I promise you I'll have him first."

"You do have a singular advantage. Merriwether tells me that even in his wildest days Gabriel showed no interest in broadening his horizons to include men. Pity. I don't intend to give up my pursuit, but I bow to your undeniable attractions."

"You were ever a realist, my dear."

"In the meantime, what are we going to do about our little celebration? Merriwether and his friends failed to secure that serving wench, and now everyone in the area is being ridiculously careful."

"It was ill judged of you to send them after her," Delilah said. "I thought we'd agreed on a well-bred virgin, not a randy housemaid. Offering her might have brought us even more misfortune."

"She wasn't going to be our sole offering, Delilah," Francis said patiently. "I'm afraid the wicker cage is a bit larger than I anticipated, and there's no time to make a smaller one. It can hold three, perhaps four people, and I do dislike wasting space. A well-bred young virgin, a lusty trollop, perhaps a strong young boy would be a fitting tribute."

"We're having enough trouble finding a well-bred virgin," Delilah reminded him.

"At least it keeps you safe, dearest. You're neither chaste nor particularly well-bred." He was rewarded with a particularly icy smile.

"We have a few days. I haven't given up hope of

some of our absent friends," Delilah murmured after a moment. "These things have a way of working out. We're dedicated to the premise of offering a sacrifice of ultimate value. I have ideas along that line."

"As do I," Francis purred.

"And we have Merriwether and his coterie to assist us. We must be patient, dear Francis. If Gabriel refuses to join us, then perhaps he might have to go, much as the idea grieves me."

"Let us not be too hasty. He has more knowledge of the Old Ways than any other man alive."

"But he doesn't share that knowledge," Delilah said, her delicious pout becoming more pronounced. "I am really most displeased with him."

"Enough to change your mind about bedding him?" It was a foolish question, and Delilah's sly smile was answer enough.

"I expect that once I manage to seduce him he'll prove much more amenable to our way of thinking. He would be unlikely to deny me anything. My lovers seldom do."

"There are times, Delilah, when you truly frighten me. Just promise me one thing, my pet. Endeavor to arrange it so that I might watch."

Delilah's perfect brow smoothed of all its discontented wrinkles as she considered Gabriel's eventual fall. "Have I ever denied you anything, my love?" she asked in a throaty voice.

He smiled sweetly at her. "I am absolutely quivering with anticipation."

She kissed him with her full, pouty lips. "I doubt we'll be disappointed."

* * *

Now that she knew where she was sleeping, Elizabeth was far from happy. It didn't matter that the cavernous room was dark and warm, it didn't matter that there was no clue to the nature of the boy who had grown up in its gloomy confines. It had been Gabriel's. Gabriel had slept in that bed, presumably on the same mattress with the same dark bed hangings. Gabriel had stood at the windows and looked out over the thick woods to the towering ruins of the old abbey, just as Elizabeth did.

She was obsessed with him, and she knew it, a completely unhealthy state of mind. After a lifetime of having no interest in the opposite sex, she found she could think of nothing else.

It wasn't as if she'd lacked for inspiration in the past. Her father's parish had abounded with males of every age and shape and temperament, and any number of brave souls had attempted to court her before Elliott Maynard's suit found favor with the Reverend Penshurst. She'd often lamented her lack of interest. Daniel Pettingrew had been kind, intelligent, handsome, and in love with her. Robert deLacey had been wealthy and showing signs of fixing his attentions upon her.

And she'd run from them, into the forest, avoiding their friendly gestures, their warm smiles, avoiding them until her father grew exasperated and welcomed Elliott Maynard as a man of God who'd provide for his recalcitrant daughter.

She had longed more than anything to please her father. To be the good, dutiful child he wanted her to be. It wasn't that he and Adelia didn't love her dearly. But neither of them could understand the fey streak in her willful soul, neither of them could accept that she didn't belong in the neat little house in the neat little village.

And her wild, secret nature and her dislike of court-ship had banished her to this place of stark beauty, and to the Dark Man, who caught her soul as no man ever had. In a way it served her right. She had thought she was immune to the lure of any man, that all she needed or wanted was in the forest. And here she was, at the edge of a darker, deeper woods than she had ever known, and he lived deep in the heart of them.

She dreamed of him. She could still feel the touch of his beautiful hands on her, taste the forbidden won-der of his mouth, shocking, against hers.

And no distraction was proving effective. She lay in his bed and dreamt of him, she walked through his childhood home and couldn't banish the dream pres-ence of an unhappy little boy. All she could do was refuse to give in to the dreams, to the constant longing for something that was impossible. She needed to con-centrate on what she could have. She needed to remem-ber that her life lay along a different path, away from the woods. Back in Dorset. Even if that wild, shameful part of her longed for the forest and the Dark Man.

They'd managed a decent enough supper with bread and cheese and more of the soup Gabriel had made. Jane had disappeared into the stables, and Elizabeth wandered through the dark, cold hallways of Herne-wood Manor, looking for something to occupy her mind.

Clearly the Durhams were not great readers. There was a library, but the leather-bound tomes were of scant interest. None of the ladies of the household seemed to read novels, and even the latest fashion books held limited appeal.

She didn't want to go back into Gabriel's chamber. She had moved her things back to the small, cold bed-room under the eaves, ignoring Jane's protests, but there had been books there, arranged according to size in a small bookcase in one corner. She didn't want to know what Gabriel had read as a child. She didn't want to learn his mind and soul. His body was disturbing enough.

But so was the long stretch of empty hours in the cold, barren house. Taking the heavy branch of candles from the kitchen table, she steeled herself, heading back up to Gabriel's deserted bedroom.

It was a strange, motley collection of books. Far too many instructive guides for proper deportment in young gentlemen, and Elizabeth would have wagered young Gabriel had paid very little attention to them. A well-used Latin primer, a collection of ancient folktales, and oddly enough, a guide to the genealogy of the royal family. She picked up the latter, but the pages were uncut, and clearly Gabriel had had no interest in it whatsoever. It seemed an odd book for a child's bedroom, but then, Gabriel had been no ordinary child.

She took *Folktales of Ancient Britain* and escaped the room for her own small chamber, settling by the fire with a blanket on her lap and began reading the tale of Beowulf and the bloodthirsty monster.

Falling asleep in her chair was definitely not a wise idea, especially in the midst of such a blood-curdling tale. She awoke hours later with a jerk, her neck cramped, her body chilled, her heart pounding from an unremembered dream. The fire had died down to mere coals, the blanket had fallen on the floor. The candles had guttered out, and she was alone in the icy shadows, with the half-remembered monsters baying at her heels.

She rose and headed for the window, peering out at

the moon-shadowed night. The woods were still and silent—no creature moved in the darkness, real or unreal, no storm threatened. And yet Elizabeth couldn't shake the feeling that something was desperately wrong.

She stubbed her foot against the bed as she made her way back across the room, banged her knee on a table, opened the door against her nose, jarring her enough to let out a small curse that would have horrified her saintly father to the tips of his toes. But no one was around to hear and admonish her, and as she faced the impenetrable darkness of the hallway she cursed again, with more emphasis, enjoying herself.

She knew what she should do. Close the door, find her way back to bed in the smothering darkness, strip off her clothes, and crawl beneath the covers. It was foolish to go traipsing around in the dead of night, when all she would find would be trouble. Look at what had happened to her when she'd given in to temptation and gone out into the forest.

She moved out into the darkened hall, heading toward Jane's room. She needed company, another human's voice reminding her that there were no such things as bloodthirsty demons. And the only other human in this huge, dark house was Jane.

Except that Jane's door was open. There was no light inside, but her fire still burned brightly enough that Elizabeth could see her high, narrow bed was empty. Somewhere in the house a clock chimed, and proper Jane Durham was nowhere to be found.

Calm, sensible Elizabeth Penshurst immediately panicked. Fortunately there was a branch of extinguished candles near the fire—she caught it up and lit it from the flames, providing herself with at least a fitful illumination, and began her search.

Jane was nowhere in the house. Not in the small front parlor that they'd just barely managed to heat, not in the cavernous kitchen with the fires banked and glowing. Not in any of the bedrooms or drawing rooms or dining rooms or servants' rooms. The huge house was deserted.

Elizabeth set the candles down on a table with deceptive calm. For all that she might not want to think about it, three young women had disappeared from the area in the last few months, including one only a few days ago. If Jane was nowhere to be found, time was of the essence. Elizabeth could scarcely go back to bed and wait—Jane was too sensible a young woman to go wandering off in the middle of the night unless she had a very good reason. She must have been taken against her will.

Elizabeth didn't even hesitate. She had to go for help, to the one place she knew in the area. She had to find her way through the haunted forest to the Monk's Tower, and warn Gabriel that his sister had vanished.

It wasn't the first time she'd ventured forth in the darkness, she reminded herself as she wrapped a heavy shawl around her shoulders. Of course, the last time she'd gone out she hadn't known about the missing women, or just how dangerous Gabriel Durham truly was. And she hadn't just awoken from a blood-curdling nightmare whose details were mercifully vague.

She had no choice. She had no notion of where the lanterns were kept, and she didn't care. She pushed open the huge front door, and the wind immediately blew out her candles. She set the silver holder down on the doorsill and stepped out into the night air, glancing up at the three-quarter moon. Clouds were scudding across it, the wind had picked up, and the landscape was alive with eerie shadows.

And Elizabeth started forward, resolutely, ignoring the hammering in her chest, fully prepared to fight demons, bloodthirsty monsters, kidnappers, and that most terrifying of all creatures, Gabriel Durham, in order to bring Jane safely home.

CHAPTER FIFTEEN

Arundel was a huge, Gothic structure that put Herne-wood Manor to shame. Once a part of Hernewood Abbey's vast holdings, it had been taken from the monks at the time of dissolution and given by Henry VIII to a loyal subject. The loyal subject in question just happened to be the former chief prior of Hernewood Abbey, and a cousin of the king besides. The monk had no difficulty in promptly renouncing his calling, and the Moncrieff family had been in residence until recently, when bad debts and worse reputation had forced the latest of that line to relocate abroad, leaving his factor to rent the rambling estate to try to keep it in good heart.

Gabriel hadn't heard good things of the Chiltons' tenure, but then, he hadn't expected to. Most of the local people had been sent off, the Londoners had brought their own servants with them, and a shifty, suspicious lot they were, according to local gossip.

Indeed, public opinion was divided as to who was the less welcome newcomer to North Yorkshire, the Chiltons, or Gabriel himself.

Not that Gabriel was a newcomer, as the local people knew quite well. Most of them had been tolerant enough when he first came back to claim his tumbledown estate, ignoring his lapse from grace and accepting his custom and the work provided with dignity. The Chiltons were more their idea of the upper classes: haughty, extravagant, high-living, and their advent was welcomed as well.

Until the rumors started, of night riders, and dead animals, and ancient white-robed Druids wandering the woods at night, and Gabriel was their logical culprit.

Peter said no one distrusted him, but Peter would think the best of almost anyone. It was only logical they suspected him, and foolishly, he wasn't about to make any explanations. The people of Hernewood ought to remember that white-robed phantoms had been wandering the ruins of the abbey for the last two hundred or so years, and they came from a time much later than the Druids. Brother Septimus and Brother Paul were Cistercians, or had been during their time on earth. For some reason they lingered in the ruins, looking out for their abbey and guiding any stray lambs to safety.

As far as Gabriel knew, he was the first person with the dubious distinction of communicating with them. He lived in their abbey, and he had once been a monk himself, albeit for a brief, contentious time. Stout, cheerful Brother Paul had welcomed him jovially, as had Brother Septimus with slightly more reserve. They watched over him as well as stray lambs, they wandered the abbey grounds at night, and every now and then they showed up in the tower to shake their heads in dismay at his wickedness.

His wickedness consisted of reading ancient texts that

the brothers considered blasphemous, drinking too much wine, and dreaming about Elizabeth Penshurst. Of course the good brothers shouldn't have had any notion of his unspoken, lascivious thoughts, but from the woeful expression on Brother Septimus's face Gabriel expected they knew far too well.

They were tied to the abbey grounds, though no one seemed to know why. He'd left them wandering the grounds as he made his way across country toward the Chiltons' estate.

It was a two-mile walk, but he had no intention of bothering with a horse. It was late, the shadows had lengthened, and if they expected him at all, they would hardly do so on foot. He could come up the back way, observing the lay of the land to see if his suspicions were correct. He'd once known Arundel fairly well— the latest Moncrieff had never been in residence, and young Gabriel would often wander through the place, dreaming of other times, other lives.

The stone wall that marked the southern boundary was higher than he remembered, with rusty-looking metal atop the wall. The gate was closed and locked, the padlock fresh and shiny, but Gabriel had no qualms about dismantling it, one of his many odd talents. He stepped through, into the overgrown tangle of one of the gardens, and paused, listening.

The house was still more than half a mile away, a huge, imposing edifice brightly lit against the encroaching darkness. It should have looked welcoming, but it didn't. He could hear the boisterous sound of male laughter, a faint scream that might have been a woman shrieking with amusement and, then again, might not.

The path to his right would take him directly to the house in less than ten minutes' time. He imagined it was close to nine, but they wouldn't come looking for him. If they did, they'd hardly expect him to be roaming their overgrown, weed-choked garden.

Instead he struck out to the left, moving deeper into the tangle, heading toward the abandoned farm buildings with an instinct both sure and blind. There was no noise to lead him, no sound to call him. Just the certain knowledge that he'd find out all he needed to know there.

Once, decades ago, Arundel had been a prosperous estate, with a home farm, hardworking tenants, a dairy, and a mill. The cows had all died from a brain sickness, the mill was closed down, and the farm had been abandoned. Now all that remained were empty buildings, their thatched roofs long fallen into disrepair, their windows boarded up, silent and dead.

There was no sign of life when Gabriel reached the front of the old barn, and yet there were no weeds growing as there would have been if the place was truly abandoned. Someone had gone to a great deal of trouble to board up the windows, though as yet no one had bothered to rethatch the roof.

He moved through the shadows, silent and unseen, coming up to the front door of the old barn, only to find the same fresh, sturdy lock barring entrance. What could be so valuable in a roofless, deserted barn that it required that kind of lock?

This one was a little more difficult to manage, and the shadows were growing darker around him, forcing him to take even longer. He scraped his hand, drawing blood, and he cursed, trying once more. This time the lock fell open, and he removed it, pushing open the door into the dusty, dark interior of the abandoned barn.

It took a moment for his eyes to adjust to the almost impenetrable darkness. Boards and broken carriages and old furniture were piled haphazardly, blocking a far doorway that led into the center of the barn. He made his way around the obstacles, to the door, half-expecting to find still another lock, but the door wasn't even properly shut.

In the distance he thought he could hear the sound of dogs, not the friendly baying of family pets, but the deep, warning growl of guard dogs, hungry for blood. He froze, telling himself it was his imagination that they were coming closer, their paws thudding on the rough plank flooring of the old barn.

He pushed the door open, into the huge room. Overhead the last of the fitful light shone down through the hole where the roof had once been, and dust swam in the air. And in front of him was a huge structure, as tall as a cottage, made of entwined wood. Wicker, he thought with chill certainty. It was a wicker cage, just as he had dreaded.

He backed away, closing the door behind him, wondering why he felt so shaken. He'd suspected they were up to something of the sort—the dead animals and the Chiltons' unsavory reputation had suggested nothing less.

But suspicion and seeing the reality of it were two different things. And the cage was huge, much larger than Gabriel had imagined. He wondered where they expected to set it. He wondered what they planned to put inside.

Common sense told him they'd be amassing cattle and hunting dogs and birds. But there was no common sense to what he'd just seen. The wicker cage wasn't made to hold animals, it was made for humans, he knew it with a kind of horrified certainty. But he had no idea how he could stop them.

He knew an instant before anyone spoke that he was no longer alone.

"Were you impressed?" Francis Chilton's soft, affected voice was directly behind him.

Gabriel turned slowly, a distant, bored expression set firmly on his face. "Should I be?" he murmured.

"I think it's quite astonishing myself," Francis said. He was wearing some kind of wizard's robe, all embroidery and jewels and bizarre colors, his golden hair tumbling to his shoulders. "It's one thing to read about it, another to actually see it. You've never seen one before, have you?"

Gabriel considered lying, then dismissed the notion. "No," he said. "And you're right—it's quite . . . impressive. Startling."

Francis smiled smugly, clearly taking it as a compliment to his own ingenuity. "Do you think it will work?" he asked anxiously.

"It depends what you plan to do with it."

"Don't be silly, Gabriel, we intend to set it on fire come Beltane, and we're hoping you'll honor us with setting the torch." Francis smiled his winning smile, exposing sharply pointed little teeth in the darkening air.

"And what do you propose to have inside the cage?" He asked it idly, not for one moment thinking that Francis would be fooled.

"Gifts to propitiate our gods. Gifts for Herne the Hunter, Belarus, god of war, even Jesus Christ himself if he's in the mood to receive an offering. Wine and wheat and rashers of bacon, gold and satins."

"And virgins, Francis?"

Francis threw back his head and laughed. "Don't be absurd, Gabriel. I doubt there's a virgin left in the entire county. I'm certain you've done your best to decrease their number."

"I've told your wife, I'm celibate."

"Yes, so Delilah informed me. I'm certain your little problem is only temporary. I gather it afflicts most men at one time or another."

Gabriel laughed, unable to help himself, but he didn't bother to correct Francis. The last thing he cared to discuss with a dedicated degenerate such as Francis Chilton was the healthy state of his cock. "I should never underestimate you, Francis."

"No," said Francis, placing a pale, elegant hand on Gabriel's arm, "you shouldn't. You'll join us, then? We're really looking forward to having you share your wisdom."

"I doubt my wisdom would coincide with yours. I have my doubts about the existence of wicker cages."

"Oh, don't be doubtful, dear boy. You've just seen one. I assure you, you didn't imagine it."

"No," said Gabriel with a faint smile, "I realize that. Did it have to be quite so large? You'll need quite a number of gifts to fill it."

"I must confess I did become a bit overenthusiastic," Francis murmured. "But never fear, we'll find all we need. One fatted calf should take up a fair amount of space."

"Dead or alive?" Gabriel asked in a dulcet tone.

"Don't tell me you're tiresome enough to object to the slaughter of animals? Do you wander around eating twigs and nuts, then, and eschew sirloin? I'm surprised at you, Gabriel. Though you don't look like John the Baptist at the moment, despite that ill-shapen mane of hair." He stroked his arm beneath the coat of black silk. "And muscles! My, my, you are a strong one, aren't you? Couldn't have gotten that way on a diet of locusts and honey.''

Gabriel just looked at him. Francis had obviously decided to see just how far he could push him, but Gabriel was immune to annoyance. He'd known men like Francis in the past, and had no quarrel with them as long as they chose their partners wisely and without coercion.

Francis dropped his arm with an extravagant moue. "You're not being very cooperative, are you, darling?"

"I'm here, aren't I?" Gabriel murmured.

"True enough. You've finally accepted one of our countless invitations. And yet, I wonder, what made you finally decide to grace us with your presence again after all these months? We so seldom see you. Have we finally worn down your resistance and your dedication to your ascetic principles, or was it something else?"

"I can't imagine what you mean, Francis," Gabriel said lazily. "I was bored."

"Perhaps," Francis murmured. "Or perhaps you wanted to distract us from those two young women left unprotected at Hernewood Manor?"

"Why should they have anything to fear from you?"

"Oh, they don't," Francis said with an airy wave of his elegant hand that was far too practiced to be convincing. "I'm in absolute terror of that old brute, your father. Though in fact, he isn't your father, is he?"

"You're a font of knowledge, Francis."

"I spent years in London, my boy, with my eyes open and my ears listening. You have royal blood in your veins, my boy. It's a wonder Sir Richard doesn't parade you about like a prized trophy."

"It's not his blood."

"True enough. Still, he was shown royal favor, to have

been given you to raise into a proper young gentleman. Though I'm not sure how well he's succeeded."

"I imagine Sir Richard is more like to consider it a royal curse."

"Well then, why didn't he just do away with you? It's easy enough to kill a child, and very few people ask questions." Francis tossed a blond ringlet over his shoulder with a practiced gesture.

"How interesting. You know this from experience, Francis?" Gabriel inquired in an even voice.

"Me? Heavens, no." Francis managed a soft, artificial laugh. "I'm merely suggesting that if you had anything to fear from Sir Richard, it would have been accomplished these ages past. I doubt he holds any ill feeling toward you."

"I'm not particularly interested in discussing Sir Richard's ill will."

"Ah, but I am. And your heritage."

"You find it far more interesting than I do, Francis. I'm the result of an unfortunate liaison between a well-bred, well-married lady and a royal duke. The situation was dealt with before the lady's husband became aware of it. Sir Richard acquired a baronetcy and an heir, and all was well."

"I do love a happy ending," Francis murmured. "But that still doesn't account for Jane. You don't mind if I call her Jane, do you? She's most obviously your kin, anyone with an eye can see that. Unfortunately on you it looks quite delicious, while her share of the family looks is, shall we say, infelicitous."

Gabriel kept his face absolutely expressionless. He'd never had any illusions about just how dangerous Francis Chilton could be, but each fresh reminder was sharply painful. "I have to wonder why you're so interested," he said.

"Why, everything about you fascinates me, dear boy. You must know that I am quite . . . enraptured by you. Foolish of me, but then, I'm an emotional creature. So tell me about dear Jane. Do you share a father or a mother? I would really doubt it would be both."

Sod off was the term that popped into Gabriel's head. If Peter knew of Chilton's impertinent questions, he'd probably beat him to a bloody pulp. But then, knowing Francis, he'd probably derive intense pleasure from such an occurrence.

"I haven't yet paid my respects to your wife. And I gather my old friend Merriwether is staying with you, along with some of his cronies. I'm looking forward to renewing our acquaintance." He started toward the house, and Francis trotted after him, undeterred.

"Merriwether's not here at the moment," he said, almost as an aside, then returned to the subject that seemed to hold far too much interest for him. "I imagine it's the mother you must share," he murmured, half to himself. "After all, if Jane came blessed by royal blood, I imagine she'd be treated better by the Durhams. Richard seems to consider her a complete nonentity, not even worth despising. You, however, somehow have earned his undying hatred."

Gabriel turned back to look at him, an innocent expression on his face. "But, Francis, you not long ago assured me that I had nothing to fear from Sir Richard. I had no idea your acquaintance with him had reached such warmth."

Francis looked highly uncomfortable, a dubious satisfaction for Gabriel. "I've barely met the man. We hardly travel in the same circles," he said in a haughty voice. "He's a country squire. Not my favorite sort of companion at all."

"I would think not. And yet you seem so knowledgeable about his family relationships and his emotions that I begin to wonder. Have you perhaps converted him to the Old Religion?''

Francis laughed with shrill merriment. ''Unlikely. He strikes me as a most predictable and conservative gentleman.''

''True,'' Gabriel agreed. ''The idea of Sir Richard as a Druid is comical.''

''Comical,'' Francis echoed jovially. They had reached a side portico of the main house, and beyond the arched doorway Gabriel could hear the sounds of raucous laughter and girlish shrieks. He suspected those shrieks were coming from male voices, and wished he were anywhere but standing with Francis Chilton breathing down his neck.

He almost begged off. Almost came up with an instantaneous headache, or a previous engagement, but his long-lost sense of duty pulled at him. These silly, useless creatures were probably quite harmless, even with their wicker cage and their animal sacrifices. Probably.

But the people of Hernewood were uneasy, frightened, and he knew he was the more obvious culprit. He needed to find out for sure there was no correlation between the three girls who'd taken off on various spring nights, make certain that nothing apart from freshly slaughtered livestock would be burned in that infernal cage. And that the Chiltons and their ilk would come nowhere near Hernewood Manor and the two women living there.

He would go to hell and back for Jane's sake. He wasn't quite sure what he'd do for Elizabeth's sake. She was driving him to distraction.

She didn't seem inclined to go back to Dorset, as he'd advised, and that left him with no choice but to walk into the lion's den that was the Chiltons' house party and see just how dangerous things truly were. If he deemed it necessary, he'd have Lizzie bound and gagged and carried back to Dorset in the back of a hay wagon.

Even now the notion appealed to him. But there was more at stake than Lizzie, more than Jane as well. Herne-wood had turned into a place of darkness, his home had been invaded, and he couldn't sit idly by while Francis Chilton and his whore-wife played their little games. He had to discover just how dangerous things really were.

Francis stepped past him and waited by the open door, a faint, supercilious smile on his elegant face, and Gabriel, who was not a violent man, knew a sudden, intense longing to plant his fist right in the middle of all that milky perfection.

He didn't, of course. He simply stepped through the door, into the den of iniquity itself, promising himself the exquisite pleasure of ruining Francis's perfect face in the near future.

CHAPTER SIXTEEN

The night was warmer than Lizzie had expected,
though the wind tugged at her skirts and pulled at her
hair. There was something about Hernewood Manor
that held the cold, as if no warmth could survive long
in its lofty rooms. The moon was strong enough to light
her path, and she moved directly toward the old abbey
ruins. There was nowhere else she could go for help—
only Gabriel would care enough to go searching for
Jane. Pray God it wasn't too late.

There was a rich scent of spring in the air—fresh
earth and growing things. It was the end of April, a time
when everything should be blossoming, though this far
north it was taking longer than Lizzie was used to. Still,
she could smell the apple blossoms freshening in the
night wind, and a part of her was comforted.

The ruined abbey loomed up in the darkness, and
she supposed she should have been frightened. The last
time she'd been in these woods she'd been terrified,

running for her life until she'd slammed into Gabriel Durham.

But these woods felt different, safer, as they grew up around the old abbey. It felt like a holy place, whether one believed in the wicked Catholics or the ancient Druids or the more conventional faith of her father. She wondered if Mr. Penshurst would recognize the sanctity of the place. He'd probably deny it in scandalized tones.

But surely there was nothing to harm her in these towering woods. She was half-tempted to slip off her shoes in order to run faster, but she resisted the urge. She needed to keep her clothes fastened around her, her shoes tightly buttoned, and if she'd had any sense at all, she'd have scoured the manor until she found some hairpins to tame her wild mane. It only reminded her of the freedom she lacked when she felt it tumble down her back.

The tower was still and dark, and for a moment she hesitated. What if he wasn't there? He had an estate somewhere nearby—it had to be more of a home than the ruined luxury of the tower. It was the logical place for him, and yet she had no idea how to find it. She couldn't go back to the manor without Jane. She couldn't abandon her without at least attempting to help.

The curving staircase was uneven beneath her feet, and she held on to the stone walls for guidance, moving slowly, feeling her way. No sound drifted to her ears, and while she was tempted to call out, the very thought of taking a deep breath and shouting made her feel even less secure on the crumbling steps. It wasn't until she reached the top landing that she dared raise her voice.

"Mr. Durham?" It seemed absurd to call him that.

She tried again, and her voice was swallowed up by the cavernous darkness around her. "Gabriel?"

She heard a fluttering overhead, and she had the wretched suspicion there might be bats hovering around. She called once more, pushing against the heavy wooden door. The climb up in the darkness had been terrifying—the notion of climbing back down was even worse.

The door swung open easily, almost as if it had help. The room was in darkness, though the moonlight filtered in one narrow window, illuminating strange, ungainly shapes.

She didn't move from the doorway. "Gabriel?" she said again, in a voice not much more than a whisper. She could remember where his bed lay—she'd spent so much time trying not to look at it during her previous visit here that it was thoroughly emblazoned in her mind. The obvious thing to do would be to head for it, to ascertain whether he was there or not.

But what if he was? What if he lay naked in that bed, waiting for her? Or even worse, what if he wasn't alone?

She almost turned and left, willing to face those wretched stairs, when she remembered why she'd come there in the first place. Jane was missing, Jane needed her, and Lizzie couldn't abandon her.

She cleared her throat, taking a tentative step into the room. "Gabriel?" she whispered. "Gabriel, are you here?"

The door slammed shut behind her, plunging her into darkness, and she screamed in panic.

"Oh, merciful heavens, please don't do that!" begged a gentle voice from the shadows. Across the room from where the bed rested, thank heavens. "I didn't mean to frighten you." He sounded almost as frightened as she did.

She peered into the darkness. The voice was unfamiliar, though obviously well educated. "I'm sorry," she said in a relatively calm voice. "I was looking for Mr. Durham."

"He's not here, my girl." Another man's voice spoke, coming from the same dark corner of the room. They were standing by the fireplace, she could vaguely see their silhouettes, one tall and thin, one shorter and rounder. "He's gone off on some wild-goose chase, instead of staying here with his studies. I despair of the boy, I do."

"Septimus . . ." the other man said in a gentle reproof. "His motives are pure."

"His actions are not," the man addressed as Septimus intoned. "As well you know it, Brother Paul. We've talked about this time and time again, and you never . . ."

"I beg your pardon," Lizzie said in a plaintive voice, loath to continue listening to this squabbling, "but I really must . . ." Her voice trailed off. "Brother Paul?" she echoed.

"Yes, my child," came the friendly voice from the shadows.

A chill ran down Lizzie's spine. "Who are you?" she demanded in a hushed voice.

"Heavens, we've been rude," Brother Paul said. A moment later a flash of light illuminated the fireplace, and a small fire blazed forth, illuminating the corner where the two men stood.

They were dressed in long white robes, and somewhere in the back of her mind she remembered the tales of Druids, with their robes and their beards and their human sacrifices, and it took all her strength of mind not to panic entirely. "Are you Druids?" she demanded, ready to run.

"Certainly not. I'm Brother Septimus, this is Brother Paul. We're Cistercian monks attached to this abbey."

"But . . . the abbey was torn down. The monks died long ago," she said helplessly.

"Well, of course," Brother Septimus said in a crabby voice. "I didn't say we were alive, did I? We're attached to the place, and don't seem able to break free. We're ghosts, child, not Druids."

Her choices were simple, Lizzie thought dazedly. She could fall down in a dead faint, run screaming from the tower and probably break her neck on the treacherous stairs, or she could calm herself and treat this as any of the other occurrences, wondrous and commonplace, that had occurred in the forest. She took a deep, shattered breath.

"Why are you searching for Gabriel, my child?" Brother Paul inquired in a gentle voice. He had a ring of white hair on his head and a sweet, innocent expression on his round face.

"You're far too innocent, brother," Septimus intoned.

"You should be ashamed of yourself," Brother Paul replied sternly. "Can't you see she's a good girl? She wouldn't have come here if it weren't of the utmost importance. What's happened, my child?"

"It's Jane. Gabriel's sister. She's disappeared, and I'm afraid the Druids might have taken her." The sheer absurdity of confiding her worst fears to a ghost did nothing to lessen her panic.

"We know who Jane is," Septimus said in a condescending tone. "We know everything about Gabriel, including who you are. As for Jane, I'm certain she's just fine. She's a girl who knows the benefits of proper behavior, unlike some young girls I can think of."

"That's enough, Brother Septimus," Brother Paul

said sternly. "Can't you see the child is distressed? We need to find Gabriel for her."

"We can't find Gabriel," his fellow monk said. "He left the abbey grounds, and there's no way we can follow him."

"We know where he went. We can show her the way."

"Highly unwise. You want to send her into that den of lechers? I think not."

"Then what do you propose we do, brother?" Brother Paul demanded with some asperity. "Sit back and do nothing to save her?"

Brother Septimus emitted a long-suffering ghostly sigh. "We can't go with her. We can't protect her. We'd be leading her into the valley of temptation with no one to aid her."

"Gabriel will be there," Brother Paul pointed out. "He'll look after her."

"Much good he'll do," he said with a sniff.

"Just tell me where he is," Lizzie pleaded. "I'll go find him myself."

"I'm afraid he's gone to Arundel, my dear," Brother Paul said in an apologetic tone. "I'm certain his motives are entirely pure, but it's nevertheless a dangerous place for a properly brought-up young lady."

"What's Arundel?" she asked, though she had the wretched feeling she knew.

"The home of Lord and Lady Chilton. A place of orgies, licentiousness, drunkenness, sloth, and evil," Brother Paul intoned. "Or so I've been told. As we've explained, we aren't actually able to leave the abbey grounds." He sounded faintly mournful at the thought of missing the chance to observe such unrepentant evil.

"How do I find it? Will I need to ride?" She tried to

keep the quaver out of her voice. The notion of climbing back onto Marigold's broad back filled her with loathing, but for Jane's sake she wouldn't hesitate.

"She might just as well take the footpath," Brother Septimus said reluctantly. "Gabriel did."

"But what if he's . . . he's forgotten himself, brother?" Brother Paul asked in a worried voice. "What if she goes to him for help and he's in the midst of some sort of drunken revelry?"

"We can only pray," Septimus murmured. He moved closer, and Lizzie noticed with fascination that he didn't seem to quite touch the ground, but instead floated a few inches off it, the hem of his robe swinging slightly in the air. "Brother Paul will see you to the edge of the grounds. You should be able to find your way from there. In the meantime I'll see if I can find what happened to dear Jane. She's a good, properly behaved girl—I'd hate to think that evil might befall her." His tone of voice seemed to leave doubts as to Lizzie's essential goodness and proper behavior, but she decided she was being too sensitive.

Following Brother Paul's sturdy form down the curving steps was a great deal easier than feeling her way up in the dark. There seemed a faint, comforting glow to his pale robes, and she moved with confidence.

The wind had picked up, tossing the leaves overhead, and she wrapped her shawl more tightly around her as she followed Brother Paul down a winding path along the hedgerow, then up into a broad field. He halted at the low stone wall that bisected it, and in the moonlight his pale face looked both faintly transparent and doleful.

"I wish I could accompany you, my dear," he said. "But we're doomed to remain on abbey grounds."

"Why? Was it some sin you committed?" she asked, knowing she shouldn't take the time to ask such pointless questions.

"Sin? Heavens, no. I expect Brother Septimus is almost entirely without sin, if you don't count his pride. And his habit of passing judgment on all and sundry. And his annoying little habit of . . ." Brother Paul stopped himself abruptly. "Well, who among us is without sin? We were no worse than some, and better than most. It's not for us to say why we're here, but simply to do our duty. I don't expect you'll see us when you return."

"Why not?"

"I'm not certain. In fact, I'm surprised you were able to see and hear us in the first place. Most people can't. Gabriel was the first one to talk to us in more than a hundred years. Trust me, one hundred years with only Brother Septimus to converse with can be very wearing."

"I can imagine."

"Follow this path for two more fields, turn right at the stile, and continue on past the rocks. Be careful there—the ledge is steep and more than one stray lamb has fallen to its death. Arundel is just beyond. You'll recognize it—it was once part of the abbey grounds until it fell upon wicked times. They didn't tear it down as they did our holy house, they simply converted it to heathen use. Nothing compared to the wickedness that goes on now, mind you. I'll pray for your safe return."

"And Jane's," Lizzie said.

"Of course, Jane's." He made the sign of the cross, then touched her lightly on the forehead in a blessing. She felt nothing but a faint draft of air. "Go along now, child. And God go with you."

And a moment later he had vanished, and Lizzie

was alone in the moonlight, at the edge of a deserted field.

Jane used to dream that Peter would come to her in her sleep. That she'd open her eyes and he'd be standing by her bed, looking down at her, and she would only have to hold out her hand and he would come to her, beneath the layers of warm covers.

She couldn't remember how young she'd been when she'd first dreamt it. Shockingly young. Plain, oversize Jane Durham had fallen desperately in love with Peter when she was eleven years old, and nothing had changed her hopeless passion or devotion. At least he didn't know. And at least she could daydream, and night dream, touch him and see him and speak to him as she longed to do, without him ever knowing her shameful longing.

She opened her eyes, and he was there, illuminated by the fire, and she almost held out her hand, smiling at him, when he spoke, shattering the illusion.

"Penelope's gone into labor," he said in rough voice. "I knew you'd want to be there."

Jane didn't even hesitate. She threw back the covers, leaping from her bed, oblivious to the thin nightdress she was wearing, oblivious to her bare feet and dishabille. All that mattered was her beloved mare. She headed for the door, but Peter stopped her, catching her about the waist as he had when they were children, young and innocent, and hauling her back.

"It's chilly out there," he said. "You can't go out like that. I'll wait outside while you get dressed."

"No! Get back to Penelope. I'll be down there as quickly as I can," she said, ripping at the row of tiny buttons that traveled up to her throat.

Peter turned away, his gesture a shocking reminder that she was stripping her clothes in front of him. "If you haven't got warm clothes and shoes, I'll bring you back and leave Penelope alone," he warned her.

"Get back to her. I promise I'll dress warmly."

Her hands were shaking as she threw off her clothes, even before he'd closed the door behind him. She only bothered with the bare minimum of covering— a chemise, an ancient wool dress, heavy stockings and leather slippers, before she raced after him, almost slipping on the narrow servants' staircase. The night air was cool and crisp, the three-quarter moon bright in the sky, and Jane didn't bother with a lamp. She knew her way to the stables, to Penelope's stall, blindfolded, and she couldn't be bothered to waste the time searching.

Penelope was down, her swollen sides heaving, her head thrashing in misery. Peter was on his knees in the straw beside her, and he glanced up at Jane briefly, as if to assure himself that she was properly dressed. He was only in shirtsleeves, the cuffs rolled back to reveal his strong forearms, and Jane felt a little shiver of apprehension as she knelt beside him.

"She's not going to die, is she?" she whispered. Afraid of the answer, knowing she could count on Peter for the truth.

"Of course not," he said, putting gentle hands on Penelope's swollen belly. "She's having a hard time of it, but she'll pull through, and the foal as well."

"I should never have bred her," Jane said miserably.

"Don't be punishing yourself, lass," Peter said sternly. "It's a risk any horse owner has to take. And there's no need to give up hope yet. She's got a good, strong heart. She'll be fine. She's a fighter, she is. Just like her mistress."

But Jane was beyond comfort. All she could do was kneel beside Peter in the fitful light of the lantern he'd hung on the side of the stall, and watch, and pray.

She'd watched a dozen colts being born, watched mares die in the process and wept for them, but never had she felt so acutely to blame, so certain disaster was the only possible outcome. She didn't have much that she could call her own, but Penelope was hers, and no one else's, and it had been her choice to have her bred. It didn't matter that Peter had told her she was strong enough to withstand the rigors, it was still Jane's fault and Jane's alone. She knelt in the straw with Peter by her side and wept slow, hot tears.

"There's no need to be grieving so soon, lass," Peter said grimly. "She's not giving up yet, and neither should you."

Jane shook her head. "She's going to die, I know it. She's the only creature who'll let me love her, and she'll die, and I'll be alone."

"You won't be alone, lass," he said. "Your brother'll be there for you. You can trust Gabriel."

She looked up at him in the lamplight, not bothering to wipe away the tears that ran down her face. This was the second time he'd seen her crying in as many days, but she was past caring. She wanted to tell him how stupid he was, how blind and stupid and careless with her tender heart. It didn't matter so much that he didn't want her, but did he have to be so completely blind to what she was feeling?

She shook her head, closing her eyes in despair. "You don't understand, Peter," she whispered. "And maybe it's better that way."

He started to say something, then stopped, and she was just as glad. His presence was the only comfort he would offer—any words would be as empty as his heart.

He cared for her, she knew it full well. Cared for her as he cared for the horses in his charge, the stable cat with her ceaseless litters of kittens, the elderly spaniel that trotted after him in hopes of a treat or a sign of affection. She was just like that spaniel, and it could only be a blessing that he hadn't noticed how needy she was.

How much she loved him.

"It's going to be a while yet, Miss," he said, and she could have hit him for that wretched "miss." "Why don't you go back to your room and I'll call you . . ."

"No!" she said fiercely, suddenly angry. "I'm not leaving her side. I don't care if it takes all night, she's not going to die without me beside her."

"Jane, she's not going to die," he said patiently.

"Can you promise me that?"

"I can't promise you anything," he said slowly.

The truth of it broke her heart. "I know," she said in a hushed voice. She moved away from him, over to the side of the stall. "I'll stay out of your way, I promise. But I need to be here. Please, Peter."

If he called her miss again she would scream. But he didn't. He simply nodded, and she curled up in the straw, leaning against the stall and closing her eyes in sudden exhaustion. Penelope was still for the moment, resting, and Jane took that moment to rest as well. She could hear Peter moving around, and a moment later something warm covered her. For a moment she thought it might be a blanket, and then she realized it smelled like Peter, like fresh air and sunlight and horses and leather. He'd wrapped his coat around her, cradling her like a baby, and she knew she should throw it off, refuse the comfort it gave her.

But she couldn't do it. She huddled down beneath

the enveloping folds, and pretended it was Peter's arms wrapped around her, the warmth of Peter's body cradling hers. She took a deep, comforting breath, and slept, in the straw, with Peter watching over her mare.

CHAPTER SEVENTEEN

There was something essentially tedious about an orgy, Gabriel decided long hours later. Not that it was a new revelation for him—he'd given up on orgies during his sojourn in London. They tended to have a distressing sameness about them, and while everyone assured each other that they were having a magnificent time, there always seemed to be an edge of desperation to the proceedings.

Besides, it was hard to keep track of your partner if there was more than one involved. He'd learned, to his regret, that sex was far more enjoyable if you actually cared about your partner. And since he was doing his absolute best to care about no one, with the possible exception of Peter and his sister, then celibacy had been the obvious choice. Nights like these were not causing him to regret his decision.

There was one benefit to all this—Delilah Chilton was somewhere in one of the many tangles of bodies, being happily serviced by a number of men. If she hadn't forgotten about him entirely, she'd at least managed to be thoroughly distracted, which was a small blessing. If only Francis decided to join in, then Gabriel would be able to escape and take himself back home to a blessedly empty bed and at least a few hours of much-needed sleep.

But Francis sat beside him in the embrasure, removed from the action but calmly observing, matching him drink for drink for one of the best clarets Gabriel had enjoyed since he'd left London, and it seemed as if he were entirely prepared to spend the entire night doing just that.

If he had to spend another ten minutes, Gabriel thought, he might very well strangle his host. "This is getting redundant, don't you think?" he murmured, desperate for distraction. "Would you care for a game of cards?"

Francis smiled. "I thought you would never ask, dear boy. Unless, of course, you'd rather we had a bit of privacy . . ."

"Francis, your attractions are formidable but, alas, not my taste. A hand or two of piquet would be sufficient, and then I really should make my way back home."

"To that tower in the woods? Really, Gabriel, if you must live in a the wilds of Yorkshire, why not simply move in with us? I dare say it's much more comfortable, and you know we'd welcome your presence among us."

"I prefer my solitude."

"Ah, solitude," murmured Francis. "Not one of my particular vices, I'm afraid. Let's adjourn to the green room. We may even find a few hardy gamesters still at it. Though I think I'd prefer to play one on one. The stakes can be so much more interesting."

At least the green room was blessedly free of copulation. The servants had been dismissed or brought into play long ago, and Francis carried the wine himself, stepping over entangled couples with mincing delicacy. The green room was stuffy, but at least the odor of sweat and perfume was less strong. Gabriel looked longingly at the leaded casement windows before taking his seat at the baize table.

"I warn you, I'm very good at cards," Francis murmured.

"I tremble to hear it. I have a bit of skill myself."

"Then we're well matched. Haven't I always said so?" Francis purred. He dealt swiftly, the cards rippling through his pale fingers.

"And what are we wagering?" Gabriel inquired in his most casual voice. Not for one moment did he think Francis was simply interested in cards. There would be another reason, a darker one, behind this.

"Let's play a hand or two and see how things go."

Gabriel nodded, taking another sip of wine. He had a hard head, but then, so did Francis. He could drink all evening and not be impaired, but he needed more than simple competence. He needed all his wits about him. He couldn't rid himself of the notion that he was playing cards with the devil, and his very soul was at stake.

Francis won the first hand, quite easily, since Gabriel was more interested in observing his style than in winning a wagerless game. Gabriel took the second one, though only by a small margin. The third hand he gave to Francis, though he made certain not to lose too badly. Francis would know he was clever enough not to make mistakes, and he didn't want the other man to realize that Gabriel had every intention of winning.

"Very well. What shall we wager? Would you care for a night in bed with my wife?" Francis suggested lazily.

"I think not. We can start with money and go from there."

"Tame," Francis murmured, his pale, colorless eyes alight with mischief. "But as you will. We'll start with a pound a point, and move from there. You're quite able to cover your bets?"

"Quite," said Gabriel. Somewhere in the distance a clock struck four, and he stifled a yawn. This was an interminably long night, but something could still be salvaged from it. He assumed, perhaps wrongly, that he could trust Francis's code of honor—if he won some concession from him, then Francis would honor it. But if Francis knew his vulnerabilities, there would be other ways to attack him. He had to be very careful indeed.

"A pound a point," he agreed. "We'll get to the more important wagers later."

Elizabeth couldn't resist temptation. At the top of the hill she slipped off her shoes and stockings, wiggling her bare toes into the cool, damp earth. She couldn't go much further than that, even though the tight neckline of her wool dress was binding, but at least she could move more swiftly along the narrow paths.

She could see the lights from Arundel at quite a distance. She'd lost all track of time, but apparently the merrymakers in residence paid no heed to normal hours of sleeping and waking. Their revelry was in full force even as the moon began to slip toward the horizon, plunging the night into unrelieved darkness.

She didn't dare stop to think, or she would have been overwhelmed by the events of the evening. She couldn't think about chatty ghosts or decadent Londoners or Gabriel's mouth or slaughtered animals. She had to concentrate on finding Jane, and none of the rest of it mattered.

The walls surrounding the Chiltons' hired estate were high, yet a door swung wide in the middle of it, one blessed piece of luck. Lizzie moved through it, leaving her shoes and stockings in a neat pile by the entrance. She couldn't afford to take the time to put them on again, and at this late hour no one would notice her feet. She could always simply bend her knees slightly to cover them.

She moved toward the house, following a pathway that led along the gardens until she came to a gate. She unlatched it with no great difficulty and pushed through, heading across a refuse-strewn courtyard that led directly up to the house.

She heard the rumble from a distance, and for a moment she thought it might be thunder. The sky was clear overhead, still lit by the setting moon, but the growling increased, and she placed an inquiring hand on her stomach, but despite her anxiety it was still. The growling grew deeper, more fierce, and she looked up to see at least three pairs of eyes glowing red in the fitful moonlight.

They moved toward her, slowly, three huge beasts, their massive paws clicking on the cobblestones, their huge jaws wide, the deep, warning sounds from their chests enough to terrify the bravest soul. They were some kind of mastiff, obviously guard dogs, and more than ready to attack.

As she looked about her she could now see scattered animal bones that the dogs had discarded, but they still looked very thin, very strong, very hungry. She wasn't that large—she'd provide no more than a snack for them.

She took a deep breath. "Poor babies," she said softly.

"Doesn't anyone feed you?" She held out her hand, calm, patient, and the largest, meanest of the bunch moved toward her with slow, lethal calm, the two others close behind him.

He lifted his huge snout to her hand, opened his massive jaws, and licked her.

She rubbed his head, now that he'd given her permission, and the others crowded around, seeking comfort as well. "Poor little ones," she crooned. "What a life you must lead here. No one to take proper care of you, no one to cuddle and run with you. And what lovely creatures you are, the three of you."

The largest one rolled over on his back, presenting his belly to be rubbed, which Elizabeth immediately did. She had always been at peace with animals. Old Peg had said it was part of her gift, but Lizzie only knew that no animal would hurt her. With the possible exception of the bad-tempered Marigold.

The dogs were loath to let her go, but she promised them a treat on her return, and after much cuddling she moved onward, through the next gate, coming up to the brightly lit house.

It was difficult to discern which was the proper entrance. She found one door, and knocked as loudly as she could, battering her hand against the ancient wood, but no one seemed inclined to answer. She doubted they could even hear her. She tried to open it herself, but it was too heavy for her to move, and she gave up, moving back in search of a smaller, more accessible entrance.

She could hear distant laughter, and the sound of breaking glass. There was no music, so they couldn't be dancing, but something was keeping the household awake, and clearly they were enjoying themselves. She wondered what they could find of such paramount interest to keep them occupied. At that hour she would have liked nothing more than to be safe in her bed.

She moved along the edge of the building, edging as close to the windows as she could. They were set high and deep in the stone walls, and thick shrubbery kept her from getting too close. She could have wept with frustration.

There had to be a way into the huge, fortresslike building, if only she could find it. Either that, or she'd simply throw herself on the ground and have a major tantrum the likes of which few had seen. Gabriel was somewhere in that building, and he was the only one she could trust to help her find Jane.

At the far corner a window stood open, and the box-wood hedge beneath it was relatively sturdy. Lizzie eyed it doubtfully. It would be rough going, and the final leap from boxwood to window ledge would be a difficult one. But she didn't seem to have any choice.

The hedge was as sturdy as she'd hoped, and twice as scratchy. It hurt her bare feet. She scrambled up it, hearing her blasted gown rip and catch, and the stone windowsill was still a good foot away from her. She had no choice but to leap for it, holding her breath.

She slammed her knees against the stone wall, but the open window provided enough purchase, and a moment later she was through, landing on the hard floor in a ball, with tattered clothes and bare feet and bloody hands. She lay there in the darkness, trying to catch her breath. She was in some sort of hallway, and no one had seen or heard her enter. With any luck she could find Gabriel and escape without running into the Chiltons or their assorted houseguests. Luck had been with her so far—she could only pray that it held.

Slowly she pulled herself to her feet, trying to smooth her abused clothing. She seemed all in one piece, albeit a barefoot, disreputable piece, but that was the least of her worries.

There were strange sounds coming from the adjoining room, grunts and noises she didn't even want to think about. The door was tightly closed, and she decided to save that particular room for later. If Gabriel was inside, she wasn't certain she wanted to find him.

Gabriel was losing. He was very good at losing—he knew just how to play his cards so that it seemed his opponent was simply enormously clever. Francis was falling for it, his vanity powerful enough to feed on his unlikely success, and Gabriel bided his time. He was baiting his trap with all the skill and cleverness he had at his command. He had no idea whether it would prove that useful in the long run, but he had every intention of trying.

"So, shall we make the wager more interesting?" Francis murmured, a few minutes before Gabriel had expected him to. His luck had obviously made him reckless. "You know how eager we are to have you join us? Your steadfast refusals have been most distressing, particularly when one considers the wisdom you have to impart. You've had a run of ill luck with the cards, but you and I both know how easily that can change. Why don't we place a small wager on the outcome of the next hand that would benefit us both? If I win, you join us in our Beltane revelries."

"And if you lose? I don't see that I have much to gain."

Francis smiled, his small, pointed teeth showing beneath his rouged lips. "You have a certain concern about those around you. It would be useless to deny it—like the priests of old, you hold family and county dear to you, and you're worried some harm may befall them. I could guarantee the safety of your loved ones."

"Could you, indeed?" Gabriel kept his voice silky calm. "And did you have any particular designs on my family?"

"Of course not, my boy. We're not monsters, you know. We're simply seekers of the truth, just as you are, and we try to follow the Old Ways, before Christianity put such a damper on things. Have you noticed that Christians never seem to have fun? Such a doleful religion."

"No, I hadn't noticed." Gabriel shuffled the cards. It was his turn to deal, and Francis was too vain to realize what an advantage that gave Gabriel. Of course Francis assumed a gentleman like Gabriel would never cheat at cards. For such a degenerate, Francis was surprisingly naive.

There was no limit to what Gabriel would do to protect his own. He would lie, he would kill, he would cheat at cards. Particularly when his opponent was a useless, decadent creature such as Francis Chilton.

It wasn't his taste for his own kind that Gabriel despised. It wasn't unheard of in the monastery where he'd spent those long years, and while not to his particular interest, he had no quarrel with those who practiced it.

But Francis was a dangerous, evil creature who preyed on the innocent and the unwilling. And whether he liked it or not, Gabriel felt the need to protect those he could. Particularly when they were his people.

"So if you mean no ill to my family or the people in this county, why should I bother with such a wager? I have nothing to gain." He continued shuffling the cards with a slow, idle gesture.

"Ah, but that's where you're wrong. Just because I

tell you they have nothing to fear doesn't mean you'll believe me. I regret that my reputation is not quite spotless in matters of truthfulness. But if we wager the safety of your family, then I'll have no choice but to honor my gaming debts, as any gentleman would.''

Gabriel took leave to doubt it. However, there was always the remote possibility that Francis would keep his word, and it was worth it to Gabriel to secure it. He would leave nothing to chance, and he had no intention of feeling even the slightest bit of guilt. After all, Francis would get what he sought as well. The only way Gabriel could be completely certain his family was safe would be to join the merry revelers. While the notion was both boring and faintly nauseating, he'd done far worse in his life and managed to survive. He could manage this as well.

"Done," he said, dealing the cards with such swift, careless grace that Francis would never guess he knew exactly which cards he was receiving.

Francis picked up his hand, a deceptively impressive selection, and smiled obliquely. "I should warn you I intend to win."

"Intentions never harmed a soul," Gabriel said idly.

"And let me assure you that your sister is completely safe from me, whether you join with us or not." There was something in his tone that caught Gabriel's attention, and his gaze shot up.

"I rejoice to hear it," he murmured.

"But of course, we didn't quite clarify where Miss Penshurst fits. She's neither a villager nor a relative, is she?"

"She's second cousin to Lady Elinor," he said carefully, making a seemingly foolish discard.

Francis's smile widened. "Which makes her no kin of yours. We'll have to wager separately for her."

Gabriel set his cards facedown on the green baize table. "I dislike being used, Francis. Miss Penshurst requires the same guarantee of safety that the others do."

"But why, my boy? What possible interest is she to you? She's no more than indifferently pretty, her lineage, while respectable, is hardly worthy of yours, and as far as I can see, no one cares about her. Why should you? Do you have a secret wish to break your celibacy between her thighs? I'm not sure I blame you—redheads can be deliciously passionate, and that one seems possessed of a certain charming fierceness."

"I feel responsible for her, nothing more." He picked up his cards again, inwardly seething. He made another seemingly careless discard.

"And yet you seem totally unconcerned about your younger sister."

"She's in London. And she has her father to look out for her."

"Not quite good enough. I think you have a tendre for the little Penshurst girl. We could arrange something, you know. If you're afraid of repercussions, there are ways to handle these things. In the dark, with the girl properly restrained, and you could take your pleasure with no one the wiser."

Gabriel met his gaze. "You're a sick bastard, Francis," he said softly.

Francis smiled. "But you're tempted, aren't you, love?" He laid down his cards. "I believe I've won."

Gabriel fanned out his cards on the table, no expression on his face. "I'm afraid you haven't, dear boy," he said, mocking the endearment. "And you won't. Ever."

Francis stared at the cards in disbelief. And then, to Gabriel's surprise, he threw back his head and laughed. "You delight me, Gabriel," he said. "You truly do. I can't deny that you've won this round, though how you managed to accomplish such a feat leaves me in awe."

"Are you accusing me of cheating, Francis?"

"Never. I simply admire a skill and deviousness that is fully equal to my own. I expect we'll have more than one chance to go at it. I'm looking forward to it immensely. Just tell me one thing. Do you have any feelings for Miss Penshurst? Do you want her?"

Silently he cursed him. If he admitted any interest, it would give Francis the edge he needed. If he denied it, it would doubtless make protecting her even more difficult. It was a question of damned if you do and damned if you don't.

"Aren't you going to answer, Gabriel? Do you want Miss Penshurst or not?"

He no longer hesitated. Lizzie was the last woman who would appeal to a degenerate such as Francis—her only value would be in how much he cared. The only way to protect her was to deny her. "Do I strike you as the kind of man to waste my time on such a plain little nobody? You may do with Miss Penshurst as you please. She's of no interest to me."

"I delight to hear you say so, dear boy," Francis murmured. "Though I expect she's not so well pleased."

He was looking past him, over his shoulder to the open doorway, and Gabriel froze. She couldn't be there, in the midst of all that profligacy, she couldn't have overheard his drawling dismissal of her.

But he knew before he turned that she was, she had. And at the slamming of the door, Francis threw back his head and laughed.

CHAPTER EIGHTEEN

Elizabeth tore down the hall blindly, too mortified to think clearly. All the doors in this strange household were tightly closed, and it had been sheer luck that the one open door had held Gabriel, calmly playing cards with Francis Chilton.

He hadn't known she was there, of course, and she'd opened her mouth to speak when Francis spied her. Something in his pale, smirking countenance had silenced her, just long enough to hear Gabriel's scathing opinion of her.

"Lizzie!" The voice behind her was a furious, insistent hiss, but she ignored him, speeding up, knowing it was hopeless, knowing he was faster than she was. She couldn't face him, not until she got her hammering heart and her ruined pride under control, and she skidded to a stop, reached for the first door she could find and opened it.

"For God's sake, no!" she heard him cry, but it was

too late. She stood frozen in the threshold of a very dark, hot room and stared at the scene in front of her in shocked amazement.

A moment later he'd put his arms around her and yanked her from the room, slamming the door shut behind them. As far as Lizzie could tell the assorted people in the room hadn't even been aware they'd been observed.

"What," she demanded in a shaken voice, "was that?"

Gabriel turned her around, not releasing her. In the darkened hall she couldn't see his expression, which meant, thank God, that he couldn't see hers. Couldn't see the utter shame that suffused her. "You're better off not knowing," he said grimly. "What in God's name are you doing here?"

She was still distracted by the odd sight beyond the closed door. "It looked like some kind of monster," she said, struggling for some kind of calm. "So many arms and legs, and . . ." She suddenly realized what else she saw in that brief glimpse. "Oh, my heavens! Were those naked people?"

"Yes," he said briefly. "And if you don't come along with me, you may be joining them, whether you wish to or not." He took her hand and started pulling her back down the hallway. She wasn't in any mood to hold hands with the foul beast, however, and she did her best to yank her hand away. It was useless. She slapped at him with her other hand, but he ignored her, simply continued dragging her down the hallway till they reached an entryway.

The door was barred—it was no wonder she'd been unable to open it from the outside. He slid the heavy bolt and pushed her outside, following a moment later and slamming the door behind him. It took her a moment to realize now was her chance to escape, when she remembered why she'd come here in the first place.

He towered over her, and even in the darkness she could sense his anger. It was nothing compared to hers, she reminded herself. She hadn't been gaming with degenerates while the rest of the household occupied itself in unholy doings. She'd been trying to save his sister's life.

"It's Jane," she said, not bothering to disguise the fury in her voice. "She's disappeared."

"And that's why you came traipsing over here in the middle of the night?" he demanded. "Haven't you any sense at all?"

"Don't you care about your sister? She could be kidnapped, murdered, she could . . ."

"Did you check the stables?" he asked with devastating calm.

"Why would she be in the stables?"

"Because she has a horse ready to foal. I expect Penelope must have gone into labor and Jane went down to help, particularly since Peter's the only one on hand. He's not going to let anything happen to her."

"How was I supposed to know that? And how can you be so certain?" she demanded hotly.

"If anything had happened to Jane, I'm certain my gracious host would have informed me. And you weren't supposed to go haring off like a wild woman, jumping to conclusions."

"I beg your pardon," she said icily. "But what can you expect from an insignificant little twit like me? I'll just get back to the house and you can continue with your entertainments . . ."

"I didn't call you an insignificant little twit," he said wearily. "I called you a plain little nobody, and I had very good reasons for doing so, which you're far too angry to realize. And I'm more than ready to leave. Come along.''

He reached for her hand again, and she slapped at him, trying to get away. He was faster than she had expected, ducking under her blows and catching her arm, drawing her tight against him. "If you hit me again," he said between his teeth, "you will very much regret it. I intend to see you safely home, reassure myself that my sister is safe, and then get a much-deserved night's sleep."

She considered kicking him, then realized it wouldn't do much good since she was barefoot. She considered sticking her tongue out at him, but that was childish and undignified. "It's almost morning," she pointed out inconsequentially.

"Then I'll get a much-deserved day's sleep," he said. "Come along."

She didn't bother fighting him—much as she wanted the excuse to hit him again, she wanted to be free of him even more. She went with him willingly enough, running a bit to keep up as he circled the house and headed for the back gardens.

He pushed open the gate that divided the mansion and pulled her into the bone-strewn courtyard. The moon had set long ago, but there was a pale pink glow in the east, enough to illuminate the courtyard and the three hungry mastiffs.

They rose, the deadly trio, advancing with menacing growls. Before Lizzie could say a word Gabriel shoved her behind him, shielding her. "Run," he said in a whispered command. "I'll distract them."

Lizzie had had enough. "Don't be an idiot," she muttered, shoving him hard in the middle of his back. She moved in front of him, just as the largest of the dogs was about to leap, and held out her hand.

"Did you think I'd forgotten you, angel?" she cooed. "I've brought you a lovely treat from the big house."

The first mastiff stepped forward, sniffed at the crumpled meat pie in her outstretched hand, and delicately lapped it into his strong jaws. "I've got some for the rest of you," she promised, emptying the deep pocket of her petticoat. It was stained with grease, but a worthy sacrifice for the poor hungry beasts.

She could feel Gabriel watching in astonishment as she rubbed their huge heads, then she turned back and fixed him with a cool glance. "Are you coming? They trust me, but animals tend to sense the difference between worthy and unworthy people, and I wouldn't count on my being able to protect you."

He tried to take her hand again, but the largest of the dogs lifted his head and emitted a short, warning growl. Gabriel wisely thought better of it, following her across the littered courtyard without another word.

He waited until they were through the tangled gardens and past the gate, out into the fields once more, before he spoke. "How did you manage to do that?"

"Animals trust me."

He made a noise of profound disbelief, but she ignored him, starting down the hillside at a fast pace, hoping against hope that he'd simply let her go. The sky was growing lighter—the pink had turned a pale, peachy beige, and birds were beginning to sing in the hedgerows. It would be full daylight in less than an hour, and the daylight would be unforgiving. She'd be hard put to keep her composure.

"Where the devil are your shoes?" was the only thing he said after a few minutes of vigorous walking.

Lizzie came to such an abrupt halt that he barreled into her, almost knocking her flat. She ignored his muffled curse, too distressed to be bothered. "I left them

back at that house," she cried. "I'll have to go back."
She whirled around, ready to run back in search of her
missing shoes when he caught her, swinging her back.

"You certainly will not," he said. "We were lucky to
get you out without anyone seeing you."

"Lord Chilton saw me," she said.

"And he's the most dangerous of all, I suspect. If
you go back for your shoes, you probably wouldn't be
allowed to leave."

"They're my only pair of shoes! I can't just abandon
them!"

"You should have thought of that before you took
them off. What in heaven's name made you do such a
ridiculous thing? Did you decide to go dancing in the
moonlight again?"

"I can run faster without my shoes," she said, her
voice sulky.

"We'll find you some new ones. I imagine one of the
women at Hernewood Manor would have shoes that fit
you. Both Lady Elinor and Edwina delight in acquiring
needless possessions."

"You don't understand . . ." she began, but he gave
her a hard little shake, silencing her.

"No, you don't understand. Don't you realize what
you just witnessed? And that kind of behavior is relatively
harmless compared to the kinds of things they're capable of."

"Why should it matter to you? I'm merely a . . . a . . ."

"Plain little nobody," he supplied.

"Thank you."

"You're welcome."

She glared up at him, but there was no pulling away
from him. The sky was growing steadily brighter, and a
soft spring breeze caught in her tangled hair, brushing
it into his face. He caught it, holding it, staring down

at the auburn strands for a long, enigmatic moment. And then he sighed.

"You'll be the death of me, Lizzie," he muttered.

"It's my fondest dream." She jerked away from him, both her arm and her hair, and started onward, back to Hernewood Manor, still holding the vain hope that he might abandon her.

He didn't, of course, which was just as well. He might be certain Jane was safely tucked up in the stables, but Lizzie wasn't so sure. On the one hand she wanted nothing more than to find that Jane was safe and unharmed. On the other, she would have given almost anything to prove Gabriel Durham wrong.

They had reached the edge of Hernewood Forest when he spoke once more. She hadn't realized how close behind her he was—he moved with such stealthy grace she could almost pretend she'd left him far behind. She ignored him, quickening her pace, but he simply reached out and caught her, turning her back to face him.

"I am getting mortally tired of your putting your hands on me," she said in a dangerous voice. The sun had just begun to peek over the towering treetops of Hernewood Forest, and she could see him quite clearly. For the first time she realized he was dressed with a modicum of propriety, in a black-silk coat and breeches, his long hair tied carelessly back. He even wore a large ring on one tanned, strong hand, and the sight of such a large emerald was incongruous. His eyes were weary, his chin was stubbled with new beard, and his mouth was grim. He looked nothing like the Dark Man, the lord of the forest, and yet everything like the Dark Man of her heart. It took an effort to summon her anger, but then she remembered his slighting words, and she hardened herself.

"How did you find me?" he asked again. "Don't tell me you guessed, I won't believe you."

"I doubt you'll believe the truth either," she said shortly. "They told me."

"And who are they? Am I supposed to guess?" He was beyond grim, he was positively cranky, like a willful boy deprived of sleep. Which, in truth, she supposed he was.

"The ghosts," she replied finally. "Who else could it be?"

He stared at her blankly. "That's not possible."

"You don't believe in them? I thought you warned me about them." He was still holding on to her arm, and she told herself she ought to break free again, but she made no move to do so. In truth, she liked the feel of his hand on her. It was annoying, restricting, and yet deliciously unsettling. As long as he touched her she felt connected to him by more than flesh, and it was both tempting and unnerving.

He was staring down at her, as if trying to read the truth in her face. "You told me you didn't believe in ghosts," he said finally. His thumb was absently stroking the soft flesh of her arm, and the faint, unconscious movement was sending waves of complicated sensations through her body. She still didn't pull away from him. She couldn't.

"Brother Septimus and Brother Paul changed my mind," she said evenly.

He shook his head in shock. "They don't show themselves to anyone else," he said. "How could you have seen them?"

"And talked to them," she reminded him. "They were lurking in your tower. Maybe if you invited more people to visit, they'd reveal themselves more often.

They probably talk to you because they haven't got any-thing better to do with their time.''

"Why were you in the tower?"

"Looking for you, of course. I thought Jane had been kidnapped. I'm still not convinced she's safe, and the longer we stand here arguing, the worse things could become.''

He still didn't move, shaking his head slightly. "They spoke to you," he repeated in a tone of disbelief.

"Obviously your ghosts don't consider me a plain little nobody," she said, remembered outrage helping her to drag her arm free from his grip. "I'm not going to stand around and argue with you. Go find your blasted ghosts and ask them yourself. I'm going to find Jane."

And she took off into the morning light, secure in the knowledge that he wouldn't be far behind.

Jane dreamed he loved her. It was an old dream, a common dream, still gloriously sweet, and she tried to hold on to it as best she could, fighting the sounds that were creeping in, trying to destroy her sleep. He was there beside her, she could hear his voice, a deep, sooth-ing rumble, and she fought hard to stay in that warm, safe place, where Peter loved her and nothing bad would ever happen.

She could feel his heart beating beneath her ear, feel his arms around her, safe and warm. Her head rose and fell slightly with the rhythm of his breathing, and all around them a faint, golden glow filled the room, bath-ing them in a perfect light. She could feel his hand stroking her hair, feel the muscle and sinew of his warm body beneath hers, and she suddenly realized she wasn't dreaming. She was curled up in Peter's arms in the stable, and he was holding her.

She lifted her head slowly, reluctantly, and his eyes opened. He smiled at her, a reluctant smile that was heartbreakingly sensual. "You caught me napping, lass," he whispered. "Do you always sleep like the dead?"

He still held her against his chest, the heavy coat draped over both of them. "Yes," she said, her voice husky. "And I snore."

"I wouldn't care," he said, looking down into her eyes for a brief, heartbreaking moment. Before she could respond he nodded toward the stall. "Don't you want to meet your new foal?"

She should have torn herself out of his arms, but instead she held very still. "The baby's born?"

"A beautiful filly. She's already standing up and feeding."

"And Penelope?" She didn't dare look.

"Right as rain, lass. Didn't I promise you?"

She turned her head then. She could see them in the misty light of dawn, mother and peacefully nursing baby. Penelope lifted her head to look at Jane, as if to ask what the fuss was all about, and then she went back to nuzzling her foal like the tender mother Jane had known she would be.

Peter had loosened his grip on her, so that she could move any time she wanted to, but he hadn't dropped his arms. It was just past dawn, and she didn't care. She was too happy to care about anything.

She leaned back against him, letting her head rest against his shoulder once more, and breathed a sigh of pure, blissful relief. "I was so frightened," she said.

"I know you were. But everything's just fine. Your only problem is what to name the baby." He pulled the coat up around her shoulders, reaching across her in something that was almost an embrace. Almost.

"I hadn't even thought. I was so certain she was going to die, and the foal with her, and I'd be alone . . ."

"Even if she died you wouldn't be alone, Janey," he said slowly.

She couldn't see his face, and she was afraid to look. His heart was beating beneath her, faster than she would have thought, and he was warm and strong and everything she'd ever wanted for as long as she could remember. "Why?" she asked in a quiet little voice she was almost afraid he heard.

But Peter could hear everything. "I'll be with you as long as you want me, lass," he said quietly, his voice deep and firm. "I'll take care of your horses and watch over you and make sure you don't come to grief. I won't let anyone harm you or make you cry."

She wanted to weep right then and there. She lifted her head to look at him, her face wry. "You're telling me you'll be my servant, Peter?"

"For as long as you want me," he said, an almost imperceptible shadow in his eyes.

He had no earthly notion of how much she wanted him, how much she loved him, and she wasn't about to tell him. The shame of it would drive him away, and she couldn't bear to lose him.

Instead she managed a wobbly smile. "Then that's forever, Peter."

For a moment she saw something else in his eyes. For a brief, heart-stopping moment she thought she saw everything she'd ever wanted, and he moved his head, his mouth coming closer, and he was going to kiss her, he was finally going to kiss her, and nothing else mattered but his lips, his mouth . . .

"Didn't I tell you?" Gabriel drawled. "Safe and sound in the stables. You scared the wits out of Lizzie, Jane."

Jane fell back, a minute too late, staring up at her

brother with unshed tears in her eyes as Peter scrambled to his feet, backing away from her as if she had the plague.

She sat absolutely still in her little nest in the straw, Peter's coat falling from her shoulders. "I'm just fine," she said in a bright, false voice. "Absolutely splendid." And she burst into tears, leaving her brother to stare at her in astonishment.

CHAPTER NINETEEN

Francis picked his way carefully around the sleeping, entwined bodies. It did his cold, nasty little heart good to see such profligacy—it brought a smile to his lips as nothing else could. Delilah was somewhere beneath a pile of bodies—he could only hope she wouldn't suffocate.

There were various ensembles in most of the bedrooms, but Francis was secure in the knowledge that no inhabitant of Arundel spent the night unsullied. Except, of course, for Gabriel Durham.

The more Francis saw of him, the stronger his obsession grew. If he had any interest in leading a comfortable life, he would have done his best to rid himself of it, but since he usually enjoyed the darker emotions, he was happy to indulge himself. He suspected that Gabriel was not going to succumb easily to his stratagems. He was far too clever and far too observant. He could see through Francis's clever attempts with no effort whatsoever. Clearly he was an adversary worthy of his mettle. Strong, handsome, possibly as brilliant as Francis himself. *Such a delicious waste of man,* he thought.

Gabriel did, however, have a weakness, a fact which gave Francis hope. Not his ungainly sister—Francis had once possessed a sister far more attractive than Jane Durham, and while he'd felt a token of affection for her, he'd barely noticed her youthful passing in childbirth. Were she still alive today, he wouldn't have hesitated in using her to his best advantage. Pretty women could be excellent bargaining chips.

Tall, ugly women were essentially useless, and he expected that Gabriel would have simply shrugged off any threat to his sister's well-being, despite his claims to the contrary.

No, Jane Durham was of no earthly use to him. But little Miss Penshurst more than compensated.

People were such odd creatures. He never could understand the human heart, and had always been most sincerely grateful that he seemed to be blessedly devoid of one. Why someone of Gabriel Durham's impressive talents and physical beauty would be interested in an ordinary girl like Elizabeth Penshurst baffled him. She had absolutely voluptuous hair, and a nice willful streak that she was obviously trying to quiet, but she dressed badly—an unconscionable sin to Francis's way of thinking—and seemed actually to belong in the country. Normally he had no use for bucolic creatures, but he had a use for this particular one.

She was a virgin, he had no doubt whatsoever about that. There was something about her eyes, about the way she moved, that told him she'd never been initiated in the art of Eros. He was half-tempted himself—it was a rare woman who inspired him, but Elizabeth Penshurst had hidden depths. It would add particular piquancy if Gabriel could be persuaded to watch, but that was probably too much to hope for. He had more important matters that required his concentration.

She had another value, apart from her virginity. Gabriel wanted her, quite desperately. And while he might sit tamely by and let them burn his sister, he'd be unlikely to ignore any threat to Elizabeth. All it would take would be some careful handling, and Gabriel could be bent to their will quite nicely.

The second floor was quiet, their guests sleeping peacefully, but Francis didn't let that bother him. He went straight to the bedroom he sought and opened the door without knocking. He knew he wouldn't interrupt anything particularly interesting, but it wouldn't have made any difference. For the time being Arundel belonged to him, and all within it were his minions.

He walked over to the head of the bed, looking down at its occupant. He wasn't alone after all—that young girl they'd snatched from the river was curled up beside him. Delilah had told him the girl was pregnant, running away from home. An added gift for the master. There were two other young women from the village at Arundel as well, though he'd lost track of their whereabouts. Willing females of the lower classes were negligible, particularly when they'd run away from home in the first place.

"If I might have a moment of your time," Francis said softly.

The man in the bed jerked awake, sitting upright. "What do you mean by coming in here?" he demanded furiously.

"To talk."

Sir Richard Durham kicked the sleepy trollop out of his bed. "Get out," he said. The girl scuttled away, her clothes clutched to her chest, eyeing them both nervously. She was wise to be nervous, Francis thought.

"What do you want?" the old man asked.

"I rather thought you'd want to hear how the night went. Your son arrived as expected."

"He's no son of mine."

"According to the law he is," Francis pointed out smoothly. "We played cards, and I found he was rather better than I expected. I'm afraid I ended up promising to leave his sister alone."

Sir Richard held himself very still in the bed. He was a big, burly man, covered with graying hair all over his thick body. Not Francis's type, and he turned his gaze away from the old man, staring out the window into the dawning day.

"That's your call, not mine. You needed a well-bred virgin, and I offered you Jane. If you don't want her, that doesn't mean I haven't fulfilled my part of the bargain," Sir Richard said fiercely.

"Ah, my dear fellow, life is not that simple. I promised Gabriel I wouldn't touch Jane. But she's not the only well-bred virgin in your household, now is she?"

"You touch my Edwina, and I'll slit your throat," he said hoarsely.

Francis laughed. "You took care to remove her from our reach, didn't you, Richard? She's off in London with her brother and mother, safe and sound. Where do they think you are, by the way?"

"In Cornwall," Sir Richard mumbled. "I've got investments in some mines out there, and I told them I needed to inspect them."

"And they believed it. Not very clever, the members of your blood family. Not nearly as clever as your false son and daughter. What do you suppose that says about your bloodlines, hmmm?"

"Elinor's a fool," Sir Richard said flatly.

"I don't doubt it. However, since the lovely Edwina is out of our reach, we shall simply have to look elsewhere. Have you forgotten there's yet another young lady in residence at Hernewood Manor?"

"That girl? Elinor's niece or whatever? What in God's name would you want with her?"

Francis breathed a weary sigh at Sir Richard's obtuseness. Elinor wasn't the only thick one in the family. "She's a passably pretty, passably well-bred virgin."

"That'll do," Sir Richard said grudgingly.

"It will do, indeed. Particularly when you take into account that Gabriel seems uncharacteristically taken with her."

"I don't believe it," Richard scoffed. "That bastard has never cared for anyone or anything."

"He learned from a master," Francis murmured. "But I'm afraid he has the most peculiar weakness for Miss Penshurst, which we can use to our advantage. He'll be so busy worrying about her, that he won't notice when his sister disappears."

"I thought you promised not to take Jane."

"Whatever made you think I would keep my promises?" Francis asked with mock astonishment. "Once we have the girl secured it should be a simple enough matter to entice Jane here as well. I'm expecting it to be quite a merry blaze."

"You'll kill them both?" Sir Richard was looking slightly queasy at the notion.

"The greater the gift, the greater good will come to us," Francis intoned. "Surely you don't object?"

"No," Sir Richard said after a moment. "I don't object."

Francis smiled. "In the meantime, I think you ought to make yourself scarce. Cornwall should be quite lovely this time of year. Go enjoy yourself, and by the time you return you'll be minus one daughter and one annoying houseguest."

"And one son," he added eagerly. "You promised."

"Gabriel will be gone as well, in flame and smoke, with nothing left behind but ashes and your assured good fortune. The gods will smile on you, Richard. Haven't I promised you'll be rewarded?"

Sir Richard had at least enough brains to look dubious. "So you say," he muttered. "I'll leave at first light."

"It is first light. Begone, Richard."

"What about the girl? She saw me . . ."

"She saw a great deal of you, quite obviously. Don't worry. There's more than enough room in the cage for a pregnant woman."

A faint shadow crossed Sir Richard's thick face, then vanished. "I'll be off, then."

"Do," Francis said sweetly.

His house was a shambles. Gabriel knew that it would be, but something made him skirt the forest and head back to the house. He needed time to think, and he wasn't in the mood to deal with ghosts popping up for a bit of conversation.

He still couldn't get over the notion that the monks had actually appeared to Lizzie. More than that, they'd spoken to her, told her where to find him. In fact, they'd sent her into the lion's den, and when he'd had enough sleep he'd tell them so in no uncertain terms.

Not that he expected to accomplish much by yelling at ghosts. During the past few months he'd often wondered whether they were simply a figment of his imagination. The stories about them had filled Hernewood

Forest for hundreds of years, and yet no one could report a reliable encounter with them.

But if they were an illusion, then they were clearly a shared illusion, and that was just as unsettling a notion. Why would the ghosts allow Lizzie to see them? Or, conversely, why would Lizzie imagine the same phantoms he did? And how would she know their names?

He was too bone-weary to worry about it now, he only knew he didn't want to go back to the tower and have to wonder whether Brother Septimus was looming over him, a disapproving expression on his transparent face. He was too tired to make sense of anything at the moment, including the knowledge that they'd come into the stables at exactly the wrong instant.

He took his time following the paths to Rosecliff Hall. The woods were deep and still around him, the animals still hiding from the threat of ritual slaughter. The more he thought about Francis Chilton's twisted variation of Druidry, the more disturbed he became. Very little of what he'd seen or sensed had anything to do with the Old Religion, but more in common with devil worship. There was no bloodthirsty Celtic god who demanded the slaughter of countless animals. As far as Gabriel was concerned, there was no being, of this world or the next, who demanded such things. But Francis clearly had found a deity who required blood, and he was embracing his newfound religion with sickening enthusiasm.

At least there was a chance he'd secured Jane's safety. Francis was, despite everything else, a gentleman. He would be unlikely to renege on gaming debts, any more than he'd cheat at cards. Gabriel could only be glad he wasn't similarly fettered by convention. He had the unfashionable belief that right was more important than gaming debts, and he had no qualms about acting on that belief.

He could hear the noise of the workmen as he approached Rosecliff—hammers, saws, voices shouting to each other. It was a blessedly normal setting, and as he passed the workmen they greeted him with the combination of deference and camaraderie he'd come to expect. That was one small blessing to all this. Despite his known interests in the Old Religion, so far no one ever suspected him of having anything to do with the slaughtered animals, the missing girls. No one, that is, with the possible exception of Lizzie Penshurst.

She'd like to believe the worst of him, and he was just as likely to encourage it. If she thought him a bloodthirsty demon and a lecher, then she'd keep her distance, which would make the temptation easier to resist.

Of course, he was a lecher, particularly where she was concerned. And he still hadn't quite decided why he should resist temptation in the first place. Apart from a long-held belief in not seducing well-bred virgins, of course, and the certain knowledge that if the Chiltons realized he was at all enamored of her, it could prove dangerous.

But Francis already knew. And enamored was one hell of a word, perilously close to love, when Gabriel had no intention of loving anyone.

The huge front hall smelled of sawdust and fresh pine. The broken leaded glass had been replaced, letting in the early-morning light, and sun motes and dust danced like faeries in the shaft of sun. *Faeries,* he thought in disgust. *First ghosts, then faeries. What else will I be seeing?*

It was a huge, rambling old place, far older, far grander than the tidy, soulless house that was Hernewood Manor. The workmen were busy in the east wing, repairing the holes in the roof, replacing rotten beams and missing windows, but the west wing was empty. He moved along the endless corridors, stopping by a window to look out over Hernewood Forest. He could see the spires of the ruined abbey just beyond the trees, but the manor was hidden. If he put his mind to it he might be able to forget it was there, forget the past and the present.

The future was in this rambling disaster of a house. He pushed open the gnarled oak door that led to the bedroom he'd chosen. It wasn't the largest or the grandest in the house, but he didn't care. It looked out over the forest, and some of the trees had grown so near that he could open the windows and touch them. The bed was a huge medieval piece, large enough for a family, and the fireplace could roast an ox. It was still, oddly enough, a friendly room, unlike the place where he'd spent his lonely childhood. Someone had made the room habitable for him—there were fresh hangings on the bed and a plump new mattress, and there wasn't a cobweb to be seen. He moved over to the window, pushing it open to let in the early-morning air. The rosebushes were growing up the side of the building, surrounding the casement windows, and he could see buds. In a week or so there would be fresh roses blooming at the windows.

He looked back at the bed and closed his eyes, cursing beneath his breath. No matter how much he tried to deny it, Lizzie was there, haunting him. He could see her, laughing, reaching out to touch the roses that would come. He could see her, small and trusting in that huge bed, waiting for him.

Except, of course, that she didn't trust him, not for one moment. And he had never heard her laugh.

He knew that she did. He knew she had a rich, beautiful laugh, full of delight and joy in the world. She would laugh in the woods, he knew it. But she wouldn't laugh for him.

He pushed away from the window, leaving it open to the fresh spring air. It was the end of April, tomorrow the May Day celebration would take over the county. Beltane, with its fires and its fertility. And he knew, to his regret, how Francis Chilton planned to celebrate it.

"Someone told me you were here." Peter was standing in the door, a remote expression on his face.

"I thought it was time to check up on the progress. It's coming along quite nicely, don't you think?" he asked idly.

"It's more than fit for human habitation. I've got a household staff lined up, ready to come in whenever you're ready."

"Ready to live a squire's life?" Gabriel said with an ironic smile. "I can't imagine it."

"This entire wing is in good shape, and the east wing's coming along as well. The water damage wasn't as bad as was first feared."

"You relieve me. Get to the point, Peter."

Peter glared at him. "There's room for guests in this place. Namely your sister."

"My sister comes equipped with a horse, a foal, and a most inconvenient second cousin," Gabriel pointed out. "Why should they come here?"

"Because they need looking after, and I . . . I have other things to do."

"Do you, now? You've developed a sudden distaste for my sister's company?"

"I haven't paid proper attention to the farm, and you've certainly let this place fall to wrack and ruin. I can't be running over to the manor at the drop of a hat."

"Afraid she'll seduce you, old friend? Jane's a wicked

temptress, but I would have thought you'd be strong enough to resist her siren's wiles."

"Damn you, Gabriel," he said fiercely. "Everything's a joke to you. I have no intention of destroying your sister's life."

"Even though I suspect she very much wants you to destroy it? I know, I know, we've had this argument countless times. I'm only sorry we chose that moment to barge into the stables. To my innocent eye it looked as if things were about to progress quite nicely."

"I can't have her, Gabriel," Peter said wearily. "That's the damnable truth of it. I want her and I can't have her. I know you can't imagine such a thing—you've never cared about anyone or anything that you couldn't get with a snap of a finger. But there are rules in society that I won't ask her to break. I won't ask her to accept being ostracized by society, and I can't live without her. You have no idea what that's like."

"Haven't I?" Gabriel murmured, gazing out the open window into the spring morning. "You don't know me as well as you thought, old friend. Which suggests you don't know Jane all that well either. She's a romantic fool, and I suspect she adores you. She'd consider the world well lost for love."

"No."

Gabriel shrugged. "Very well, then you and I will resist temptation together. But bringing them into the house will hardly make things easier. Why don't we send some of this excellent staff you've acquired over to the manor house? They can make life more comfortable for them, and we won't have to worry."

"I thought of that. They won't go. Sir Richard's made too many enemies," Peter said flatly. "The only way to protect them is to bring them here."

"Protect them from what? I'm not certain it's any

safer here than anyplace else. And how will you like having Jane so close, day and night?"

"I'll survive. Knowing I can look out for her."

Gabriel shook his head. "I think we're asking for trouble, my friend."

"I want them safe," Peter said stubbornly.

Gabriel considered it for a long, careful moment. Bringing Jane into his house was an excellent way to ensure she'd find her way into Peter's bed, and if that happened, honor assured that Peter would marry her and the problems would be resolved. Jane would be deliriously happy at Peter's home farm, raising children and horses, if only Peter's conscience could be assuaged.

Lizzie was a different matter, but he was a philosophical man. With luck she'd simply decide to head back to Dorset, and he could forget about her. Couldn't he? Quite easily, he supposed.

"So be it," he said in a careless voice. And he turned back to the window, his eyes on his lonely tower, feeling his safe, solitary life spiral out of control.

CHAPTER TWENTY

"I'm not going anywhere," Lizzie said flatly. "Certainly not into his den of iniquity. I think it would be much better if I simply returned to Dorset."

"A most excellent idea," Gabriel said promptly, looking extremely bored. "I'll make arrangements. Perhaps Jane could accompany you, then continue on to London. It's been years since you've left Yorkshire, Jane, and it would do you a world of good."

"No," Jane said. "I'm not leaving here, and neither is Lizzie."

"I could have Peter accompany you." He tossed it off casually, a subtle bribe, but it didn't work. The two women sat in the chilly front parlor of Hernewood Manor, looking at him as if he were the Antichrist, and neither of them seemed the slightest bit inclined to do his bidding.

"Peter would have something to say about that, I'm sure," Jane replied, unmoved. "I doubt he would want to leave his farm, and he has as little use for London as I do. And I'm not leaving Penelope and her new filly, so you needn't bother arguing.''

''All right,'' he said, never expecting to triumph in this particular battle. ''We'll bring the horses over to Rosecliff. The stables are in good condition, and the farm's nearer by, so Peter can keep a watch on them.''

Jane was wavering, thank heavens. ''I still don't see why we can't stay here.''

He wasn't about to tell her just how dangerous it was, cheek by jowl with the Chiltons' lively doings. She had enough to worry about.

''This place is far too remote for two young women to be staying here without any staff or any sort of protection.''

''You could move in here,'' Jane suggested.

''No!'' Lizzie and Gabriel protested in unison.

''Then I'll have to insist you come to Rosecliff until Durham returns. Last night was an example of what could happen. Lizzie went haring off, in a panic because she couldn't find you, and we're only lucky she didn't run into any worse trouble than she did.''

Jane turned an inquisitive look at Lizzie. ''You didn't tell me you ran into trouble. What happened?''

Lizzie glared at him, a faint flush staining her cheekbones. ''Absolutely nothing. I went to the Chiltons in search of your brother, found him, and brought him back.''

''You went to Arundel? In the middle of the night? Lizzie, you must be mad!''

''I was worried about you.'' Her voice was defensive.

''And therein lies the problem. With no servants, no one to rely on but each other, the situation is dangerous indeed. The obvious answer is for you to come to Rosecliff and Lizzie to return home to the bosom of her loving family." He kept his face averted. He had no idea what his condescending dismissal of her might do, but he wasn't willing to take any chances. She had already heard him refer to her as a plain little nobody, and she'd believed him quite handily. She should take this latest act in stride.

"I fail to see why we should come to your tumbledown house while you stay in the woods," Jane said stubbornly. "How would that improve our situation?"

"I've moved into the house. And it's not tumbledown. It may need a bit of repair, but it's far more comfortable than this miserable place."

"I'm not going anywhere without Lizzie," Jane said stubbornly. Gabriel was just about to tear his hair with frustration when she turned to her cousin. "Please come with me, Lizzie. I don't think I could bear it if you weren't there. I need you."

They were magic words, Gabriel realized. Lizzie's stubborn, delicious mouth softened, and her gorgeous green eyes grew troubled. "But Jane . . ."

"I need you," she said again, his wicked sister sealing the trap. Gabriel knew a moment's fraternal pride. Docile Jane was more capable of getting her own way than he would have thought.

"For a day or two," Lizzie said finally. "Just until we can make arrangements to get me back to Dorset. The mail coach comes through tomorrow, and . . ."

"That's the first of May. People take that holiday seriously around here—I doubt the coach will be running," Gabriel said, inwardly cursing the timing. "I'll send you back in one of my carriages."

She looked at him in astonishment. "You have carriages?"

"And horses to pull them," he said irritably. "What did you think?"

"I thought you were the Dark Man," she said flatly.

He was silenced only for a moment. "And so I am. But there are horses and at least one carriage capable of taking you back to Dorset whenever you're ready to go." He was sounding almost too eager, a mistake, and he knew it. He wanted her gone, quite desperately. Out of harm's way. Out of his reach.

And Lizzie knew it. She smiled with deceptive sweetness. "I'm certain I'll be more than happy at Rosecliff," she said. "There's no hurry in getting me back to Dorset."

"Bless you, Lizzie," Jane said with a bright smile.

Curse you, Lizzie, Gabriel thought, keeping his expression suitably bored. He'd have to find some other way to get rid of her. It was already May eve, and apart from locking her in the cellars, he couldn't fathom a way to keep her out of the woods. Where the Chiltons could find her and lure her away to God knew what. And she called his household a den of iniquity!

"I'll be honored by your company," he murmured, keeping the irony out of his voice. He rose, sketching a polite bow, for all the world as if this were a normal social gathering and he were an ordinary gentleman. The women rose as well, polite as ever, and he paused, glancing down at Lizzie's feet. Her gown brushed the floor, and he had no idea whether she'd found anything to replace her shoes.

He'd ask her later. Once she was under his roof, and he had all the time in the world, perhaps he'd see for himself. If she wouldn't leave for Dorset on her own, he could think of one very simple way to drive her away, and he had no qualms about acting on it. Once Jane was safely ensconced in his house, Miss Elizabeth Penshurst would have no choice but to leave in a huff or risk seduction and ruination. He couldn't see her standing still for that.

"I'll send someone with a carriage," he murmured.

"Send Peter," Jane said.

"I expect Peter will want to see to the horses. Don't worry, Jane. Everything will be all right." He didn't know why he said it, but she was looking so forlorn, and he needed to keep from looking at Lizzie, glaring daggers into his back.

He was rewarded with Jane's sunny smile, and he wondered how anyone could think his tall sister plain. "I have faith, Gabriel."

He could have told her that was her problem. But he merely kissed her on her cheek, wondering what Lizzie would do if he attempted something similar with her. Probably kick him.

Lizzie sat back down in the small, uncomfortable chair by the hearth. Since they had been totally unable to keep a fire going, it seemed a foolish place to sit, but she was too distracted to do more than wonder at it. She kept her skirts down over her stockinged toes, thanking a merciful providence that Gabriel hadn't commented on her lack of shoes. He'd been looking, she knew it, and she'd done her best to keep her hem to the floor, refusing him a curious peek. He was truly a wretched human being, and if she had any sense at all, she'd leave his vicinity and Yorkshire entirely as soon as she could.

The only problem was that he seemed far too eager to have her leave, and Lizzie found she could be completely contrary. He might consider her unworthy of his attention, but that didn't mean he couldn't find her quite annoying. He wanted her gone, and the last thing she was going to do was accede to his wants. Any of them. Particularly when Jane so desperately wanted her to stay.

"You think I'm foolish, don't you?" Jane said when she returned.

Lizzie summoned a smile. "Why should I?"

"Longing for what I can't have. Such a waste of human emotion, my brother would tell me."

"And what is it you want, Jane?" Lizzie knew the answer full well—she had eyes to see and a heart to listen. But she wanted to hear Jane say it, admit to it out loud.

Jane's mouth quivered in a wry smile. "Peter," she said. "I want Peter."

The simplicity of it was breathtaking. Heartbreaking. A thousand complications popped into Lizzie's mind, and then vanished. "Then," she said, "you should have him."

Gabriel had never in his entire life made such a scatterbrained, chuckleheaded mistake, he thought hours later, immured in the half-refurbished library, the tightly closed doors unable to keep the sound of female voices from his sensitive ears. Lizzie hadn't just arrived in his torn-apart house. She had taken it over, bringing in spring flowers, throwing open the windows, tossing dusty window hangings out into the bright sunlight and setting a small army of servants to scrubbing the derelict kitchen. Jane had watched with wonder, then quickly banished herself to the stables to watch over her precious mare and foal, leaving no one to protect Gabriel from the harridan who seemed determined to ruin his life.

She was doing it on purpose, he knew it. She moved

through the house like a whirlwind, working just as hard as the servants, and he found he was too devout a coward to object. He could face almost anything but a woman bent on cleaning. He knew just how far his objections would get him, which was nowhere. He couldn't very well expect them to live in such clutter and disarray, and he was entirely unwilling to see to the housekeeping himself. He told himself if she wanted to do the work and make the arrangements, then it was her business, but he couldn't resist listening for the sound of her footsteps on the old floors, the lilt of her voice.

The servants seemed to like her as well, which surprised him. Yorkshiremen didn't take kindly to southerners, nor to strong-minded women, and Lizzie was both. Then again, there was an earthiness and an honesty about her that would appeal to the country folk. That appealed to him, no matter how much he fought it.

He knew perfectly well why she was doing it. She was determined to keep him at bay, and striding through his house like an ancient warrior goddess summoning her troops was as good a defense as any. Most men would do exactly what he was doing—cower out of sight.

What she didn't realize was that he liked strong women. What she didn't realize was that it would take a great deal to make him not want her, and taking over his household, as if she truly belonged there, was not the way to do it. It only tempted him further to believe in the possibility of something he had always refused to consider. He was made to live alone in the forest, with his books and his ghosts. He wasn't made for domesticity.

When he finally emerged from his lair the place had been transformed, and he halted, stricken in ways he couldn't even begin to understand.

The glow of candlelight was warm and welcoming,

and somewhere in the distance he could smell roasting fowl and sweet spices. The house smelled of beeswax and lemon, and though the windows had been closed against the rain that had begun to fall, a fresh breeze still lingered, and the panes of glass were spotless. He closed his eyes, and the scent of fresh flowers teased at his nostrils. He could hear voices, he could hear Lizzie, and she was laughing, as he knew she would laugh, deep and rich and full, and he wanted her with a ferocity that left him angry and shaken.

He didn't want to face her. He didn't want to see her, talk to her. Be tempted by her. He wanted nothing more than to stop thinking about her, stop caring.

He might just as well have wished he could stop breathing.

"What a wretched night," Francis murmured, glancing out into the rainswept darkness. "I almost hesitate to send you out in such weather."

Delilah set her brush down, turning to look at him. "I'm not particularly delighted to be going. Why can't Merriwether see to it?"

"You know perfectly well he's on his way back from London. We need a little assurance that all will go according to plan tomorrow. You know I'm a careful man—I dislike leaving anything to chance."

"This house is filled with people. Surely someone else could be sent?"

He picked up her slender hand and kissed her fingertips. "No one I trust as much as you, dearest. I'm certain you're more than capable of convincing the two girls to come with you. After all, what possible harm could you do? Whereas some of our friends might be a bit more . . . suspect."

Delilah pouted. "I'd be far more interested in seeking out Gabriel."

"Once we have the girls, Gabriel will follow. It's really quite simple, dearest. I wish you would remember."

Delilah made a face. She had developed a deep fondness for opium, which made her huge eyes deliciously dreamy. It had yet to leave a mark on her exquisite face, but that time would come. Eventually Francis would be forced to do something about it, but in the meantime it made her marvelously compliant.

"I'll go," she said mutinously. "But I won't like it. I don't see why it can't wait till tomorrow."

"Beltane is tomorrow, my precious. Besides, I don't trust Sir Richard, and you know I'm a stickler for details. Come, my precious, give your devoted husband a kiss and do as he asks you. I promise you shall be well rewarded."

Delilah's greedy little face lit up. "Presents?"

"Lots of presents, darling. Haven't I always taken good care of you?"

"Yes, Francis," she murmured.

"Then go, love, and bring me back two well-bred innocents."

"Yes, Francis," she said again. And she kissed him full on the mouth.

He waited until she left the room before he brought out his lavender-silk handkerchief and carefully wiped his mouth. She'd worn off a bit of the rouge. That could be overlooked; her sudden, tiresome affection was another matter.

It wouldn't be for long, however. Everyone knew that the more cherished the gift, the more valuable the reward. What better gift to Belarus than one's own sweet wife? He'd hoped to make her pregnant first, but that had failed, most likely with her complicity. But she was still lovely enough to make a suitable offering, and he could even feel a pang of regret. It would grieve him to part with any of his favored possessions, and Delilah was certainly one of his treasures.

But there would be others as well. He'd find a more fertile, docile wife, get himself an heir, and then dispense with her. Edwina Durham was vapid, pretty, and vain enough to be a perfect candidate, but he still rather fancied her for the wicker cage. Then again, it would keep Sir Richard well in line. He would willingly marry his precious daughter off to Satan himself if her husband was also an earl.

And this time, he wouldn't be far off, Francis thought with a gentle laugh. Not far off indeed.

CHAPTER TWENTY-ONE

As far as Lizzie could tell, Gabriel was nowhere within the acres and acres of tumbledown house. She looked from one end to the other, picking her way over construction debris and uneven flooring, a branch of candles held high to light her way, but she couldn't find him anywhere. Outside the rain pounded against the windows, inside everything was bright and clean and warm, no thanks to him; but Gabriel was nowhere to be found.

Jane had wisely retired to bed, the sleepless night having taken its toll, and Lizzie promised she would soon follow.

But something stopped her. She found her way into the library, the one room she hadn't dared enter during her flurry of cleaning, and curled up in a large leather chair by the fire. Waiting for him.

She wasn't precisely sure what she would say when she finally had a moment alone with him. His casual

dismissal of her the night before still wounded, his seeming eagerness to send her back to Dorset only made
things worse. If she had any sense, any pride, she would
pack her things and leave immediately, even if she had
to do so on foot.

But she couldn't. Something tied her to this place,
something strong and powerful. It wasn't simply her
infatuation with Gabriel, and she no longer denied that
that shameful state existed. It went beyond silly girlish
dreams to something deeper and stronger. She couldn't
rid herself of the notion that she somehow belonged
here. She couldn't turn her back on the woods and the
trees, the land and the people, any more than she could
let Gabriel dismiss her from his life. Even if that was
the wisest move she could possibly make.

She kicked off the riding boots which now had to
suffice for everyday footwear, and curled her feet up
under her. There was plenty of fuel in the house—the
wood scraps from the new construction and the ancient
wood that had recently been replaced kept the fires
going strong. It wasn't that cold a night, but the rain
brought a certain dampness to the air, and she shivered
anyway.

This was a huge, sprawling, impractical, ridiculous
house. It was almost like a fairy castle, lost in the middle
of an enchanted wood, and any landholder with sense
would hack away the overgrown trees and put in a neatly
landscaped park.

She would kill him if he did.

She felt like killing him anyway. The neglect of this
place was shameful, wicked. A house needed to be lived
in, looked after, cherished. She doubted if all the living
and cherishing could make a difference in the cold
stones of Hernewood Manor, which was, without a
doubt, the bleakest, dourest place she'd ever been. Per-

haps Gabriel didn't know the difference, didn't know a house could be filled with light and life. It was still no excuse to abandon this place.

He'd also missed a very fine dinner, which annoyed her no end. His own sister had demonstrated heretofore unknown culinary talents and made an apple pie with her own strong hands, and yet neither Peter nor Gabriel had bothered to show their faces to praise her. Jane was pale-faced and subdued, and Lizzie had simply gotten angrier as the hours passed.

For all she knew he could be hiding in a cupboard. She didn't care. Sooner or later he'd come back to his refuge, and she'd be waiting, ready to trap him.

Of course, he was even more likely to go back to the bedroom upstairs, but she certainly had enough sense not to lie in wait for him up there. She still couldn't quite believe that that was his room, even though Jane assured her it was. It was a strange room, all twists and turns, nooks and crannies, odd windows and peculiar corners. Far less grand than some of the other rooms, except for that massive bed that looked as if it were a thousand years old. The room hardly befitted the master of the house, and it was Lizzie's favorite place in the whole house. Another strike against him, unreasonable though it was.

The sound of the rain was soothing, beating against the stone. She hadn't realized how weary she was— she'd barely slept the night before, and then spent the greater part of the day working on Gabriel Durham's massive house. It was little wonder she was tired.

She tried to summon her earlier anger, that which had fueled her through the day, but it had vanished, lulled by the warmth of the fire and the sound of the rain. He wouldn't even make an appearance, she thought hazily. She ought to take herself to bed and deal with him in the morning.

And that's exactly what she would do, she promised herself. In just a few more moments, she would open her eyes and go upstairs. In just a few . . .

"I'm getting married."

Gabriel eyed Peter with a doubtful expression. "You are?" He glanced at the mug of hard cider, his fifth, then back at Peter's. "And what did Jane say?"

"I haven't told her."

"Don't you think you should ask her first?" Gabriel said.

"Why should I? I'm not marrying her."

Gabriel nodded. "I misunderstood. I hadn't realized you'd formed a passionate attachment elsewhere. Who's the lucky girl?"

"I haven't decided. Maybe one of the Twickham girls."

Gabriel hooted with laughter. "I don't need to worry about stopping you—your mother would never let you get away with such foolishness."

"I'm not afraid of my mother," Peter said with the great dignity of one who had had too much hard cider.

"You should be. Alice terrifies me, and always has," Gabriel said devoutly.

"She doesn't frighten Janey."

"What is that apropos of? You aren't marrying Jane, are you?"

"I wouldn't insult her by asking."

Gabriel laughed heartlessly. "You'll find out what an insult is when she hears of this plan. I think you underestimate my sister. As a matter of fact, I'm certain you do."

"It's none of your business," Peter said.

"The future happiness of my sister? It is indeed. You can't expect me to stand aside and let you muck everything up."

"What do you intend to do about it?" Peter demanded belligerently.

"What any sensible man would do. Tell your mother on you."

Peter looked torn for a moment, and Gabriel wondered if they were actually going to come to blows for the first time in several years. This time he'd have the advantage—he hadn't had nearly as much to drink as Peter had. But then, he didn't have a hopeless love to try to forget, now did he? Did he?

Peter put his head down on the table, and a moment later began emitting deep snores. Gabriel surveyed him a moment longer, then rose. He hated to leave the huge, comfortable kitchen of the home farm, but he couldn't put if off any longer. Despite the downpour, he'd have to go back sooner or later. It was late enough, past eleven, that both his sister and the meddlesome Lizzie should be long since retired, and he could go to his study and finish off the night with a glass of brandy and the devout prayer that he'd manage to get rid of his beautiful nemesis by the next morning.

He certainly didn't like the idea of sleeping under the same roof as she. He had the melancholy suspicion she'd taken the old nursery, a rambling, light-filled room that was far too close to his quarters for his comfort. If he hadn't already seen her in her night rail, he'd have a lot easier time of it. He'd seen her in even less—that thin shift had exposed the most arresting shadows on her body. He had to admit she had a lovely body. High breasts, perhaps not quite as large as he preferred, but large enough. A small waist, nicely rounded hips

and buttocks, and long legs that could cover miles of
hillsides with no difficulty. As the sky had lightened this
morning he had allowed himself the dubious treat of
watching her move through the morning mist, and that
picture had stayed in his thoughts ever since.

The rain had let up a bit when he started for the main
house. The home farm had once been a prosperous part
of the Rosecliff estate, and the tenants had kept it in
better heart than the mansion. Once Gabriel returned
to Hernewood he'd given the farm to Peter as minor
enough compensation. Peter could get more out of land
and animals than any other living soul, and the farm
would thrive under his care. It would be something to
leave his children. It would be a place fine enough
and prosperous enough to bring even a highborn wife,
though Peter was stubbornly refusing to realize it.

But Gabriel put no conditions on Peter's ownership.
It was simple remuneration for years of loyalty and
friendship. He wouldn't force the man to take his sister
as well, even if it was more than obvious that Peter was
desperately in love with her.

He should have known that life would never be simple. All he wanted was a quiet glass of brandy, a little
bit of reading, and a decent night's sleep. But when he
walked into the ramshackle study he saw Lizzie, curled
up in a huge leather chair, sound asleep.

He was about to turn on his heel and leave when
something stopped him. Some dark, wicked part of him,
rising up, tempting him. She was a fool and a half if
she thought he was harmless.

He moved across the room, slowly, silently, until he
stood over her. Her face was delicately flushed from the
firelight, and her breasts rose and fell with each sleeping
breath.

He leaned down in front of her, putting his hands

on the arms of the chair, trapping her there. He could make her run screaming back to Dorset—it would be simple and enjoyable. All he had to do was put one hand on her breast, the other beneath her skirt, and she'd wake up and slap him.

For some reason he was loath to do it. She looked so peaceful, so trusting, that some lost part of him hated to destroy that trust, even if it was the best way to keep his sanity and keep her safe. He told himself her peacefulness was deceptive—the moment she opened her eyes and started in on him he'd have no qualms at all.

But for a long, painful moment he simply looked at her and wondered why certain things could never be.

Odd, how people sensed they were being watched, even in their sleep. She opened her eyes, slowly, sleepily, looking up at him as if she somehow expected him to be there.

"What . . . ?" she began, but he didn't let her finish. He jerked her up roughly, into his arms, silencing her question with his mouth.

There was no seductive tenderness in him, and she fought, struggling against his tight embrace, but he simply trapped her arms between their bodies. She tried to jerk her face away, but he caught her chin in one strong hand, holding her mouth still for him, and he kissed her, slow and hard and deep, with insulting, deliberate precision. She didn't have the sense to try to bite him, a blessing, that. He was already half-mad with the taste and the scent and the feel of her, and if she'd bitten him he would have lost what dubious self-control he still maintained.

This was an act, he reminded himself, feeling her breasts against his chest as she fought and struggled. He was doing this to fill her with disgust, to make her run away. It didn't matter that her struggles were making his cock like iron—she'd had that effect on him anyway, whether she was rubbing up against him or screaming blue murder.

He lifted his head, looking down at her. She was breathless, her eyes were filled with angry tears, and her lips were damp, swollen from his rough mouth. She didn't deserve that, he thought. She deserved soft, loving kisses, not punishment, but she didn't deserve it from him.

"Please," she said in a strangled voice. "Don't."

He kissed her again, moving her body so that he pressed her against the wall, pinning her there. She tried to kick him, but she was barefoot, and he barely noticed. He pushed his tongue into her mouth, and she shuddered, with revulsion, he hoped, even as he grew harder and hotter and more needy. He could do this, he could survive, as long as he made her hate him.

He slid his hand between their bodies, covering her breast. The material of her dress was old, thin, and he tore it without hesitation, ripping the bodice downward. She gasped against his mouth, but he didn't care. He wanted to taste her breasts, he wanted to put his mouth between her legs, he wanted to take her every way he'd ever thought of and a hundred more.

She made a strange, choking noise, and suddenly he stopped, frozen. He put his hands on her face, pulling back to look at her. Tears were streaming down her pale skin, and he knew he'd accomplished his desire. She hated him.

All he had to do was step back, smirk, and make some lightly insulting comment. It would be so simple, and it would finish the night in fine style, complete her disgust of him and send her running back home to her father. All he had to do was move.

She looked into his eyes, frozen in time and space.

And then, to his shock, she slid her arms around his neck and kissed him, kissed him with her pale bruised mouth and her pale, bruised heart. Kissed him as he'd never deserved to be kissed. Kissed him with love.

He shoved her away from him as if she were poison. "Go back home, Lizzie," he said in a strangled voice. "There's nothing for you here."

"You're here," she said simply.

He could have her. It was that simple, that devastating. All he had to do was hold out his arms to her, and she would come to him, strip off her clothes for him, do anything he wanted. She would do it, and she would do it for love. And the very notion terrified him.

He looked at her, and out of the deep recesses of his past he summoned a cool, condescending smile. "Not interested, love," he said. And he turned and walked from the room, praying he had the strength to keep going.

He slammed out of the house, back into the night, the steady rain, and when he reached the edge of Herne-wood Forest he broke into a run, faster and faster, running as if the wild dogs of Arundel were snapping at his heels. The wild dogs that Lizzie had tamed with little more than a gentle touch and a soft word. The woods gathered around him, dark and welcoming, the smell of the rain and the tangy scent of fir trees, the oaks and the ash and the alder surrounding him. It was the home he knew, the home he trusted, the only place that was truly his. The warmth and laughter at Rosecliff was a lie, a fantasy. Beneath it all were cold, empty rooms where he'd lived all his life. He belonged in the forest, in the woods, in the rain. He belonged alone, without warmth, without love.

It was pouring rain by the time he reached the tower, but he knew the steps better than he knew himself, and he raced up them in the pitch dark with unerring skill. He didn't bother closing the door behind him once he stumbled into his lair. Locked doors wouldn't keep the ghosts out, and no one else would be fool enough to come after him. The rain had gathered force, coming down heavily, and he was soaked. He ripped off his shirt and sent it sailing, remembering the last time he'd been caught in a rainstorm, and who had sheltered here with him.

He was safe from her, he who was seldom afraid of anything. There were still a few coals in the fire, and he kicked it into life, tossing fresh wood on top of it. He didn't bother with the candles—he knew what his tower room looked like. Like a mad monk's cell, full of light and color and rich, decadent furnishings. The bed was far smaller than that monstrosity in his bedroom, covered with velvet throws and animal furs, and he threw himself down on it, cradling his head in his arms and watching the fire. He would stay there forever, stay there until he damned well pleased, and nothing, and no one would make him go home.

"What are you doing here?" It was Brother Septimus, of course, looking disapproving. He seemed to have no other expression on his ghostly face.

"I live here," Gabriel snapped.

The old monk shook his head. "Not any longer. Go home, my boy. The answer lies there."

"I'm not looking for answers, I'm looking for peace. Go away and haunt someone else. Go bother Lizzie, since you seem so fond of her," he said irritably, closing his eyes to shut out the apparition.

"She won't see us again. Not unless you foul things up even more than you have."

His eyes flew open. "Go away," he said again. "Or I'll have you exorcised."

"We're not demons, Gabriel," Brother Paul said in a plaintive voice. "And we'd like nothing more than to move on to the next realm. Unfortunately we have no idea how to accomplish such a feat."

Gabriel groaned. "Brothers, have mercy on me. I haven't slept in days, a crazy woman has taken over my house, and my sister seems doomed to a life of miserable spinsterhood. If she even makes it that far, considering what the Chiltons might be planning. Just leave me in peace for a few short hours."

"I don't approve . . ." Brother Septimus began earnestly, and Gabriel rolled over on his stomach and covered his ears, shutting out the sepulchral tenor. Everything was silent, and after a moment he opened one eyelid. No apparitions, nothing to disturb him. The rain was pelting against the sides of the tower, ensuring that he wouldn't be disturbed. He had escaped the worst temptation he had ever faced, and no one would dare follow him.

With a sigh of pure pleasure he closed his eyes again and drifted into a sweet, erotic dream.

CHAPTER TWENTY-TWO

Lizzie stood in the center of Gabriel's ramshackle library, numb with shock. Her mouth hurt. Her breasts burned. Her chest ached. And in her heart burned an anger so deep she shook with it.

Down the endless corridors she heard the door slam, and she knew he had gone out into the rain again, running away from her, running away from himself.

She'd be damned if she'd let him.

She stepped over her discarded boots. She didn't bother with any kind of coat—the rain was so heavy it would simply soak through. She followed him, barefoot, into the storm, her sheer fury guiding her.

He could be a thousand different places, but she knew exactly where he'd gone. Into the woods, back to his tower, back to his ghosts, where he could be safe from life, from caring, from her.

Not this time.

She slipped on the stone steps, smashing her face

against the wall, but she scarcely noticed it, so intent was she on getting to the top of the tower and telling Gabriel Durham exactly what she thought of him. How dare he kiss her like that? How dare he walk, no, run away from her when she offered him her heart and soul? He'd be lucky if he escaped with his life.

She would have enjoyed slamming the door open to announce her arrival, but it was already ajar. She had to make do with stomping inside and slamming it behind her. It was hard to stomp in bare feet, and the door was too heavy to slam properly.

He was lying on the bed, shirtless, watching her out of hooded eyes. She strode over to him, putting her hands on her hips. "You," she said, "are a royal bastard."

"In fact," he said, "I am."

It stopped her cold. "I beg your pardon?"

"My father was one of the king's many brothers. I'm not quite sure which one, and I don't suppose it matters. I was seen to as befits one of my heritage, dumped on Sir Richard for a good price. It's little wonder I lack some of the subtleties of kindly behavior."

She shook off her momentary surprise. "That's no excuse," she snapped. "I don't care how miserable and unloved you were, you still have no right to go around making other people feel miserable and unloved."

"Is that what I did to you?" He sat up, and she wished he hadn't. The firelight gilded his strong shoulders, gleamed in his long, damp hair. "Do you feel unloved, Lizzie?"

"You tried to rape me."

"I don't think so. If I had planned on actually raping you, nothing would have stopped me. And I suspect it wouldn't have ended up being rape."

She slapped him, the sound shocking in the night

air. The force of her blow knocked him back, but it
didn't wipe the faint smile from his face. Lizzie's hands
were shaking with rage, and she knew a moment's grati-
tude that there was nothing sharp near at hand. She
definitely would have stabbed him.

"What would you call it then?" she said icily. "Vigorous flirtation?"

"I thought it was obvious," he said wearily. "I was
trying to drive you away. You're a remarkably hard
woman to get rid of."

The words hit her with the force of a blow. She backed
away from the bed, and a chair seemed to appear behind
her. She collapsed into it, numb with too many emotions.

"Oh, God," she said softly, lost in pain as the realization washed over her.

He swung his legs over the side of the bed, staring at
her in sudden concern. "Oh, God, what?" he said.

She was too mortified to say another word. The room
was dark beyond the glow of the firelight, and she
wanted to sink back into the shadows, to simply disappear like a phantom. She lifted her head suddenly.
"Where are the ghosts?"

"Watching us," Gabriel said. "Why are you looking
like that?"

"Like what?"

"Like you just swallowed a spider."

It made her laugh, when she never wanted to laugh
again. "Maybe I did," she said hoarsely. She needed to
get up, get out of there before she disgraced herself
even more thoroughly. She'd been so stupidly wrong,
so blindly certain that he cared about her beneath his
cool, untouched exterior.

But he hadn't. Not even on the most shameful of
levels. He didn't even want her as a whore—he'd only

kissed her to disgust her. Not because he wanted to kiss her. No wonder he'd run away when she kissed him back.

"I should go," she said vaguely, trying to push herself out of the chair, but her limbs felt strangely heavy.

"What's wrong with you?" he demanded, climbing out of the bed and coming toward her. She flinched when he approached, and he halted, staring at her in consternation.

"Just give me a moment," she whispered.

He stepped back in baffled frustration, and she closed her eyes, trying to pull herself together. It wasn't the end of the world, she told herself. She'd made a complete fool of herself, but it wasn't the first time, and it doubtless wouldn't be the last. Old Peg had warned her to beware of the Dark Man, and she'd woven all sorts of unspoken romantic fantasies about him. When all Old Peg meant was beware making a bloody fool of yourself.

She heard him talking, and she jerked her head up, but he was across the room, deep in shadows, talking to nothing in a hushed, angry voice. At least, she thought it was nothing. If she sort of unfocused her eyes she could almost see the outline of two monkish figures, but she didn't want to start thinking about that again, and she deliberately blinked.

Gabriel turned back to look at her, a strange expression on his face. "I need to get you home."

She rose, pushing against the arms of the chair, suddenly determined. "I'm fine. You don't need to trouble yourself any further . . ."

She was halfway across the room when the door slammed, and she heard the sound of a bar being dropped in place.

Gabriel was nowhere near the door. His response was

immediate and blasphemous, and he raced across the room, pushing against the door and cursing wildly. He turned and looked at her, pushing his hair out of his face. "They've locked us in," he said in a grim voice.

"Who? The Chiltons and their friends? I didn't hear anyone . . ."

"Not the Chiltons. Worse."

She was about to say with automatic calm that she didn't believe in ghosts, when she remembered that she did. "But why?"

He moved away from the door, but not before giving it one last kick. "They're sick of being here."

"I can't blame them, but why lock us in? Did they want company?"

He went to stand in front of the fire, and she watched for a moment as the flickering flames cast strange golden shadows across his chest. And then she averted her gaze, deliberately.

She went instead to the door, pushing on it, but it held fast. "It won't do you any good," he said in a low voice. "They're not going to let us out until they're good and ready."

"Ask them why not."

"They're gone. I can't ask them anything. They said you were the key, and then they vanished."

She pushed her damp hair away from her face in helpless frustration. "If I have to spend any more time trapped with you, I'm going to jump out the window," she said in a deceptively calm voice.

"You wouldn't fit."

She glared at him. The truth of the matter didn't help things. The high medieval tower only had very narrow slits, not much more than arrow loops, and she doubted a child would be able to slip through. "All right," she said. "Do you know why they locked us in here? Did they happen to share that vital information before they vanished in a puff of smoke?''

"They did."

"Well, then, whatever you need to do to get us out of here, go ahead and do it," she said irritably.

He looked at her. A long, slow, considering look that she could see quite clearly through the shadows. And then he started toward her.

She backed up against the door. "No," she said flatly.

"They're a romantic pair. They think we belong together, and they're locking us in until we realize it."

"You're demented."

He shrugged, his shoulders smooth and golden in the firelight. "Not me. They're the ones who think it."

"Well, convince them of the truth. You wouldn't touch me if your life depended on it. You had to steel yourself to put your hands on me, and that was in a desperate effort to get rid of me . . . what are you laughing at?"

He was standing right in front of her, too much flesh, too much heat, and he blocked her view, there was nowhere she could look away from him. "Lizzie, Lizzie," he said, shaking his head in amused disbelief. "Is that what you really think?"

"That's what you told me . . ." Her voice disappeared in a squeak when he reached out and cupped her face, pushing her damp hair away from it. He frowned, staring down at her.

"You've hurt yourself," he said, touching her bruised cheek with infinite gentleness.

"I fell." There was no way she could escape from him—the door was at her back, and he was blocking her.

His hands were as gentle on her as they'd been rough

before. "I wish you hadn't followed me," he said in a soft voice.

"I hate you."

"No, you don't." There was soft certainty in his voice. "Why do you think I want to drive you away from here?"

"Because I'm an annoying inconvenience."

His beautiful mouth quirked up in a smile. "That, too," he said. "But first and foremost I wanted to get you safely back home. This is a dangerous place—Francis Chilton is quite mad, and there's no telling what kind of foul things he has planned. I can count on Peter to keep Jane safe, but I wanted you gone so I wouldn't have to worry about you."

"I'm not your responsibility."

"You are," he said flatly. "Whether I like it or not, you matter to me."

She didn't want to hear this. She didn't want his hands stroking her face, she didn't want him standing so close, when her knees were weak, and her brain was weak, and she wanted wicked, sinful things.

"No," she said, but he went on, inexorable.

"There's another reason I want to drive you away, an even stronger reason. Don't you want to know why?"

"No."

"Because you reach inside my soul and make me want to care. Because I could fall in love with you, and I don't believe in love. Because you've thrown everything I've wanted and everything I believe into such a mess that I don't know my arse from my head, and all I can think about is you."

She didn't move, frozen. It was everything she wanted, it was nothing at all. His thumb grazed her mouth, and she wanted to kiss him, her lips trembling with the effort to keep them still.

"You're soaked," he said, reaching up to unfasten

the buttons at her throat. "You need to get out of these wet things."

"No," she said again.

He ignored her, and she couldn't bring herself to stop him. She kept her hands by her side, unable to move.

"I'm going to make love to you," he said in a calm, detached voice. "You know that, don't you? It's been taken out of my hands. Tomorrow night is Beltane, and if you're not a virgin, you won't be any use to them. It's the least I can do," he said lightly, pushing the dress from her shoulders.

"Good of you," she whispered, "but such a sacrifice is unnecessary."

He kissed her collarbone as he exposed it, and she trembled. He kissed the base of her throat, the swell of her breasts above the thin chemise. "The ghosts won't let us out until I do," he murmured against her skin.

"Will they watch?" Her voice was strangled, as his hands unfastened her corset with a deftness no man should possess.

She could feel him smile against her skin. "They're holy men," he said. "They'll leave us to get on with things."

"I won't . . ." she said, as her gown tumbled to the floor at her wet, bare feet.

"You will," he said, and he scooped her up in his arms, holding her against the hot, sleek hide of him as he carried her across the room to the bed.

He set her down with infinite care, settling her against the furs and velvets, and for a moment she lay still, quiet, waiting. Her father's sermons echoed in her head, and Old Peg's warnings as well. The Dark Man stood over her, watching her, and he would take her soul.

And she would give it, gladly.

"Do I need to tie you to the bed?" he asked her.

"Do you want to?"

He laughed. "Not this time. Maybe later."

"Later?" He was tying his long hair back with a leather thong, for all the world as if he were a man about to get down to serious business. Which she supposed he in fact was.

He knelt on the bed, straddling her, reaching for the hem of her shift. She immediately caught it, holding it down. "Do I have to take this off?"

"Yes, you have to take it off," he mimicked her.

She bit her lip, lay back, and closed her eyes—prepared to endure.

She quivered when she felt the warm night air touch her skin. Or maybe it was the heat of his gaze, she couldn't be sure. She'd have to open her eyes to find out, and she wasn't about to do that. She was going to lie there, still and quiet, and let him do the inevitable, because there was no way out, and because she wanted him to. But that didn't mean she was going to participate.

He picked up one of her limp hands and placed it on his stomach, on his hot, smooth skin. He rubbed it across his chest, over his stomach, her fingers drinking in the sleek, smooth texture of him, and then he moved her hand down, to the rigid column of flesh beneath the soft material of his breeches.

She jerked her eyes open in outrage, trying to pull her hand away, but his grip was tighter than she realized, and a faint, triumphant smile lit his dark face as he held her there against that part of him.

"This is a two-person activity, Lizzie. You're not going to lie back and sleep through it." He moved her hand up and down against that hard flesh, and it seemed to grow even larger and harder beneath her hand. "When we're finished there won't be a part of your body I haven't touched. There won't be a part of me you won't know as well, or be afraid of. When we're finished . . ." he paused, looking down at her, his voice raw. "Hell, I don't think we'll ever be finished."

She could think of only one way to stop him, when she didn't want him to stop. Her eyes looked up into his. "I'm in love with you," she said, shocked at the words she hadn't even dared speak to herself. "If you do this, you'll never be rid of me."

"I know," he said. "I know." And he leaned forward and kissed her mouth with such tenderness that she wanted to weep.

His mouth was cool, wet against hers, a shock of teeth and lips and beard stubble. He cradled her face as he kissed her, his long fingers stroking her, holding her, as he set his mouth against hers, wooing, teasing, tasting, taking. He seemed in no hurry to do anything but kiss her, and she slid her arms around his torso as he covered her, and she kissed him back, her tongue touching his in shameless need.

He kissed her ears, he kissed her elbows, his mouth an instrument of delight and torture. When he put his head to her breasts and sucked at her she jerked in shocked pleasure, hot and wet and burning.

She cradled his head against her, threading her fingers through his long hair, pulling it free of the leather thong and letting it fall around them like a curtain of silk. She moaned in protest when his mouth left her breast, but he cupped her with his hands, his fingers deftly squeezing, and she felt a strange little shock go through her, and she cried out in surprise.

She heard him laugh, a sound of pure, masculine satisfaction, and she wondered vaguely what had pleased him so. And then he put his mouth between her legs, and she was past rational thought.

It didn't matter that what he was doing was dark, wicked, perverse. He cradled her hips with his hands and used his tongue, his mouth, his teeth on her, claiming her in ways she'd never even imagined, and she was past shame and denial in a dark forest of hot, wet need.

This time the strange shock was stronger, and she jerked against the bed, but he held her still, and he kept on, until she couldn't breathe, and the forest closed around her, and she felt her body arch off the bed in a powerful convulsion.

And then he was lying over her, between her legs, pressing against her, his flesh resting against hers, invader against fragility, heat and strength against hot, damp need. He caught her legs and pulled them around his hips, and she felt him enter her, a strange, needy, frightening sensation.

She cried out, but he covered her mouth with his, and pushed deeper, slowly, slowly, but she was so wet there was little resistance, until he stopped, holding himself perfectly still, rigid.

She could feel the tension rocketing through his body as he fought to control himself. He lifted his head, and his beautiful face was convulsed in a grimace of desperate control. And suddenly her fear vanished, and she needed him, all of him. Now.

She slid her hands around his sweat-slick waist to his flat buttocks, and arched against him. "Yes," she whispered finally. "Please."

The pain was fierce, fast, fleeting, and he filled her, pushing her hard against the mattress as he took her, and she cried out in mingled grief and joy.

He kissed her then, soft, hurried kisses of comfort and need, and after a moment she kissed him back, her mouth clinging to his, as he began to move, pulling out, then pushing deep inside the very heart of her.

She felt lost, in some sort of mindless haze of pleasure, his tongue in her mouth, his body tight in hers, rocking with a slow, deliberate rhythm that made her want to scream, want to claw and beg and weep.

He moved faster then, sensing her urgency, unable to slow himself. It was too much for her, and she wanted to beg him to stop, but no words would come, only *please* and *Gabriel* and *yes*.

He slid his hand between the bodies and touched her, hard, at the very moment he slammed in deep. "Now," he said in a tight voice, and Lizzie shattered, as he thrust deep inside her, filling her, bathing her with his hot, wet essence.

He rolled over on his back, bringing her with him, still buried deep inside her, his hands clamped to her hips, keeping her still. She had no strength to push away from him, and no desire to do so. She simply sprawled across his body and slept.

She didn't sleep long. He woke her, taking her from the back, pushing in deep until she shattered, weeping her release into the velvet throw. He made her sit astride him and take him that way, so that he could kiss her and touch her breasts while she controlled the strength and depth of his thrusts. He taught her to take him in her mouth, and she liked it. He did it all without a word, and when they were momentarily sated they slept, with her head on his stomach, his arms cradling her, her curtain of tangled hair covering them both.

CHAPTER
TWENTY-THREE

She lay curled up on top of him, smooth and sleek and utterly exhausted. He couldn't keep himself from stroking the soft skin of her back, even though he didn't want to wake her. God knows she had little enough sleep, and very few people could get by with as little as he could. Particularly when she'd spent such a physically and emotionally energetic night.

He was hard again, which frankly astonished him. He was like a seventeen-year-old boy, in a constant state of heat, and the more he had of her the more he wanted. He forced himself to let her be—she had to be sore and aching after such a night, and he'd put her through too much as it was. But he couldn't rid himself of the fear that tonight would be their only night.

It was no longer night, and hadn't been for a long while. A fitful sunlight was streaming through the narrow window slits, and he imagined it was close to midmorning. Was Jane in a panic, having discovered them missing? Or would Peter jump to the obvious conclusion and set her mind at ease.

The tower door was ajar. He didn't know when during the long night it had swung open silently on its massive hinges, and he didn't particularly care. Once he'd accepted the fact that he was going to have her, nothing could have stopped him. Nothing except Lizzie.

"Yes," she'd said in his ear. "Yes," against his lips. "Yes," when she took him in her mouth.

He stifled his instinctive groan. He wasn't going to take her again, he'd sworn to himself he'd let her have some peace, but her touch, the soft weight of her body draped across his, the even cadence of her breathing was driving him insane.

He was able to slide from underneath her without waking her. She was so exhausted she could probably sleep for days, he thought, climbing out of bed and stretching with a slow, luxurious stretch.

He realized he had a stupid, idiotic grin on his face, like some damned monkey. He tried to wipe it off, but it just stuck there. He felt ridiculous—he was half-tempted to slam his hand against the stone wall just to stop his stupid smile.

He looked back at Lizzie, sprawled gracefully in his bed, her flame red hair wrapped around her pale body. He frowned when he saw the bruise on her face, the one that had come when she'd tripped, running out into the rain after him. He felt guilty about that. But not in the slightest bit guilty about the marks on her body that he'd left during their endless night. Any more than she should feel guilty about the bite mark in his shoulder that she'd inflicted without knowing.

He had to stop thinking about it. About her. He moved to the window. The rain had stopped, but the sky was gloomy and overcast, an ugly, sullen day for the first of May. He could always pray for rain. A steady downpour would ruin Francis's little celebration quite nicely.

But he couldn't count on that. He needed to find Peter, to make sure he kept Jane safe. He'd been muttering something extremely stupid about marrying one of the Twickham girls, but this morning should have brought common sense along with a blinding headache.

Lizzie would be fine right where she was, and she probably wouldn't awaken for hours. He had time to make sure Jane was protected, and then get back to her. He wasn't certain what he could do about Francis's bizarre plans, but he could deal with that later. There'd be no fires until night—he had time to come up with a way to stop Francis if he needed stopping.

There were no signs of the ghostly matchmakers when he stepped outside the tower. From a distance he could hear the faint sound of birds, and he felt suddenly hopeful. It had been too long since he'd heard the sounds of animals in these woods. Francis and his little tricks had frightened them into hiding.

But some of them were becoming brave enough to emerge. It was a good sign.

Jane walked slowly along the road, her head down, her shawl wrapped tightly around her tall body. She heard the carriage in the distance, and for a moment she considered diving into the underbrush, hiding while whoever it was drove past. She couldn't bear to face one more person on the darkest day of her life.

Odd, May Day was supposed to be bright and sunny, full of the joy of spring and new life. Today her life, or at least any hope of happiness, had officially ended.

She glanced over her shoulder on the off chance that she could still manage to hide. She didn't recognize the carriage—it was a large, closed one, without any identifying crest or pattern. She had no idea whether the coachman had spied her trudging up the narrow road or not, and she didn't care. Without hesitation she slipped into the woods, sliding down a shallow embankment and ending up against a stand of saplings. It was dark and quiet there, blessedly peaceful, and no one would see as she wept.

It hadn't begun that awfully. She'd woken up early, and immediately gone to the stables to see Penelope and her foal, both of them looking strong and healthy. She cursed herself for the slight pang it gave her, watching the mare's maternal love. Jane had wanted babies of her own for so long it had almost ceased to hurt. But she didn't want just any babies. She wanted Peter's.

"You shouldn't be here, Miss," he'd said, coming up out of nowhere. She turned with a welcoming smile on her face, one that quickly died once she looked at him. He looked sick, pale and sweating, and angry.

"Are you all right, Peter? You look ill."

"I'm fine, Miss. Don't trouble yourself about the likes of me," he said, and his Yorkshire accent was very broad, surprisingly so. "I'll take care of the horses, you take care of yourself. You should be getting back to the house, now."

"But, Peter . . ."

"You're to wish me happy," he said abruptly, in that strange, angry voice. "I'm to be married."

And just that simply her life had ended. "M . . . married?" she'd stammered.

"Aye. Time for me to start a family. I've got the home farm to think of, and me mum's not getting any younger. I have to think of meself, you know. I won't be coming back to Hernewood Manor once your father comes home. You'll have to find someone to replace me."

"I . . . I don't understand," she said dizzily.

"What's to understand, Miss? Servants leave their masters all the time. They get married and raise families. It's no concern of yours." He turned his back to her, fiddling the bucket of feed he'd brought with him.

"Obviously not," she said in a hollow voice. "Well, I wish you all the best, Peter. When's the happy day?"

"I'll let you know, Miss." His voice was muffled. "It'll only be family and the people from the village, none of the gentry. I'm sure you'd understand that well enough. Classes just don't mix properly."

"No," she said, numb and dead inside, "I suppose they don't."

She'd managed to keep her calm when she walked from the stable into the gray morning air. He hadn't told her who he was marrying, maybe he'd simply made it up for some bizarre reason of his own. And then she'd seen the stout, cheerful form of his mother, Alice.

She'd looked up, suddenly hopeful, and Alice's face had crumpled. "Ah, lass," she said, and put her arms around Jane, pressing her head to her ample bosom.

She'd cried then. In the middle of the farmyard, with servants all about and Peter not that far away, she cried in Alice Brownington's arms, as Alice stroked her head and murmured, "There, there, lass," and other words of meaningless comfort. And when Jane's tears finally slowed, and she lifted her face, Alice simply shook her head sadly. "I only wish it could be different, love."

She'd never known she possessed such dignity. She'd managed a wry smile, despite her red and swollen eyes. "So do I, Alice," she whispered. And then she took off, running down the road, away from watching eyes and pitying looks, until she wound up where she was now, hiding.

The carriage stopped, and she cursed beneath her breath, a word she'd learned from Peter, long ago, when they'd been children together and life had been so simple. It had Peter, Jane, and Gabriel against the world. Now it was Peter against Jane, and the world had won.

She heard the carriage door open, and she froze, hoping she'd blend with the woods around her. She should have known it would be too much to hope for, given the wretchedness of her day so far. And she should have known it would be the last person she wanted to see.

"Miss Durham?" Delilah Chilton's light, piercing voice floated down to her. "Oh, Jane, dear. I know it's you. I can see you quite clearly. Come up, do."

So much for blending with my surroundings, Jane thought miserably. She lifted her head. "Hullo, Lady Chilton," she called out in a muffled reply. "I'm afraid I'm rather busy right now. I promised my . . . my brother's cook that I'd find some herbs. This is the only place they grow, and they're most useful . . ."

"Don't be ridiculous, Jane," Delilah snapped. "You don't know anything about herbs. Besides, I've been looking for you. It's important."

Something in Delilah's tone of voice broke through her misery, and she scrambled to her feet, peering up through the foliage. "Has something happened?" she demanded urgently. "Is Lizzie all right? I haven't seen her all morning, and I didn't stop to think . . ."

"She's perfectly fine," Delilah said smoothly. "She simply lost her way when she was out for a walk, and ended up at Arundel. I persuaded her to stay for lunch, and promised I'd bring you back to join us."

"She lost her way? That doesn't sound like Lizzie," Jane said, climbing back up the embankment. Delilah took in her twig-strewn clothing, her swollen face, but simply gave her a deceptively sweet smile.

"Well, she's a newcomer to this area, she can't be expected to know where one person's lands end and another's begin. Come along, dear. I think she's a bit anxious, being surrounded by so many gentlemen. You would provide a great comfort."

The door to the huge black carriage stood open, waiting. Two of Lady Chilton's servants stood by, large, hulking men dressed in funereal black as well. They looked entirely capable of forcing her into the carriage if she didn't choose to go willingly.

Once that thought entered her mind she couldn't dismiss it. Jane took one step forward, then suddenly whirled around, diving back toward the bushes.

She hadn't realized how anyone so large could be so quick on his feet. In less than a minute she was bundled into the carriage, her ankles and wrists tied with stout rope, a dry, dusty cloth silencing her screams. They dumped her on the floor of the carriage, and then Lady Chilton climbed in, stepping around her quite delicately as the door closed behind her, plunging the carriage into an eerie, unnatural gloom. There were dark covers on the window, shutting out the light, and no one had lit the tiny lamps.

"Don't worry, Jane," Delilah's soft, sweet voice murmured. "If your dear friend Lizzie isn't at Arundel yet, she will be soon. You can keep each other company until your sister arrives." Delilah leaned closer, and her oversweet, musky perfume washed over Jane. "No need to be frightened, darling. You're just being invited to participate in our May Day celebrations, which I'm certain you'll enjoy enormously. Such a nice, well-bred, pure young creature like you."

Jane kicked out with her legs, connecting with Lady Chilton's long silken skirts. Delilah let out a little shriek of pain, then laughed. "I'll pay you back for that, my girl. You can count on it."

The ride in the dark seemed endless. Jane could scarcely breathe around the smothering gag, and every now and then Delilah would give her a little kick with her pointy-toed shoes, which she'd follow with an eerie trill of laughter. By the time the carriage finally came to a halt Jane was ready to scream.

They hauled her out like a sack of potatoes and tossed her over someone's burly shoulder. The world swung crazily about her as they carried her into the house, and she saw a crowd of people, mostly men, who seemed to be watching the proceedings with unholy amusement.

"Ah, you've brought her," Francis Chilton's light, affected voice greeted her. "Set her down, Joseph, and let me take a look at her. Maybe she's more presentable than I thought."

She felt herself put on her feet, but her ankles were tied too closely together, and she toppled over onto the floor, unable to break her fall. The room shook with thunderous laughter, and she glared up mutely.

"What say you, Merriwether?" Francis murmured.

"She's not as pretty as your little prize, is she? Still, she's a virgin, how could she not be, and as well-born as her sister."

She didn't recognize the beefy man who stepped forward and peered down into her face. "Is this the other daughter? Durhams?" he demanded.

"Of course," Francis said smoothly. "I thought you realized we were going for both. Two well-bred innocents are better than one, and if things work out according to plan, we might even have three."

Merriwether stepped back. "I don't know whether she's innocent or not, and I don't care," he said. "But she ain't well-bred."

"Don't be ridiculous," Francis said, affronted. "You mean that old story about Gabriel and his sister? I'm fully aware that the Durhams are not their real parents. There's royalty in their blood, which makes it even better."

"In Gabriel's blood, not this one. They've got the same mother. I should know, because I bedded her some years past, and she was a corker, even in her fifties. She's dead now, of course, but she was a talkative one. Gabriel's father was one of the royal dukes. But this one was sired by a stable lad."

"A stable lad?" Francis said, horrified.

"She's no better born than half the servants around here," he said flatly.

Jane didn't move. If she hadn't been bound and gagged she would have leapt up and thrown her arms around the disgusting gentleman who'd once tupped her mother. She was deliciously, gloriously lower class, and if she survived the next few days, she planned to celebrate her fall from grace in no uncertain terms.

Francis shrugged. "So we burn a baseborn virgin as well. I doubt the gods will mind."

"Seems an awful waste with the other one," Merriwether said. "Don't you think we might have a go at her? I mean, once she's burned up, how is anyone to know whether she still had her maidenhead or not?"

"Don't be crass," Francis said with a sniff. "When you bring a gift to Belarus you cannot soil it first. Really, how often must I explain how these things are done?"

"How do you know how these things are done?" Merriwether said in a cross voice. "What made you such an expert and all?"

"I learned from Gabriel," he said in a silky voice.

"Ah," said Merriwether, accepting it. "And will he be here for the Beltane fire?"

"Oh, he'll be here," Francis said in a soft, purring voice. "You can trust me on that."

They locked her in a small, dark room in an outbuilding near a kennel of growling dogs. "Don't try to escape, love," one man said as he untied the ropes around her ankles. "Them dogs would just love a tasty handful like you."

She didn't make the mistake of kicking at them. She sat on the narrow bed, still and silent, biding her time. "Someone will bring you something to eat," the man called Merriwether said. "And maybe we'll have a little surprise for you. A nice visitor to cheer your spirits."

"My brother will come looking for me," she said with icy calm.

"Your brother doesn't give a damn about anybody, and never has. Didn't you hear Francis—he taught him everything he knows. Cheer up, though, Miss Durham. I'll see if we can't do something to make sure it won't hurt."

"What won't hurt?"

"Why, the fires. The fires of Beltane. We're Druids,

and we burn our sacrifices in the fires of Beltane. And you're one of the chosen ones."

She didn't scream. She didn't say a word, she just sat there, numb, as the door closed behind them.

She was still sitting there, an endless time later, when someone unlocked the door and stepped inside. It was Maudie Possett, a tray of food resting on her slightly swelling belly, looking both wary and smug.

"Maudie!" Jane breathed. "Everyone's been so worried about you! No one had any idea you were here. You've got to get away from here. You've got to help me . . ."

"I don't 'got to do' anything," she said, setting the tray down on the edge of the bed. "I like it here just fine. They treats us nice here, me and Josie and Mary. They're real sweet, except for that old bastard." She laughed nervously. "But then, you'd know all about that, wouldn't you? Mean old man, he is."

"Who is?"

But Maudie wasn't going to answer any questions. "Eat your food and be quick about it. I haven't got all day. There's a gentleman waiting for me, and I do mean a real gentleman. Treats me nice, he does. Says he'll give me money for me baby."

Jane shuddered in horror. "Maudie, these people are evil."

Maudie grimaced. "And what would you know about evil, Miss? You who've always had a full belly and a roof over your head?"

"I know evil when I see it," she said in a low voice. "And it's all around us."

Maudie shrugged. "Suit yourself. I've got things to do. I'll be back for the tray. Don't you get any ideas, now. There's no way out. The dogs run loose, and I wouldn't want to come up against them. They're mean, and they starve 'em. They'd tear you apart as soon as look at you."

"I won't be going anywhere." It was a lie. That was the second time she'd been warned about the dogs. If they were that dangerous, they wouldn't have bothered to tell her, they would have simply let her find out for herself.

Maudie slammed the door behind her, locking it securely. Jane looked at the tray of food, feeling her stomach revolt at the very thought of eating. She forced herself to pick up the piece of stale bread—she hadn't eaten since last night, and if she was going to get out of here, she needed her strength.

Her throat was so dry she could barely manage to choke it down, but she forced herself, leaning back on the sagging iron bed and surveying her surroundings. There was only a small, horizontal window set high in the wall. The walls were thick, and there was no help to be had in this wretched place. She would simply have to hope Maudie would forget to lock the door when she came back for the tray.

The moment the idea came to her Jane thought better of it. Maudie was a silly girl, but not stupid. She wouldn't forget anything so crucial. If Jane had any sense at all, she'd hide behind the door when Maudie returned. If it came to a struggle, she didn't know who would win. Jane was taller, but Maudie was wiry and tough, having worked hard all her life. And Jane didn't know if she could bring herself to hit a pregnant woman for fear of hurting the child.

She had to try something. She heard the footsteps outside her prison, and she scampered off the bed. There was nothing she could use as a weapon but her bare hands, so she would simply have to rely on the element of surprise.

She stood poised, waiting, as the door opened inward, ready to leap.

And then stopped in shock as her beautiful, golden-haired sister Edwina walked into the room, for all the world as if she were at a garden party.

CHAPTER
TWENTY-FOUR

"Well, you've screwed this up royally, love," Francis said with acid in his voice. "Where's the other girl, then?"

Delilah shrugged, blissfully unconcerned. "Does it matter? Sooner or later Gabriel will come looking for his sister, and then we can snatch the girl."

"I'm not so certain he'll come after her at all. And I'm not willing to wait. Send Merriwether after the red-head. He did an excellent job bringing darling Edwina from London—I imagine an unprotected young lady out in the country would be child's play."

"Ask him, darling," Delilah said, admiring her reflection in the mirror. Her eyes were wide, and ever so slightly glazed. "I'm sure he'll be more than happy to help you."

Francis surveyed his exquisite wife for a long, thoughtful moment. He would miss her, he truly would. He had never known a woman quite as soulless, quite as unrepentant as she. She enchanted him with her total lack of morality, but all things had to end sooner or later. He wasn't a man to waste his time with useless regrets.

He leaned down and kissed her gently on the temple. "You look ravishing, my pet," he murmured.

Her perfect mouth curved in a small, wicked smile. "I know."

She would miss him, she truly would. Francis had been the perfect husband for her, beautiful, wealthy, and without a shred of decency. But he'd made one thing very clear: To gain the most from the ceremony, you must sacrifice the most. Slitting the throat of a pregnant serving girl could hardly be considered a worthy gift when a handsome, adoring husband stood nearby.

Besides, she'd begun to tire of married life. She was still young, still exquisitely beautiful, and she was growing weary of trailing along in Francis's wake. She wanted to go back to civilization, to London, the beautiful, grieving, extremely wealthy widow. She'd always looked good in black.

And she would mourn him, quite sincerely. But all things must come to an end, sooner or later, and it was past time for her to move on.

If Francis knew, he would understand. Why, he was more than capable of doing the same.

No, she need feel no guilt whatsoever. A generous amount of opium in his wine, a little slip, and he'd go up in flames, a simply grand offering. And the next day she'd read her future in his ashes.

She giggled softly. Coming to Yorkshire hadn't been quite as big a waste of time as she had once thought.

It was dreary, tedious, but it would provide her freedom. It was worth the months of boredom.

Lizzie opened her eyes in sudden shock. She was lying completely naked in Gabriel Durham's bed, and there wasn't an inch of her that didn't throb, ache, or itch. She was sticky, scratched, and sore, and completely horrified by the memory of what had passed between them last night.

At least, she knew she should be. Particularly since it was midafternoon and she'd been abandoned, left alone in the old tower without a word. Her torn dress was halfway across the room, her shift lay on the floor beside the bed, and the door stood open to the outside. She wondered if she'd dreamt that locked door. She wondered if she'd dreamt everything.

She crawled out of bed, too weary to do more than that, and looked down at her body. No, she hadn't dreamt it. He'd taken her maidenhead last night, he'd taken her every way he could think of and ways she couldn't even imagine. She pulled back the velvet throw and saw her blood staining the sheet.

She yanked her shift back around her, shivering in the warm air. She found her dress, doing it up as best she could, when she heard footsteps on the stairs. For a moment she knew absolute panic. She couldn't face him. She couldn't look at him after last night, the things he'd done to her, the hot, needy words he'd spoken. For a moment she considered hiding, anywhere rather than face him, but a last remnant of pride stiffened her backbone, and she stood straight and tall in the middle of the room, waiting for him.

It was no relief when an absolute stranger walked through the door. He was a burly, well-dressed man, past his first youth, with a corpulent belly and a flushed, degenerate face. He didn't seem surprised to see her.

"Are you looking for Gabriel?" she asked in a deceptively calm voice. "I imagine he's up at Rosecliff Hall . . ." The man was ignoring her. No, that wasn't strictly true. He was paying no attention to her mindless babbling, but he was watching her quite closely. He came up to her, standing too close, then looked past her to the bed. To the bloodstained sheet.

"Shit," he said. "He's had his fun, then, hasn't he?"

Lizzie didn't move, frozen in fear. It wouldn't have done her any good if she had—he was blocking her way. The man sighed. "We don't need to tell Francis you're not still virgin, now do we?"

"I don't know what you're talking about," she said in a cool voice that failed to disguise her panic. "Please leave."

"Oh, I'll leave, my little darling. And I'll be taking you with me. Virgin's blood or not, you can go in the cage with the others, and who's to know in the long run?"

"Cage?" Too late she remembered Gabriel's gruesome stories. She made a sudden, darting movement, but he caught her easily in one meaty hand. She kicked back at him, knocking over a chair, and he cursed. She tried to scream, but his arm swung out, and everything went black.

"Where the hell is Jane?"

Peter was studiously ignoring him, intent on the horse he was leading. "Can't say as I know, sir," he muttered in that damned, subservient voice of his. "I haven't seen Miss Jane since early this morning."

Gabriel resisted the impulse to flatten him, much as

he was tempted. He was an inch or two taller than Peter, but there was no guarantee he could still best him in a fight. And he had more important things to worry about.

"You saw Jane this morning? What time?" he demanded.

"I haven't the faintest idea, sir."

"Call me 'sir' one more time, and I won't answer for the consequences," Gabriel said in a dangerous tone of voice.

"I quake at the very thought, *sir,*" Peter said, his expression defiant and bleak. He led the horse into the ring and set him free, closing the gate behind him.

"Don't you understand, you pride-blind idiot?" Gabriel exploded. "Jane's gone missing. I can't find her anywhere in the house, no one's seen her all morning . . ."

"I saw her," Peter said in an emotionless voice. "I told her I was getting married."

"You crazy bastard. Were you still drunk?"

"For once I was showing some common sense. I don't know where Jane got the notion that there might be any future between us, but you and I both know better."

"I don't know any such thing."

"Then you're a fool," Peter said bitterly.

"I'd rather you called me a fool than 'sir,' " Gabriel said. "And I'm not interested in arguing with you right now. We have to find Jane."

"I'm not doing any such thing. You know how women are—they shed a few tears, then get on with things. Your sister may have imagined a few tender feelings for a stable lad, but given time she'll realize she's much better off this way."

"I don't know if she has time, damn you! It's May Day—Beltane for the pagans—and God only knows what the Chiltons have in mind to celebrate. I just came back to make sure Jane was safe, only to find she's disappeared."

"They wouldn't touch her," Peter said in a soft, savage voice.

"They would. If I know Francis Chilton, he'll be looking for a virgin sacrifice, and as far as I know, Jane is the only girl in the area to fit that description."

"What about her cousin?"

Gabriel didn't even blink. "I left her at the tower— she should be safe enough. For God's sake, Peter, stop worrying about your pride and concentrate on Jane. God knows what they might do to her if they get their hands on her."

Peter had frozen. "Jane's not in the house?"

"No one's seen her since she went racing off down the road this morning. I was hoping she might be off someplace with you . . ."

"I'll kill them."

"After we make sure Jane is safe," Gabriel said. "In the meantime I'll go get Lizzie and bring her back to the house where she can be guarded."

"What if Jane's gone to the tower? Wouldn't she run to her brother for comfort?"

Gabriel breathed a sigh of relief. "You're right, I never thought of that. She's probably with Lizzie right now, cursing all men. Come along."

"There's probably no need . . ."

"Come along, Peter, or I'll tell Jane just how damnably in love with her you are."

"You're crazy," Peter muttered.

He kept up that litany all the way back through the woods to the abbey ruins, cursing Gabriel and his antecedents, his taste, his education, his sexual habits, and anything else he could think of. Gabriel roundly ignored him. As long as Jane was safe, anything else could be dealt with in its own time.

Peter's quarreling came to a halt a few yards from the base of the tower. "Someone's been here," he said.

"Thank God!" Gabriel breathed. "I should have realized Jane would have come straight here . . ."

"No." Peter's voice was strange. "I'm talking about a carriage and horses. And it looks as if someone was dragged."

Gabriel had already disappeared into the shadowy tower, taking the steps three at a time. He came to a halt just inside the door as a feeling of cold, bitter fury washed over him. The place was a shambles of overturned furniture. Lizzie hadn't given up without a fight.

He didn't turn when Peter came up behind him. "They've taken her, Peter. I think they've taken them both."

"I'll kill the bastards," Peter said with devastating calm. "If they've harmed a hair on Janey's head . . ."

"We've got to find them first," Gabriel said in a calm icy voice. "Then you can kill them."

"Oh, my God, Edwina!" Jane cried, moving toward her younger sister with arms outstretched to embrace her.

Edwina immediately ducked, a discontented expression marring her lovely face. "Whatever are you doing here, Jane? And in this horrid room?"

"Edwina, we're in danger. We have to get away from here as fast as we can. Are they keeping you locked up?"

"Locked up? Of course not. That delightful Mr. Merriwether brought me down from London, and he's been everything that's charming. I wasn't certain I wanted to come back here at first, but now I'm not the slightest bit sorry I agreed to it. This is a very elegant house party, quite the first level of society, and I'm enjoying myself enormously. But I still don't know what you're doing here."

Jane looked at her silly younger sister in frustration. For not the first time she realized that they truly were no kin at all, neither in blood nor in spirit, but she still felt responsible. "Edwina," she said slowly, "understand this. These people are wicked. They mean us both harm. We have to get away. If you're not locked in, it should be very simple for you. I intend to crawl out the window the moment they leave me alone. I was afraid I couldn't fit, but the casing is loose, and I'm certain I can break it free. But I can't leave here unless I'm sure you're safe as well."

"I don't think you're supposed to leave," Edwina said stiffly. "You're an important part of some celebration they're planning tonight, and if I were you, I wouldn't be so quick to miss a chance like this. It's not often gentlemen want to spend time with you."

"Edwina, you silly little fool, they don't want to spend time with me, they want to kill me. They want to sacrifice me to their gods, and they probably want to do the same thing to you."

Edwina laughed, a lovely trill of silver-toned laughter. "You're mad as a hatter, Jane." She went back to the door and knocked on it with a peremptory fist. It opened immediately, revealing Lord Chilton, magnificent in lavender satin.

"And how is the sisterly reunion going?" he purred.

"She says you plan to sacrifice her to the gods," Edwina said brightly. "Can you imagine such a thing?"

Chilton's smile widened. "You can see why we have

her locked up here. She showed up, raving about blood sacrifice and Druids. With your family away there was nothing we could do but try to detain her. We're so glad you came to keep her company."

"If I'd known that's why Father sent for me, I wouldn't have come," Edwina said mutinously, glaring at Jane. "Why couldn't he be here himself?"

"He was needed elsewhere, my pretty. There's tea in the drawing room. Why don't you let your sister rest? It may settle her mind."

Edwina smiled up at him, her face dazzling. "That would be lovely. But you'd best be careful with Jane. She told me she's planning to escape through the window—it's not as secure as you think. We don't want a madwoman roaming the countryside."

Lord Chilton gave her an approving smile. "We don't, indeed. You go on ahead, my dear, and I'll see to your sister."

Edwina disappeared without a backward glance, leaving the two of them alone. For a moment Jane considered whether she had a chance of overpowering him. He was slight, effete, but he was also male, and there was a good chance he was stronger than she was.

And then she saw the men outside, and she held still, unwilling to give them any reason to put their hands on her again.

Francis strolled up to her, a faint smile on his pale face. "You were going to leave our hospitality so soon, Jane? We certainly can't have that." He glanced at the narrow window, then back at her. "I'm not sure we have time to put bars in place. I think we'll simply have to shackle you to the bed. It's iron—it should hold you quite securely."

"And you just happen to have shackles?"

Francis's smile was dreamy. "You'd be surprised at

how useful they can be. And how much fun." To her horror he leaned forward and kissed her full on the mouth. "Don't worry, Jane. Perhaps I'll let Merriwether break your neck before we put you in the cage. As long as we can keep him from beneath your skirts we'll do just fine. We need a virgin, and I'm considering keeping your sister as a little playmate. She's so delightfully shallow."

Jane rubbed her mouth, and Francis's lip rouge stained her hand. "You can't . . ."

"I can do anything I please," he said sweetly. "Joseph, bring the chains."

"I'm going to kill them," Peter said grimly. "I'll rip their fuckin' throats out with me bare hands."

"I'm afraid someone like Francis would enjoy that," Gabriel said with deceptive calm. "Besides, there are two of us and more than a dozen of them. Brute force won't carry the day, no matter how satisfying it might be."

It was getting perilously close to dusk. The two men were just inside the back garden gate. No one had noticed the broken lock, no one had bothered to fix it. They were far too busy with other things, and Gabriel could only imagine what sorts of things they might be.

Jane was somewhere down there, and had been for countless hours. The only bright spot was that Francis was determined to sacrifice an innocent in his bloody wicker cage—no one would be raping his sister during the long hours of her captivity.

He wouldn't think of Lizzie. When he did, the white-hot rage filled him, and he couldn't think clearly. He needed all his wits about him to extricate the women safely, and thinking about Lizzie made him crazed. He couldn't afford that.

"They've moved the wicker cage into an oak clearing near the abbey ruins," he said evenly. "They'll be convening there by full dark, so we have that long to get Jane out."

"Why would they go to the abbey?"

"Sacred ground," Gabriel said grimly. "With someone like Francis Chilton a little knowledge is a dangerous thing. Hernewood Abbey was built on the grounds of an old Druid temple, and there were probably even more ancient worshipers there before the Druids. There's an oak grove that's a perfect concentric circle, and they've built some sort of pit filled with tinder and wood and placed the cage atop it. It should burn quite handily."

"Bastards," Peter muttered.

"You've got to get Jane out of there before they come for her. Take her and run. As long as I don't have to worry about Jane I can concentrate on Lizzie."

"Won't they be wanting her for a virgin sacrifice as well."

"No," Gabriel said flatly. "Not since last night."

Peter gave him a measuring look. "Jane's not going to be pleased with you."

"You worry about Jane. I'll take care of the rest."

CHAPTER TWENTY-FIVE

They'd only chained her wrists to the bedstead. It didn't matter—there was nothing she could do with her feet to free herself. Her wrists were raw, bleeding from her useless attempts to pull free. Her bones were simply too blasted big. A frail little flower like Edwina would have slipped through the iron rings with little difficulty. Jane's wrists stuck fast.

It was growing dark. All afternoon she'd listened to them coming and going, the low mutter of conversation, the occasional cheery laugh that was somehow even more chilling. She wondered if Peter even knew she was missing. If he even cared. He was probably off courting his intended, without a thought for her. She'd hate the girl, if she even knew who she was. Peter hadn't told her, and Jane hadn't asked.

She heard the noise at the window but at first dismissed it, convinced it was more of the strange bangings that had come from beyond the small room where she was being held. And then the room darkened still further, as the narrow row of window was blocked out, and someone fell forward into the room.

She had the presence of mind not to scream. Who would help her, anyway? The shadowy creature rose from the floor, coming toward her, and she bit her lip, prepared to scream anyway if he touched her.

"What have they done to you, lass?" Peter's voice was barely more than a whisper of sound, and his cool, rough hands touched her face with tender concern.

She could feel tears come, the tears she had fought all afternoon, and she tried to stop them. In the shadows he wouldn't see them, but he would feel them coursing down her cheeks. "You have to get away, Peter," she said urgently. "Get help. I'm all right for now—they're not going to touch me until later. Please, Peter."

"I'm not leaving without you." He reached under her shoulders and tried to pull her up toward him, off the bed. The chains held, yanking her back with a noisy clatter, and she muffled her shriek of pain.

"You can't," she said, breathless. "I'm chained here, and there's no way I can get free. You've got to go find Gabriel, find help."

"Gabriel's already here. They've got Lizzie as well, though God knows where they're keeping her. I promised I'd get you out while he finds a way to get to her." He yanked at the chains, rattling them with noisy fury, but they were well oiled and impossible to break.

"Rattle 'em all you like," a rough voice called from outside. "Won't do you a speck of good, lass."

"Peter," she whispered, "you have to leave."

"I'll find something to cut the shackles," he said, moving away from the bed on silent feet. "I'll be back as quickly as I can."

She closed her eyes in despair. There wouldn't be

enough time, and she knew it. They both knew it. "Peter," she said, "there's no time. It's almost dark, and they'll come for me. You could stop them. You could save me."

"Anything, lass," he said. "Just tell me."

It was the hardest thing she ever said. "They only want a maiden, Peter. I'm no good to them if I'm not an innocent."

He froze in the darkness, and she couldn't see his expression. It was one small blessing. "What are you asking me for, Janey?"

"I'm saying if you want to save my life, you'll have to bed me. There's enough time for that and not much more." It sounded ridiculous even to her ears, and she turned her face away, waiting for him to mock her.

All was silent for a moment. And then he sighed, a deep, shaken sound. "I wouldn't want this for you, lass. You deserve far better."

"I don't deserve to die."

He moved toward the bed. "No, lass, you don't," he said in a rough, strained voice. "And better me than one of those drunken brutes out there." She could only see his silhouette in the shadows, but she could see him slowly reach for the fastening of his breeches.

She closed her eyes, letting the tears fall now, feeling them slide down her face as she listened to the rustle of his clothing. His hands touched her legs, and she jumped, then stilled as he slowly pulled her skirts up. Biting her lip in the darkness. Telling herself this was right. If it didn't save her life, at least she would take something of him to her grave.

"Janey, I don't want to do this to you," he said, his big rough-skinned hands incredibly gentle on her legs, her thighs. Touching her as no man had ever touched her.

"I'm begging you, Peter."

He hesitated a moment longer, then moved on top of her, lying stretched out over her body, her skirts bunched up between them. His body was hot, strong between her thighs, bare flesh against her partially covered skin. He reached between her pantalets and touched her, and she braced herself.

"Can you do it, Peter?" she asked belatedly. "They say men can't just do it anytime they want. I never thought . . ."

"Hush, lass," he whispered against her ear, and she felt him testing the entrance to her womanhood, smooth and strong. "I can do it."

He pushed in, hard, with one smooth thrust that broke past the frail barrier of her virginity, stopping when he was lodged deep inside her. His face was buried in her neck, and his entire body was trembling, his muscles taut. She held very still, waiting, and after an endless minute he let out a tight, shaky breath. "That's it, lass," he said in a raw voice. "I'll let you be . . ."

"No!" Her voice was barely a thread of sound, but there was no missing her anguish. "Finish it."

"You're no longer a maid, Janey," he said tightly. She could feel the tension thrumming through his muscles as he tried to keep utterly still, tight inside her body.

"But I'm not yet a woman. I love you, Peter. Finish it."

He kissed her then. Her first kiss, when he was already buried deep inside her body, and then he began to move, gently, controlling his infinite strength, until shudders began to wrack his body, and he moved faster, thrusting deeper, harder, and she welcomed him, all of him, tears pouring down her face.

He reached up and clasped her shackled hands, holding them in a tight grip, and he uttered a strangled cry, filling her with sweet warmth.

He was still for a moment. And then he kissed her eyes, her tear-stained cheeks, her nose, and she kissed him back, a strange, bubbling joy filling her. "You'll have to marry me, you know," she whispered. "Forget about your village lass, if she even exists. You've ruined me, and now you've got to do the right thing by me, or Gabriel will horsewhip you."

"Janey, you're a lady . . ."

"My father was a stable lad," she said. "I have it on good authority. I'm no better bred than you are. Your mother was a farm girl, your father was a lord, and we're both bastards. It makes us perfectly matched."

He was silent for a moment. "You've figured this all out?"

"I've had time to think, lying here. Will you marry me?"

For a moment he didn't move, and she knew real fear. And then he leaned down and kissed her eyelids. "Janey, you've held my heart for longer than you can even guess. You should have far better than the likes of me, but I'm not going to let you go. You'll marry me, and be damned to everyone."

"Be damned to them," she echoed, and kissed him. "Go find Gabriel now, and get me out of here."

Jane lay still on the narrow bed and waited for them. Her body ached, a glorious, triumphant pain, and she knew there was blood on the mattress beneath her. He'd covered her with loving tenderness when he'd left, and she'd waited until he was well and truly gone before she kicked the covers off and lay there, waiting.

It was after dark when they came for her. They were

wearing white robes, and she recognized Francis Chilton at their forefront, flanked by one of the thickset men who'd put the shackles on her and another, taller man whose face was hidden by his cowled hood.

"There you are, my sweet," Francis cooed, lifting his candelabra up high to illuminate the small room. "I know you're tired of waiting . . ." His voice trailed off as he saw her. "You bitch," he spat.

"Apparently she didn't have to wait," the tall man said, and she knew his voice. Gabriel.

Francis handed him the candelabra with calm deliberation. And then, in a sudden frenzy threw himself on the thickset man, screeching like a woman as he tried to strangle him.

"You randy pig, Merriwether, don't you have any brains at all?" he screamed, slamming the heavier man against the wall. "We needed a virgin, damn you, even a baseborn one would be better than none at all."

"I didn't touch her," Merriwether protested in a wheedling voice. "I like 'em younger and plumper."

Francis released him abruptly, straightening his robe with a fastidious gesture. "I don't believe you." He turned away from him, stalking toward Jane, where she lay shackled to the bed.

She didn't bother to shield the triumph and tears on her face. "You're too late," she said, glaring at him.

His sulky expression smoothed over, and he reached down and stroked the side of her neck. She shivered in disgust. "Don't let it distress you, my dear Miss Durham," he murmured. "We'll still burn you. Even a despoiled virgin has some value to the gods. And you've failed to take one important thing into account."

"What's that?" She didn't want to ask, but she couldn't keep herself from voicing the question.

"We'll simply take your sweet, innocent little sister as well. Edwina will make a perfect gift for the gods."

"No!" Jane gasped.

"Yes," Francis said cheerfully. "It will be a lovely blaze." He turned away. "Unlock her shackles, Merriwether, but keep your John Thomas in place. There'll be plenty of prettier women left for afterward." And he stalked from the room.

The man she knew was Gabriel paused for a moment, as if he wanted to say something, but Merriwether came toward her, reaching for the shackles. He looked over his shoulder to the other man. "You want a piece of this? You heard what he said. It would be worth your life to go against him when he's in that kind of mood."

"You might remember that as well." Gabriel's voice was muffled beneath the folds of cloth.

"I told you, it wasn't me. And if I'd been stupid enough to touch her in the first place, I certainly wouldn't do it again," Merriwether said in a righteous whine. "I'm not ready to die."

"Aren't you?" Gabriel murmured. And despite the warmth of the room, Jane shivered.

CHAPTER TWENTY-SIX

They fed her, and Lizzie ate. They gave her fresh water, and she washed up as best she could. And then she sat in the corner, quiet and docile, waiting for the first moment when they didn't watch her. It was a long time coming.

Dusk was late in the north country. She was tied to an ornate chair in one of the many rooms at Arundel, with no choice but to watch as everyone scurried back and forth, intent on their preparations.

They seemed harmless enough, a group of unprepossessing gentlemen of various ages and appearance, all of them looking slightly the worse for wear from drink and celebration. None of them looked at her directly, and when she tried to speak to them the servants came and stood over her, separating them. She wondered whether they really knew what Francis Chilton had planned for her. Whether evil truly existed on such a grand scale, or simply reposed in the soul of one strange man and his beautiful, greedy wife.

They were dressed in flowing white robes made of the finest linen, with pointed cowls covering most of their faces. Only Francis had his hood back, exposing his long blond curls as they tumbled down his back.

He came up to her, followed closely by a very tall man in enveloping robes, and cupped her face with his cold hands. "The time has come, my pretty one. Fate has done its best to interfere with my plans, but I'm not so easily denied. You'll burn tonight, my dear. For a righteous cause." His voice was low, not carrying to the other gentlemen, and Lizzie wondered why.

"What righteous cause?" she snapped.

He stroked her face with his too soft fingers. "Why, the righteous cause of my future well-being and the good fortune of all these fine gentlemen. The gods must be propitiated on Beltane if we're to be guaranteed power and prosperity."

"The gods? What gods?"

Francis shrugged. "I don't really care which ones, as long as they grant me my wishes. Perhaps it's Belarus the warrior god, or even Belial the demon. Either way he has a fierce appetite that must be quenched, and you are the girl to do it for me. You and the others."

"Others?"

"That slut, Jane. Another randy whore—they found her amidst the bloody sheets, deflowered and unworthy. I'll cut the throat of the man responsible when I find him. But in the meantime she'll go as well, and we still have a proper virgin." He pinched her face, hard. "No, not you, pet. Though I would have liked the chance to sample you. You would have been great fun to discipline."

"Who else?"

The loud shriek answered her question. Perfect Miss Edwina Durham was being dragged along between two white-robed cultists, kicking and struggling and screaming imprecations. "Sorry to give you such infelicitous company, but you and Jane can hold hands as the fire surrounds you."

"You're a sick bastard," she said calmly.

He looked pleased. "Flattery," he murmured. "Come along." He'd already untied the ropes that held her to the chair.

"Gabriel will kill you," she said fiercely.

Francis stepped back, a smug smile on his face. "Gabriel will drag you to the fire, my pet." And the tall man behind him pulled back his hood, and it was Gabriel, with no expression on his cool, beautiful face.

"Take her, Gabriel," Francis ordered.

Gabriel made no move. "I think you're forgetting who's in charge here, Francis," he said.

"Ah, yes, the mighty chief of the Druids, font of all wisdom and knowledge," Francis sneered. "We've gone beyond your puny research, Gabriel. Gone into a whole new realm, and you can either join us or"—he paused for the maximum dramatic effect—"you can join her."

Gabriel's eyes glanced over her, dismissing her. "Hardly much of a choice, is it?"

"Then show your loyalty. Bring her. But don't have any second thoughts. My brethren will be watching you to make certain you don't let her escape."

"Francis," Gabriel said with a weary sigh, "we're both men of the world. She's a well-bred young lady, and I despoiled her. Nothing would suit me better than to have her conveniently disappear in a puff of smoke."

Francis's smile exposed his sharp white teeth. "I knew you were my kind of man. Now if you'd only realize it, love, we could be quite happy together. In the mean-

time, bring the tiresome creature, and we'll have a Beltane fire to remember.''

Gabriel hauled her to her feet, his hand an iron grip
on her arm as he dragged her in the wake of the shuffling men. He'd pulled his cowl back over his head, and
Lizzie tried to tell herself it wasn't Gabriel dragging her
to her death.

The death march through the woods was slow and
stately. There was no moon that night; it was hidden by
the thick clouds overhead. There was no promise of
rain, either. No deluge would put out their unholy fire
and stop their wickedness. There was no one to save
them, and Lizzie wasn't sure she even cared.

She saw Jane stumbling along, another white-robed
man leading her, but in the thick darkness she couldn't
catch her eye. It didn't matter. Edwina was shrieking
and making enough noise to distract anyone, and Lizzie
found herself with the uncharitable wish that someone
would shut the silly twit up. If she had to die, she at
least wanted to die without Edwina's yammering in her
skull.

She was barely aware when they crossed the boundary
from Arundel into the forest of Hernewood. She could
see the ruined abbey spires in the distance, too far away
for help. And who was there left to help them? Peter,
perhaps, but he was devoted to Gabriel. For all Lizzie
knew he might be one of the white-robed ghouls who
were now chanting beneath their breath as they
marched onward.

The chanting didn't drown out Edwina. Lizzie
couldn't decide which was more unnerving, the sepulchral chant or the high-pitched wail. She didn't particularly care. Gabriel's grip on her arm was painfully tight,
needlessly so. He should realize she had no chance of
escape.

The procession halted when they reached a small glade, the white-robed Druids forming a circle inside it. There was a deep pit, and a large cage atop it, and she could only presume it was made of wicker. It looked as if it would burn very quickly.

She looked up at the tall man beside her, but his face was averted. He seemed almost oblivious to her presence beside him, except for that crushing grip on her arm. If she survived, she'd have bruises, she thought dazedly. Bruises to join the other marks he'd left on her body.

"Light the fire, Merriwether!" Francis declaimed, raising his white-robed arms to the sky. A man stepped forward, a torch in one beefy hand, and tossed it into the middle of the cage. It began to burn, the flames spreading, slowly at first.

"We give these offerings in the name of Belarus, of Belial, of all the gods of war and power," Francis intoned.

"Where are the animals?" Lizzie heard one man mutter. "Aren't we going to put animals in there?"

"Bring forth the virgin!" Francis cried out.

Edwina Durham had stopped her wretched screaming for the time being, but this brought forth a fresh outcry. She was dragged forth between two of the Druids, and during the struggle the smaller one's hood fell back, exposing Delilah Chilton's silky black curls.

There was a gasp from the crowd. "You didn't say anything about sacrificing women," someone muttered. "Damn it, it's indecent."

"The time for small sacrifices is past!" Francis shouted. "Bring her!"

"Nooooo!" The scream was blood-curdling, as Sir Richard Durham stumbled into the grove, ripping at his white robe. "Leave her be, damn your black soul!

You promised. You promised you'd take Jane, you filthy bugger."

"Father!" Edwina shrieked, holding out her arms to the old man in a piteous plea for mercy. Sir Richard stumbled toward her, yanking her away from Delilah and knocking her to the ground. Merriwether surged forward with his torch, aiming it straight for Sir Richard's face, when a sudden, horrified hush fell over the crowd. Even Merriwether stopped where he was at the edge of the pit, staring up at him in disbelief.

In the midst of the flaming cage floated two white-robed creatures, one tall and thin, one short and round.

"Druids," someone muttered in horror. "Real Druids."

"Cease this mockery!" Brother Septimus's voice rang out in sepulchral splendor. "Or you will all spend eternity in these flames!"

Lizzie stared in numb disbelief. Behind her the fake Druids scattered, running for their lives. She quickly searched through the firelit darkness for Jane, only to see her running away, her hand held tight in the hand of her Druid captor, who looked suspiciously like Peter. But Gabriel's grip hadn't loosened—there would be no escape for her. Francis lifted his arms to the sky, his blond curls rippling down his back. "Fools!" he shouted. "Run, if you must." Merriwether was still standing at the edge of the pit, frozen in fright, and Francis kicked at him. "Throw the bitch into the fire. Take her, you fool."

His kick was an error in judgment. Merriwether toppled over backwards, into the flames, with a strangled scream that echoed throughout the night until it dissolved into merciful silence.

Francis looked around him in frustrated fury. He leapt

for Edwina, but Sir Richard had her other arm and was pulling just as hard.

"Ow, you're hurting me!" Edwina screamed. "Let go of me, you brutes."

"Edwina!" Sir Richard said in a broken voice, making one more mighty effort. Francis's hold broke, and Edwina and Sir Richard went tumbling to the ground. Edwina lay there, shrieking and screaming. Sir Richard didn't move. It took Lizzie a moment to realize that she and her captor were almost alone in the flame-lit clearing. The Druids had all scattered, Jane had escaped, and only Francis and Delilah remained.

And Gabriel, holding her so tightly her arm had gone totally numb.

Francis started toward them. "Are you going to turn on me, Gabriel? Is your midnight-hour entry into the fold all a lie as well?" He sounded almost remote, as if the answer to his question didn't particularly matter.

Gabriel lifted his other hand from beneath the folds of the robe, the hand that wasn't holding her arm in a death grip. He had a small pistol, and Lizzie had no doubt whatsoever that it was primed and ready. It was pointing straight at Francis's heart.

"What do you think, love?" Gabriel said in a lightly mocking voice.

Francis shook his head. "You disappoint me, Gabriel, you really do. I expected better things of you, than to have you besotted with this ordinary female. And that's it, isn't it?"

"Besotted is as good a word as any," he said in an even tone of voice. "Take your wife and get out of here, Francis. You haven't killed anyone yet, and I have no interest in adding to my sins. Leave."

Francis Chilton had a smile like an angel. His rouged mouth curved up, and he advanced on the stunned

Delilah. She was standing by the edge of the flaming pit, staring into Merriwether's funeral pyre, a dazed expression on her face.

"My love," Francis said, taking her arm, "you heard Gabriel. I'm afraid our time here is at an end. Our followers have all abandoned us."

She looked up at him. "They have, haven't they?"

"But that still doesn't mean Beltane is a lost cause. I can still offer a sacrifice of my most beloved." His hands tightened on her slender shoulders, and he pushed her toward the flames.

But she was ahead of him, her foot snaking behind his ankle, tripping him. "My thoughts exactly, my dear," she cooed.

For a moment they hung, suspended, on the edge of the flames. "Bitch," he spat at her.

"Bastard," she hissed back.

And they toppled over into the fire, a moment before the flaming wicker cage collapsed on top of them.

Lizzie suddenly realized Gabriel wasn't holding on to her any longer. She fell to her knees on the hard ground, hugging herself in shock and horror, as Gabriel walked away from her, over to the fallen body of the man who had once been his father.

Edwina was lying in the dirt, having what seemed perilously close to a temper tantrum, screaming and kicking in mindless fury. Gabriel hauled her upright with surprising gentleness. "Your father's dead, Edwina."

"Ewww!" Edwina shrieked. "I don't want to touch him. I hate dead people. I want to go home. I want to go back to London right this minute. I hate it here. I hate you, Gabriel, and I hate Father, and I hate Yorkshire, and I hate everybody. I hate you I hate you I hate you."

Somewhere Lizzie found hidden strength. She rose to her feet and started toward the weeping child. "Let me take care of this," she said to Gabriel, the first words she'd spoken to him all day. And taking Edwina's shoulder, she turned her and socked her in the jaw.

Edwina's tears vanished, and her mouth dropped open in shock. "You struck me!" she said. "You actually dared strike me. I shall have a bruise, I know it . . ."

"If you don't shut your mouth, I'll hit you again," Lizzie said quite calmly. "And I will enjoy it immensely."

Edwina's mouth slammed shut. Gabriel had moved past her, kneeling by Sir Richard's fallen body and closing his staring eyes. He looked up and met her eyes with a dispassionate gaze.

"There are times, Lizzie, when I think I could love you," he said.

And for one brief moment Lizzie considered pushing him after the Chiltons.

CHAPTER
TWENTY-SEVEN

Lizzie had the sudden, very real need to be taken care of. To be soothed and petted and cosseted, stroked and reassured and pampered. The trip back to Rosecliff Hall had been accomplished in the back of a farm wagon, with the semihysterical Edwina sitting on the seat beside Gabriel. It would have been Lizzie's luck to ride in back with Sir Richard's corpse, but Edwina flatly refused to travel anywhere with her deceased father, and Lizzie had ended up riding amidst the straw in solitary splendor.

Gabriel had disappeared moments after they arrived back at Rosecliff Hall. Peter and a rumpled-looking Jane met them, with Peter taking the horse and Jane dealing with Edwina, who immediately took one look at her older sister and began screeching once more. Jane was far more sympathetic, putting her arms around Edwina and leading her into the house as she flashed an apologetic look at Lizzie, standing forlornly in the midnight courtyard.

For a moment Lizzie considered bursting into noisy tears as well, perhaps even throwing herself on the ground in a tantrum to rival Edwina's earlier efforts. But there was manure on the ground, and she really didn't have the energy. The best she could manage was a trembling sort of sniff.

"There, there, dearie, you come along with me." A woman appeared at her side, all maternal comfort and practicality. "You've had a rough time of it, and that's the truth, but Alice will see to you, just trust me. A warm bath, a nice cup of tea, and you'll be feeling right as rain."

"I don't think so," Lizzie said in a quavering voice.

"Oh, you're stronger than you think," Alice said. "We'll get you cleaned up, then I'll go find Mr. Gabriel and give him a piece of my mind. Imagine just abandoning you here when you need some taking care of."

"I do," Lizzie said. "And I hate him."

"Of course you do, lass," Alice said warmly. "We all hate our menfolk half the time, and God knows they deserve it. I'm that cross with my Peter for letting Miss Jane get taken up by those monsters, and I'm going to sort him out as well, if Jane doesn't see to it. If you leave men to run the world they always mess it up, don't they, love?"

Lizzie could only manage a heartfelt nod of agreement.

"Besides, you don't really want Mr. Gabriel looking after you, now do you? There are times when you need another woman seeing to your needs." She kept up a soft, running monologue of comfort as she led Lizzie upstairs to a bathroom with a tub full of steaming, rose-scented water. "Now you take as long as you like, Miss

Elizabeth," Alice murmured. "If you need some help, just give a call. I'll lay out some fresh nightclothes for you and bring you something to eat, and then I need to see to the others."

"Are you Peter's mother?" Lizzie yanked at her dress, sending the buttons flying across the floor. She didn't care. She never wanted to wear the wretched thing again.

"I am."

"Jane loves him," Lizzie said, abandoning her own misery in favor of a nobler quest. "You can't let him ruin both their lives because of something foolish like pride."

Alice smiled fondly at her. "Don't you worry, lass. I'll see to him. I believe in letting young people find their own way, but if a boy's determined to be blind, then he needs his mother to set him straight. He'll marry her, lass, and be glad of it."

Lizzie managed a weary smile, stripping off the rest of her clothes and climbing into the tub with a loud sigh of pleasure so intense it was almost painful. And then she caught Alice staring at her with a troubled expression on her face, Lizzie's bloodstained shift in her capable hands.

"Did they hurt you, lass?" she asked quietly. "Did they force you . . . ?"

Lizzie shook her head, glad her loose hair tumbled around her to hide her face. "No, they didn't touch me," she said.

"Then . . . Gabriel," Alice said after a moment's realization. "It seems I have another young man to sort out as well."

"No," she said brokenly. "Don't . . . he didn't . . ." Her voice trailed off.

"Didn't what?" Alice asked gently.

"Didn't do anything I didn't want him to," Lizzie confessed, bursting into tears.

Alice wrapped her comforting arms around Lizzie, ignoring the soapy water that drenched her sleeves. "Men," she muttered in a dire tone that boded no good for Gabriel Durham.

Lizzie stayed in the tub till the water cooled, soaping and rinsing her hair, scrubbing at her skin with a vengeance. Her tears dried, and her temper rose. She wasn't quite certain what she was completely furious about— Gabriel had saved her life, even if he'd taken his own sweet time about it, and if he'd made it clear he'd felt nothing more than passing lust for her, she had only herself to blame. She was ruined, thoroughly and completely, and the fact brought her a slight comfort. She could refuse Elliott Maynard with impunity now, and if her father pushed for a reason, she could always admit the devastating truth.

It wouldn't come to that. She would go home and be a dutiful daughter, and live out her days the perfect maiden aunt. Unless she happened to be pregnant.

She wouldn't even consider that shocking possibility. Or the even more disastrous realization that she wished she were. She wanted a baby, his baby, almost as much as she wanted him.

She was crazy, that's what she was. She was exhausted, upset, and totally out of her mind. What she needed was sleep. A soft bed, warm covers, and hours and hours of peace. In the morning she'd have regained her senses. He didn't want her, and she had too much pride to go where she wasn't wanted.

Alice had left her clean linen, and she pulled the soft shift over her still-damp body, doing her best to dry her hair on the thick, rough towels. There was a heavy, quilted robe, obviously masculine in design, and she hated to think to whom it belonged. But she couldn't traverse the corridor in only her shift, so she pulled it around her, resisting the impulse to stroke the soft material as it draped her body.

As promised, there was a pot of hot tea in her room, a plate of small cakes, and a glass of fresh milk. She forced herself to nibble at one of the cakes, and there was nothing so bad that a cup of tea didn't make it better. There was a faint light in the inky black sky, and it took her a moment to realize that it was approaching dawn.

She slipped off the robe and climbed up into her bed, pulling her legs up toward her body and wrapping her arms around her knees. The room was almost too warm, and she should open the window and let in the fresh night air, but she couldn't move. She was afraid that if she looked out over the forest she would soon leave, she might cry. She was afraid she would find her way back out there, barefoot and in her shift, when she needed to stay safe and secure in her bed.

She blew out the candle beside her bed and leaned back against the pillows, closing her eyes. Waiting.

She might have fallen asleep. When she opened her eyes he was standing a few feet away from the bed, staring at her. He'd bathed as well—his long hair was wet and pulled back from his elegant face, and he was dressed in a loose white shirt and breeches. Barefoot, as she was.

She sat up, giving him her most defiant look. "What do you want?" she asked in a suitably cranky voice.

"I . . . just wanted to make certain you were all right. Alice said you were crying." His smile was wry. "She said it was my fault."

"I'm perfectly fine. Just in need of sleep." It was

a pointed statement, designed to get rid of him. She couldn't bear to look at him without touching him.

"I know. I'm having a bit of trouble sleeping myself."

"Warm milk will do wonders."

"I don't want warm milk," he said in a stiff voice. "I want you." He sounded as if he'd rather eat nails than admit it.

"Then that is a great tragedy," she said, "because you can't have me."

"I already did. Several times, if I recall correctly."

She ignored the blush that mounted to her cheeks. In the dawnlit room he probably wouldn't be able to see it, which was scant comfort. "Go away, Gabriel," she said in a cross voice. "Leave me in peace."

He spun around and moved toward the open door, then paused. "You told me you loved me," he said.

"A moment of temporary insanity." She could only fight him for so long. Her heart was breaking, and all he could do was argue. Why couldn't he simply scoop her up and take her, leaving her no choice in the matter?

"Love me again, Lizzie," he said softly. "I've been alone for too long."

She was lost, and she knew it. He knew it as well. He held out his hand to her, forcing her to make the choice. "Come to bed with me," he whispered. "I need you."

And she went, barefoot, in her shift, holding his hand, down the darkened corridors of Rosecliff to his room, to his bed, loving him.

He took her tenderly this time, kissing her with deep, slow, unhurried kisses, as if the whole night stretched before them instead of brash light of a new dawn filling the room. He took her sweetly, with murmured endearments and gentle caresses. He took her leisurely, playing languid, erotic designs on her flesh with his mouth and tongue.

And then he took her hard, with a sudden roughness they both wanted, as if he were angry for needing her, as if she were angry for loving him.

And then he was gone, and she was alone, in his big tumbled bed, in the harsh, glaring light of day.

CHAPTER
TWENTY-EIGHT

Six long weeks passed, and it was time to say good-bye to the ghosts, good-bye to the woods. Lizzie had stayed in Hernewood long past any reasonable time, and she had to leave.

It didn't matter that Peter and Jane kept insisting she didn't disturb their newly wedded bliss. She knew that she didn't. The rambling house that Peter owned was neat, tidy, waiting to be filled with children, and from the sounds that carried through the lonely corridors in the night, Peter and Jane were doing their best to fill it.

She could see Rosecliff from her window. The roses were out now, covering the house, warming it. It still looked like a castle in an enchanted forest, but now it seemed to her eyes like a happy enchantment. She could only hope they would keep it so for Gabriel when he returned.

It was past time for her to leave. To go back to Dorset

and be the good, sweet, unimaginative girl her parents
so desperately wanted. She could do that, for them. She
wouldn't marry Elliott Maynard, or any other man, but
she could be the perfect maiden, the spinster of the
parish, her parents' solace and help in their declining
years. She could spend the rest of her life in quiet, dull
captivity, and she would never again run barefoot in
the woods. There was no babe in her belly, there was
no joy in her heart.

There was no word from Gabriel, and in truth, she
didn't expect it. When she'd awakened in his bed the
next morning, she was alone. He was gone, without
another word to her, taking the hysterical Edwina and
her father's body back to London, not even staying for
Peter and Jane's hasty wedding. He was the heir now,
whether he wanted it or not, the head of the family
and he had responsibilities, Jane said in vain excuse.
She was sure he hadn't really wanted to leave.

But Lizzie knew him far better than his sister did. He
was running again, and she would let him go this time.
There were times when she could almost convince herself that wild, endless time had never happened, that it
was nothing more than a shameless dream. And the
moments of hot, ceaseless longing would come less
often, as would the deep tear in her heart. She had
even managed to laugh yesterday, a good sign that she
would eventually mend, at least partially.

She had already told Jane and Peter she was leaving,
and their pleas and arguments had fallen on deaf ears.
Her bags were packed, and Peter would drive her to
York to meet the London coach. In the meantime, she
had to say good-bye to the forests that felt like home.
The woods that she would never see again. The monks
who had already left.

She walked swiftly through the trees, following the

paths that she knew so well by now. Hernewood Manor
was a shell, if that. All the furnishing and possessions
had been packed and shipped to London in a dazzlingly
short time. Lady Durham would not be returning, nor
would the twins. The manor belonged to Gabriel now,
and he could do with it as he pleased.

And what he pleased was to order it torn down. Half
the stone was scattered over the fields, the stone that
had first come from the ruined abbey. Brother Septimus
and Brother Paul were free. They had finally earned
their rest, long gone to their overdue reward.

She said good-bye to them in the ruined nave of the
old building. She went nowhere near the tower that
now stood abandoned. There were some things even
she could not do.

She should head back, she knew she should, but these
were her last moments, and she lingered. No one would
come in search of her, they were all busy with their
duties and responsibilities. She slipped off her shoes
and stockings, leaving them in a neat pile.

A rabbit hopped by, pausing a moment to look at
her, then moved onward. The creatures of the forest
had returned, now that the evil had passed, and Lizzie
knew a deep, loving relief.

The earth was warm and spring-soft beneath her bare
feet. She would wear shoes for the rest of her life, but
not now. She moved deeper into the woods, humming
softly to herself, a song about faithless love and found
love, and when her eyes filled with tears she switched
to something bawdy as she danced in the woods one
last time, at one with the magic that lived there.

She spun, lightly, she dipped and twirled, singing
nonsense songs under her breath. And she turned, one
last time, and came to a dead stop. Gabriel stood in a

shaft of sunlight between a stand of tall trees, watching her.

He was wearing the clothes she'd first seen him in—a rough white shirt and dark breeches, his hair loose and far too long. He held her shoes and stockings in his hand.

She faltered, feeling the color flood her face and body. At least she hadn't given in to temptation and shed her dress as well. If he'd caught her dancing in her shift, she might just as well have died.

"You're still here," he said in a tone of wonder.

"Not for long." She prided herself on how calm she sounded, when she wanted to scream at him. "The ghosts are gone."

He nodded, seemingly distracted. "The manor house needed to be torn down. It was built from the old abbey, and the ghosts couldn't leave until it was in pieces."

"Why?"

He shrugged. "I don't know."

"Where were you . . ." She stopped herself mid-tirade. "Never mind. It's none of my concern."

"I love you, Lizzie Penshurst," he said abruptly.

She paused, not believing her ears. "You love me?" she echoed in stark disbelief. Her outrage bubbled over. "You seduce me, almost kill me, and then run off without a word, and now you tell me you love me?"

He managed a wry smile. "I knew you'd take it well."

"And where have you been all this time? Did you just come to this momentous conclusion, or have you been carrying such a burden around with you for a while?" She was furious with him, utterly and completely enraged. She had been ready to give him up, ready to live a life of mournful sacrifice, and now he came back to tell her he loved her! It was unforgivable.

"I had things to do in London," he said calmly. "And

I was rather hoping I'd grow out of it. However, it seems to be a permanent affliction, so I think you'll have to marry me."

"Marry you?" This was getting more and more ridiculous. "I can't possibly marry you."

"Why not? Your father gives his blessing."

"Because I don't give mine," she snapped.

"And why not? Don't you love me? Did you come to my bed simply to trifle with my affections? Not kind of you, love. I've a gentle soul, easily wounded. Surely you must hold some tender feeling for me?"

"You have the soul of a monster," she said. "I hate you."

"Of course you do. Come here, Lizzie."

He was halfway across the clearing, and the sun speared down among the trees, filled with dancing motes of light.

"I could make your life a living hell," she warned him.

"I'm counting on it. I love you with all my heart and body and soul. You can spend the rest of your days tormenting me."

She walked across the clearing, the sunlight dappling around her, came up to him in the woods. He was even taller than she remembered, and then she realized she was barefoot, as always. He dropped the shoes and reached out for her, cupping her face with beautiful hands. "Marry me, Lizzie. Let me love you."

"Yes," she said, kissing his hands, kissing his mouth. "Yes."

EPILOGUE

Yorkshire, 1817

It was the first truly warm day in spring, and Gabriela Durham went into the woods to dance.

She should have outgrown her love of the forest, and she knew it. After all, she was a mature young lady of eighteen and a half, with a London Season already behind her, and two perfectly desirable gentlemen vying for her favors. She could marry either one of them, and she supposed she ought to. After all, it was what was expected of her. After the scandalous behavior of her grandparents it had taken her more conventional parents a great deal of effort to reestablish the name of Durham in society, and Gabriela was ready to reap the benefits of all that hard work. She would make a suitable, wealthy marriage, even though money was in abundance, and she would be a suitable, well-bred wife.

If only she didn't take after her grandmother Lizzie.

Her own mother, a warmhearted, easily exasperated woman of steady temperament, had often despaired of her impossibly fey mother-in-law, known by one and all, servant and landholder alike, as Lizzie, and while she seldom showed it, she was terrified of her father-in-law, the notorious Gabriel Durham.

Gabriela had never been afraid of her grandfather. After all, she'd been named for him, despite her mother's objections, and she knew perfectly well he was as devoted to her as he was to his entire family. Even her uneasy and ungrateful mother.

And Gabriela's mother had learned to tolerate her in-laws' eccentricity, their predilection for pagan religions, and their embarrassingly obvious affection for each other. Since they stayed out of society, preferring their own motley assortment of friends, Richard and Mary Durham could only pretend they didn't exist.

But Gabriel and Lizzie were gone now, having lived happily and well into their eighties. Their prodigious offspring had scattered across the world, leaving their eldest, Richard, to manage the vast estate and marry well.

And now it was Gabriela's turn. When she went back to the house she knew what awaited her. Adrian Grant had written to her father, and Paul Taylor had sought an interview that very morning. There was no way she could come up with any more excuses.

She came to the circle of oaks and slipped off her shoes and stockings. There were whispered tales of Druids in these parts, but Gabriela had always ignored them. She knew the woods, better than she knew her own heart. There was no danger to her here.

She was humming beneath her breath, an old, old song, about faithless love and found love, and she danced barefoot in the circle of trees. Until she saw him watching her.

He could have been standing there since she arrived, so still was he. He blended with the woods, his skin dusky from the sun, his mop of curly hair streaked with brown and gold. He wore rough clothes, and he was tall, motionless, his eyes alive in his quiet face as he watched her.

"Who are you?" She asked the question abruptly, embarrassed at being caught, wondering where her shoes were. "What are you doing on my father's land? Are you a poacher?"

"I'm no poacher," he said, his voice low and beguiling, faintly touched with a northern burr. "I stopped to watch a faery dance in the woods."

"I'm no faery," she said. She knew him, in her heart if not in her mind. "You're Patrick Brownington."

"I'm Patrick," he agreed. He lifted his head to look at her more clearly, and she felt a sudden tug, sharp and sweet, inside her. He had brown eyes and a beautiful face, and years ago, when they were only children, he'd told her he would marry her and they would live in the woods. How could she have forgotten him?

"You're a very grand lady now, Gabriela," he said. He was some sort of distant cousin, though his lineage was a bit too shady for her mother, and he had every right to call her by her name in that soft, easy voice of his. "Are you married?"

"Would a married woman go running off into the woods?" she countered.

"If she was looking for what she lacked at home, she would. If she had any sense. Have you forgotten your promise?"

"What promise is that?" She knew, and he did, that she hadn't forgotten.

"You said you'd marry me and live in the woods when we were old enough. I think we were ten and twelve at the time." The hint of laughter in his voice made it clear he wasn't about to hold her to it. Just a distant relative, remembering an innocent time.

"Are you here to claim me, Patrick?" she asked. His family owned a tidy estate nearby, one that had prospered over the years, but he came from yeoman stock, and she could look much higher. And so her mother had often reminded her.

He tilted his head sideways. "I just might be," he said softly.

Gabriela thought of Adrian Grant with his grand estates and his pale, elegant face. She thought of Paul Taylor and his dark beauty and fierce temper and his beautiful house in Sevenoaks.

She looked at Patrick Brownington and a weight lifted from her shoulders, and she flashed him a dazzling smile. "Good," she said.

And once more, barefoot on the thick carpet of leaves, she began to dance.

ROMANCE FROM JO BEVERLY

DANGEROUS JOY   (0-8217-5129-8, $5.99)

FORBIDDEN   (0-8217-4488-7, $4.99)

THE SHATTERED ROSE (0-8217-5310-X, $5.99)

TEMPTING FORTUNE (0-8217-4858-0, $4.99)

ROMANCE FROM JANELLE TAYLOR

YOU WON'T WANT TO READ
JUST ONE—KATHERINE STONE

ROOMMATES   (0-8217-5206-5, $6.99/$7.99)
No one could have prepared Carrie for the monumental changes she would face when she met her new circle of friends at Stanford University. Once their lives intertwined and became woven into the tapestry of the times, they would never be the same.

TWINS   (0-8217-5207-3, $6.99/$7.99)
Brook and Melanie Chandler were so different, it was hard to believe they were sisters. One was a dark, serious, ambitious New York attorney; the other, a golden, glamourous, sophisticated supermodel. But they were more than sisters—they were twins and more alike than even they knew . . .

THE CARLTON CLUB   (0-8217-5204-9, $6.99/$7.99)
It was the place to see and be seen, the only place to be. And for those who frequented the playground of the very rich, it was a way of life. Mark, Kathleen, Leslie and Janet—they worked together, played together, and loved together, all behind exclusive gates of the *Carlton Club*.

Available wherever paperbacks are sold, or order direct from the Publisher. Send cover price plus 50¢ per copy for mailing and handling to Kensington Publishing Corp., Consumer Orders, or call (toll free) 888-345-BOOK, to place your order using Mastercard or Visa. Residents of New York and Tennessee must include sales tax. DO NOT SEND CASH.